Praise from England for *Remote Control*

"McNab takes his new job every bit as seriously as his old."
                    —*The Times* (London)

"An enjoyably gritty thriller...With more than a back-handed compliment to Frederick Forsyth's storytelling style, McNab enjoys the minute research for his locations."
                    —*The Scotsman*

"[McNab's] prose has the authenticity that comes from being an SAS veteran and the narrative races along."
                    —*Express* (London)

By Andy McNab

BRAVO TWO ZERO
IMMEDIATE ACTION
REMOTE CONTROL*

*Published by Ballantine Books

REMOTE CONTROL

Andy McNab

BALLANTINE BOOKS • NEW YORK

A Ballantine Book
Published by The Ballantine Publishing Group
Copyright © 1997 by Andy McNab

All rights reserved under International and Pan-American Copyright Conventions. Published in the United States by The Ballantine Publishing Group, a division of Random House, Inc., New York. Originally published in Great Britain by Bantam Press, a division of Transworld Publishers Ltd., London.

www.randomhouse.com/BB/

Library of Congress Catalog Card Number: 99-91022

ISBN 0-345-42806-4

Manufactured in the United States of America

First American Hardcover Edition: June 1999
First American Mass Market Edition: January 2000

10   9   8   7   6   5   4   3   2   1

GIBRALTAR: SUNDAY, MARCH 6, 1988

We didn't know which of the three was going to detonate the bomb. All Simmonds had been able to tell us was that it was a big one, and that it would be initiated remotely.

For now, though, there was nothing to do but wait. The security service had triggers out on the checkpoints with mainland Spain. Until the players were sighted, Pat, Kev, and I were to stay exactly where we were: sitting outside a cafe just off Main Street, drinking coffee, looking and listening.

The spring air was crisp and clear under a blindingly blue Mediterranean sky, the morning sun just starting to make it comfortable enough for shirtsleeves. The trees that lined the square were packed with birds so small I couldn't see them among the foliage, but they made enough noise to drown out the sound of traffic going up and down the main drag, just out of sight. It was strange to think that this small outpost, on the tip of southern Spain, was still under British jurisdiction, a last bastion of Empire.

Through my earpiece I heard Euan make a radio check to the operations room. Everything he said on the net was very precise, very clear, very calm. Euan was the tidiest man in the world. If you sat on a cushion he would puff it up again the moment you stood up. Dedication was his middle name.

I heard a loud hiss of air brakes and looked up. A tour bus had turned into the square and was parking about twenty yards away. The sign in the windshield said YOUNG AT HEART.

I didn't pay much attention. I was bored, looking for things to do. The laces on one of my running shoes had come undone. I bent down to do them up and got a jab in the ribs from the hammer of the 9mm Browning. The holster was covert, inside my jeans; that way, only the pistol grip would be in view if I pulled open my black nylon bomber jacket. I preferred to have my pistol at the front. A lot of the guys wore theirs on the side, but I could never get used to it. Once you find a position you like, you don't change; you might be in deep shit one day, go to draw your weapon and it isn't there—it's several more inches to the right and you're dead.

I had an extended twenty-round magazine protruding from the pistol grip. I also had three standard thirteen-round mags on my belt—if fifty-nine rounds weren't enough, I shouldn't be doing this for a living.

The senior citizens began getting off the bus. They were typical Brits abroad, the men dressed almost identically: beige flannels, sensible shoes, and a V-neck sweater over a shirt and tie. Most of the women were in polyester slacks with elastic waistbands and a sewn-in crease down the front. They all had flawless, blow-dried, jet black, white, or blue-rinsed hair. They spotted the cafe and started to move as a herd toward us.

Pat muttered, "Fuck me, the enemy must be getting desperate. They've sent the Barry Manilow fan club. Friends of yours, grandad?" He grinned at Kev, who offered him a finger to swivel on. Whether you like it or not, you have to quit the SAS—the Special Air Service—at the age of forty, and Kev had just a year or two of his contract with the Regiment left.

The young at heart settled down at nearby tables and picked up the menus. It was now decision time for them—whether to have dessert or go for a sandwich, because it was halfway between coffee break and lunchtime and they didn't know which way to jump.

The waiter came out, and they started talking to him one syllable at a time. He looked at them as if they were crazy.

On the net I heard, "Hello, all call signs, this is Alpha. Radio check, over." Alpha, who was located in the ops room, was our controller. When we'd flown in sixty hours ago, our team of eight SAS soldiers and support staff had requisitioned rooms in the accommodation block at HMS *Rooke*, the British naval base in the docks, and turned them into living space.

Kev responded quietly into his concealed microphone: "Golf."

Pat: "Oscar."

I heard Euan: "November."

My turn came: "Delta."

The elderly Brits started taking pictures of themselves. Then they were swapping cameras so they could appear in their own photographs.

Slack Pat got up and said to one of them, "Here y'are, love, want me to take one of all of you?"

"Ooh, you're from England, are you? Isn't it nice and warm now?"

Slack was in his early thirties, blond-haired, blue-eyed, good-looking, clever, articulate, funny; he was everything I hated. He was also six feet two, and one of those people who naturally shit muscle. Even his hair was well toned; I'd seen him climb into his sleeping bag with his hair looking groomed and perfect and wake up with it in the same condition. Pat's only saving grace, as far as I was concerned, was that when he stood up, there was nothing where his ass should have been. We used to call him Slack because he had lots of it.

He had just started doing a Richard Avedon when we got: "Stand by, stand by!" on the net from one of the female triggers. "That's a possible, a possible—Bravo One toward the town square."

Alpha came back, "Roger that. Delta, acknowledge."

I got to my feet, gave two clicks on the radio transmitter that was wired into my jacket pocket, and started walking. It was pointless all three of us moving at this stage.

Families on their Sunday *paseo* strolled across from my left. Tourists were taking pictures of buildings, looking at maps, and scratching their heads; locals were sitting down, enjoying the weather, walking their dogs, playing with their grandchildren. There were two men with comfortable-looking beer bellies, old and not giving a fuck, smoking themselves to death. Pants with big suspenders, shirt and undershirt, soaking up the March sun.

I wondered how many of them would survive if the bomb went off just here.

I was just starting to get in my stride when a very fired up male trigger shouted: "Stand by, stand by! That's also a possible Bravo Two and Echo One at the top end of Main Street."

This got me quite excited.

I listened for Euan. His task in this operation was the same as mine: to confirm the "possibles" with a positive ID. I imagined him sauntering along the sidewalk like me. He was short, with an acne-scarred face and the world's biggest motorcycle, which he could just about keep upright because his toes only brushed the ground. I liked to take the piss out of him about it as often as I could. I knew the guy like a brother—in fact, probably better; I hadn't seen any of my family for more than ten years. Euan and I had been young soldiers together; we'd passed Selection at the same time, and we'd been working together ever since. The fucker was so unflappable I always thought his heart must have been only barely beating. I'd been with him in Hereford when the police arrived to tell him that his sister had been murdered. He just said, "I think I'd better go to London then and sort things out." It wasn't that he didn't care; he just didn't get excited about anything. That sort of calm is contagious. It always made me feel secure to have guys like him around me.

I hit Main Street and spotted Bravo One right away.

I got on the net: "Alpha, this is Delta. That's confirmed— Bravo One, brown pinstripe on faded blue."

He always wore that brown pinstriped suit jacket; he'd had it for so long that it sagged in the pockets, and there were constant creases in the back from wearing it in a car. And the same old faded and threadbare jeans, the crotch halfway down between his balls and his knees. He was walking away from me, stocky, slight stoop, short hair, long sideburns, but I recognized the gait. I knew it was Sean Savage. Bomb maker number one for the Provisional Irish Republican Army—PIRA.

I followed him to a small square at the bottom end of Main Street, near the governor's residence, where the band of the resident British infantry battalion would fall out after the changing of the guard. It was where Simmonds suspected the PIRA team might plant their bomb.

Alpha, the base station controlling the operation for now, repeated the message so that everyone knew which direction Savage was walking in. I knew that Golf and Oscar—Kev and Slack Pat—would soon start moving up behind me.

There were six or seven cars parked up against the wall of an old colonial building, taking advantage of the shade. I saw Bravo One push his hand into his jacket pocket as he headed toward them. For a split second I thought he was going for the initiation device.

Without checking his stride, Savage focused on one vehicle in particular and headed toward it. I moved slightly to the right so I had a clear view of the license plate.

"Alpha, this is Delta," I said. "That's Bravo One now at vehicle Mike Lima 174412."

I pictured Alpha with the bank of computers in front of him in the control room. He confirmed, "Roger that, Mike Lima 174412. That's a white Renault Five."

"It's on the right, third car from the entrance," I said. "That's nose in."

By now the keys were in Savage's hands.

"Stop, stop, stop. Bravo One at the car, he's at the car."

I was committed to passing him quite close now—I couldn't just change direction. I could see his profile; his chin and top lip were full of zits, and I knew what that meant. Under pressure, his acne always blew up.

Savage was still at the Renault. He turned, now with his back to me, pretending to sort his keys out, but I knew he'd be checking the telltales. A sliver of Scotch tape across a door, things arranged in a certain way inside the vehicle; whatever, if they were not as he had left them, Savage would lift off.

Kev and Slack Pat would be somewhere near the entrance to the square, ready to "back." If I got overexposed to the target, one of them would take over, or if I got in deep shit and had a contact, they would have to finish it—and we'd all worked together long enough for me to know that, as friends as well as colleagues, they'd let nothing stand between them and the task.

The buildings were casting shadows across the square. I couldn't feel any breeze, just the change in temperature as I moved out of the sunlight.

I was too close to Savage now to transmit. As I walked past the car I could hear the keys going in and the click of the lock.

I headed for a wooden bench on the far side of the square and sat down. There were newspapers in a trash can next to me; I picked one out and pretended to read, watching him.

Savage made a suspicious move and I got back on the net: "Alpha, this is Delta—that's his feet outside, he's fiddling underneath the dashboard, he's fiddling under the dashboard. Wait . . ." I had my finger on the button, so I was still commanding the net. Could he be making the final connection to the bomb?

As I was doing my ventriloquist act, an old guy wandered toward me, pushing his bike. The fucker was on his way over for a chat. I took my finger off the button and waited. I was deeply involved in the local newspaper but didn't have a clue what it said. He obviously thought I did. I didn't want to stick around and discuss the weather, but I wasn't going to just blow him off either because he might start jumping up and down and draw Savage's attention.

The old guy stopped, one hand on his bike, the other one flailing around. He asked me a question. I didn't understand a word he was saying. I made a face that said I didn't know what the world was coming to, shrugged, and looked down again at the paper. I'd obviously done the wrong thing. He said some angry shit, then wheeled his bike away, arm still flailing.

I got back on the radio. I couldn't exactly see what Savage was doing, but both of his feet were still outside the Renault. He had his ass on the driver's seat and was leaning underneath the dash. It looked as if he was trying to get something out of the glove compartment—as if he'd forgotten something and gone back to get it. I couldn't confirm what he was doing but his hands kept going into his pockets.

Everything was closing in. I felt like a boxer—I could hear the crowd, I was listening to my seconds and the referee, I was listening for the bell, but mostly I was focused on the boy

I was fighting. Nothing else mattered. Nothing. The only important people in the world were me and Bravo One.

Through my earpiece I could hear Euan working like a man possessed, trying to get on top of the other two terrorists.

Kev and Slack Pat were still backing me; the other two boys in our team were with Euan. They'd all still be satelliting, listening on the net so as to be out of sight of the targets, but always close enough to back us if we got in trouble.

Euan closed in on Bravo Two and Echo One. They were coming in our direction. Everybody knew where they were; everybody would keep out of the way so they had a clear run in.

I recognized them as soon as they turned the corner.

Bravo Two was Daniel Martin McCann. Unlike Savage, who was well educated and an expert bomb maker, "Mad Danny" was a butcher by trade and a butcher by nature. He'd been expelled from the movement by Gerry Adams in 1985 for threatening to initiate a campaign of murder that would have hampered the new political strategy. It was a bit like being kicked out of the Gestapo for cruelty. But McCann had supporters and soon got himself reinstated. Married with two children, he had twenty-six killings linked to his name. Ulster Loyalists had tried to whack him once, but failed. They should have tried harder.

Echo One was Mairead Farrell. Middle class and an ex–convent schoolgirl, she was, at thirty-one, one of the highest-ranking women in the IRA. See her picture and you'd think, aah, an angel. But she'd served ten years for planting a bomb in Belfast and reported back for duty as soon as she was released. Things hadn't gone her way; a few months earlier her lover had accidentally blown himself up. As Simmonds had said at the briefing, that made her one very pissed off Echo One.

I knew them both well; Euan and I had been working against them for years. I got on the net and confirmed the ID.

Everybody was in place. Alpha would be in the control room with the senior policeman, people from the Foreign Office, people from the Home Office, you name it, every man and his dog would be there, everybody wanting to put in their two cents' worth, everybody with their own concerns. We could only hope that Simmonds would be looking after ours. I'd met the Secret Intelligence Service desk officer for Northern Ireland only a couple of days earlier, but he certainly seemed to be running our side of the show. His voice had the sort of confidence that was shaped on the playing fields of Eton, and he measured his words slowly, like a big-time attorney with the meter running.

We wanted the decision made now. But I knew there would be a big debate going on in the ops room; you'd probably have to cut your way through the cigarette smoke with a knife. Our liaison officer would be listening to us on his radio and explaining everything that we were doing, confirming that the team was in position. At crunch time, it was the police, not us, who'd decide that we go in. Once it was handed over to the military, Kev would control the team.

The frustration was unendurable. I just wanted to get this over.

By now Farrell was leaning against the driver's door, the two men standing and facing her. If I hadn't known differently I'd have said they were trying to chat her up. I couldn't hear what they were saying but their faces showed no sign of stress, and now and then I could hear laughter above the traffic noise. Savage even got out a packet of mints and passed them round.

I was still giving a running commentary when Alpha came back on the net. "Hello, all call signs, all call signs, I have control, I have control. Golf, acknowledge."

Kev acknowledged. The police had handed over; it was Kev's show now.

The targets started to move away from the vehicle, so I pushed the button four times.

Golf came back: "Stand by, stand by!"

That was it; we were off.

I let them walk toward the main square, and then I got up. I knew we wouldn't lift them here. There were far too many people around. For all we knew, the players might want to go out in a blaze of glory and start dropping the civilians, take them hostage, or, even worse, go into kamikaze mode and detonate the device.

Alpha came back on the net. "Hello, all call signs, all call signs—cancel, cancel, cancel! I do not have control! Cancel! Golf, acknowledge."

At once I heard Kev's not-so-formal reply: "What the fuck's going on? Tell me—what's going on?"

"Wait . . . wait . . ." Alpha sounded under pressure. There were voices in the background. "All stations, all stations, the police need another ID, they need to be sure. Golf, acknowledge."

What do they want, introductions? *"Hi, I'm Danny, bomber and murderer, I enjoy traveling and working with children."*

We were in danger of losing them if we didn't act soon.

Alpha came back: "All stations, ATO is moving to check the vehicle. Delta, we need that confirmation." The ATO is the ammunitions technical officer.

I acknowledged. There was obviously some sweating going on in the ops room. The boss was getting a hard time from the police; it sounded like a chimpanzees' tea party in there.

The terrorist team would be crossing the border within minutes. Once they were on the other side, they could detonate the bomb with immunity.

I was now on the other side of the road, and wanted at least to get parallel to them so I could see their faces again. I had to reconfirm the players, then stick with them.

More activity on the net. I could hear the tension in Alpha's voice now, telephone lines ringing, people milling about.

Kev cut in: "Fuck the ops room, let's keep on top of them until someone somewhere makes a fucking decision. Lima and Zulu, can you get forward?"

Zulu came on the net for himself and Lima, very much out of breath: "Zulu and Lima, we . . . we can do that."

"Roger that, move up, tell me when you're there."

Kev wanted them beyond the health center. They were running hard to get ahead of the targets; they didn't care who saw them as long as the players didn't. But we still hadn't got control.

Kev came back on the net: "Alpha, this is Golf. You need to get your finger out now—we're going to lose them. What do you want us to do?"

"Golf, wait, wait . . ."

I could still hear noise in the background: lots of talking, more telephones ringing, people shouting instructions.

Everything went quiet.

"Wait . . . wait . . ."

All I could hear now was the background noise of Alpha on my radio, plus my pulse pounding in my head. Then, at last, the voice of Simmonds—very clear, a voice you wouldn't argue with. I heard him say to Alpha, "Tell the ground commander he can continue."

"All call signs, this is Alpha. I have control. I have control. Golf, acknowledge."

Kev got on the net, and instead of acknowledging, said, "Thank God for that. All call signs, if they get as far as the airport, we'll lift them there. If not—on my word, on my word. Zulu and Lima, how's it going?"

They came back on the net. "That's us static at the junction. We can take." They were at the intersection of Main Street and Smith Dorrien Avenue, the main approach road to the crossing into Spain. The players were moving toward them.

I could lift off soon. I'd done the job I'd been brought here to do. I prepared myself for the handover.

But then they stopped.

Fuck. "Stop, stop, stop!" I said. "That's Bravo One, Two and Echo One static."

Everybody was closing in. *Come on, let's lift them here and now.*

Savage split from the other two and headed back the way they'd come, toward the town center. It was all going to rat shit. We had two groups to control now, and we didn't know who had the detonation device.

Kev arrived to back me. On the net, I could hear the other two players being followed toward the border by the rest of the team as I moved in to take Savage. He turned left down an alleyway.

I was just about to get on the net when I heard a police siren, followed by gunfire behind me.

At the same instant Euan came on the net: "Contact! Contact!"

Then more shots.

Kev and I looked at each other. *What the fuck was going on?* We ran around the corner. Savage had heard the shots, too, and turned back toward us. Even at this distance I could see his eyes, big as plates and jerking like he was having a seizure.

There was a female pedestrian between us. Kev shouted, "Stop, security forces! Stop!"

With his left hand, he had to push the woman over to the side and bang her against the wall to keep her out of the way. She was going down, blood pouring from her head. At least she wouldn't get up and become a target.

She began screaming. We had Kev hollering and screaming at Savage, and all the people in the area were starting to scream. It was turning into a gang fuck.

Kev flicked back the right side of his sport jacket to reach the pancake holster over his kidneys. We always put a bit of weight in a pocket—a full mag is good—to help the jacket flick back out of the way.

But I wasn't really looking at Kev; I was looking at Savage. I could see his hand moving to the right side of his jacket. He wasn't some knuckle-dragging moron from the backstreets. The moment he saw us, he knew the score. It was decision time.

Kev drew his pistol, brought it up, and prepared to fire.

Nothing.

"Stoppage! Fuck, Nick, fuck, fuck!"

Trying to clear his weapon, he dropped on one knee to make himself a smaller target.

That was when everything seemed to go into slow motion.

Savage and I had eye-to-eye. He knew what I was going to do; he could have stopped, he could have put his hands up.

My bomber jacket was held together with Velcro, so at times like this I could just pull it apart and draw my pistol.

The only way a weapon can be drawn and used quickly is by breaking the whole movement into stages. Stage one, I kept looking at the target. With my left hand I grabbed a fistful of bomber jacket and pulled it as hard as I could toward my chest. The Velcro ripped apart.

At the same time I was sucking in my stomach and sticking out my chest to make the pistol grip easy to access. You get only one chance.

We still had eye contact. He started to shout, but I didn't hear. There was too much other shouting going on, from everyone on the street and the earpiece in my head.

Stage two, I pushed the web of my right hand down onto the pistol grip. If I got this wrong, I wouldn't be able to aim correctly: I would miss and die. As I felt my web push against the pistol grip, my lower three fingers gripped hard around it. My index finger was outside the trigger guard, parallel with the barrel. I didn't want to pull the trigger early and kill myself. Savage was still looking, still shouting.

Savage's hand was nearly at his pocket.

Stage three, I drew my weapon, in the same movement taking the safety catch off with my thumb.

Our eyes were still locked. I saw that Savage knew he had lost. There was just a curling of the lips. He knew he was going to die.

As my pistol came out I flicked it parallel with the ground. No time to extend my arms and get into a stable firing position.

Stage four, my left hand was still pulling my jacket out of the way and the pistol was now just by my belt buckle. There was no need to look at it; I knew where it was and what it was pointing at. I kept my eyes on the target, and his never left mine. I pulled the trigger.

The weapon report seemed to bring everything back into real time. The first round hit him. I didn't know where—I didn't need to. His eyes told me all I wanted to know.

I kept on firing. There is no such thing as overkill. If he could move, he could detonate the bomb. If it took a whole magazine to be sure I'd stopped the threat, then that was what I'd fire. As Savage hit the ground I could no longer see his hands. He was curled up in a ball, holding his stomach. I moved forward and fired two shots at the head. He was no longer a threat.

Kev ran over and was searching inside Savage's coat.

"It's not here," he said. "No weapon, no firing device."

I looked down at Kev as he wiped the blood off his hands onto Savage's jeans.

"One of the others must have had it," he said. "I didn't hear the car go up, did you?"

In all the confusion I couldn't be sure.

I stood over them both. Kev's mother came from southern Spain; he looked like a local: jet black hair, about five feet ten inches, and the world's bluest eyes. His wife reckoned he was a dead ringer for Mel Gibson, which he scoffed at but secretly liked. Right now his face was a picture; he knew he owed me one. I wanted to say, "It's OK, these things happen," but it just didn't seem like the time. Instead I said, "Fucking hell, Brown, what do you expect if you have a name the same color as shit?"

As I spoke we put our safety catches on, and Kev and I swapped weapons.

"I'm glad I won't be at any inquest." I grinned at Kev. "You'd better start getting your shit together."

He smiled as he got on the radio and started to send a situation report. It was all right for him and the others, but Euan and I shouldn't have been here. We had to vanish before the police arrived. We had been flown in from doing undercover work in Northern Ireland with Fourteen Intelligence Group; it was illegal for its members to operate anywhere else. If either of us were caught in Gibraltar, there would be a shit storm.

The ops room at HMS *Rooke* was about fifteen minutes away on foot. I tucked Kev's weapon inside my jeans and started walking fast.

The mood was subdued aboard the C-130 as it lifted from the tarmac at 11 P.M. that night.

Spanish police had found PIRA's car bomb in an underground parking garage in Marbella, thirty miles away, across
the Spanish border; 145 pounds of Semtex high explosive
and an unattached timing device preset at 11:20 A.M., the time
the Gibraltar guard-changing ceremony ended and the soldiers dispersed in the square. The white Renault had been a
blocking vehicle after all.

When Simmonds came over, Pat said, "As far as we knew,
they had the means to detonate a bomb big enough to separate Gibraltar from the mainland. All it would have taken was
one press of a button. If there's going to be an inquest, fuck it.
Better to be tried by twelve, I say, than carried by six."

Deafened suddenly by the roar of the C-130's engines, I
glanced at Kev, Pat, Euan—and tried to forget what I was
going back to. A house isn't a home when there are no pictures on the walls.

Back when we were in the Persian Gulf, Pat had a battle
cry: "All for one and one for all." We'd laughed when he used
it, but he was right on target. Any one of us would put his life
on the line for the others. I cracked a smile; with these guys
around me, who needed family? Without a doubt, I thought,
this was as good as it was ever going to get.

1

NINE YEARS LATER

If you work for the British intelligence service (also known as the Firm) and get formally summoned to a meeting at their headquarters building on the south bank of the River Thames at Vauxhall, there are three levels of interview. First is the one with coffee and cookies, which means they're going to give you a pat on the head. Next down the food chain is the more businesslike coffee but no cookies, which means they're not asking but telling you to follow orders. And finally there's no cookies, and no coffee, either, which basically means that you're in deep shit. Since leaving the SAS in 1993 and working on deniable operations, I'd had a number at every level, and I wasn't expecting a nice frothy cappuccino this particular Monday. In fact I was quite worried, because things hadn't been going too well.

As I emerged from the subway station at Vauxhall the omens weren't exactly with me, either. The March sky was dull and overcast, preparing itself for the Easter holiday; my path was blocked by roadworks, and a burst from a jack-hammer sounded like the crack of a firing squad. Vauxhall Cross, home of what the press call MI6 but which is actually the Secret Intelligence Service, is about a mile upstream from the Houses of Parliament. Bizarrely shaped like a beige and black pyramid that's had its top cut off, with staged levels, large towers on either side, and a terrace bar over-looking the river, it needs only a few swirls of neon and you'd swear it was a casino. It wouldn't look out of place in Las Vegas. I missed Century House, the old HQ building near Waterloo station. It might have been 1960s ugly, square with loads of glass, net curtains, and antennae, and not so handy to the subway, but it was much less pretentious.

Opposite Vauxhall Cross and about two hundred yards across the wide arterial road is an elevated section of railway line, and beneath that are arches that have been turned into shops, two of which have been knocked through to make a massive motorcycle shop. I was early, so I popped in and fantasized about which Ducati I was going to buy when I got a pay raise—which wasn't going to be today. What the hell, the way my luck was going I'd probably go and kill myself on it.

I'd fucked up severely. I'd been sent to Saudi to encourage, then train, some Northern Iraqi Kurds to kill three leading members of the Ba'ath party; the hope was that the assassinations would heat everything up and help dismantle the regime in Baghdad.

The first part of my task was to take delivery in Saudi of some former Eastern bloc weapons that had been smuggled in—Russian Draganov sniper weapons, a couple of Makharov pistols, and two AK assault rifles, the parachute version with a folding stock. All serial numbers had been erased to make them deniable.

For maximum chaos, the plan was to get the Kurds to make three hits at exactly the same time in and around Baghdad. One was going to be a close-quarters shoot, using the Makharovs. The idea was for the two boys to walk up to the family house, knock on the door, take on whatever threat presented itself, make entry into the house, zap the target, and run.

The second was going to be a sniper option. The target saw himself as a big-time fitness freak; he'd come out and have a little jog around a track, all of about four hundred yards. He emerged from his house every day in a lime green, fluffy velour tracksuit, did one lap, and that was his training for the day. The boys were going to hit him just as he started to sweat and slow down—which by the look of him would be after about a hundred yards. I would be on this one to coordinate the hit so that both fired at once.

The third target was going to be taken out on his way to the ministry. Two bikes would pull up at stoplights and give him the good news with their AK-47s.

I landed up in Northern Iraq without any problems and started the buildup training. At this stage not even the Kurds knew what their task was going to be. The Draganov sniper rifles were a heap of shit. However, the weapon is never as important as the ammunition, which in this case was even worse, Indian 7.62mm. Given a free hand I would have wanted to use Lapier, manufactured in Finland and the best in the world for sniping because of its consistency, but Western rounds would have given the game away.

The Indian ammunition was hit and miss—mostly miss. On top of that the Draganovs were semiautomatic rifles. Ideally, you need a bolt-action weapon, which is not only better for taking the hit, it also doesn't leave an empty case behind because it stays in the weapon until you reload. However, it had to be Russian shit that they were zapped with, and it had to be deniable.

Once all three jobs went down, the weapons were to be dumped and destroyed. They weren't. On the AK there is a forward leaf sight, with a serial number scratched underneath it. I had been told that all serial numbers had been removed at the source, and had taken the information at face value. I didn't check—I fucked up.

The only way to save the situation as far as London was concerned was to kill the Kurd teams I'd been training. It was damage control on a drastic scale, but it had to be done. Detail counts. If the Iraqis could trace the weapons, they might make the UK connection. If they then captured the Kurds, who just happened to mention that they had been trained by a Westerner called Nick, it wouldn't take a mastermind to figure out which country he came from. It actually pissed me off to have to kill them, because I'd gotten to know these guys really well. I was still wearing the G Shock watch one of the snipers had given me. We'd had a bet when we were on the range, and he lost. I knew that I could beat him, but still cheated because I had to win. I'd really gotten to like him.

Back in the UK there had been an internal inquiry; everybody was covering their ass. And because I was a K, they

could land it all on me. The armorers and technicians from
the intelligence service said it was my fault for not checking.
What could I say? I didn't even exist. I was bracing myself to
take the hit.

I entered Vauxhall Cross via a single metal door that fun-
neled me toward reception. Inside, the building could be mis-
taken for any high-tech office block in any city—very clean,
sleek, and corporate. People who worked there were swiping
their identity cards through electronic readers to get in, but I
had to go over to the main reception desk. Two women sat behind thick bulletproof glass.

Through the intercom system I said to one of them, "I'm
here to see Mr. Lynn."

"Can you fill this in, please?" She passed a ledger through
a slot under the glass.

As I signed my name in two boxes, she picked up a telephone. "Who shall I say is coming to see Mr. Lynn?"

"My name is Stamford."

The ledger held tear-off labels. One half was going to
be ripped off and put in a plastic badge container, which I
would have to pin on. My badge was blue and said ESCORTED
EVERYWHERE.

The woman came off the phone and said, "There'll be
somebody coming down to pick you up."

A young clerk appeared minutes later. "Mr. Stamford? If
you'd like to come with me." He pressed the elevator button
and said, "We're going to the fifth floor."

The whole building is a maze. I just followed him; I didn't
have a clue where we were going. There was little noise
coming from any of the offices, just people bent over papers
or working at PCs. At the far end of one corridor we turned
left into a room. Old metal filing cabinets, a couple of six-
foot tables put together, and like in any office anywhere, the
cups, packets of coffee and sugar, and a milk roster. None of
that for me, though—in free-fall talk, I'd just stand by and accept the landing.

Lieutenant Colonel Lynn's office was off to one side of the
larger area. When the clerk knocked on the door, there was a

crisp and immediate call of "Come in!" The boy turned the handle and ushered me past him.

Lynn was standing behind his desk. In his early forties, he was of average build, height, and looks but had that aura about him that singled him out as a high achiever. The only thing he didn't have, I was always pleased to note, was plenty of hair. I'd known him on and off for about ten years; for the last two years his job had been liaison between the Ministry of Defense and SIS.

It was only as I walked farther into the room that I realized he wasn't alone. Sitting to one side of the desk, obscured until now by the half-open door, was Simmonds. I hadn't seen him since Gibraltar. What a professional he'd turned out to be, sorting out the inquest and basically making sure that Euan and I didn't exist. I felt a mixture of surprise and relief to see him here. He'd had nothing to do with the Kurd job. We might be getting the coffee after all.

Simmonds stood up. Six feet tall, late forties, rather distinguished-looking, a very polite man, I thought, as he extended his hand. He was dressed in corduroy trousers the color of Gulden's mustard, and a shirt that looked as if he'd slept in it.

"Delighted to see you again, Nick."

We shook hands and Lynn said, "Would you like some coffee?"

Things were looking up.

"Thanks—milk, no sugar."

We all sat down. I took a wooden chair that was on the other side of the desk and had a quick look around the office while Lynn pressed the intercom on his desk and passed the order on to the clerk. His office was at the rear of the building and overlooked the Thames. It was a very plain, very functional, very impersonal room save for a framed photograph on the desk of a group I presumed were his wife and two children. There were two Easter eggs and wrapping paper on the windowsill. Mounted on a wall bracket in one corner was a television; the screen was scrolling through world news headlines. Under the TV was the obligatory officers' squash racquet and his jacket on a coatrack.

Without further formalities Lynn leaned over and said, "We've got a fastball for you."

I looked at Simmonds.

Lynn continued, "Nick, you're in deep shit over the last job, and that's just tough. But you can rectify that by going on this one. I'm not saying it'll help, but at least you're still working. Take it or leave it."

I said, "I'll do it."

He'd known what I was going to say. He was already reaching for a small stack of files containing photographs and bits of paper. As a margin note on one of the sheets I could see a scribble in green ink. It could have been written only by the head of the Firm. Simmonds still hadn't said a word.

Lynn handed me a photograph.

"Who are they?"

"Michael Kerr and Morgan McGear. They're on their way to Shannon as we speak, then flying to Heathrow for a flight to Washington. They've booked a return flight with Virgin, and they're running on forged Southern Irish passports. I want you to take them from Shannon to Heathrow and then on to Washington. See what they're up to and who they're meeting there."

I'd followed players out of the Irish Republic before and could anticipate a problem. I said, "What happens if they don't follow the plan? If they're on forged passports, they might go through the motions just to get through the security check—then use their other passports to board another flight and fuck off to Amsterdam. It wouldn't be the first time."

Simmonds smiled. "I understand your concern, and it is noted. But they will go."

Lynn passed me a sheet of paper. "These are the flight details. They booked yesterday in Belfast."

There was a knock on the door. Three coffees arrived, one in a mug showing the Tasmanian Devil, one with a vintage car on it, and a plain white one. I got the impression Lynn and Simmonds were on their second round.

Simmonds picked up the plain one, Lynn picked up the car, and I was left with the Tasmanian Devil running up a hill.

"Who's taking them from Belfast to Shannon?"

Simmonds said, "Actually, it's Euan. He has them at the moment. He'll hand over to you at Shannon."

I smiled to myself at the mention of Euan's name. I was now out of the system and basically just used as a K on deniable operations. The only reason I did it was to finance the other things I wanted to do. What they were I didn't know yet; I was a thirty-seven-year-old man with a lot on his mind, but not too much in it. Euan, however, still felt very much part of the system. He still had that sense of moral responsibility to fight the good fight—whatever that meant—and he'd be there until the day he was kicked out.

Simmonds handed me the folder. "Check that off," he said. "There are thirteen pages. I want you to sign for it now and hand it over to the air crew when you've finished. Good luck," he added, not meaning it at all.

"Am I going now?" I said. "I don't have my passport with me—*fastball* isn't the word."

Lynn said, "Your passport's in there. Have you got your other docs?"

I looked at him as if I'd been insulted.

Passport, driver's license, credit cards are the basic requirements for giving depth to a cover story. From there the K builds up his own cover by using the credit cards to buy things, or maybe make direct payments for magazine subscriptions or club memberships. I had my cards with me as always, but not my passport. The one Simmonds handed me had probably been specially produced that morning, correct even down to visas and the right degree of aging.

I didn't have time to finish my coffee. The clerk reappeared and took me downstairs. I signed for the documents in the outer office before I left; thirteen pieces of paper with the information on them, and I had to sign each sheet. Then I had to sign for the folder it was in. Fucking bureaucracy.

A car was waiting for me outside. I jumped in the front; when I was a kid I'd look at people being chauffeured and

think, *Who the fuck do they think they are?* I talked shit with
the driver, probably bored him silly; he didn't really want to
talk, but it made me feel better.

A civilian Squirrel was waiting on the pad at Battersea
heliport, rotors slowly turning. I had one last job to do before
boarding; from a pay phone I called up the family who covered for me, people who'd vouch for me if I was ever up
against it. They'd never take any action on my behalf, but if I
got lifted I could say to the police, "That's where I live—
phone them, ask them."

A male voice answered the phone.

"James, it's Nick. I've just been given a chance to go to the
States and visit friends. I might be a week or two. If it's more,
I'll call."

James understood. "The Wilmots next door had a break-in
two days ago and we're going to see Bob in Dorset over the
Easter weekend."

I needed to know these things because I would if I lived
there all the time. They even sent the local paper to my accommodation address each week.

"Cheers, mate. When you see that son of yours next
weekend, tell him he still owes me a night out."

"I will . . . Have a nice holiday."

As we skimmed over the Irish Sea I opened the briefing pack
and thumbed through the material. I needn't have bothered.
All they knew for certain was that two boys had booked
tickets to Washington, D.C., and they wanted to find out why.
They wanted to know who they were meeting and what was
happening once they met. I knew from experience that the
chances of failure were great. Even if they kept to the script
and landed in D.C., how was I going to follow them around?
There were two of them and one of me; as a basic antisurveillance drill they were sure to split up at some point. But hey,
the Firm had me by the balls.

Judging from one of the documents, it seemed that we'd
reached the time of the year when all good PIRA fund-raisers
headed for the dinner circuit in Boston, New York, Washington, D.C.—even down as far as Tucson, Arizona, to catch

Irish American sympathizers who'd retired to the sun. It seemed that the seizure of ten tons of explosives and weapons during the search of a warehouse in north London last September had produced a financial crisis. PIRA wasn't exactly asking its bank for an overdraft yet, but the increase in legitimate fund-raising in Northern Ireland was an indication that they were sweating. There were also other, less public, ways of raising cash. I was sure my new friends were part of that.

Apart from that, I was still none the wiser about the job. I had no information on the players' cover stories, or where they might be going, inside or outside D.C. All I knew was who they were and what they looked like. I read that Michael Kerr had been a member of the South Armagh ASU (Active Service Unit). He'd taken part in four mortar attacks on Special Forces bases and in dozens of shootings against the security forces and Protestants. He'd even gotten wounded once but escaped into the South. A tough nut.

The same could be said for Morgan McGear. After a career as a shooter in the border area of South Armagh, the thirty-one-year-old subcontractor had been promoted to PIRA's security team, where his job was to find and question informers. His favored method of interrogation was a Black & Decker power drill.

2

The helicopter was operated by a civilian front company, so the arrival procedure at Shannon, the Irish Republic's premier airport, was no different than if I'd been a horse breeder coming to check the assets at his stud farm in Tipperary, or a businessman flying in from London to fill his briefcase with European Union subsidies. I walked across the tarmac into the arrivals terminal, went through Customs, and followed the exit signs, heading for the taxi stand. At the last minute I doubled back into departures.

At the Aer Lingus ticket desk I picked up my ticket for Heathrow, which had been booked in the name of Nick Stamford. When choosing a cover name it's always best to keep your own first name—that way you react naturally to it. It also helps if your last name begins with the real initial because the signature flows better. I'd picked Stamford after the battle of Stamford Bridge. I loved medieval history.

I headed straight to the shop to buy myself a bag. Everybody has hand luggage; I'd stick out like the balls on a bulldog if I boarded the aircraft with nothing but a can of Coke. I never traveled with luggage that had to be checked in because then you're in the hands of whoever it is who decides to take bags marked Tokyo and send them to Buenos Aires instead. Even if your baggage does arrive safely, if it reaches the carousel five minutes after the target's, you're fucked.

I bought some toothpaste and other odds and ends, all the time keeping an eye out for Euan. I knew that he'd be glued to Kerr and McGear, unless they'd already gone through the security gates.

24

The departures lounge seemed full of Irish families who were going to find the Easter sun, and newly retired Americans who'd come to find their roots, wandering around with their brand-new Guinness sweatshirts, umbrellas, and baseball caps, and leprechauns in tins and little pots of grow-your-own shamrock.

It was busy, and the bars were doing good business. I spotted Euan at the far end of the terminal, sitting at a table in a coffee shop, having a large frothy coffee and reading a paper. I'd always found "Euan" a strange name for him. It always made me think of a guy with a kilt on running up and down a hill somewhere, tossing a caber. In fact, he was born in Oxford, and his parents came from Surrey. They must have watched some Scottish movie and liked the name.

To the left was a bar. Judging by where Euan was sitting I guessed that was where the players were. I didn't bother looking; I knew Euan would point them out. There was no rush.

As I came out of the pharmacy, I looked toward the coffee shop and got eye-to-eye. I started walking toward him, big grin all over my face as if I'd just spotted a long-lost pal, but didn't say anything yet. If somebody was watching him, knowing he was on his own, it wouldn't look natural for me just to come up and sit next to him and start talking. It had to look like a chance meeting, yet not such a noisy one that people noticed it. They wouldn't think, *Oh, look, there's two spies meeting,* but it registers. It might not mean anything at the time, but it could cost you later.

Euan started to stand and returned my smile. "Hello, dickhead, what are you doing here?" He gestured for me to join him.

We sat down, and since Euan was sponsoring the RV (rendezvous), he came up with the cover story. "I've just come to see you from Belfast before you fly back to London. Old friends from schooldays." It helps to know you both have the same story.

"Where are they?" I said, as if asking after the family.

"My half left and you've got the bar. Go right of the TV.

They're sitting—one's got a jean jacket on, one a black three-quarter-length suede coat. Kerr is on the right-hand side. He's now called Michael Lindsay. McGear is Morgan Ashdown."

"Have they checked in?"

"Yes. Hand luggage only."

"For two weeks in Washington?"

"They've got suit bags."

"And they haven't gone to any other check-in?"

"No, it looks like they're going to Heathrow."

I walked over to the counter and bought two coffees.

They were the only Irishmen at the bar, because everybody else was wearing a Guinness polo shirt and drinking pints of the black stuff. These two had Budweisers by the neck and were watching soccer. Both had cigarettes and were smoking like ten men; if I'd been watching them in a bar in Derry, I'd have taken it as nervousness, but Aer Lingus has a no-smoking policy on its flights; it looked as if these boys were getting their big hit before boarding.

Both were looking very much the tourist, clean-shaven, clean hair, not overdressed as businessmen, not underdressed as slobs. Basically they were so nondescript you wouldn't give them a second glance, which indicated that they were quite switched on—and that was a problem for me. If they'd been looking like a bag of shit or at all nervous, I'd have known I was up against second- or third-string players—easy job. But these boys were Major League, a long way from hanging around the docks on kneecapping duty.

There were kids everywhere, chasing and shouting, mothers screaming after two-year-olds who'd found their feet and were skimming across the terminal. For us, the more noise and activity the better. I sat down with the drinks. I wanted to get as much information as I could from Euan before they went through security.

On cue, he said, "I picked McGear up from Derry. He went to the Sinn Féin office on Cable Street and presumably got briefed. Then to Belfast. The spooks tried to use the listening device but didn't have any luck. Nothing else to report, really. They spent the night getting drunk, then came down here. Been here about two hours. They booked the flight by credit card, using their cover names. Their cover's good. They've even got their Virgin luggage tags on; they don't want anything to go wrong."

"Where are they staying?"

"I don't know. It's all very last-minute and Easter's a busy time. There're about ten Virgin-affiliated hotels in D.C.; it's probably one of them—we haven't had time to check."

I didn't write anything down. If you write stuff down, you can lose it. I'd have to remember it. "Is that all?" I asked.

"That's your lot. I don't know how they're going to transfer from the airport, but it looks like they're off to D.C., big boy." Subject closed, as far as Euan was concerned. It was now time to talk shit. "You still see a lot of Kev?"

I took a sip of coffee and nodded. "Yeah, he's in Washington now, doing all right. The kids and Marsha are fine. I saw them about four months ago. He's been promoted, and they've just bought the biggest house in suburbia. It's what you'd call executive housing."

Euan grinned, looking like Santa Claus with white froth on his top lip. His own place was a stone-walled sheep farmer's cottage in the middle of nowhere in the Black Mountains of Wales. His nearest neighbor was two miles away on the other side of the valley.

I said, "Marsha loves it in D.C.—no one trying to shoot holes in the car."

Marsha, an American, was Kev's second wife. After leaving the Regiment he'd moved to the States with her and had joined the Drug Enforcement Administration. They had two young kids, Kelly and Aida.

"Is Slack Pat still over there?"

"I think so, but you know what he's like—one minute he's going to learn how to build houses, and the next minute he's going to take up tree hugging and crocheting. Fuck knows what he's doing now."

Pat had had a job for two years looking after the family of an Arab diplomat in D.C. It worked out really well—he even got an apartment thrown in—but eventually the children he was minding grew too old to be looked after. They went back to Saudi, so he blew off his job and started bumming around.

The fact was, he'd made so much money during those two years he wasn't in a hurry.

We carried on chatting and joking, but all the time Euan's eyes flickered toward the targets.

The players ordered another drink, so it looked as if we were going to be sitting here for a while. We carried on spinning the social shit.

"How's year ten of the house building program?" I grinned.

"I'm still having problems with the boiler."

He'd decided that he was going to put the central heating in himself, but it was a total screwup. He'd ended up spending twice as much money as he would have, had he paid someone to do it.

"Apart from that, it's all squared away. You should come down some time. I can't wait to finish this fucking tour; then I've got about two more years and that's it."

"What are you going to do?"

"As long as it's not what you're doing, I don't care. I thought I'd become a garbageman. I don't give a fuck, really."

I laughed. "You do! You'll be itching to stay in; you're a party man. You'll stay in forever. You moan about it all the time, but actually you love it."

Euan checked the players, then looked back at me. I knew exactly what he was thinking.

I said, "You're right. Don't do this job; it's shit."

"What have you been up to since your Middle Eastern adventure?"

"I've been on holiday, got some downtime in, did a bit of work for a couple of the companies, but nothing much, and to tell you the truth it's great. Now I'm just waiting for the outcome of the inquiry. I think I'm in deep shit—unless this job gets me out."

Euan's eyes moved again. "It looks like you're off."

The two boys must have started to sort themselves out at the bar.

I said, "I'll call you after this is finished. When are you back in the UK?"

"I don't know. Maybe a few days."

"I'll give you a call; we can arrange something. You got yourself a woman yet, or what?"

"You've got to be drunk! I was going out with someone from the London office for a while, but she wanted to make me all nice and fluffy. She was starting to do my washing and all sorts of shit. I really didn't get into it."

"You mean she didn't iron a crease in the front of your jeans?"

Euan shrugged. "She didn't do things my way."

Nobody did. He was the sort of guy who folded his socks instead of putting them inside each other, and stacked his coins in their denominations. Since his divorce he'd become Mr. I'm-going-to-have-the-best-of-everything. People even started to call him Mr. Ikea—you name it, track lights, entertainment center, the whole nine yards. The inside of his house was like a showroom.

I could tell Euan was watching the two players pick up their gear and walk away from the bar.

I took my time; no need to get right up their ass. Euan would tell me when to move.

"Do a one-eighty," he said. "Look to the right, just approaching the newsstand."

I casually got to my feet. It had been great to see him. Maybe this job would turn out to be a waste of time, but at least I'd seen my closest friend. We shook hands, and I walked away. Then I turned, looked ninety degrees to the right, and spotted them, suit bags over their arms.

The departures lounge looked like an Irish craft fair. I was starting to feel out of place; I should have gotten myself a Guinness hat.

What was I going to do once I got to D.C.? I didn't know if somebody was going to pick them up, whether they were taking a cab or the bus, or, if they'd managed to get a hotel, whether transport was included. If they started moving around the city, that would be fun, too. I knew Washington a bit but not in any great detail.

They were still smoking like fiends. I sat in the lounge and picked up a paper from the seat. McGear started scrabbling about for change in his pocket as they talked to each other, standing at the bar. He was suddenly looking purposeful; he was either going to go to the slot machines or the telephone.

He got a note out and leaned over to the bartender; I could see him asking for change. I was sitting more or less directly behind them and about twenty feet back, so even if they turned their heads forty-five degrees to either side, I still wouldn't be in even their peripheral vision.

McGear walked toward the slot machines but continued on past. It must be the telephone.

I got up and wandered over to the newsstand, pretending to check the spinning rack of newspapers outside.

He picked up the phone, put a couple of pound coins in, and dialed. He got the number from a piece of paper, so it wasn't one that was well known to him. I looked at my G Shock; it was 4:16 P.M. The display was still on dual time; if there were any Iraqis in the lounge needing to know the time in Baghdad, I was their man.

I checked my pockets for coins; I had about two and a half quid; I would need more for what I was going to do, so I went in and bought a newspaper with a twenty-pound note.

McGear finished his call and went back to the bar. Those boys weren't going anywhere; they ordered more beer, opened their papers, lit another cigarette.

I gave it a couple of minutes, then strolled over to the phone McGear had been using. I picked up the receiver, threw in a couple of pound coins, and looked for a number on the set. I couldn't find one; not to worry, it would just take a bit longer.

I dialed a London number and a woman's voice said, "Good afternoon, your PIN number, please?"

"Two-four-two-two." The digits were etched into my memory; they were the first half of the army number that I'd had since I was sixteen.

She said, "Do you have a number?"

"No. This line please."

"Wait."

I heard a click, then nothing. I kept my eyes on the players and fed the phone. Within a minute she was back.

"What times are you interested in?"

"I'd like to book it from four-thirteen up till now."

"That's fine. Do you want me to call you, or will you call back?"

"I'll call back. Ten minutes?"

"Fine. Good-bye."

And that was it. No matter where you are in the world, you can dial in and the Firm will run a trace.

I phoned back ten minutes later. We went through the same PIN number routine, then she said, "Nothing until four-ten. A Washington, D.C., number. Washington Flyer Taxis, USA."

As she recited the number, I jotted it down, hung up, and immediately dialed.

"Good morning, Washington Flyer Taxis, Gerry speaking. How may I be of assistance today?"

"Yes, I wonder if a Mr. Ashdown or a Mr. Lindsay has booked a taxi. I just want to make sure they're going to get to a meeting on time."

"Oh yes, sir, we've just had the booking. Collect from Dulles, arriving on flight number—"

I cut in. "Are you going to drop them off at the hotel or are they coming straight to me at Tyson's Corner?"

"Let me see, sir . . . They're booked for the Westin on M Street, Northwest."

"All right, that's fine. Thank you."

Now all I had to do was try to get to the Westin before them. Things were looking OK. Either that, or the fuckers had spotted me and were playing a deception.

The flight to London Heathrow was getting ready to board. I watched them get up, find their tickets, and walk. I followed.

On something like this you always travel club class so you're at the front of the aircraft. You can then choose either to sit down and watch people boarding or let them through ahead of you and come in later on. At the destination, you can wait for the target to come off the aircraft and naturally file in behind—or get out of the way beforehand so that you're ready to make the pickup once you're out of arrivals.

I thought about a drink but decided against it; I might have to start performing as soon as we got to the other side. These guys seemed very professional, so chances were they weren't going to be doing any work after all the Bud they'd been putting away. But still, no drink for me.

I settled into my seat and started to think about Kev and his family. I'd been there when he first met Marsha; I was best man at their wedding and was even godfather to Aida, their second child. I took the job seriously, though I didn't really know what I was supposed to do on the God front.

I knew I'd never have any of my own kids; I'd be too busy running around doing shit jobs like this one. Kev and Marsha knew that, and really tried to make me feel part of their setup. I'd grown up with this fantasy of the perfect family, and as far as I was concerned Kev had it. The first marriage fell apart, but this one seemed absolutely right. His job with the DEA was now mostly deskbound in D.C. He loved it. "More time with the kids, mate," he'd say. "Yeah, so you can be one!" I'd reply. Luckily Marsha was the mature and sensible one; when it came to the family, they complemented each other really well. Their home at Tyson's Corner was a healthy, loving environment, but after three or four days it would get too much for me and I'd have to move on. They'd make a joke of it; they knew I loved them but somehow couldn't handle people showing so much affection. I guessed that was why I'd always felt more comfortable with Euan. We were both made from the same mold.

As for Slack Pat, he was completely off the scale. Half the world seemed to be his best friend, and he was still working on the others. Even when he opened the fridge door and the light came on he'd have to launch into some sort of chat-up routine. When he started the bodyguard job in Washington, a real estate agent took him to look at an apartment in Georgetown, by the university. The way he told the story, he saw a building with people coming in and out.

"What's that then?" he asked.

"One of the best restaurants in Washington," she said. "Half of Congress seems to go there."

"Right, I'll take it," he said. The moon was in a new quarter or some shit like that and I thought for a while he reckoned he'd turned into Donald Trump. He told me he used to eat there every day and knew every waitress by name. He'd even started going out with one of them. Maybe it was her who got him into drugs. I hadn't seen it myself, but I'd heard he had a problem. It made me sad. We'd all seen the results of addiction during our time in Colombia. Pat had called them losers. Now it seemed he was one himself. Hopefully it was just one of his phases.

3

The transfer at Heathrow had been easy. The boys didn't get stopped at the security checks—probably because Special Branch had been informed—and the flight to Dulles had taken off on time.

I hoped McGear and Kerr were going straight to the hotel. I hoped they'd be playing the good tourists and wouldn't blow it by not checking in. If I ever lost a target, I'd look in all the places where he might be—his place of work, the pub, where the kids go to school, where he lived, or even the bookie's. I needed to know as much as I could about them, because once you're inside your target's mind you can second-guess every movement, even understand why they do what they do. Unfortunately, all I knew so far about McGear and Kerr was that they liked drinking Budweiser and must be dying for a smoke. So I had to start with the hotel.

I needed to get in front of them. That shouldn't be a problem, since club class had its own shuttle to get us to the terminal ahead of the herd. However, since they'd prebooked a transfer, I'd need to grab a cab PDQ if I was going to beat them to M Street. I could have booked one of my own when I spoke to Washington Flyer, but I'd tried to do that in Warsaw once in similar circumstances, only to come out and find the two drivers fighting over who to take first, me or the target. It was the taxi stand for me from then on.

I came out of arrivals through two large automatic doors and into a horseshoe of waiting relatives held back by steel barriers, and limo drivers holding up name boards. I carried on through the bustle, turned left, and walked down a long ramp into heat and brilliant sunshine.

There were lots of people waiting for taxis. I did a quick calculation; the number of passengers didn't go into the limited number of cabs. I wandered toward the rear of the rank and waved a twenty-dollar bill at one of the drivers. He smiled conspiratorially and hustled me inside. Another twenty soon had me screaming along the Dulles access road toward Route 66 and Washington, D.C. The airport and its surroundings reminded me of a high-tech business park, with everything green and manicured; there'd even been a lake as we exited the terminal. Suburbia started about fifteen miles from the airport, mainly ribbon development on either side of the Beltway—very neat wooden and brick houses, many still under construction. We passed a sign for the Tyson's Corner turnoff and I strained my neck to see if I could see Kev's place. I couldn't. But, as Euan would have said, executive housing all looks the same.

We crossed the Potomac and entered the city of monuments.

The Westin on M Street was a typical upscale hotel, slick and clean, totally devoid of character. Walking into the lobby, I got my bearings and headed left and up a few stairs to a coffee lounge on a landing that overlooked the reception area; it was the only way in and out. I ordered a double espresso.

A couple of refills later, Kerr and McGear came through the revolving door. Looking very relaxed, they went straight to the desk. I put down my coffee, left a five-dollar bill under the saucer, and wandered down.

It was just a matter of getting the timing right; there was a bit of a line at the desk, but the hotel was as efficient as it was soulless and now had more people behind the reception desk than were waiting to be served.

I couldn't hear what McGear and Kerr were saying, but it was obvious they were checking in. The woman looking after them was tapping a keyboard below desk level. Kerr handed over a credit card; now was the time to make my approach. It makes life far easier if you can get the required information this way rather than trying to follow them, and there was no way I was going to risk a compromise by getting in the elevator with them. I only hoped they were sharing a room.

To the right of them at the reception desk was a rack of postcards advertising everything from restaurants to bus tours. I stood about two yards away, with my back to them. There was no big deal about this; it was a big, busy hotel—they weren't looking at me, they were doing their own stuff. I made it obvious I was flicking through the postcards and didn't need help.

The woman said, "There you are, gentlemen, you're in room four-oh-three. If you turn left just past the pillars, you'll see the elevator. Have a nice day!"

All I had to do now was listen to their conversations while they were in their room, and to make that happen I went to the bank of pay phones in the lobby and dialed the Firm.

A woman's voice asked me for my PIN number.

"Two-four-two-two."

"Go ahead."

"I'd like a room, please. The Westin on M Street, Washington, D.C.—four-oh-one or four-oh-five, or three-oh-three or five-oh-three."

"Have you a contact number?"

"No, I'll call back in half an hour."

They would now telephone the hotel using the name of a front company and request one of the rooms I'd specified. It didn't really matter whether the room was above, beside, or below the targets', as long as we could get in and plant surveillance devices.

I went back to the raised lounge area and read a few of the leaflets and postcards I'd picked up, all the time watching the exit onto M Street.

I ran through a mental checklist of surveillance equipment to ask for. I'd fit the first wave of gear myself: wall-mounted listening devices, phone-line devices, both voice and modem, and cables that fed into the TV in my room to relay pictures. They'd take me only about three hours to rig up once the Firm had dropped them off.

The second wave, once McGear and Kerr had vacated their room for the day, would be fitted by technicians from the Firm. In their expert hands, a hotel-room TV could become a camera, and the telephone a microphone.

Half an hour later I called the contact number and again gave my PIN number. There was a bit of clicking, then the strains of a string quartet. About five seconds later the woman came back again.

"You are to lift off and return today. Please acknowledge."

I thought I'd misheard her. There was a conference at the hotel given by the Norwegian board of trade, and all the delegates were exiting for coffee.

"Can you repeat, please?"

"You are to lift off. Please acknowledge."

"Yes, I understand, I am to lift off and return today."

The phone went dead.

I put the phone down. Strange. There had even been a memo in green ink from the head of the service about this—the fastball job that had now come to a sudden halt. It wasn't unusual to get lifted off, but not so quickly. Maybe Simmonds had decided these people weren't that important after all.

Then I thought, *So what, who gives a fuck? They wanted me to do the job; I've done it.* I called the travel agency and tried to get a flight out of Dulles. The only one I could get on was the British Airways at nine-thirty-five, which was hours away. Kev and Marsha were only an hour down the road toward the airport, so why not?

I dialed another number, and Kev answered. His voice was wary, until he recognized mine. "Nick! How's it going?" He sounded really happy to hear me.

"Not too bad. I'm in Washington."

"What are you doing? Nah, I don't want to know! You coming to see us?"

"If you're not busy. I'm leaving tonight, back to the UK. It'll be a quick stop and hello, OK?"

"Any chance of you getting your ass up here right away? I've just got the ball rolling on something, but I'd be interested to know what you think. You'll really like this one!"

"No problem, mate. I'll hire a car at the hotel and head straight over."

"Marsha will want to go into *cordon bleu* overdrive. I'll tell her when she gets back with the kids. Have a meal with us,

then you can go on to the airport. You won't believe the stuff
I've got here. Your friends over the water are busy."

"I can't wait."

"Nick, there's one other thing."

"What's that, mate?"

"You owe your goddaughter a birthday present—you
forgot again, dickhead."

Driving west along the freeway, I kept wondering what Kev
could want to talk to me about. Friends over the water? Kev
had no connection with PIRA that I knew of. He was in the
DEA, not the CIA or any antiterrorist department. Besides, I
knew that his job was far more administrative than fieldwork
now. I guessed he probably just needed some background
information.

I thought again about Slack Pat and made a mental note to
ask Kev if he had a contact address for the assless one.

I got on the interstate. Tyson's Corner was the junction I
had to get off at—well, not really; I wanted the one before but
I could never remember it. The moment I left the freeway I
was in leafy suburbia. Large houses lined the road, and just
about every one seemed to have a seven-seat minivan in the
drive and a basketball hoop fixed over the garage.

I followed my nose to Kev's subdivision and turned into
their road, Hunting Bear Path. I continued on for about a
quarter of a mile until I reached a small parade of shops
arranged in an open square with parking spaces, mainly little
delis and boutiques specializing in candles and soap. I bought
candy for Aida and Kelly that I knew Marsha wouldn't let
them have, and a couple of other presents.

Facing the shops was a stretch of vacant ground that
looked as if it had been earmarked as the next phase of the development. On and around the churned-up ground were
trailers, big stockpiles of girders and other building materials, and two or three bulldozers.

Far up on the right-hand side among the sprawling houses I
could just about make out the rear of Kev and Marsha's
"deluxe colonial." As I drove closer I could see their Ford
Windstar, the thing she threw the kids into to go screaming to

school. It had a big furry Garfield stuck to the rear window. I couldn't see Kev's company car, a Caprice Classic that bristled with antennae. They were so ugly only government agents used them. Kev normally kept his in the garage, safely out of sight of predators.

I was looking forward to seeing the Browns again even though I knew that by the end of the day I'd be more exhausted than the kids. I got to the driveway and turned in.

There was nobody waiting. The houses were quite a distance apart, so I didn't see any neighbors, either, but I wasn't surprised—D.C.'s bedroom suburbs were quite dead during weekdays.

I braced myself; on past form, I'd get ambushed as soon as the car pulled up. The kids would jump out at me, with Marsha and Kev close behind. I always made it look as if I didn't like it, but actually I did. The kids would know I had presents. I'd bought a little Tweety-Pie watch for Aida, and Kelly's was the Goosebumps kids' horror books numbers thirty-one to forty—I knew she already had the first thirty. I wouldn't say anything to Aida about forgetting her birthday; hopefully she'd have forgotten.

I got out of the car and walked toward the front door. Still no ambush. So far, so good.

The front door was open about two inches. I thought, *Here we go, what they want me to do is walk into the hallway like Inspector Clouseau, and there's going to be a Kato-type ambush.* I pushed the door wide open and called out, "Hello? Hello? Anyone home?"

Any minute now the kids would be attacking a leg each.

But nothing happened.

Maybe they had a new plan and were all hidden away somewhere in the house, waiting, trying to muffle their giggles.

Inside the front door there was a little corridor that opened up into a large rectangular hallway with doors leading off to the different downstairs rooms. In the kitchen to my right I heard the sound of a female voice singing a station jingle.

Still no kids. I started tiptoeing toward the noise in the kitchen. In a loud stage whisper I said, "Well, well, well—I'll have to leave . . . seeing as nobody's here . . . What a shame, because I've got two presents for two little girls . . ."

To my left was the door to the living room, open about a foot or so. I didn't look in as I walked past, but I saw something in my peripheral vision that at first didn't register. Or maybe it did; maybe my brain processed the information and rejected it as too horrible to be true.

It took a second for it to sink in, and when it did my whole body stiffened.

I turned my head slowly, trying to make sense of what was in front of me.

It was Kev. He was lying on his side on the floor, and his head had been battered to shit by a baseball bat. I knew that, because I could see it on the floor beside him. It was one he'd shown off to me on his last visit, a nice light aluminum one. He'd shaken his head and laughed when he said the local rednecks called them Alabama lie detectors.

I was still rooted to the spot.

I thought: *Fucking hell, he's dead—or should be, looking at the state of him.*

What about Marsha and the kids?

Was the killer still in the house?

I had to get a weapon.

There was nothing I could do about Kev at the moment. I didn't even think of him, just that I needed one of his pistols. I knew where all five of them were concealed in the house, always above child level, and always loaded and ready, a magazine on the weapon and a round in the chamber. All Marsha or Kev had to do was pick up one of the weapons and blast anyone who was pissed off at Kev—and there were more than a few of those in the drug community. I thought, *Fuck, they've got him at last.*

Very slowly, I put the presents on the floor. I wanted to listen for any creaking of floors, any movement at all around the house.

The living room was large and rectangular; against one wall was a fireplace. On either side of it were alcoves with bookshelves, and I knew that on the second shelf up, on the right, was the world's biggest, fattest thesaurus, and on top of that, tucked well back out of view, just above head level but close enough to reach up for, was a big fat gun. It was positioned so that as you picked it up it would be in the correct position to fire.

I ran. I didn't even look to see if there was anyone else in the room. Without a weapon, it wouldn't have made much difference.

I reached the bookcase, put my hand up, and took hold of the pistol, spun around, and went straight down onto my knees in the aim position. It was a Heckler & Koch USP 9mm, a fantastic weapon. This one even had a laser sight under the barrel—where the beam hits, so does the round.

I took a series of deep breaths. Once I'd calmed myself, I looked down and "checked chamber." I got the topslide and pulled it back a bit. I could see the brass casing in position.

Now what was I going to do? I had my car outside; if that got reported and traced, there'd be all kinds of drama. I was still under my alias cover; if I got discovered, that meant the job got discovered, and then I'd be in a world of shit.

I had a quick look at Kev, just in case I could see breathing. No chance. His brains were hanging out, his face was pulped. He was dead, and whoever had done it was so blasé they'd just thrown the baseball bat down and left it there.

There was blood all over the glass coffee table and the thick shag pile carpet. Some was even splattered on the patio windows. But strangely, apart from that, there wasn't much sign of a struggle.

4

I had to make sure Marsha and the kids weren't still here, tied up in another room or held down by some fucker with a gun to their heads. I was going to have to clear the house.

If only room clearing were as easy as Don Johnson made it look in *Miami Vice*: run up to the door, get right up against the doorframe, jump out into the middle of it, pistol poised, and win the day. A doorway naturally draws fire, so if you stand in one, you're presenting yourself as a target. If there's a guy waiting for you there with a shotgun, you're dead.

The first room I had to clear was the kitchen; it was the nearest, plus there was sound there.

I was on the opposite side of the living room from the kitchen door. I started to move along the outside wall of the room. I stepped over Kev, not bothering to look at him. The pistol was out in front of me; it had to be ready to fire as soon as I saw a target. Where your eyes go, the pistol goes.

I mentally divided the room into sections. The first was from the couch halfway across the living room, a distance of about twenty feet; I got there and froze by a big TV stereo setup, which gave me a bit of cover while I cleared the door that led back to the hallway. It was still open.

There was nothing in the hallway. As I moved through, I closed the door behind me. I approached the one to the kitchen. The handle was on the right-hand side; I couldn't see the hinges, so it had to open inward. I moved across to the hinged side and listened. Just above the sound of my breath and that of my heart thumping, I could hear some bonehead going on about "Injured at work? Fight for compensation through our expert attorneys—and remember, no win, no fee."

My pistol arm wasn't completely stretched out but the weapon was still facing forward. I leaned over to the handle, turned it, gave the door a push, and moved back. Then I opened it a bit more from the hinge side to see if there was any reaction from inside the kitchen.

I could hear more of the radio and also a washing machine—turning, stopping, turning. But nothing happened.

With the door now open just a few more inches I could see a small part of the kitchen. I moved forward and pushed the door fully open. Still no reaction. Using the doorframe and wall as cover, I edged around slowly.

As the angle between me and the frame increased, I gradually saw more of the room. I took my time so I could take in the information in stages. If I had to react, being two yards away from the doorframe would not affect my shooting, and if it did, I shouldn't be in this business anyway. Using my right thumb, I pushed the laser sight button. A small dot of brilliant red light appeared on the kitchen wall.

I leaned my body over to present as small a target as possible. If anyone was in the kitchen, all they'd see was a very nervous bit of head, and that would be what they'd have to react to, not the full Don Johnson.

The room was like the *Marie Celeste*. Food was still on the side in the middle of preparation. Kev had said Marsha was going to cook something special. There were vegetables and opened packs of meat. I closed the door behind me. The radio was now playing some soft rock and the washing machine was on spin. The table was half-set—and that really upset me. Kev and Marsha were very strict on the kids' chores; the sight of the half-set table made me feel sick inside because it heightened the chances of the kids being either dead or upstairs with some fucker who had a 9mm stuck in one of their mouths.

I moved slowly to the other end of the room and locked the door to the garage. I didn't want to clear the bottom of the house only for the guys to come in behind me.

I was starting to sweat big-time. Were Marsha and the kids

still in the house, or had they made a run for it? I couldn't just leave. The fuckers who'd done that to Kev would be capable of anything. I was starting to feel my stomach churn. What the fuck was I going to find upstairs?

I went out into the hallway again. As I moved, I had my pistol pointing up the stairs, which were now opposite me. The last room uncleared downstairs was Kev's study. I put my ear to the door and listened. I couldn't hear anything. I did the same drill and entered.

It was a small room, just enough space for some filing cabinets, a desk, and a chair. Shelves on the wall facing the desk were full of books and photographs of Kev shooting, Kev running, that sort of stuff. Everything was now on the floor; the filing cabinets were open and paper strewn everywhere. The only thing not ripped apart was Kev's PC. That was lying on its side on the desk, the screen still showing the British army screensaver I'd sent him for a laugh. The printer and scanner were on the floor beside the desk, but that was where they had always been.

I went back out and looked at the stairs. They were going to be a problem. They went up one flight, then turned back on themselves just before hitting the landing. That meant that I'd have to be a bit of a Houdini to cover my ass getting up there. I wouldn't use the laser now; I didn't want to announce my movements.

I put my foot on the bottom step and started to move up. Fortunately, Kev's stair carpet was a thick shag pile, which helped keep the noise down, but still it was like treading on ice, testing each step gently for creaks, always placing my feet to the inside edge, slowly and precisely.

Once I got level with the landing, I pointed my pistol up above my head and, using the wall as support, moved up the stairs backward, step by step.

A couple of steps; wait, listen. A couple more steps; wait, and listen.

There was only one of me, and I had only thirteen rounds to play with, maybe fourteen, if the round in the chamber was on top of a full magazine. These guys might have semiautomatic weapons for all I knew, or even fully automatic. If they did and were there, it would not be a good day out.

The washing machine was on its final thundering spin. Still soft rock on the radio. Nothing else.

Adrenaline takes over. Despite the air-conditioning, I was drenched with sweat. It was starting to get in my eyes; I had to wipe it with my left hand, one eye at a time.

The girls' room was facing me. From memory there were bunk beds and the world's biggest shrine to *Pocahontas*— T-shirts and posters, sheets and bedspreads, and even a doll whose back you pressed and she sang something about colors.

I stopped and prepared for the worst.

I reached for the handle and started to clear the room. Nothing. No one.

For once the room was even clean and tidy. There were piles of teddy bears and toys on the beds. The theme was still *Pocahontas*, but *Toy Story* was obviously a close second.

I gradually came out into the hallway, treating it as if it were a new room because I didn't know what might have gone on in the half-minute since I'd left it.

I slowly moved to the next bedroom with my back nearly touching the wall, pistol forward, eyes watching forward and rear, thinking: *What if—what do I do if they appear from that doorway? What if . . . what if?*

As I got nearer to Kev and Marsha's room, I could see that the door was slightly ajar. I couldn't actually see anything inside yet, but as I moved nearer I started to smell something. A faint, metallic tang, and I could smell shit as well. I felt sick. I knew that I'd have to go in.

As I inched around the doorframe I got my first glimpse of Marsha. She was kneeling by the bed, her top half spread-eagled on the mattress. The bedspread was covered with blood.

I sank to my knees in the hallway. I felt myself going into shock. I couldn't believe this was true. This was not happening to this family. Why kill Marsha? It should have been Kev they were after. All I wanted to do was throw my hand in and sit down and cry. But I knew the kids had been in the house. They might still be here.

I got a grip of myself and started to move. I went in, forcing myself to ignore Marsha. The room was clear.

The next job was the master bathroom. I went in, and what I saw made me lose it, totally fucking lose it. *Bang,* I went back against the wall and slumped onto the floor.

Blood was everywhere. I got it all over my shirt and hands; I sat in a pool of it, soaking the seat of my pants.

Aida was lying on the floor between the bath and the toilet. Her five-year-old head had been nearly severed from her shoulders. There was just three inches of flesh left intact; I could see the vertebrae still holding on.

Turning my head away and looking out of the bathroom, I could now see more of Marsha. I had to hold back my scream. Her dress was hanging normally, but her tights had been torn, her panties were pulled down, and she had soiled herself, probably at the point of death. All I saw at this distance of about fifteen feet was somebody that I really cared for, even loved maybe, on her knees, her blood splattered all over the bed. And she'd had the same done to her as Aida.

I was taking deep breaths and wiping my eyes. I knew I still had another two rooms to clear—another bathroom and the large storeroom above the garage. I couldn't give up now because I might wind up getting dropped myself.

I cleared the other rooms and half-collapsed, half-sat on the landing. I could see my bloody footprints all over the carpet.

Stop, calm down, and think.

What next? Kelly. Where the fuck was Kelly?

Then I remembered the hiding place. Because of the threats to Kev, both kids knew where they had to go and hide in the event of a crisis.

The thought brought me to my senses. If that was where Kelly was hiding, she was safe for the time being. Better to leave her there while I did the other stuff I had to do.

I got up and started to move down the stairs, making sure that, as I moved, I had my pistol pointed. As I descended I could see the blood I had left on the wall and carpet where I'd sat. I was almost willing the attackers to appear. I wanted to see the fuckers.

I got a cloth and a trash bag from the kitchen and started to run around the house wiping door handles and any surfaces where I might have left fingerprints. Then I went over to the patio sliding doors and closed the curtains. I didn't want anybody to discover this mess before I was well out of it, hopefully on a plane back to London.

I took a quick look at Kev and knew I was back in control. He was now just a dead body.

I went back upstairs, washed the blood off my hands and face, and got a clean shirt and a pair of jeans and running shoes from Kev's closet. His clothes didn't fit me, but they would do for now. I bundled my own bloodstained stuff into the trash bag that I'd take with me.

5

Kev had shown me the "hidey-hole," as he called it, built under an open staircase that led up to a little makeshift loft stacked with ladders. The kids knew they had to hide there if ever Kev or Marsha shouted the word "Disneyland!"—and they were never ever to come out until Daddy or Mommy came and got them.

I headed to the garage. Pushing the door slightly, I could see the rear of the large metal doors to the right. The garage could easily have taken three extra vehicles besides Kev's company car. "Fucking thing," I remembered Kev saying, "all the luxury and mod cons of the late nineties, in a car that looks like a nineteen-sixties fridge."

The kids' bikes were hanging from frames on the wall, together with all the other clutter that families accumulate in garages. I could see the red laser dot on the far wall.

I moved in and cleared through. There was no one here.

I went back to the area of the staircase. Chances were she wasn't going to come out unless her mom and dad came for her, but as I moved I started to call out very gently, "Kelly! It's Nick! Hello, Kelly, where are you?"

All the time the pistol was pointing forward, ready to take on any threat.

Moving slowly toward the boxes, I said, "Oh well, since you're not here I'll go. But I think I'll have one more look, and I bet you might be hiding underneath the staircase in those boxes. I'll just have a look . . . I bet you're in there . . ."

There was a pile of large boxes. One had contained a freezer, another a washing machine. Kev had made a sort of cave with them under the staircase and kept a few toys there.

I eased the pistol down my waistband. I didn't want her to see a gun. She'd probably seen and heard enough already.

I put my mouth against a little gap between the boxes. "Kelly, it's me, Nick. Don't be scared, I'm going to crawl toward you. You'll see my head in a minute, and I want to see a big smile . . ."

I got down on my hands and knees and kept talking gently as I moved boxes and squeezed through the gap, inching toward the back wall. I wanted to do it nice and slowly. I didn't know how she was going to react.

"I'm going to put my head around the corner now, Kelly."

I took a deep breath and moved my head around the back of the box, smiling away but ready for the worst.

She was there, facing me, eyes wide with terror, sitting curled up in a fetal position, rocking her body backward and forward, holding her hands over her ears.

"Hello, Kelly," I said very softly.

She must have recognized me, but didn't reply. She just kept on rocking, staring at me with wide, scared eyes.

"Mommy and Daddy can't come and get you out at the moment, but you can come with me. Daddy told me it would be OK. Are you going to come with me, Kelly?"

Still no reply. I crawled right into the cave until I was curled up beside her. She'd been crying; strands of light brown hair were stuck to her face. I tried to move them away from her mouth. Her eyes were red and swollen.

"You're in a bit of a mess there," I said. "Do you want me to clean you up? Come on, let's go and get you sorted out, shall we?" I got hold of her rigid hand and gently guided her out into the garage.

She was dressed in jeans, a denim shirt, running shoes, and a blue nylon fleece. Her hair was straight and just above her shoulders, a bit shorter than I remembered it; she was quite lanky for a seven-year-old, with long, skinny legs. I picked her up in my arms and held her tight as I carried her into the kitchen. I knew the other doors were closed; she wouldn't see her dad.

I sat her down on a chair at the table. "Mommy and Daddy

said they had to go away for a while but asked me to look after you until they come back, OK?"

She was trembling so much I couldn't tell if her head was nodding or shaking.

I went to the fridge and opened it, hoping to find some comfort food. I found the world's largest Easter egg. "Mmm, yum—do you want some chocolate?"

I'd had a good relationship with Kelly. She was a great kid, and that wasn't just because she was my pal's daughter. I smiled warmly, but she just stared at the table.

I broke off a few pieces and put them on one of the side plates that she'd probably been setting earlier with Aida. I found the Off switch on the radio; I'd had enough relaxing soft rock for one day.

As I looked at Kelly again I suddenly realized I'd fucked up. What was I going to do with her? I couldn't just leave her here: her family was lying dead all over the house. But more important, she knew me. When the police arrived she'd be able to say, "Nick Stone was here." They'd soon find out that Nick Stone was one of Daddy's friends; the house was littered with photographs with me in them. And if they did arrest the grinning drunk in the barbecue shots, they'd find that for some strange reason he wasn't Nick Stone at all—he was Mrs. Stamford's little boy.

Kev's jacket was hanging over one of the chairs. I said, "Let's wrap you up in your dad's coat; that'll keep you nice and warm." At least she'd have something of her dad's; with luck it would cheer her up.

There was just a little bit of whimpering in reply. She was almost in rigor mortis with shock, though at least she had turned her head to look at me now. This was where normally I would have let Marsha take over, because a child's mind was far too complicated for me to work out. But I couldn't do that today.

I wrapped the coat around her and said, "Here you are; get this around you. Look, it's your dad's! Don't tell him, eh, ha ha ha!" I felt something solid in one of the pockets and checked. "Oh good, look, we can phone him up later."

I looked out the window—no movement. I picked up the

trash bag, grabbed Kelly's hand, then realized that to reach the front door I'd have to come out of the kitchen and into the hallway.

"Just sit there a second," I said. "I've got to do something."

I had a quick look to make sure the doors were closed. I thought again about fingerprints, but if I'd missed a set, there was nothing I could do about it now. My only thought was to get out of the area and keep Kelly away from the cops until I'd sorted things out.

I went back and got her and checked the front of the house again for movement. She seemed to be finding it hard to walk. I had to grip Kev's coat by the collar, half-dragging her toward the car.

I put her in the front passenger seat and smiled. "There you go; that's nice and warm. Better look after your dad's coat for him. Keep it nice for when you see him."

Then I threw the trash bag in the back, settled into the driver's seat, put my seat belt on, and turned on the ignition. We drove off at a really sensible pace, nothing outrageous, nothing likely to be noticed.

We'd gone only a few hundred yards when I thought of something; I looked across at her and said, "Kelly, put your seat belt on. Do you know how to do that?"

She didn't move, didn't even look at me. I had to do it for her.

I tried to make small talk. "It's a nice day today, isn't it? Yep, you'll stay with me a while; we'll get everything sorted out."

Silence.

My mind switched back to the matter in hand. What was I going to do? Whatever I decided, I knew it was no good where we were at the moment. We needed to lose ourselves in a crowd. I headed for Tyson's Corner.

I turned to Kelly and smiled, trying to be the happy-go-lucky Uncle Nick, but it just wasn't happening. She was staring anxiously out the window as if she was being wrenched away from all her familiar landmarks and seeing them for the last time.

"It's OK, Kelly." I tried to stroke her hair.

She jerked her head away.

Fuck it, just let her get on with it; with luck I'd be able to drop her off somewhere before too long.

I turned my thoughts to Kev. He'd said he had a bit of a problem with my "friends over the water." Could it have been PIRA that'd killed him? What the hell for? It was highly unlikely that PIRA would start messing about like that, not in America. It was too professional to bite the hand that was feeding it.

Other things weren't adding up. Why wasn't there a struggle? Both Marsha and Kev knew where the weapons were. Why weren't they used? Why was the front door ajar? There was no way that would have happened. People didn't just wander in off the street into Kev's house; they had to be invited in.

I felt a rush of anger. If the family had been killed in a car crash, that would have been one thing. If the killers had come in and maybe shot them, I'd be upset, but, at the end of the day, if you live by the sword, you must be prepared to die by the sword. But not like this. They'd been hacked up for no reason that I could see.

I forced myself to think rationally. There was no way I could phone the police and explain my version. Although I'd been lifted off, I was still operating in another country without its consent. Getting caught would be a big no-no. The operation here would be seen as a sign of betrayal and would create distrust between the two security communities. There was no way the Firm would back me up; that would defeat the whole purpose of deniable ops. I was on my own.

Looking at my passenger, I knew I had a problem. As we drove toward Tyson's Corner I realized what I had to do. I saw a Best Western hotel on the left and an open-plan mall on the right. I had to dump the car, because that was one of the connections between me and the house. I needed somewhere to leave it that wasn't isolated, somewhere without video cameras. As well as the shopping mall and its massive parking lots, on the outskirts was a drive-thru Burger King with its own parking.

It was all very well abandoning a vehicle in the middle of

hundreds of others in a parking lot during shopping hours. But at night, it might be the only car left there and was going to stick out, and it would be checked out by police patrols. What I was after was an area that was really busy, day and night. Streets or multilevel parking garages were out, because nine times out of ten they have video cameras to stop muggings and car theft. Many multistory parking lots have a camera that takes a picture of the license plate and driver as you enter. At any major junction and along most major thoroughfares, there are traffic video cameras. If my car had been found outside Kev's house, the first thing they'd do was study the traffic videos and parking lot photography.

"Shall we get a burger and some shakes?" I suggested. "Do you like milk shakes? I tell you what, I'll park and maybe we'll even go shopping."

Again it would be no good driving into the Burger King parking lot, stepping out, and then walking a few hundred yards to the shopping mall—that isn't normal behavior. It might stick in people's minds and be recalled at a later date, so I wanted to make the two of us look as natural as possible.

"Strawberry, chocolate, or vanilla—which one do you want?"

No reply.

"Strawberry? Go on, I'm going to have a strawberry."

Nothing.

I parked. The place was pretty full. I cupped my hand under her chin and gently turned her face so that she was looking at my big smile. "Milk shake?"

There was a faint movement of her head, or maybe it was a nod of appreciation. Not much, but at least it was a reaction.

I carried on with the bullshit. "You just sit here then; I'll get out, I'll lock the car, go and get the milk shakes. And then I tell you what, we'll go into the shopping mall. How about that?"

She looked away.

I continued as if she'd given me a positive response. I got out of the car and locked her in. I still had the pistol tucked down in my waistband, concealed by Kev's jacket.

I went into the Burger King, got two different flavor milk shakes, and came straight back to the car.

"Here we go then, chocolate or vanilla?"

She kept her hands by her sides. "I tell you what, I'll have the vanilla; I know you like chocolate."

I put the shake in her lap. It was too cold for her legs; as soon as she lifted it up I said, "Come on, then, let's go to the shops. You can bring that with you."

I got her out, closed the door, and locked up. I did nothing about our fingerprints; no matter how hard I tried, I'd never get rid of them all, so what was the point? I opened the trunk, pulled out the bag with the bits and pieces I'd bought at Shannon, and threw in the trash bag full of bloodstained clothing.

It looked like rain. We walked toward the shopping mall; I kept on talking to her because the situation felt so awkward. What else do you do, walking along with a kid who doesn't belong to you and doesn't want to be with you?

I tried to hold her hand but she refused. I couldn't make an issue of it with people around. I gripped the shoulder of the jacket again.

There was everything in the shopping center from a computer discount warehouse to an army surplus store, all housed in long one-story units that were like islands in a sea of parking lot.

We went into a clothing store, and I bought myself some jeans and another shirt. I'd change as soon as I'd had a shower and got Aida's blood off my back and legs.

At an ATM I drew out three hundred dollars, the maximum allowed on my credit card.

We came back out to the parking lot but didn't return to the car. I kept a firm grip on her as we walked toward the hotel across the road.

As we got nearer I could see that the Best Western was in fact farther away than I first thought, separated from the main drag by a row of single-story office buildings. Our view was of the rear of the hotel.

Looking each way, it was obvious that the junctions that would lead us around to the front of the hotel were miles away. I decided to take a shortcut. The traffic was heavy, and the road system hadn't been designed for people on foot. I gripped Kelly's hand as we dodged to the median strip and waited for another gap. I looked up at the sky: it was very overcast; rain couldn't be far away.

Drivers, who had probably never seen pedestrians before, beeped furiously, but we made it to the other side and scrambled over small railings onto the sidewalk. More or less directly in front of us was a gap between two office buildings. We went through and crossed a short stretch of vacant ground that brought us into the hotel parking lot. As we walked past the lines of vehicles I memorized the sequence of letters and numbers for a Virginia plate.

The Best Western was a large four-story rectangle, the architecture very 1980s. Every elevation was concrete, painted the world's weirdest off-yellow. As we walked up to the reception area, I tried to look inside. I didn't want them to see us coming from the direction of the parking lot, because it would be odd to walk all that way without first checking that they had a room, and then unloading our bags. I hoped Kelly would stay silent when we were inside; I just wanted to do the business and walk out again as if we were going to see Mommy back in the car.

Inside the lobby I got hold of Kelly and whispered, "You just sit there. I'm going to get us a room." I gave her a tourist brochure that was lying on one of the chairs, but she ignored it.

In one corner, by the coffee machine and cream, was a large TV. A baseball game was on. I went over to the receptionist, a woman in her mid-forties who thought she was still twenty-four, who was watching the screen, probably fantasizing about her chances with one of the pitchers.

All smiles, I said, "I need a family room just for one night, please."

"Certainly, sir," she said, an honors graduate from Best Western's charm school. "If you'd like to fill out this card."

As I started to scribble I said, "How much is a room, anyway?"

"That's sixty-four dollars, plus tax."

I raised an eyebrow to make it look as if that was a lot of money to a family man like myself.

"I know," she smiled. "I'm sorry about that."

She took my credit card and I filled in the form with crap. I'd been doing this for donkey's years, lying on hotel forms, looking relaxed as I wrote but in fact scanning about four questions ahead. I filled in a car registration, too, and for number of occupants put two adults and a child.

She handed back my card. "There you are, Mr. Stamford, it's room two-twenty-four. Where's your car?"

"Just around the corner." I pointed vaguely to the rear of the hotel.

"OK, if you park by the stairs where you see the Coke and ice machines, turn left at the top of the stairs, and you'll see room two-twenty-four on the left-hand side. You have a nice day now!"

I could have described the room even before I ran the key card through the lock and opened the door. A TV, two double beds, a couple of chairs, and the typical hotel designer's obsession with dark wood veneers.

I wanted to get Kelly settled quickly so I could use the phone. I pressed the remote and flicked through the channels, hoping to find Nickelodeon. Eventually I found some cartoons. "I remember this one; it's good—shall we watch it?"

She sat on the bed, staring at me. The expression on her face said she didn't like this outing too much, and I could understand that.

"Kelly," I said, "I'm going to leave you for just a couple of minutes, because I've got to make a phone call. I'll get a drink while I'm out. What would you like, Coke? Mountain Dew? Or do you want some candy?"

There was no reaction, so I just went on. "I'm going to lock the door, and you're not to answer it for anybody. Nobody at all, OK? I'll use the key to get back in again. You sit there and enjoy yourself and I'll just be about five minutes, OK?"

Still there was no reaction. I hung the DO NOT DISTURB sign on the door handle, made sure I had the key card, and left.

I was heading for a phone booth I'd seen in the street because I didn't want her to hear the telephone conversation I was about to have. I didn't know much about kids, but I knew that when I was seven nothing had gone unnoticed in my house. On the off chance that it wasn't PIN-protected, I took Kev's mobile from his jacket pocket. I pressed the Power button and it demanded a PIN number. I tried two basic ones—the usual factory default, four zeros, and then 1 2 3 4. Nothing. I couldn't try anymore; with some phones you can try the wrong PIN only three times and then it automatically cuts out and you need to go back to the dealer to get it rectified. I turned off the power and put it back in my pocket. I'd ask Kelly about it later.

I turned left through the parking lot and headed for the phone booths out on the street. I spent a few moments sorting out in my mind what I wanted to say, and then I dialed London.

In veiled speech I said, "I've just finished work and I'm in Washington to visit an old friend. I used to work with him ten years ago. He's now working here for the US government." I outlined the problem and said that Kelly and I both needed help.

Veiled speech is not some magical code; all you're trying to do is intimate what is going on, yet at the same time throw off a casual listener. You're not going to fool any professional eavesdroppers—that's what codes and onetime pads and all the rest of it are for. But all London needed to know was that I was in deep shit; I had Kev's child, and needed sorting out. ASAP.

"Fine, I'll pass that message on. Have you a contact number?"

"No. I'll call back in an hour."

"OK, good-bye."

These women never ceased to amaze me. They never ever got worked up about anything. It must be hard work being their husbands on a Saturday night.

I put down the phone and felt a bit better as I strolled over to a gas station. I knew the Firm would work everything out. They might have to call in some big-time favors in the US to detach me from this shit, but what are friends for? They'd pull out all the stops, not so much to get me off the hook, as to make sure their operation was covered up.

I was trying to look on the bright side, which was more than the weather was doing. It had started to drizzle when I left the hotel, and that had now turned to light rain. With luck the Firm would pick up both of us tonight. Kelly would be taken care of, and I would be whisked back to the UK for another interview without coffee and cookies.

I bought some food and drink at the gas station to keep us out of the public eye in restaurants, and a few goodies to pass the time, then crossed the road and went back to the hotel. At the Coke machine I went up the stairs, turned left, and knocked on our door.

As I opened it I said, "I've got loads of things—I've got candy, sandwiches, chips—and I've even got you a Goosebumps book to read."

I figured it was better to buy stuff to occupy her mind rather than try to cuddle or console her. I'd have felt really uncomfortable with that anyway.

She was lying on the bed exactly where I'd left her, staring in the direction of the television set, but not really watching, her eyes glazed over.

As I put everything down on the other bed I said, "Right, I reckon what you need now is a nice hot bath. I've even bought some Buzz Lightyear bubble bath."

It would give her something to do, and maybe relax her out of the catatonic state she was in. Apart from that, when I handed her over to the Firm I wanted them to see that I'd made an effort and that she was all nice and clean. After all, she was my friend's kid.

I turned the taps on and called back into the room, "Come on then, get undressed."

She didn't reply. I went back into the bedroom, sat at the end of the bed, and started undressing her. I thought she might resist, but instead she sat placidly as I pulled off her shirt. "You do your jeans," I said. She was only seven, but I felt awkward about taking those off. "Come on, undo your buttons." In the end, I had to. She was miles away.

I carried her into the bathroom. Good old Buzz Lightyear had done his job; the bubbles were halfway to the ceiling. I tested the water, lifted her into the bath, and she sat down without a word.

"There's loads of soap and shampoo," I said. "Do you want me to help you wash your hair?"

She sat stock-still in the water. I gave her the soap, which she just stared at.

It was nearly time to call London again. At least I wouldn't have to go to a phone booth for this one; she'd be out of earshot in the bath. Just in case, I kept the TV on.

There was some weird and wonderful cartoon on: three characters in jeans, half man, half shark, who said things like "Fin-tastic!" and "Shark time!" Apparently they didn't kick ass, they kicked dorsal. *The Street Sharks.* The opening credits finished and I dialed London.

Immediately I heard "PIN number, please?"

I gave it. She went, "One moment."

A few seconds later the phone went dead.

That was strange. I dialed again, gave my PIN number, and again got cut off.

What the fuck was going on? I tried to reason with myself, tried to tell myself that this was just a fuck-up. But really, inside, I knew the truth. It had to be deliberate. Either that, or maybe, just maybe, the phone line was down. No good thinking about it. Take action.

I went into the bathroom. "The phone's not working," I said. "I'll just go down to the one on the corner. Is there anything else we need from the store? I tell you what, we'll go down there later on, the two of us, together."

Her gaze didn't leave the tiles at the end of the bath.

I lifted her out and put a towel around her. "You're a big girl now. You can dry yourself." I took the hairbrush from the bag and dragged Kelly into the bedroom. "Once you've done that, brush your hair, and make sure you're all dry and dressed when I come back. We might have to go somewhere. Don't open the door for anyone, OK?"

There was no answer. I pulled out the phone jack and left.

7

I was feeling apprehensive as I walked across the parking lot. I'd done nothing wrong, so why were they cutting me off? Was the Firm going to stitch me up? I started to go through all the scenarios in my head. Did they think I was the killer? Were they cutting away now as a prelude to denying everything?

I got to the phone, dialed, and the same thing happened. I slowly put down the receiver. A low wall made up part of the entrance to the hotel; I went and sat down. I needed to think hard. It didn't take long to decide that there was only one option, and that was to phone the embassy. I'd be breaking every rule in the book. I wouldn't even bother going through all the protocol; I dialed 411 and got the number. I got straight through.

"Hello, British Embassy. How may I help you?"

"I want to talk to LOSO."

"Excuse me?"

"LOSO. Liaison officer, special operations."

"I'm sorry, we don't have an extension number for that name."

"Get hold of the defense attaché and tell him there's somebody on the phone who wants to speak to LOSO. It's really important. I need to speak to him now."

"Hold on a moment." She put me on hold and I waited.

Another woman came on the line. "Hello, how may I help you?"

"I want to talk to LOSO."

"I'm sorry, we have no one of that appointment."

"Then put me through to the DA."

"Sorry, the defense attaché is not here. Can I help you? Would you like to give me a name and contact number?"

I said, "Listen, this is the news. I want LOSO or the DA to pass this on. I've tried to phone in on my PIN number. My PIN number's two-four-two-two, and I'm getting blanked off. I'm in a really bad situation at the moment and I need some help. Tell LOSO or the DA that if I don't make contact with London, I'm going to expose what I've got in my security blanket. I will call back in three hours' time."

The woman said, "Excuse me, could you repeat that?"

"No, you're recording—the message will be understood. All you've got to do is pass that on to the DA or LOSO, I don't give a fuck which one. Tell them I'll call London on the PIN line in three hours' time."

I put the phone down. The message would get to them. Chances were the DA or LOSO was listening anyway.

Some of the operations I'd been on had been so dirty that no one would want them exposed, but that could cut two ways: it also meant that someone like me would be expendable if things weren't working too well. I'd always operated on the basis that if you were involved in deniable operations for the intelligence services and hadn't prepared an out for the day they decided to shaft you, then you deserved everything you got. The head honcho knew that Ks had security blankets, but everybody denied it—the operators denied it, the Firm denied it. I'd always been sure that the Firm put as much effort into trying to find where the blackmail kit was hidden as they did into the operations themselves.

I'd committed myself now. It was a card I could play only once. No way would I be living an easy existence after this. I was finished with the Secret Intelligence Service and would probably have to spend the rest of my life in a remote mountain village in Sri Lanka, looking over my shoulder.

What if the Firm decided to admit to the Americans that there'd been an op they'd forgotten to mention? Would they take the rap on the knuckles, then say, "This man killed one of your officers"? No, it didn't work that way. The Firm wouldn't know if my blanket was a bluff or not, or, if used, how much damage it could do in the hands of the press.

They'd have to take it as real; they'd have to help. They had no choice. We'd get lifted by the Firm, I'd be flown back to the UK, and then I'd take up basket weaving until they forgot about me.

Kelly was lying on the bed with a towel wrapped around her when I got back to the room. The cartoon had finished, and there was some sort of hard-hitting news-type voice on, but I didn't pay much attention to it. I was more interested in getting a response from this little girl. It seemed that I was fast running out of friends; she might be just seven years old but I wanted to feel she was on my side.

I said, "We've got to hang around for another hour or two, and then somebody's coming to . . ."

And then it hit me. The no-nonsense, New England female voice was saying, ". . . brutal murders and a possible kidnap . . ." I switched my attention to the screen.

She was black and in her mid-thirties. Her face was on camera, with Kev's house in the background and the Windstar still in the drive. Police were milling around two ambulances with flashing lights.

I grabbed the remote and hit the Off button. "Kelly, naughty girl." I grinned. "You haven't cleaned your neck. Just you go and do it right this minute!"

I nearly threw her into the bathroom. "And don't come out until I tell you to!"

I hit the On button and kept the volume low.

The woman said, ". . . neighbors report seeing a white man in his late thirties, around five-foot-ten to six feet tall, medium build, with short brown hair. He arrived at the house in a white Dodge with Virginia plates at approximately two forty-five today. We now have Lieutenant Davies from the Fairfax County Police Department . . ."

A balding detective was standing beside her. "We can confirm that there was a male fitting that description, and we're appealing for more witnesses. We need to know the whereabouts of the Browns' seven-year-old daughter, Kelly."

A picture came up on the screen of Kelly standing in the garden with Aida, with a spoken description. The broadcast cut back to a studio shot of the two anchors saying that the family was a victim of what appeared to be drug-related murders. A family portrait appeared on the screen. "Kevin Brown was a member of the Drug Enforcement Administration . . ." The anchors expanded the piece into a discussion about the drug problem in the D.C. area.

There was no sound of splashing water from the bathroom. Kelly would be out again any minute. I started flicking channels. Nothing more on the murders. I switched back to children's TV and went into the bathroom.

I hadn't heard any splashing because Kelly wasn't washing. She was on the floor, under the sink, in the same fetal position I'd found her in at Kev's, hands over her ears to block out the news she'd just heard on the TV.

I wanted to pick her up and comfort her. The only thing was, I didn't know how. I decided to appear unaffected by her condition. "Hello, Kelly." I smiled. "What are you doing down there?"

Her eyes were shut so tight I could see the creases in her face. I picked her up in my arms and started to walk back into the bedroom. "Hey, you look sleepy. Do you want to watch TV or just go to bed?" It sounded like crap to me but I just didn't know what else to say or do. Best pretend it hadn't happened.

I took the towel off to get her dressed. "Come on, let's get some clothes on and your hair combed." I was really fighting for words now.

She just sat there. Then, as I started to pull her shirt on, she said quietly, "Mommy and Daddy are dead, aren't they?"

Getting her arms into the shirt suddenly became very interesting. "What makes you say that? I told you, I'm just looking after you for a while."

"So I'm going to see Mommy and Daddy again?"

I didn't have the words to use, or the guts to tell her. "Yes, of course you will. It's just that they had to go away really quickly. I told you, it was too late to pick you up, but they asked me to look after you. As soon as they come back I'll take you to Mommy and Daddy and Aida. I didn't know it was going to take this long; I thought it was going to be only a couple of hours. But they will be back soon."

There was a slight pause as she worked through it all. I got her panties and placed her feet in them and pulled them up.

"Why didn't they want to take me, Nick?" She sounded sad at the thought.

I moved over to the chair and picked up her jeans. I didn't want her to see my eyes. "It isn't that they didn't want to take you, but there was a mistake made, and that's why they asked me to look after you."

"Just like *Home Alone*!"

I turned around and saw that she was smiling. I had to think about that one. "Yeah, that's right, just like *Home Alone*. They left you by mistake!" I remembered watching it on a flight. Shitty film but good booby traps. I busied myself with her jeans again.

"So when are we going to see them?"

I couldn't spend all day picking up two bits of clothing. I did a half turn and walked back toward the bed.

"That won't be for a while yet, but when I spoke to them just now they wanted me to tell you that they love you, and they're missing you, and to do everything I say and be a good girl."

There was a beaming smile on her face. I wished I had the courage to tell her the truth.

I said, "Kelly, you must do what I say, do you understand that?"

"Yeah, I understand."

She nodded, and I saw a little child needing affection.

I gave her my best attempt at a smile. I looked into her eyes. "Come on, cheer up. Let's watch TV."

We both went back to watch the *Power Rangers*, with a can of Mountain Dew. I couldn't take my mind off the news broadcast. Kelly's photograph had been on the TV. The receptionist, the clothing store clerk, anyone might remember her. Surely the embassy had called London by now, surely every fucker knew what was going on because it was splashed all over the news. No need to wait three hours before making the call.

I'd have to go to the outside phone again because I didn't want Kelly to hear. I put Kev's jacket on, slipped the TV remote control into a pocket, told her where I was going, and left.

As I came to the stairs by the Coke machine I looked down. Two cars had pulled up outside the reception lobby. Both were empty, but their doors were still open as if the occupants had piled out in a hurry.

I looked again. Besides a normal radio antenna each vehicle had a two-foot antenna on the back. One of the cars was a white Ford Taurus, the other a blue Chevy Caprice.

There was no time to think, just to turn around and run toward the rear fire exit like a man possessed.

8

Now wasn't the time to worry about how they'd found us. As I ran, the options started to race through my mind. The obvious one was to leave Kelly where she was and let them pick her up. She was a millstone around my neck. On my own, I could get away.

So why did I stop running? I wasn't too sure; instinct told me that she had to come with me.

I doubled back and burst into the room. "Kelly, we've got to go! Come on, get up!"

She'd been drifting off to sleep. There was a look of horror on her face because of my change of tone.

"We've got to go!"

Grabbing her coat, I picked her up in my arms and started toward the door. I snatched up her shoes and stuffed them into my pockets. She made a sound, half-frightened, half-protesting.

"Just hold on!" I said. Her legs were wrapped around my waist.

I came out onto the landing. I closed the door behind us, and it locked automatically. They'd have to break it down. I did a quick check down the corridor, not bothering to look below to see what was happening. I'd know soon enough if they were behind us.

I turned left and ran to the end of the corridor, turned left again, and there was the fire exit. I pushed the bar and it opened. We came out onto an open concrete staircase at the rear of the hotel, facing the shopping mall about a quarter of a mile away. Kelly started to cry.

There was no time to be nice. I got hold of her head so that her face came right up to mine. "People have come to take you away, do you understand that?" I knew it would frighten her, and that it would probably fuck up her mind even more, but I didn't care about that. "I'm trying to save you. Shut up and do what I say!"

I squeezed her cheek hard and shook her face. "Do you understand me, Kelly? Shut up, and hold me very tight."

I buried her face in my shoulder and lunged down the concrete stairs, looking for my escape route.

Ahead of us lay about forty yards of rough grass, and beyond that a six-foot chain-link fence that looked old and rusty. On the other side of that was the rear of the long row of office buildings that faced the main road. Some were brick, some were plaster, all different styles built over the last thirty years. The rear administration area was strewn with clutter and large Dumpsters.

There was a pathway running across the empty ground, and it went through at a point where a whole section of the chain-link fence had crumpled or been pulled down. Maybe the hotel and office workers used it as a shortcut.

Carrying Kelly was like having a rucksack on the wrong way. That was going to be no good if I had to run fast, so I threw her around onto my back, linking my hands under her butt so I was carrying her piggyback. I got to the bottom of the stairs and stopped and listened. No sound of them shouting or breaking down the door yet. The urge was just to run for it across the grassy dirt toward the gap in the fence, but it was important to do this correctly.

Still with Kelly on my back, not bothering to tell her what was happening, I got onto my hands and knees. I lowered myself to within about a foot of the floor and slowly stuck my head around the corner. There was a chance that once I'd seen what was happening, I'd choose a different route.

The two cars had pulled up to the bottom of the staircase by the Coke machine. The fuckers were obviously upstairs. I didn't know how many of them there were.

I realized that the ground was in fact dead ground to them now, and started running. The rain had been light but constant, and the ground was muddy. It was reasonably well looked after, littered only here and there with bits of paper, old soft drink cans, and burger wrappers. I kept heading for the gap in the chain-link fence.

Kelly was weighing me down; I was taking short, quick strides and not bending my knees too much, just enough to take her weight, bending forward from the hips. She made involuntary grunts in time with the running movements as the wind was knocked out of her.

We reached the broken section of fence, which was buried in the mud. I heard the screech of tires, then the sound of protesting suspension and bodywork. I didn't bother looking around, just dug deep to try to lengthen my stride.

Once through, we were faced with the rear of the office buildings. I couldn't see the alleyway we'd come through earlier. I turned left, looking for any other route through to the main drag. There had to be one somewhere.

Now on asphalt, I could make good speed, but Kelly started slipping. I shouted, "Hold on!" and felt her tense up more. "Harder, Kelly, harder!"

It wasn't working. With my left hand I got hold of both her wrists and pulled them down in front of me toward my waist. She was nice and tight on me now, and I could use my right hand to pump myself forward. My priority was to make good speed and distance. They would be out and running soon. I needed that alleyway.

It's a strange thing when people are being chased. Subconsciously they try to get as much distance as they can between themselves and their pursuers, and, whether it's in an urban environment or a rural one, they think that means going in a straight line. In fact, what you need to do is put in as many angles as possible, especially in a city or a town. If you come to an intersection with four options, it makes the chasers' job more difficult: they have a larger area to cover and have to split forces. A hare being chased in a field doesn't run in a straight line; it takes a big jump, changes direction, and off it goes again—the pursuers are gaining momentum in a straight line and all of a sudden they have to change direction, too, which means slowing down, reevaluating their position. I was going to be that hare. As soon as I got to the end of the alleyway I was going to hang a left or a right, I didn't even know which yet, and run as fast as I could until I found other options.

I found the alley. No time to think if it was the right decision—just make one. I could hear shouting behind me, maybe 100 to 150 yards away. But it wasn't directed at me. They were too professional for that. They knew it wouldn't have any effect. I heard the cars turning around. They'd be trying to cut me off. I ran.

By now I was out of breath, with this seven-year-old on my back. My mouth was dry, and I was breaking into a sweat. Kelly's head was banging onto the back of mine, and I was holding her so tight her chin was digging into my neck; it was starting to hurt her and she was crying.

"Stop, stop, Nick!"

I wasn't listening. I reached the end of the alley and ran into a totally different world.

In front of me was a narrow road that ran the length of the office buildings, and on the other side of it a grass embankment that went downhill to the main drag. Beyond that lay parking lots and the malls. Traffic noise drowned out Kelly's cries. The flow of vehicles was fast in both directions, despite the wet road. Most had their headlights on, and their wipers on intermittent. I stopped.

We must have looked a sight, a man with a shoeless child on his back, puffing and panting down the grass slope, the child moaning as her head banged on the back of his. I climbed the railings at the side of the main drag; now we were playing chicken with the traffic. Cars sounded their horns or braked sharply to avoid us. It seemed my new name was fuck, nut, or jerk. I didn't acknowledge anybody, even the ones who'd saved our lives by braking; I just kept on running.

Kelly was screaming. The traffic scared her as much as the running. All her young life she'd probably been warned about playing near the road, and here she was on a grown-up's back, cars and trucks swerving all around her.

Crossing the railings at the far side, I was also starting to worry. Kelly was slowing me down, without a doubt, and I still had quite a distance to run to get to safety. I ducked and weaved through the parking lot, using the height of the pickups and minivans to block us from their view.

At the far right of the mall I could see a computer superstore, CompUSA, and that was where I headed. There's always a good chance that a large store on a corner site will have more than one entrance. I expected there to be one on the other side, maybe at the rear, so even if they saw me going in, they'd have problems.

I knew the store would be hard for them to deal with, because I'd had to do this sort of thing myself in Northern Ireland. If a player went into a shopping center, we would send only one guy in with him, then rush to seal up all the exits. It was hard enough when we knew a target, let alone having to find and identify him. If he was doing antisurveillance drills, he could go up an elevator, leave by one exit, go back in through another and up an elevator two floors, down one floor, then wander out into a parking lot, and he's gone. If these boys were professional, they'd start sealing the exits as soon as they saw where I'd gone. I had to be quick.

We went in through the wide automatic doors. The store had aisles and aisles of office equipment, computers, and software. I went past the checkout counters without taking a cart, still with Kelly on my back. The place was packed. I was standing there drenched with sweat, chest heaving up and down as I fought for breath. Kelly was crying. People started looking at us.

Kelly moaned, "I want to get down now!"

"No, let's just get out of here."

I took a look behind and could see two men coming across the parking lot. In their suits they looked very much like plainclothes police, and they were running purposefully toward the store; they'd be heading to block off the exits. I had to put in some angles, had to get that confusion going.

I ran down a couple of aisles crammed with CD-ROM games, turned right, and ran along the exterior wall, looking for an exit. Fuck it, there wasn't one. The warehouse seemed to be one big sealed unit. I couldn't go back out the way I'd come in, but if I didn't find another exit, I was going to spend the rest of the day running around the shop in circles.

One of the young assistants looked at me, turned away, and went trotting down the aisle, obviously looking for the manager or a security guard. Seconds later two men in shirt-sleeves with name badges started to approach us. "Yes, excuse me? Can we help you?" all very polite, but in fact meaning *"What the fuck are you doing in our store?"*

There was no time to answer. I ran toward the rear of the store, looking for loading bays, emergency doors, open windows, anything. At last I saw the sign I was hoping to see: FIRE EXIT. I ran at it, pushed it open, and the alarm went off.

We were outside. We were on a platform, obviously used for deliveries, where trucks could back in and unload.

I ran down the four or five metal stairs and hit the ground. As I started to run to the left I shouted at Kelly to hold tight.

The rear of the shopping mall was deserted, just a long stretch of administration areas, with Dumpsters, bins, and even a trailer detached from its truck and being used as a storeroom. There were piles of cardboard boxes and bulging trash bags everywhere, a day's worth of garbage. Beyond the blacktop was a chain-link fence surrounding the whole area, and probably about fifteen feet high. Then vacant ground with trees and bushes. On the other side of that, I guessed, would be more parking and more stores.

I felt like a trapped rat. I had only two exits now, the access roads at either end of the long line of stores.

I couldn't get over the fence with Kelly on my back; if I tried to throw her over, she'd break her legs. I started to run to the left, along the rear of the stores, heading toward one of the access roads. It was no good—they'd had too much time to react; the road would be sealed.

I had to make a decision quickly. I moved toward one of the collection areas of Dumpsters, bagged-up garbage, and cardboard boxes.

I lifted her from my back and positioned her in among it all, throwing boxes over the top of her and moving others to fill in the gaps on each side.

She looked at me and started to cry.

I said, "Disneyland, Kelly! Disneyland!"

She stared at me, tears rolling down her cheeks, and I threw a couple of boxes over the top.

"I'll be back, I promise."

As I ran I looked at the trailer that was right up against the fence. It was a huge thing, the height of a truck. Without fifty pounds of young girl on my back, running toward it was like floating on air. At last I was in control. I felt as if I'd lost a ball and chain.

I sprinted like a maniac, using the cover of the bins and Dumpsters. I suddenly spotted the trunk of a car jutting out from one of the loading bays. It was a mid-1980s model, not one of the cars that had been chasing me. I'd check the ignition for keys, and if I was out of luck, I'd cross the open ground to the container.

A truck was parked up near another loading bay. I started

73

to run past it. A guy was running full tilt the other way, and we smashed our heads together. We both went down.

"Shit!" I looked at him through blurred eyes. He had a suit on. There was no way I was going to take a chance. I staggered to my feet and charged at him, banging him up against the car. He tried to wrap himself around me.

As I was pushing into him I could feel with the side of my face that his body was solid. This fucker had covert body armor on.

I pinned him up against the car, moved back a step, and pulled my weapon, flicking on the laser sight with my thumb.

Then, dazed, I sank back to my knees. I was seeing stars and my head was spinning; he was probably in exactly the same state. He looked down at me, confused, trying to make a decision. I aimed the sight onto his face.

"Don't do it," I said. "Don't waste your life on this, it's not worth it. Get your hands up—now!"

As his hands moved I could see he was wearing a wedding ring. "Think about your family. It's not worth dying over this. Number one, you're wrong, it wasn't me. Number two, I'll kill you. Put your hands on your head."

My head was clearing. What the fuck was I going to do now? Their cars would be here soon.

"Stay on your knees," I said. "Turn right. Move to the back of the vehicle."

I got up off the ground and stumbled behind him. My eyes were still smarting as if I'd been hit with CS gas.

We were between the loading bay and the car. He knew the score and hopefully was thinking of his wife and kids. I switched my pistol into my left hand, moved into him, and quickly jabbed the pistol muzzle into his armpit, twisting it into the material of his jacket. I felt his body tense and heard a little grunt.

"I'll explain the facts of life to you," I said. "This weapon is screwed into your clothes. I've got my finger on the trigger and the safety catch is off. If you fuck around, you'll kill yourself. Understand?"

He didn't react.

I said, "Come on, this isn't difficult. Do you understand me?"

"Yes."

"Place your hands on your head."

With my right hand I took his weapon. Mine had only one magazine. He was carrying a Sig .45 in a pancake holster over his right kidney, and three magazines on his belt. The Sig is an approved weapon of the FBI.

He was in his mid-thirties, straight off the set of *Baywatch*: blond, tanned, fit, good-looking, square-jawed. I could smell soap and baby lotion. This guy wanted to keep his skin soft. Or maybe he had a baby. Who cared? If he moved he'd be dead.

There was a white wire behind his ear, linked to an earpiece.

"Who are you?" I said. Not that it made any difference whether he was FBI or D.C. police.

No reply.

"Listen, whatever you think, I did not kill that family. I did not kill them—do you understand?"

Nothing. I knew I wouldn't get *Baywatch* man to talk. In any event, there wasn't any time to waste trying.

I took the radio, and the cash from his wallet. Then, with the pistol still in his armpit, I whispered loudly over my shoulder, "Stay where you are, Kelly! Don't worry, I'm coming!" I gripped him harder. "Kelly, I said we're going to go in a minute!" If they thought Kelly was still with me when I legged it, maybe they'd move on and search a fresh area.

I turned back to him and said, "I'm going to untwist this now. Don't fuck with me—it's not worth it." I gradually released my pistol, making sure I could fire at any moment. I was behind him, with the weapon now pointing at his head. He knew that.

I said, "You know what I've got to do next, don't you?"

There was a slight nod of acceptance.

I picked up an iron support from a pile of discarded shelving and gave him the good news where his neck met his shoulder. That sent him right down. For good measure I gave him a few kicks to the head and balls. At the end of the day, he wasn't going to be more pissed off with me because of this kicking; he probably already wanted to kill me. But I had to keep him from raising the alarm. A professional like this would be expecting it anyway; if the roles were reversed, it would be him doing the honors. It would certainly fuck him up for about ten minutes, and that was all I needed.

I came out from behind the car, had a quick look around. Nobody in sight. I ran toward the trailer; there was a large trash can beside it that I could use as a springboard. I jumped, threw myself upward, and got my arms onto the roof. I scrambled up. From there it was just a fifteen-foot drop to freedom.

A sign pointed the way to Maylords Boardwalk. I turned left and ran along the grass embankment, past the trash cans, and into another parking area. I went straight toward the boardwalk because it promised cover. I was looking for a rest room, and with luck there would also be an exit to the other side of the mall.

The boardwalk seemed to be a minimall with mainly shoe and greeting card boutiques. I found the block of conveniences by the coffee shop about a third of the way down the arcade. Looking farther down, I could see there was another exit to the boardwalk. I went into the men's room.

Two guys had just finished pissing and were now washing their hands. I went straight into one of the stalls and sat there while I waited to calm down.

I put the earpiece in my ear and switched the radio on. I didn't get much at all, it was broken up, but that meant nothing. I was probably in a dead spot.

I used toilet paper to wipe the blood and mud off my shoes and pants, and cleaned myself up as much as possible. When I was sure the other two had gone, I went out to the sinks, pressed the faucet, and washed my hands and face. I still wasn't getting anything but fuzz on the earpiece.

I headed for the coffee shop, bought a cappuccino, and sat down about three tables back. From there I could watch both exits to the boardwalk. I didn't look out of place with the wire in my ear because so many store detectives and security guards wore them.

They sparked up on the net. They were talking freely as if the radio were secure, not using codes. There was a jack on the radio for the key gun—the device that sends the chosen encryption codes to the radio. Once this has been done to two or more sets, they can talk together securely. Everybody else would just hear fuzz.

I listened to some of them checking around the back, where the boy had been dropped, and others in places that I couldn't identify. What I couldn't hear was a base station, a central control. I started to wonder about that. Then I thought, Why was it these guys and not uniformed police had turned up at the hotel? I was supposed to be a kidnapping murderer; in situations like this I'd expect to see heavily armed SWAT teams leaping from Chevy vans. I realized it was this that had made me run back for Kelly without even knowing it. I should have checked the boy I'd dropped for any ID. Never mind, it was too late now.

How did they find me so quickly at the Best Western? Had my call to London been traced to our room? Impossible: too quick. Was it my credit card when I checked in? Unlikelier still. Only the Firm would have known the details of my cover documents, and they wouldn't have turned me in because they'd be too worried about the Americans finding out about their deniable ops. So it must have been the receptionist—she must have watched the news and recognized Kelly's photograph. But even then, it didn't add up somehow. I started to feel very uneasy.

These boys weren't a Mickey Mouse group. When I bumped into *Baywatch* man, he'd been wearing a double-breasted jacket and it was open. But it was only now, thinking about it, that I realized that in fact it hadn't been open at first. There had been a Velcro fastening.

I heard more radio traffic. They'd found him. *Baywatch* man's name was Luther, but whoever the boss was on the ground, he didn't really care too much about Luther's condition. He just wanted to know if he was able to talk.

"Yeah, he's OK."

"Is he alone?"

"Yeah, he's alone."

"Did he see the target?"

"No, he says he didn't see the target but they're still together."

"Does he know what direction they went?"

There was a pause.

"No."

I imagined Luther sitting on the ground with his head against the car, getting patched up and feeling pretty pissed off at me. In the background I could hear him mumbling information. He sounded almost drunk.

The sender said, "No idea of the direction. And one more thing—he's armed. He had a sidearm with him and he's also taken Luther's . . . Wait . . ."

I heard a click, then whoever was with Luther came back on the net; his voice was very agitated. "We've got a problem—he's got the radio! He's got the radio!"

The boss came back on: "Fuck! Everybody, all stations, cut comms! Close down now! Out."

The earpiece went dead. They were going to turn the radios off and refill with a new code. Luther's radio was obsolete. What I wouldn't have given now for a key gun.

Luther said he hadn't seen the target, so it was Kelly they were after, not me. My face burned with anger. These were the people who'd killed Kev, they had to be. This chase was nothing to do with law enforcement; this was about people who wanted to finish the job. Maybe they thought Kelly had seen them.

By now I had finished my coffee and the waitress had whisked the cup away. I was starting to be a pain in the ass here; other people were waiting for my table. I went back into the rest rooms. The TV remote control was still in my pocket. That went into the trash can, along with the useless radio.

What about Kelly? What did I have to gain by going back? What if they'd found her, disposed of her, and were waiting for me to pick her up? That was what I would have done. I could think of lots of reasons why I shouldn't go back.

Shit.

I walked back toward the mall exit. Looking left across the dead ground, I could just about see the roof of CompUSA. The parking lot was still full, and it was raining harder now. I turned up the collar of Kev's jacket and looked toward the main drag. I could see a Wendy's like a desert island in the middle of the parking lot. It was coffee time again. I checked the route ahead for any sign of my new friends and again used tall vehicles as cover.

I took my burger and coffee over to a window seat. I couldn't see the rear of the buildings, but I could see the nearer of the two access roads, the one I'd been running toward when I met Luther. Better than nothing. The Wendy's had a play station, which was great cover; kids screamed around in a tub of multicolored tennis balls while their parents sat it out, just like me. I tried not to think of Kelly hiding among the Dumpsters, scared, wet, cold, and hungry.

I sat and stared out the window at the rain. I remembered the times I'd been bad as a child and got a spanking from my stepfather and been put in the shed for the night. I'd been terrified of the rain beating down on the clear plastic roof; I'd sat there curled up, thinking that if the rain could get me, then so could the bogeymen. As a soldier and as a K I had been shot at, beaten up, imprisoned; I'd always been scared, but nothing like those times as a child. I thought of Kelly abandoned in her makeshift hiding place, rain beating down on the cardboard. Then I cut it from my mind. She'd get over it. I shouldn't let it concern me; I'd done worse things.

Still looking out the window, I saw the white Taurus come out from behind the mall onto the access road, stop at the intersection, and turn with the flow of traffic. It was four up by the looks of things, all suits, though in the rain it was hard to be certain. Four up was a good indication that they were lifting off: if they were taking Luther to the hospital, there'd be three at most inside, one driving, one looking after the casualty. The others would have stayed behind. I was beginning to feel a decision coming on.

I'd have to change my appearance, and I'd have to do it on the cheap—I had about five hundred dollars in total, and would be needing every cent.

I finished my coffee and went back to the boardwalk. I found a clothing store and bought a thin cotton raincoat that folded up to about the size of a handkerchief. I also bought a Kangol hat, the sort it was fashionable to wear the wrong way so the brim was hanging down the back of your neck and the logo was in front.

I then went to an Hour Eyes and bought a pair of display glasses with thick rims. Glasses really change the shape of your face. Whenever I'd needed an appearance change on a job, a haircut and glasses had always done the trick. Wearing a different color and giving yourself a different shape was the minimum required.

I went back to the rest rooms to sort myself out. I ripped

out the inside of the raincoat pocket with my teeth. My newly acquired Sig .45 was down the front of my jeans, with the mags in my pockets. If the shit hit the fan, I could draw the weapon and fire through the coat.

I wanted to use the last three-quarters of an hour of daylight reconning the garbage area. The lift-off might have been a ploy; I wanted to assure myself that nobody was lying in wait. The idea would be to do a complete 360 degrees around the target area, but before that I wanted to go back and give the hotel another look; I wanted to see if there were any police cars outside, to confirm whether it had been an official lift. If Luther and his friends were after a murder suspect, the cops should be up there by now, dusting for prints and taking statements.

I put on my disguise and looked in the mirror at the world's hippest dude—well, nearly. If people looked closely, they would think I was the oldest swinger in town. I turned the cap around with the brim now forward, and off I went. I walked straight across the parking lot, crossed the main drag at the intersection, and worked my way back to the Best Western along the roads. I saw nothing. Everything looked perfectly normal; not a police car in sight.

As I walked back I thought about the state that Kev, Marsha, and Aida had been left in. Why hack them to bits? Luther and his friends weren't dopeheads, they were pros; they did nothing without a reason. They must have wanted it to appear drug related to cover their asses. Given the number of attempts on Kev's life in the past, it would have been perfectly plausible for the police to assume that one of them had finally succeeded, and that the perpetrators had then gone overboard and slain the whole family as a warning to others. But I knew that wasn't the explanation. They had killed Marsha because they'd have had to assume that Kev had passed on whatever he knew, and then they'd had to kill Aida simply because they didn't want witnesses. Kelly owed her life to their having not seen her. It was probably only after the news reports that they realized they hadn't finished the job, that there might be a witness after all.

The way they'd butchered Aida brought back to me a story

about the American "hearts and minds" program in Vietnam. In one region they'd injected the children of a village against smallpox. The Viet Cong came along a week later and cut each child's arm off. It worked: no more hearts and minds programs for them. Sometimes the end justifies the means. I had a sort of respect for Luther and company, but I knew I mustn't fuck around with these people—they were too much like me.

Rush hour was now in full swing; it would be dark soon. The stores were still open and the area was packed with people. It was great for me; it made me just another sucker.

As I walked I had my head down against the rain. I reached the Wendy's parking lot. This time I was nearer the fence; wiping my new glasses, I looked across the low ground as the rear of the mall came into view.

There was a loud hiss of brakes as a truck backed up to a loading bay. Three other trucks were already parked alongside the car where I'd met Luther. But again, just as at the hotel, there were no police investigating the crime scene. Maybe they didn't like the weather.

Only the bays that were in use were lit. The group of bins where I'd hidden Kelly was pretty much in shadow. One was being filled with the old metal shelving I'd used on Luther. Even from where I was, I could hear the loud crash and clatter. Kelly must be petrified down there.

No need for a 360; I'd seen enough. As I looked forward deciding where to go now, I watched a bus pull up by a shelter, take on passengers, and drive off again. Maybe that was our way out of here.

But if they'd found Kelly and set an ambush, where was I going to run? I had to work out an escape route. Hijacking cars doesn't work so well in a built-up area—it attracts too much attention. Better to use the crowds and confusion. I picked three possible routes.

Hanging around increased the chance of getting busted, so I decided to lift off from the area for a while. I continued on to the stores. I thought I'd get some stuff for Kelly; she'd be needing an appearance change, too. She'd been on the news; she was famous now.

I bought her a nice big floppy hat. I wanted to tuck her hair up out of the way and hide her face as best I could. I also bought her a thinly padded pink three-quarter-length coat to cover those skinny legs, and a completely new set of clothes to fit a nine-year-old. She was tall for her age, so I thought I'd better get the larger size. Almost as an afterthought, I bought myself some new jeans and a T-shirt.

With a handful of shopping bags I retraced the route along the fence. As I walked away from the stores, their lights still reflected on the wet asphalt of the parking lot. The traffic was slow on the main drag, windshield wipers on full speed.

As I got to the fence I looked left. There was no change.

I kept on walking. As I got level with the stores, the access road started to rise up to meet me. The fence stopped. I turned left down a slippery grass embankment and onto the road that led to the back of the stores. I followed the fence again as I dropped down into the vacant lot.

The rain had turned the dust into mush. I now had the fence to my left and the loading bays to the right. I kept on walking, fighting the temptation just to run to Kelly, grab her, and get the hell out of there. That's what gets people caught or killed.

My eyes must have looked as if I were plugged into the power lines. They were darting everywhere, getting as much information into my head as possible. I wanted to see this ambush before it was sprung. I was committed now. If push came to shove, I'd fucking shove.

What if Kelly wasn't there? I'd call 911 and say I'd seen that girl from the news wandering around the area. Hopefully the cops would get her before Luther's pals did. That was if they hadn't already. I'd then have to take my chances when the Nick Stone manhunt began. Whoever had her would then have my name.

I got to within about twenty yards of the bins, still walking at the same steady pace. I didn't even look around now, because that took time and effort.

I came up to the bins and started to lift away the boxes. "Kelly, it's me! Kelly! See, I told you I'd come back."

The cardboard was soaking wet, coming apart in my hands. As I pulled the last of it away, I could see she was more or less exactly in the position I'd left her. Curled up, sitting on some dry cardboard. My mind flashed back to how she'd looked when I'd found her in the garage. At least she wasn't rocking, with her hands clamped over her ears. She was dry; maybe the bogeyman had got in, but at least the rain hadn't.

I stood her up and put her new coat around her shoulders. "I hope you like pink," I said. "I got this for you, too." I put the hat on her head to preserve whatever was left of her body heat.

She put her arms around me. I hadn't been expecting it; I didn't know how to react. I just kept talking to her. She cuddled me harder.

I readjusted the hat. "There, that'll keep you nice and dry. Now let's go and get you a bath and something to eat, shall we?"

I had the bags in my left arm. She gripped my left sleeve as we walked. It was awkward, but I needed to keep my right hand free to draw my pistol.

The bus was about half full with shoppers and bulging shopping bags. Kelly was cuddled up beside me in the window seat. Her hat was doing its job; her hair was tucked up, and the dropped brim covered her face. I was feeling good. I'd saved her from Luther and his buddies. I'd done the right thing.

We were on our way to Alexandria, an area I knew to be south of downtown D.C. but within the Beltway; we were going there because that was what had been on the destination sign of the first bus to arrive.

Everyone was fed up and wet, and the bus was well misted up. I leaned across and used my sleeve to wipe away the condensation, but it didn't help much. I looked toward the front, where the windshield wipers were working overtime.

The priority was a hotel; we'd have to check into one within the next hour or so, because the later in the day I left it, the more unusual it would look.

"Nick?"

I didn't want to look at her because I knew what she was going to ask.

"Yes?"

"Why were those men chasing you? Did you do something wrong?"

I could feel her looking at me under her hat.

"I don't know who they are, Kelly. I just don't know." Eyes still fixed on the clear patch of windshield, I said, "You hungry?"

In the corner of my eye, I could see her hat moving up and down.

"Not long now. What do you want—McDonald's? Wendy's?"

She nodded for both, then mumbled something. I was still looking out the window. "What's that?"

"Mickey D's."

"Mickey D's?"

"McDonald's! You're so out of it!"

"Ah, OK—that's what we'll get."

I went back to my thoughts. I would only use cash from now on; I had to assume the worst, which was that we'd been traced through my credit card. Despite that, I'd still call London again. Deep down, I guessed that they'd probably already consigned my records to the shredder, but what did I have to lose?

We drove past a place called the Roadies Inn. It fit the bill. I didn't have a clue where we were, but that didn't matter; I'd sort that out later. I signaled the driver that we wanted the next stop.

When the Roadies Inn had been built in the 1960s it probably looked like a million dollars. Now even the grass outside looked faded, and on the red neon VACANCY sign the *V* and the *N* were flickering. Perfect.

I peered through the screen door to the lobby. A woman in her twenties was behind the reception desk, smoking, and watching a TV that was on the far wall. I only hoped we hadn't had star billing on the news. Looking past her into the back office, I saw a bald, overweight man, probably late fifties, working at a desk.

"I want you to wait just here, Kelly." I pointed to the wall of the hotel under the upstairs landing that acted as a patio.

She didn't like it.

"I won't be long," I said, starting to walk backward toward the doors. "Just wait there; I'll be right back." By now I was at the door. I pointed at her as if I were training a puppy. "Stay, OK?"

The desk clerk was wearing jeans and a T-shirt. Her hair was the blondest I'd ever seen, apart from the roots. She glanced away from the TV and said on autopilot, "Hello, can I help you?"

"I'm looking for a room for maybe three or four nights."

"Sure, for how many?"

"Two adults and a child."

"Sure, one moment," and she ran her finger down the register.

The news was on. I turned and watched, but there was nothing about the murders. Maybe we were already old news. I hoped so.

"Can I have your card?"

I pulled a face. "Ah, that's where we have a problem. We're on a fly-drive vacation, and we've had our bags stolen. We've been to see the police and I'm waiting for replacement cards, but I'm just running on cash at the moment. I understand you have to have it for the record, but maybe if I pay in advance, and you disconnect the room phone?"

She was starting to nod her head, but her expression was still the wrong side of sympathetic.

"We're really stuck." I played the wet and sorrowful Brit abroad. "We've got to go to the British consulate tomorrow and sort out our passports." I brought out some twenty-dollar bills.

It seemed to take a while for it all to sink in. "I'm so sorry to hear about that." She paused, waiting for more chemicals to interact in her brain. "I'll get the manager."

She went into the office, and I watched her talking to the bald guy at his desk. From their body language I got the impression he was her father. I felt a drop of sweat roll down my spine. If they refused us a room, we were stranded maybe miles from the next motel and would need to start ordering taxis and raising our profile.

Hurry up! I turned and looked outside but couldn't see Kelly. Fuck, I hoped Mr. Honest Citizen wasn't about to storm in demanding to know who'd left a little girl all alone outside in the rain. I quickly walked to the door and stuck my head outside. She was still there, standing where I'd asked her to.

I came back to the reception desk just as Dad appeared from the back office. The woman was on the telephone, taking a reservation.

"Just making sure our car isn't blocking the way." I grinned.

"I hear you have a problem?" Dad had a vacant smile on his face. I knew we were OK.

"Yes." I sighed. "We've been to the police and contacted the credit card companies. We're just waiting for it to get sorted out. Until then, all I've got is cash. I'll pay for the next three days in advance."

"That's no problem."

I was sure it wasn't. There was no way our little cash transaction would be finding its way onto the books. What some people call white trash, Kev used to call "salt of the earth"; they might take a while to understand things, but money is money in any language.

He smiled. "We'll keep the telephone on for you."

I played the thankful Brit and checked in, then Kelly and I bounded up two flights of concrete and cinder-block stairs.

Kelly hesitated outside the room, then looked at me and said, "Nick, I want to see Mommy. When can I go home?"

Shit, not that again. I wished more than anything that she could go and see Mommy. It would be one less problem. "Not long now, Kelly," I said. "I'll get some food in a minute, OK?"

"OK."

Once inside, I lay down on the bed and thought out the priorities.

"Nick?"

"Yes?" I was looking at the ceiling.

"Can I watch TV?"

Thank God for that.

I reached over to the remote and quickly checked the channels, making sure I wasn't going to catch us both on the news. I found Nickelodeon and stuck with it.

I'd made a decision. "I'm going out now to buy us something to eat," I said, my mind on the one option that hadn't yet been closed. "You stay here, the same as before. I'll put the DO NOT DISTURB sign on the door, and you make sure that you don't open it for anybody. Do you understand?"

She nodded.

The phone booth was next to a Korean grocery store. It was

still drizzling; I could hear the noise of tires on wet asphalt as I crossed the road.

I pushed in a couple of quarters and dialed.

I got "Good evening, British Embassy. How may I help you?"

"I'd like to speak to the defense attaché, please."

"May I say who's calling?"

"My name is Stamford." Fuck it, I had nothing to lose.

"Thank you, one moment please."

Almost immediately, a no-nonsense voice came on the line: "Stamford?"

"Yes."

"Wait."

There was a long continuous tone; I was starting to think I'd been cut off again. Then, thirty seconds later, I heard Simmonds. My call must have been patched through to London. Unflappable as ever, he said, "It seems you're in a spot of trouble."

"*Trouble*'s not the word."

In veiled speech I told him everything that had happened since my last call. Simmonds listened without interruption, then said, "There's not really a lot I can do. Obviously, you understand the situation I'm in?" I could tell he was pissed off with me big-time. "You were told to return immediately. You disobeyed an order. You should not have gone to see him, you know that." He was still cool about it all, but under the veneer I knew he was boiling.

I could just picture him behind his desk in his crumpled shirt and baggy cords, with the family photo and maybe Easter eggs for his family on his desk, next to a pile of red-hot faxes from Washington that had to be attended to.

"It's got nothing on the situation I can put you in," I said. "I've got stuff that would make your lot look not very British at all. I'll blow it to whoever wants to listen. It's not a bluff. I need help to get out of this shit and I want it now."

There was a pause: the patient parent waiting for a child to stop its tantrum.

He said, "Your position is pretty delicate, I'm afraid. There is nothing I can do unless you have some form of proof that you're not implicated. I suggest you make every effort to discover what has happened and why, then we can talk and I might be able to help. How does that sound to you? You can carry out your threat, but I wouldn't recommend it."

I could feel his hand tighten around my balls. Whether they complied or called my bluff, I'd be spending the rest of my life on the run. The Firm does not like being strong-armed.

"I've got no choice really, have I?"

"I'm glad you see it like that. Bring what you find."

The phone went dead.

My mind racing, I wandered into the shop. I bought a bottle of hair color—one wash in, twelve washes out—and a hair-trimmer gadget. I also bought a full range of washing and shaving supplies because we couldn't look like a couple of scruffies at large in D.C. Then I filled the basket with bottles of Coca-Cola and some apples and candy.

I couldn't find a Mickey D's and ended up in a Burger King. I bought two meal deals, then went back to the hotel.

I knocked on the door as I opened it. "Guess what I've got—burgers, fries, apple pies, hot chocolate, coffee for me . . ."

By the wall next to the window was a little circular table and PVC chairs. The shopping bags went on the bed; I dumped the burgers on the table with a flourish, like a returning hunter. Ripping the bags open to make a tablecloth, I tipped the fries out, opened the ketchup, and we both dived in. She must have been starving.

I waited until she had a mouthful of burger. "Listen, Kelly, you know how grown-up girls are always dyeing their hair and cutting it and all sorts of stuff? I thought you might like to try it."

She couldn't have looked less interested.

"What do you fancy, a really dark brown?"

She shrugged.

I wanted to get it done before she understood too much of what was happening. The moment she'd finished her hot apple pie, I led her to the bathroom and got her to take off her shirt. I tested the shower temperature and leaned her over the sink, quickly wetting her hair, then toweled and brushed it. I got the trimmer going but I wasn't entirely sure what I was doing. I realized it was for beards, really, and by the time I'd got the hang of it her hair looked like shit. The more I tried to sort it, the shorter it was getting. Soon it was up around her collar.

As I studied the bottle of dye, trying to read the instructions, she said, "Nick?"

I was still reading the bottle and hoping I wasn't about to turn her hair into a ginger fuzzball.

"What?"

"Do you know those guys who were chasing you?"

I was the one who should have been asking questions.

"No, I don't, Kelly, but I will find out." I thought about it, put the hair dye down. I was standing behind her; both of us were looking at each other in the mirror. Her light blue eyes were now not so red around the edges. That only made my brown ones even more dark and tired-looking. I looked at her a while longer. Finally, I said, "Kelly, why did you go to the hidey-hole?"

She said nothing. I could see in her eyes that she was starting to question my hairdressing skills.

"Did Daddy shout 'Disneyland'?"

"No."

"Then why did you go?" Already this was getting too intense for me. I needed to do something. I picked up the dye.

"Because of the noise."

I started to comb the dye in.

"Oh, what noise was that?"

She looked at me in the mirror. "I was in the kitchen but I heard a bad noise in the living room and I went and looked."

"What did you see?"

"Daddy was shouting at the men and they were hitting him."

"Did they see you?"

"I don't know, I didn't go in the room. I just wanted to shout to Mommy to come and help Daddy."

"And what did you do?"

Her eyes went down. "I couldn't help him." When she looked up again, I saw her face was burning with shame. Her bottom lip started to wobble. "I ran to the hidey-hole. I wanted to go to Mommy but she was upstairs with Aida, and Daddy was shouting at the men."

"You ran to the hidey-hole?"

"Yes."

"Did you stay there?"

"Yeah."

"Did Mommy come and call for you?"

"No. You did."

"So you didn't see Mommy and Aida?"

"No."

The picture of the two of them dead flashed into my mind.

I put my arms around her as she sobbed. I said, "Kelly, you couldn't have helped Daddy. Those men were too big and strong. Probably I couldn't have helped him, and I'm a grown-up. It's not your fault Daddy got hurt. But he is OK and wants me to look after you until he is better. Mommy and Aida had to go with Daddy. There just wasn't any time to get you."

I let her cry a bit, then asked, "Did you see any of the men who were chasing us today?"

She shook her head.

"Did the men who were with Daddy have suits on?"

"I think so, but they had like painting clothes over them."

I guessed what she meant. "The sort Daddy would wear to paint the house?" I did the actions of putting on a pair of overalls.

She nodded.

"So do you mean they had suits on underneath, but had the painting things on top?"

She nodded again.

I knew it; these boys were good—they were players. They hadn't wanted to get nasty red stuff all over their nice suits.

I asked her how many men came out and what they looked like. She was confused and scared. Her lip started to quiver again. "Can I go home soon?" She was fighting back the tears.

"Yes, very soon, very soon. When Daddy is better. Until

then, I'm looking after you. Come on, Kelly, let's make you look like a big girl."

After a rinse I combed her wet hair and got her dressed right away in her new clothes. If we had to move, I needed her dressed, so I told her that the only things she could keep off were her hat, coat, and shoes.

She inspected herself in the mirror. The new clothes were much too big and her hair was—well, she didn't seem too sure.

We watched Nickelodeon, and eventually she fell asleep. I lay staring at the ceiling, going through the options, or rather, trying to kid myself that I had some.

What about Slack Pat? He would certainly help if he could, as long as he hadn't turned into some drugged-up New Age hippie. But the only way I could think of contacting him was through the restaurant he used to rave about. The way he described it, he practically lived there. The problem was, I couldn't remember the name of it, just that it was on a hill at the edge of Georgetown.

What about Euan? He was no good yet because he'd still be operating in Northern Ireland, and there was no way I could make contact with him until he was back in England.

I looked over at Kelly. That was how she would have to live now, always dressed, ready to run at a moment's notice. I put the comforter over her.

I piled all the trash together and put it in the wastebasket, made sure the sign was still on the door and her shoes were in her pockets. I checked chamber in both weapons—the 9mm in Kev's jacket and the Sig in my waistband. No doubt Kelly was going to be in all of tomorrow's papers, but at least if the shit hit the fan we were ready to go. I knew my escape route and would not hesitate to shoot my way out.

I got my new clothes out of the bag and took them into the bathroom. I shaved, then undressed. I stank; Kev's things were stained with blood from Aida or Marsha, I couldn't remember which. The sweat had thinned it, spreading it right up the back and shoulders of his shirt and the inside of his jeans. Everything went into a plastic laundry bag, which I'd throw away in the morning. I had a long, hot shower and washed my hair. Then I got dressed, checked the door lock, and lay on the bed.

I woke up at about 5:30 in the morning after a terrible night's sleep. I wasn't sure if all the bad stuff was a dream. The only good result was that I remembered the name of Slack Pat's restaurant.

I thought again about money. I definitely couldn't use credit cards because I had to assume they'd either been frozen or would be used as a trace. It was cash or nothing—not easy in the West nowadays. Pat, if I got to him, would fund me, but I knew I'd have to take advantage of any spare time to get hold of more. Kelly was snoring big-time. I picked up the key card, gently closed the door behind me, checked that the sign was up, and went looking for a fire extinguisher.

12

As I passed the open door to the chambermaid's storeroom I spotted half a dozen wedge-shaped door stops on a shelf. I helped myself to a couple.

I found the fire extinguisher on the wall by the elevators. I quickly unscrewed the top of it and removed the carbon dioxide cylinder, a nine-inch black steel tube. I put it in my jacket and walked back to the room.

I put the three spare magazines for the Sig .45 in the left-hand pocket of Kev's jacket and decided I was going to keep the USP in the room. I hid it in the toilet tank. A weapon can stand getting wet in the short term. I just didn't want her to find it and start putting holes in herself.

I dozed some more, woke up, and dozed again. By 7 A.M. I was bored and hungry. Breakfast was included in the room price, but to get it I'd have to go downstairs to the lobby.

Kelly started to stir. I said, "Good morning. Do you fancy something to eat?"

She was all yawny, sitting up and looking like a scarecrow because she'd gone to sleep with wet hair. Immediately I put the TV on for her, because I didn't really know what to say. She looked down at her clothes, trying to work it out.

"You fell asleep," I laughed. "I couldn't even undress you last night. Hey, it's like camping, isn't it?"

She liked that. "Yeah." She smiled, still sleepy.

"Shall I go and get you some breakfast?"

She didn't look up, just nodded at the television.

"Remember, you must do this every time; you never ever open the door. I'll come back using the key. Don't even open the curtains, because the cleaning ladies will think it's OK to

95

come in, and we don't want to talk to anyone, do we? I'll leave
the DO NOT DISTURB sign, OK?"

She nodded. I wasn't sure how much of it had gone in. I
picked up the tray the ice bucket was on, put on my glasses,
and went down to reception.

It was already fairly crowded: people with RVs who
couldn't be bothered to sleep in them, and salesmen looking
clean, fresh, and straight out of the "appearance counts" section of the manual.

The breakfast area was made up of two or three tables by
the coffeepots under the TV. I took three packets of cereal,
bagels and muffins, some apples, then two cups of coffee and
an orange juice.

The desk clerk had just finished her shift and came over. "I
hope everything goes OK with your passports and all." She
smiled, helping herself to a bagel.

"I'm sure it'll be fine. We're just going to concentrate on
having a good vacation."

"If you need any help, you just come and ask."

"Thanks." I walked over to the desk and picked up a com-
plimentary *USA Today*. I also helped myself to a book of
Roadies Inn matches from a whole bowl of them and a paper
clip that was in a big ashtray full of elastic bands and office
supplies, and went back to the room.

Ten minutes later Kelly was munching on her cereal, glued
to Nickelodeon. I said, "I'm going out for about an hour. I've
got to do stuff. While I'm away, I want you to wash up and be
all nice and clean for when I get back, and have your hair
brushed. Are you going to be all right on your own, with your
big-girl haircut?"

She shrugged. "Whatever."

"What are your favorite colors?"

"My favorite colors are pink and blue."

"Well, we've got the pink." I pointed at the coat hanging up
with her shoes sticking out of the pockets. That had been a bit
of luck. "Now I've got to get you something blue."

I gave my glasses a quick clean with toilet paper, put them
back in their case and into Kev's jacket, then put my long
black raincoat over the top, checking the pocket for the

cylinder. I checked my pockets and took out the loose change. I wanted to cut down on noise, and always felt better anyway with as little as possible dragging around my clothes.

I got my Kangol hat in my hand, and I was all ready to go.

"I won't be long. Remember, let no one in. I'll be back before you know it."

It had stopped raining, but the sky was still gray and the ground wet. The road was choked with cars heading into downtown D.C. It's a people town; the sidewalks were busy, too.

I walked briskly to keep pace with the office workers, each with their "Got to get up, got to get going" expression, looking all the time for the ideal place to make some money quickly and get back to the hotel before Kelly started panicking.

It was too early for a shopping mall, since they didn't open until tenish. And I wasn't in an area with a lot of hotels—they were all farther downtown. There were fast-food outlets but with normally just one way in and out, and too much rest room traffic, they wouldn't be a good choice. A service station would do, as long as it had an outside bathroom that could be opened only with a key obtained from the cashier.

I'd been wandering around for maybe twenty minutes. I walked through a couple of gas stations that were busy enough, but they were modern, with inside rest rooms.

Eventually I found what I was looking for, an outdoor rest room with a sign on the door that said KEY AT DESK. I checked to make sure that the door was locked, then I walked on.

I was looking for two things now: somewhere natural to watch the pumps from, and my escape route. Farther up, on the other side of the road, was a run of lawyers' offices, credit unions, insurance brokers, in wonderful 1930s brick detached houses; in between were what looked like well-used alleys. I crossed over, walked down one, and came out onto the parallel street; turning right, I followed the road to an intersection, turned left, then right again up another alley. The whole area was perfect for angles and distance. I made my way back to the gas station by a different route.

There was a bus stop across the street, about a hundred yards away. I strolled along to it, stood in a doorway, and

waited; it had to look natural, I had to have a reason to be
doing what I was doing. There were two or three people
waiting, then the line got gradually longer, a bus came, and
we were back to two or three again. I looked at the destination
sign of each bus as it approached, looked fed up that it wasn't
the one I wanted, and got back in the doorway.

People don't carry much cash with them nowadays, especially here in the land of the credit card. The ideal target
would be a tourist—they tend to carry more cash and
traveler's checks—but there weren't likely to be many in this
part of town.

Over a period of about thirty minutes there'd been four or
five possibles going in to fill up their cars, but unfortunately it
seemed that none of them was in need of a shit. I thought
about Kelly; I hoped she was sticking to the script.

A white guy in his late twenties drove up to the pumps in a
new Camaro. It carried thirty-day plates while waiting for the
new registration. He was wearing a baggy track suit that was
red, blue, green, orange, and six other colors, and the world's
most flamboyant basketball shoes to match. His hair was
shaved at the sides, with the rest pointing skyward. The sound
system was booming out bass that I could almost feel vi-
brating from across the street.

He filled up and went in to pay. When he came out he was
carrying what looked like a small length of two-by-four. He
turned left toward the rest room. This was my boy.

I stepped out of the doorway, turned my collar up, and
headed across the road. He was putting his wallet into his
track top and zipping up. I'd already checked the garage surveillance cameras; they wouldn't be a problem: they were focused on the pumps to catch drive-aways, not on the far end
of the building to catch toilet paper thieves.

As I left the doorway I was a man who needed a piss and
couldn't wait any longer for his bus to arrive. It was unlikely
to register with anybody at the bus stop; first thing in the
morning people are brooding about the day's work ahead, or
about their mortgages or kids or the wife's headache the night
before. They're not going to worry too much about a guy
going into a toilet. I walked toward the door with just enough

spring in my step to look like the man with the world's fullest bladder and went in.

The room was about twelve by twelve, fairly clean, reeking of bleach. Dead ahead were two urinals, with a sink and a wall-mounted paper-towel dispenser. My boy was in one of the two stalls to the right.

I could hear the sound of zippers being undone, the rustle of a general sorting out, and a little cough. I closed the door behind me and jammed in the two door stops with my shoe. No one would be getting in or out of here unless I wanted them to.

I stood at the urinal and made it look as if I were taking a leak. My hands were in front of me, but holding the steel cylinder. I'd keep my back to him until he came out to wash his hands.

I stood there for three or four minutes. I heard him pissing. It stopped, then nothing. This character was taking too long. I swung my head to the right as if to look out of the small, barred window but carried on with the motions of pissing in case for some reason he could see me and was being hesitant about leaving the stall.

Then, casually looking right behind me, I saw something really bizarre. Through the gap between the bottom of the door and the floor I could see one foot, which seemed to be his right, on the ground and facing the toilet. His tracksuit pants weren't bunched around his ankles. I thought, *Weird position, but there you go.* Then I noticed that the door was open an inch. He hadn't locked it.

I wasn't going to stop and figure it out. Clenching my right fist around the cylinder, and with my left hand out to protect myself, I started quickly but quietly toward the door. At the last minute I took a deep breath, dropped my shoulder, and barged in.

He banged up against the wall, screaming, "What the fuck! What the fuck!" His hands went out to try to keep himself from falling and the door held; his bulk was blocking it.

I had to barge in again. The hard and fast rule of mugging is to be exactly that: hard and fast. Putting all my weight behind the door, I had him pinned up against the wall. He was a big boy; I had to be careful, I could get fucked over here. I grabbed a handful of his gelled hair with my left hand and pulled his head over to the left, exposing the right side of his neck.

You don't just use your arm to hit somebody. I needed to get as much weight as I could behind the cylinder, the same as a boxer using his hips and the top half of his body to power the swing. I brought the cylinder up in my right and swung my whole body around as if throwing a downward right hook and cracked him just below the ear. The idea was just to take him down, not kill him or give him brain damage for the rest of his days; if I'd wanted to do that, I'd have cracked him over the head a few times. As it was, it wouldn't be his best day out, but tough shit—wrong place, wrong time.

It had been a good hit. He groaned and went down. He was fucked, and without a doubt he would have had star bursts in his eyes, that crackling and popping sensation you get when you go down semiconscious. He'd just want to curl up and get under the comforter and hide. That was why I'd used the cylinder instead of a gun. You can't predict people's reactions to a pistol. He might have been an undercover cop with a gun himself, he might have been some kind of heroic, take-a-chance citizen. Not that it mattered now. The old ways are the best.

He'd banged his head on the tank and smashed his nose; blood was pouring down his chin. There was a high-pitched, childlike moan coming from him. He was in shitty shape but he'd live. I gave him another one for good measure; I wanted him down and well out. He stopped making a noise.

I put my left hand on his head and held it facing away from me. I didn't want him to be able to ID me. With my right hand I got under his belly and twisted his tracksuit top around toward me, unzipped it, and pulled out his wallet. Then I started to feel down his pockets in case he had another big wad stashed away there. My fingers closed around a plastic bag that filled the ball of my hand. I pulled out what looked like enough white powder to send the guy's entire neighborhood into orbit, all in neat little plastic wallets ready for sale. No good to me; I left it on the floor.

It was then that I realized what he'd been up to while I was at the urinal. Wrapped tight around his left arm was a rubber tube, and there was blood dripping from a small puncture wound. He must have had his left leg up on the toilet seat to support his arm while he was shooting up. I saw the hypodermic on the floor.

As I stood up, my pants felt wet and I looked down. He'd had the last laugh. I'd made him lose control of his bodily functions and he'd pissed himself. And I'd been kneeling in it.

I picked up the key from the floor. That, too, was covered in piss. He was starting to come around a bit; there were a few moans and groans. I got hold of his head and banged it against the toilet to give him the message to stay where he was for a while.

I stepped back from the stall. There was no time to try to clean my jeans. I went to the main door, retrieved the doorstops, put them in my pocket, came out, and locked the door behind me. I tossed the key into some shrubbery.

I was out of breath and a bit of sweat dripped down the side of my face, but I had to make myself look calm and casual. If another customer happened to come around the corner to use the toilet, I'd say it was out of order.

As I crossed the street I glanced left and behind me. Nothing. I wouldn't look back again. I'd soon know if something was going on because I'd hear all the screaming and shouting, or the sound of people running toward me. Then I'd have to react—but at the end of the day, I was the one with the big fucking gun.

I passed the bus stop and carried on toward the first alley. After two more turns I took my coat off, wrapped it around the cylinder, and folded the whole lot up. I took the cap off and folded that into the coat as well. I kept on walking, found a trash can, and got rid of my bundle. I was a new man, or I would be as soon as I put on my glasses.

Once on the road again, I got out the wallet as if I were checking whether I had my credit card. I opened it up and found that I was a family man; there was a very nice picture of me, my wife, and two kids—the family of Lance White. I didn't think Mrs. White would be too pleased with the state of me when I got home.

There was about $240 in the billfold; White had either just been to an ATM or done some early-morning deals. There were also a couple of credit cards, but I wouldn't keep them; it would be time-consuming to sell them, and if I tried to use them it could only be in the next hour or so—but why run the risk of the police doing a trace and ending up with my description from a sales clerk? The rest of the stuff was shit, bits of paper with phone numbers on them. Probably his client list. As I passed another trash can I dumped everything except the cash.

I now had just under $400 in my pocket, enough for the next few days in case I couldn't contact Pat or he didn't come up with the goods.

The piss on my pants was starting to dry up a bit as I walked, but it stank something awful. It was time for a change of clothes.

I reached the Burger King and all the other shops near the hotel. I was in and out of a discount shop in about fifteen minutes, with a duffel containing a new coat, jeans, sweatshirt, and underwear, all bought with cash. Kelly had also got a complete new set of clothes, down to underpants and undershirts.

I had a quick look at my watch on the way up to the room. I'd been gone about two hours and fifteen minutes, a bit longer than I'd said I'd be.

Before I even got to the door I could see it was ajar. I looked down and saw a pillow keeping it open. I could hear the TV.

Pulling my pistol, I went against the wall, the weapon pointing toward the gap. I felt disbelief, then shock. I felt emptiness in my stomach, and then I felt sick.

13

I moved into the room. Nothing.

I checked on the other side of the bed in case she might be hiding there. Maybe she was playing some game with me.

"Kelly! Are you in there?" My voice was serious, and she'd have known it.

No reply. My heart was pumping so hard my chest hurt. If they had her, why hadn't they jumped me by now?

I felt sweat slide down the side of my face. I started to panic, thinking about her in her house, her father being beaten, scared, screaming for her mommy. I understood that feeling of desperation when you want someone to take all the scary things away.

I forced myself to stop, calm down, think about what I was going to do. I came out onto the patio again and turned left. I'd come from the right and hadn't seen anything that way. I broke into a run, calling, "Kelly! Kelly!" in a loud semishout. I turned the corner, and there she was.

She was just leaving the Coke machine, wrestling with the pull tab on a can. The "look at me, aren't I a big girl?" smile soon changed when she saw me, weapon in hand, looking as serious as cancer.

For one moment I was going to read her the riot act, but I bit my lip.

She was looking suddenly sad and sorry for herself. Getting herself a can of Coke was the first thing she'd done all on her own since our adventure had begun, and I'd ruined it by coming back so soon. Leading her back to the room, I kept looking around the open square to make sure we hadn't been seen.

There were empty potato chip bags and other crap on the floor; it looked like a scene out of *Animal House*.

I sat her on the bed while I went and ran a bath. When I came back she still had a long face. I sat beside her. "I'm not cross with you, Kelly, it's just that I worry if I don't know where you are. Will you promise me not to do it again?"

"I promise," she nodded. "But only if you promise not to leave me again."

"I promise. Now get undressed for a bath." I picked her up and basically threw her in the bath before she had time to think.

"Do you wash your own hair or get somebody to do it?" I asked. I didn't have a clue.

She looked like she was going to cry.

I said, "Do you want me to wash it for you?"

"Yes, please." I wondered what was going on in that little mind of hers.

I got out the shampoo and started in; she moaned about the soap in her eyes and that the suds were tickling her ears, but I could tell she loved the attention. I couldn't blame her; she hadn't had much lately. Her world had been turned upside down, and she didn't even know it yet.

"You stink!" Kelly made a face as she caught the smell of Lance White's bladder on my clothes.

"These clothes are a bit old," I said. "Make sure you get all the shampoo out of your hair, and wash yourself with soap."

She looked as if she was having fun. I was glad somebody was. Walking into the bedroom, I called behind me, "Then I want you to put some clean clothes on. There're knickers and an undershirt on the bed."

"What're knickers?"

"These." I picked them up and walked back to show her.

"They're not, they're panties!"

Kelly was a water baby. That was great for me; the longer she was in the bath, the less time I had to spend dealing with her. I was finding it quite tiring, having to clean, dress, talk, answer questions. I left her splashing around for another half an hour, then dragged her out and told her to go dry herself.

I got in the shower, shaved, and got changed, bundling

all my old clothes and Kelly's into a plastic laundry bag and stowing it inside the duffel. I'd get rid of it at the first opportunity.

We were both in the bedroom. She was dressed. Her shirt buttons were in the wrong holes; while I was undoing them and sorting them out, I realized she was looking disapprovingly at me.

"What's the problem?"

"Those jeans. They're for losers. You should get 501s like Daddy."

On top of everything else, I had the fashion police after me. She went on, "You can't get 501s in my size. That's what Mommy says anyway. She doesn't wear jeans; she's like Aida—she likes dresses and skirts."

In my mind's eye I saw Marsha kneeling by her bed. I turned away for a moment so she couldn't see my face. I sat on the bed and said, "Kelly, do you know your dad's code number for his phone? I don't—I've tried it loads of times—I've pressed one-one-one-one, two-two-two-two, I've pressed them all and I still don't know. Have you got any idea?"

She stared at me for a few moments, then nodded.

"Right! What are the numbers then?"

She didn't say anything. She seemed to be working something out in her mind. Maybe she wondered if she'd be betraying her daddy by telling me.

I pulled the phone from my pocket, turned it on, and said, "Look! What does it say? PIN number! Do you know what numbers your daddy puts in?"

She nodded, and I said, "Come on, you show me then." She pressed the buttons, and I watched her fingers.

"One-nine-nine-oh?" I said.

"Nineteen-ninety, the year I was born," she beamed.

We were in business. I fetched the Yellow Pages from one of the drawers and sat on the edge of the bed.

"What are you looking for?" she asked.

"A restaurant called Good Fellas," I said. I found the address. "We're going to go there and look for Pat."

I thought about phoning the place and asking about him,

but they'd probably just blow me off. In any case, that could trigger a series of events I'd know nothing about until we were both suddenly lifted. It would be better to go there.

I put my glasses on and she giggled. I got her coat and held it for her to put on. As she turned around I noticed she still had the label dangling off her jeans; I ripped that off, then checked that nothing else looked out of place—just like any other unfashionable dad taking his daughter out for the day.

I put my jacket on, checked for the mags and phone, and said, "Do you remember Pat?"

"No. Who is she?"

"It's a him; he's a man called Patrick. Maybe you've seen him with Daddy?"

"Is Pat going to take me home?"

"You will be going home soon, Kelly. But only when Daddy is better and if you're a good girl and do what I say."

Her face went moody and sullen. "Will I be home by Saturday? I'm going to Melissa's party. She's having a sleepover."

I carried on. There was nothing else I could do. I didn't have the skills to coax her out of her mood.

"Pat came around to your house. Surely you remember Pat?"

"And I got to buy her a present. I've made her some friendship bracelets, but I want to get something else."

"Well, we're going to try to find Pat today because he's going to help us get you home. Maybe we'll have time to do your shopping, OK?"

"Where is Pat?"

"I think he might be in the restaurant. But you've got to be really quiet when we get there, OK, and not talk to anyone. If anybody talks to you, I want you just to nod your head or shake it, OK? We've got to be really careful, otherwise they won't tell me where Pat is, and then we might get into trouble."

I knew she'd be all right on the dumb act. She'd done what I'd said by the bins. I felt bad talking about her going home, but I couldn't think of a better way of controlling her behavior; and anyway, with any luck I wouldn't be there when she was finally told the truth.

There were a couple of other jobs to do before we left the room. I took the bottom left-hand corner of the blanket on my bed and folded it in a neat, diagonal pleat. Then I took a matchstick from the book I'd picked up in reception and wedged it between the wall and the long, low chest of drawers that the TV rested on. I put a pen mark the size of a pinhead on the wall and covered it with the matchhead. Finally I placed the paper clip in one of the drawers under the TV and turned the volume up a shade.

I had a quick look around the room to make sure we hadn't left anything compromising lying around; I even put the Yellow Pages back in the drawer. The pistol was still in the toilet tank, but there were no problems with that; there was no reason for a cleaner to come in, let alone the cops with a search warrant.

I picked up a couple of apples and candy bars and put them in the pocket of my brand-new three-quarter-length blue coat. Then I closed the door, checked the DO NOT DISTURB sign, and off we went.

We took a taxi to Georgetown. It would have conserved funds if we'd taken a bus, but this way meant less exposure to commuters or pedestrians. The driver was Nigerian. The map of the city on the front passenger seat didn't instill much confidence, and he could just about speak English. He used what few words he had to ask me where Georgetown was. It was like a London cabbie not knowing Chelsea. I patiently pointed on the map. By my guess it was about thirty minutes away.

It was spitting with rain, not enough to keep the wipers on but enough to make him give them a flick every minute or so. Kelly munched on a candy bar and I kept an eye out for other motels. We'd have to move again soon.

We sat in silence for a few minutes until it occurred to me that the driver would expect to hear us talking. "When I was your age I hadn't been in a taxi," I said. "I don't think I went in one until I was about fifteen."

Kelly looked at me, still chewing on the candy. "Didn't you like taxis?"

"No, it's just we didn't have much money. My stepfather couldn't find a job."

She looked puzzled. She looked at me for a long time, then turned her head and looked out the window again.

The traffic was clogging the exit for Key Bridge. Georgetown was just on the other side of the Potomac; it would have been quicker to get out and walk, but it made sense to stay out of sight. By now Kelly's face would have been in the newspapers, maybe even on posters. The police would be putting in a lot of time and effort to find her abductor.

I leaned over the front seat, picked up the map, and directed the driver to the river end of Wisconsin Avenue, the main north-south drag. I remembered Georgetown as almost self-contained, with a genteel and quaint feel to the town houses that had reminded me of San Francisco. The sidewalks were redbrick and uneven, and every car seemed to be a BMW, Volvo, or Mercedes. Every house and store had a prominent sign warning that the property was guarded by a security firm. Try breaking in and you'd have a rapid-response team down on you before you even had time to rip the leads from the back of the VCR.

Wisconsin is a wide street with shops and houses on either side. We found Good Fellas about four blocks up the hill on the right-hand side. As restaurants go it looked like one of the moody, designer-type places: the whole front was black, even down to the smoked-glass windows; the only relief was the gold lettering above the door. It was now nearly lunchtime; all the staff would have punched in.

We entered through two blackened glass swing doors and were hit by the frosty blast of air-conditioning. We were at one end of a dimly lit hallway that ran the length of the front. Halfway down was a young receptionist sitting at her desk, looking very upscale and friendly. I was impressed with Pat's taste. The girl smiled as we walked toward her, Kelly's hand in mine.

As we got closer I realized that the smile was a quizzical one. By now she was standing up, and I could see she was dressed very smartly in a white shirt and black pants. "Excuse me, sir," she said, "we don't . . ."

I held up my hand and smiled. "That's fine, we haven't come for lunch. I'm trying to find a friend of mine called Patrick. He used to come here a lot, maybe six or seven months ago. Does that ring a bell? As far as I know, he was going out with one of your staff. He's an Englishman, speaks like me."

"I don't know, I've only been here since the beginning of the semester."

Semester? Of course, we were in Georgetown, the university area; every student was also a waiter or waitress.

"Could you maybe call somebody, because it's really important that I make contact with him." I winked conspiratorily and said, "I've brought a friend of his—it's a surprise."

She looked down and smiled warmly. "Hi, do you want a mint?" Kelly took a small handful.

I went on, "Maybe one of the people in the back might know him?"

While she was thinking about it, a couple of guys in suits came in behind us. Kelly was looking up at them, lumps in her cheeks. "Hi, little lady," one of them laughed. "You're a bit young for this, aren't you?"

Kelly shrugged. Not a word.

The receptionist said, "Excuse me a moment," and went off to do her hostess bit, opening the door beyond the desk for somebody else to meet the two diners and take them to their table.

She came back and picked up the phone. "I'll call."

I looked down and winked at Kelly.

"We've got somebody here with a child, and they're looking for an Englishman called Patrick?" she said, then listened to the response.

She put the phone down. "Someone'll be here in a minute."

It rang again almost immediately, and she took a reservation.

Kelly and I just stood there. A minute or two later a waitress appeared from the dining room. "Hi, follow me."

Things were looking up. I got hold of Kelly's hand, and we went through the door to the dining room.

People here obviously liked eating in semidarkness, because all the tables were lit only by candles. Looking around,

I noticed that all the waitresses seemed to be wearing snug white T-shirts that exposed their midriffs, with tight shorts and sneakers with little ankle socks.

On the right-hand side against the wall was a bar with overhead lighting. The two suits were the only two customers. In the middle of the room I noticed a small raised stage, with spotlights above.

I laughed to myself: nice work, Pat!

Ass or no ass, Slack had always been successful with women. At the time of Gibraltar he was single like me, and rented the house next door. For about a year he'd been having what he called a "relationship," but we all knew better. They'd met at a Medieval Night fancy dress party; at four o'clock the next morning I was woken by the sound of a vehicle screeching up outside his house, then doors slamming and lots of giggling and laughing. We lived in a small subdivision, the sort of houses they threw up in about five minutes all through the eighties, so I could hear his front door crashing and thought, here we go. Then I heard a bit of music, and the toilet flushing, which is always nice at four in the morning. Then lots more laughing and giggling, and they were at it. At noon the next day I was in the kitchen washing up when a taxi pulled up, and that was when Queen Elizabeth I and one of her ladies-in-waiting came scuttling out of Pat's front door, hair all over the place, looking incredibly embarrassed as they jumped into the cab hoping no one would see them. When we grilled him, it turned out he was doing it with a mother and daughter combo. We hadn't let him hear the end of it ever since. Now it looked as though he'd got his own back.

One of the girls waved to Kelly. "Hi, honey!" Beneath her T-shirt was what looked like a dead heat in a zeppelin race.

Kelly was loving it. I held her hand tight. As we followed the girl, Kelly looked up at me and said, "What is this place?"

"It's a kind of bar where people go to relax after work."

"Like TGI Friday's?"

"Sort of."

We came to another set of double doors and went through into a world of bright light and clatter. The kitchens were on the right, full of noisy chaos; on the left, offices. The walls were dirty white plaster with gouge marks from where they'd been knocked by furniture.

Farther down the corridor we came to another room. Our friend led us in and announced, "Here he is!"

This was obviously where all the girls hung out—in some cases, literally. If I'd had to imagine a changing room in a lap-dancing bar, I'd have thought of seminaked girls in front of mirrors with big bulbs around the edges, but this didn't fit the bill at all; it was much more like somebody's living room. It was clean, with three or four couches, a couple of chairs, a few mirrors. There was a NO SMOKING sign that I could smell was observed, and bulletin boards full of university meetings and goings-on.

Everybody went "Hi, how are you!" to Kelly.

I looked at a policewoman wearing a skirt that was very nonregulation length. "I'm trying to find an Englishman called Pat. He told me he came here a lot."

Kelly was getting dragged away by two of the girls. "What's your name, honey?" There was nothing I could do to stop it.

I said, "Her name's Josie."

They were all in their fantasy outfits. One held out a Native American outfit, with fringed buckskin sleeves, feathers, the lot. She said to Kelly, "Do you like this?" and started to dress her. Kelly's eyes widened with excitement.

I kept on talking with Washington's finest. "It's just that there's been a big mess-up on the dates. We were supposed to meet Pat so he and Josie could go on vacation. It's no problem; I'll look after her, but she really wants to see him."

"We haven't seen Pat forever, but Sherry'll know, they used to go out. She's late but she'll be here any minute. If you want to hang out, that's fine. Help yourself to the coffee."

I went over and poured myself a cup and sat down. I watched Kelly giggling. For me, this should have been like dying and going to heaven, but I was tense about Kelly letting something slip.

I could see textbooks lying around. There was one girl on a

couch who looked as if she'd come out of a Turkish harem; she was there with her laptop, tapping away at her thesis.

Twenty minutes later the door burst open and a girl carrying a black sports bag ran in like a thing possessed, out of breath, hair everywhere.

"Sorry I'm late, girls. I wasn't on first, was I?"

She started to take her shoes off, catching her breath.

The policewoman called over, "Sherry, this guy wants to know where Pat is. Have you seen him lately?"

I stood up. "I've been trying to find him for ages. You know what he's like, he's all over the place."

"Tell me about it." She started to take her jeans off in front of me as casually as if we'd been married ten years. "He's been away for a while. I saw him about a month ago when he got back." She shot a glance at Kelly and back at me. "You a friend of his?"

"We go way back."

"I guess he won't mind. I've got his number here, if I can find it."

Dressed now only in her bra and panties, she rummaged through her bag as she talked. She looked up at one of the other girls and said, "What number am I?"

"Four."

"Christ! Can somebody go ahead of me? Can I go number six? I've got no makeup on yet."

There was a grunt from behind the laptop. It seemed the Turkish harem girl was going on fourth now.

Sherry tipped out an Aladdin's cave of a handbag. "Here we are."

She handed me a restaurant card with an address and telephone number scribbled on the back. I recognized the writing.

"Is this local?" I asked.

"Riverwood? About fifteen minutes by car, over the bridge."

"I'll give him a buzz—thank you!"

"Remind him I'm alive, will you?" She smiled with weary hope.

I went over to Kelly and said, "We've got to go now, Josie!"

She stuck out her lower lip. "Aww." Maybe it was being in the company of other females, but she looked more relaxed than at any point since we'd driven away from the house. "Do we have to?" she pleaded with big round eyes that were covered in makeup. So were her lips.

"I'm afraid we must," I said, starting to wipe it off.

The Indian maiden said, "Can't we keep her here? We'll look after her. We'll show her how to dance."

"I'd like that, Nick!"

"Sorry, Josie, you have to be much older to work here, isn't that right, ladies?"

They helped Kelly get all her feathers off. One of them said, "You work real hard at school, honey. Then you can work here with us."

They pointed to a quicker way out, through the service exit at the back. As we were leaving, Kelly looked up and said, "What do they do, anyway?"

"They're dancers."

"They dance in bikinis? With all those feathers? How come?"

"I don't know," I said. "Some people like watching that sort of thing."

Just as we got to the exit I heard Sherry shout, "Pat's daughter? The lying bastard!"

14

We walked back down the hill, looking for somewhere to sit out of the rain. A place that looked more like a house than a restaurant had a sign calling itself the Georgetown Diner. We went in.

We sat in the three-quarters-empty cafe, me with a coffee, she with a Coke, both deep in thought—me about how to make contact with Pat, she most probably about growing up and going to college, dressed like Pocahontas. Our table was by a rack of greeting cards and local drawings for sale. It was more like an art gallery than a coffee shop.

"We can't just turn up at Pat's address because we might compromise him," I thought aloud to her. "And I can't phone him because they might have made the connection between us, and there could be a tap on his phone and a trigger on the house."

Kelly nodded knowingly, not understanding a word I was saying but pleased to be part of grown-up stuff instead of being abandoned or dragged around.

"It's so annoying because he's only fifteen minutes away," I went on. "What can I do?"

She gave a little shrug, then pointed at the rack behind me and said, "Maybe send him a card?"

"Good idea, but it would take too long."

Then I had a brainstorm. "Well done, Kelly!"

She grinned from ear to ear as I got up and bought a birthday card showing a velvet rabbit holding a rose. I asked for a pen and went back to the table. I wrote: "Pat—I'm in deep shit. Kev is dead and Kelly is with me. I need help. IT

WAS NOT ME. Call me from a public phone ASAP. Nick." I
wrote down the number.

I sealed the envelope and wrote down Pat's address, then
asked to borrow the cafe's Yellow Pages. I found what I was
looking for; it was on the same street, seemingly within
walking distance. We put on our coats and left. It had stopped
raining, but the sidewalk was still wet. I checked the street
numbers; we had to go downhill toward M Street.

The courier office was next door to a weird and wonderful
New Age shop with a windowful of healing crystals that
could change your life. I wondered which one they'd suggest
if I went in and described my circumstances. Kelly wanted to
stay outside and look in the window, but I wanted her with
me; people might look twice at a child on her own outside a
store and something might register. There was also the risk of
someone in the shop identifying her, but it was a question of
balance between exposing her and making best use of her as
cover.

"Can you get this to my friend after four o'clock today?" I
said to the guy at the desk. "We're in real big trouble because
we forgot to send his birthday card, aren't we, Josie?"

I paid the fifteen-dollar fee in cash, and they promised to
bike it around just after 4 P.M. I needed the intervening two
hours to prepare for a meeting.

We went into the Latham Hotel. I'd guessed my accent
wouldn't stick out in here, and I was right; the large reception
area was full of foreign tourists. I sat Kelly in a corner and
went to the information desk.

"I'm looking for a mall that would have a Fun Zone or a
Kids Have Fun," I said.

It turned out there were about half a dozen of them in and
around the D.C. area; it was just a matter of looking up all the
different addresses in the city guide I'd been given. There was
one at the Landside Mall, not far from the Roadies Inn. I
hailed a taxi; this time the driver knew where he was going.

The idea of Kids Have Fun is that you drop your kids off for a
few hours while you go off on your big shopping frenzy. I'd
gone once with Marsha to pick up Kelly and Aida from one.

The children get a name tag on their wrist that they can't re-move, and the adult is given an ID card that means they're the only person who can collect the child. The girls had been acting up the morning I went, and I remembered that as we approached the center Marsha had grinned at the travel agent's across the way and said, "I always think that's brilliant positioning—the number of times I've been tempted to drop the kids off and pop in for a one-way ticket to Rio!"

The mall was shaped like a large cross, with a different de-partment store—Sears, Hecht's, JCPenney, Nordstrom—at the end of each spur. There were three floors, with escalators moving people up and down from the central hub. The food court was on the third floor. It was as busy as it was massive, and the heat was nearly tropical—probably on purpose, to send you to the drink counters.

I spotted Kids Have Fun on the Hecht's spur. I turned to Kelly. "Hey, do you want to go in there later? There's videos and all sorts of stuff."

"I know. But I want to stay with you."

"Let's go in and have a look anyway." I didn't want to put her in there yet because I didn't even know if we were going to get the phone call or not, but I'd still have to do the recon.

I went up to the desk. "Do we need to reserve to come in?"

Apparently not; we just had to turn up and fill out a form. I figured that if I did get a phone call at four, I'd have only half an hour at the most to hide her. I had to assume the worst-case scenario, which was that they knew Kev's mobile number and were waiting to intercept it and listen to me giving Pat direc-tions. I wanted Kelly away from that area and safe. Also, I couldn't be sure about Pat. He might call the police when he got the card. Or he could be part of a trap. I had to be careful, but at the same time I was desperate to see him.

I could see her looking around. It didn't look that bad. We walked out.

"You can come with me now, but I have to go on my own later, OK?"

She looked pissed. "Whyyy?"

"Because I have to do stuff, OK? You can help me now, though."

At last I got a smile. "Oh, OK. You won't be long, will you?"

"I'll be back before you know it."

Kelly and I started walking around, doing recon without her realizing it.

"What are we looking for, Nick?"

"A store with cameras and telephones."

We covered the whole mall, eventually finding a store on the first floor. I bought a battery charger for the mobile phone. Kelly decided not to buy another present for Melissa after all; she'd just pick up the friendship bracelets from home. I didn't comment.

At five of four I took the phone from my pocket and turned the power on. The battery and signal strength were fine. I was ready.

At ten after four it started ringing. I pressed Receive. "Hello?"

"It's me."

"Where are you?"

"In a phone booth."

"At five o'clock, I want you to come to the Landmark Mall in Alexandria. I want you to enter via JCPenney, go to the center hub, take the escalator to the third floor, and go straight toward Sears. OK so far?"

There was a pause as it was sinking in. "OK."

"On the left-hand side there's a restaurant called the Roadhouse. Go into the Roadhouse and get two coffees. I'll see you there."

"See ya."

I turned the power off.

Kelly said, "Who was that?"

"Remember I talked about Pat? I'm going to see him later—that's good, isn't it? Anyway, are you ready for Kids Have Fun?"

She was going whether she liked it or not. If Pat were setting me up, this place would soon be swarming with cops.

I filled out the form with the names we were using at the hotel. Kelly was studying the obstacle course with padding and plastic balls to break your fall. There were video areas where a huge variety of films were being shown, a juice dispenser, rest rooms. It looked very well organized. The place was packed. I could see hosts who were playing games with the kids and doing magic tricks. Seeing as she'd been doing nothing but watching children's TV for God knows how many hours, Kelly should be into all that. The downside was the danger of her talking, but I had no choice. I paid my money, plus a twenty-dollar deposit for the magic key to reclaim my child.

I asked her, "Do you want me to stay for a while?"

She was dismissive. "You can't stay. This is just for kids." She pointed at a warning sign that said: BE CAREFUL, PARENTS. DON'T GO NEAR THE PLAYTHINGS BECAUSE YOU MIGHT TRIP OVER THEM AND HURT YOURSELF.

I squatted, looking into her eyes. "Remember, your name's Josie today, not Kelly. It's a big secret, OK?"

"Yeah, OK." She was too busy looking into the play area.

"I'll be back soon. You know I'll always be back, don't you?"

"Yeah, whatever." She was dragging herself away. Her face was toward me but her eyes were looking the other way. A good sign, I thought, as I headed off.

I took the escalator to the third floor. I got myself tucked in the corner table of a cafe and ordered an espresso and a Danish.

I knew that if Pat was late, he wouldn't move into the rendezvous. The SOP—standard operating procedure—was that he'd wait an hour. If that didn't happen, it would be the same routine tomorrow. That's the great thing about working with people you know.

I looked at my watch. It was two minutes to five. Looking down the escalators, I could see the JCPenney spur joining the hub. On my floor I could also see the entrance to Sears and the Roadhouse.

At about two minutes past I saw Pat below me, walking in from the direction of JCPenney. He was sauntering along, casual and unhurried, wearing a brown leather bomber jacket, jeans, and running shoes. From this distance he looked unchanged, just a bit thinner on top. I looked forward to laying into him for that.

He'd been at JCPenney right at five; I also knew he would have been putting in his own antisurveillance drills en route, driving into the parking lot early to check it out, even sitting in his car to time it right. Pat might have his head in the clouds, but when he had to perform, he was shit-hot. At the moment my only worry was not about what was in his head but what might be up his nose.

He walked onto the escalator; I looked away. I wasn't interested in him now; I was watching everywhere else, checking to see if he was being followed. By covering his back I was protecting my own. I had the easy part, being the third party, aware. The biggest problem would be for the surveillance operators who were following him, trying not to get spotted by me.

In an urban environment it's always best to meet people where there's a lot of pedestrian traffic. It looks normal, people meeting people. The downside is that if there is any surveillance on you, they can blend in a lot easier, too. However, it is chaos for them because you can walk in and out of stores, stop at a counter, move on, then turn around and go back to another counter. So if you're going to RV with somebody to talk, go shopping.

Pat came up the last escalator, standing ahead of a group of teenage girls. They got off and turned left into the Baskin-Robbins. Pat went right. There were only four escalators, two up, two down. I couldn't see anyone who looked like an operator.

I watched him go into the Roadhouse. I gave it another five minutes, checked again, made sure the girl saw me throw my three dollars on the table, and left. Once on the Sears spur I got on the right-hand side of the walkway, which gave me a better view of the Roadhouse on the left, and that in turn gave me more time to tune in and look about to see if there were any men in Victoria's Secret looking out of place as they flicked through the ladies' lingerie.

I still couldn't be sure about Pat. But I didn't get nervous about that sort of thing; it was a drill—I'd done it so many times. I looked at it technically, in terms of "what ifs?" What if they lift me from the direction of Sears? What if they come out from the stores on each side of me? "What ifs" stop you freezing like a rabbit in the middle of the road when the lights hit you. They get you out of that initial danger. In this particular case, I'd draw my weapon, move out of the danger area through Sears or the escalators, and make a run for it.

I entered the Roadhouse and saw Pat closer up. Age was getting to him. He was only forty, but he looked eligible for some kind of pension.

He was sitting at a twin table on the far left-hand side, with two cappuccinos in front of him. There were about a dozen other people talking, eating, and yelling at their kids. I went over, pulled out the five-dollar bill that I had ready in my pocket, put it on the table, and said, with a big flashy smile, "Follow me, mate."

If he were intending to turn me in, I was just about to find out.

I was sponsoring the RV so he didn't say anything, he just came with me. We went over to the far wall to where the rest room sign was; as we went through the door we came into a long corridor, with the rest rooms at the end on the left-hand side. I'd reconned this already with Kelly. To the right was another door, which led into Sears. These were shared rest rooms, and that was why I'd chosen them. I opened the door, let Pat through, and followed him into the babywear department. We took the escalators down, putting in angles and distance. It might not work all the time, but it was the best I could do.

From the perfume counter on the first floor it was straight into the parking lot. Then we started to walk along the sidewalk toward a string of smaller stores and snack bars.

Not a word had been said. No need; Pat knew what was happening.

We walked into a SubZone, a very clinical, spotlessly clean franchise selling subs with the world's largest supply of hot fillings. I told Pat to order me a drink and a cheese and meat special. The place was full. That was good; it made life more complicated for anybody looking.

I said, "Sit over there at that table, mate, facing the rest rooms, and I'll be back in a minute."

He stood in line to order.

I went through the door to the rest rooms and on to the far end, where there was a fire escape. I wanted to be sure it hadn't been obstructed by a trash can or anything since I last checked. The fire-escape door was alarmed, so I wasn't going to test it to make sure it would open. I'd done my recon, so I knew what was on the other side and where to run.

Pat was already sitting down with two coffees and an order ticket. I was getting caffeine overload. I was also starting to feel like shit; the heat of the shopping mall and now this place, and the energy expended in this last two days, were taking their toll. But I had to keep on top of that, because this was an operation.

I sat down opposite him in the booth, looking beyond him at the glass storefront. I could see everybody coming in and out, and had a pillar and Pat as cover. I wanted to dominate the area because I needed to see what was going on.

I looked at Pat and decided not to josh him about his hair. He looked wrecked and wasted. His eyes were no longer clear and sharp but red and clouded. He'd put on weight, and there was an overhang pulling at his T-shirt and flopping over his belt. His face looked puffy; I could only just make out his Adam's apple.

I said, "The reason why we're here is that I've come over on vacation, to see you, and we're shopping."

"Fine."

I still had to test him, in case he was wearing a wire.

"If there's a drama, I'm going to go through there." I pointed toward the rest rooms. I was waiting for him to say, "Oh, what, you're going to go to the bathroom?" for the benefit of anybody who might be listening in. But he didn't. He just said, "OK." I was as sure as I could be that I was safe. There was no more time to mess around.

I said, "You OK, mate?"

"So-so. Put it this way: a bit fucking better than you. How did you find me?"

"Sherry, at Good Fellas." I looked at him and he smiled. "Yeah, good catch, Pat!"

His smile got bigger. "Anyway, what's the score?"

"I've got every man and his dog after me."

"So it seems." His red eyes twinkled.

I started explaining and was still in full flow when the girl brought over the subs. They were huge, big enough to feed a family.

"What the fuck did you order?" I said. "We're going to be here all day!"

Pat was hungry, fighting with the hot cheese as it sagged between his mouth and the sub. It made me wonder when he'd last eaten.

I was too busy chatting to eat. I said, "Look, mate, to tell you the truth, all I want to do is get the fuck back to the UK— but that's going to be a pain in the ass. I need to know what's going on, I need to know why this is happening. Do you remember Simmonds?"

"Yeah. He still in?"

"Yes. I've been in contact with him. I've even said that if the Firm doesn't help me, I'll open up my security blanket."

Pat's eyes widened. "Wow, that's big boys' stuff! You really are in heavy shit. What did Simmonds have to say to that?" His shoulders went into a slow roll as he laughed through a mouthful.

I went on for another fifteen minutes. At the end of it Pat said, "Do you think that PIRA might have dropped Kev?" He had finished his sub and was now picking at mine. He made it clear he wanted a few bites. I pushed it over.

"Who the fuck knows? I don't know, I really don't know. I can't see it myself. Can you make any sense of it?"

"The buzz around D.C. was that there was some American involvement in Gibraltar in 'eighty-eight." He was picking the pickles and tomatoes out of my sub.

"What sort of involvement?"

"I don't know. It's got something to do with the Irish American vote, all that sort of shit. And PIRA gearing up funds from Noraid by getting into the drug market."

I wondered how Pat knew. Maybe that was where he got his supply? The thought made me sad.

My mind ticked over a bit more. Pat just kept on attacking my sub. "Maybe that's where the connection with Kev comes in," I said. "DEA, drugs—what do you think?"

"Maybe. The Brits have been giving the Americans a hard time for years over Noraid giving money to PIRA, but the Yanks can't fuck around with all those millions of Irish American votes."

I sat back and studied his face. "Go on."

"I've heard that PIRA buys cocaine and gears it up once they get it out of the US. It's been going the rounds for years—there's nothing new in that. But maybe it's a starting point for you. I mean, fucking hell, you're the brainy one, not me."

It made sense; if you've got some money and you're a terrorist organization, of course you're going to buy drugs, sell them, and make a profit. And there was no way the Americans were going to attack Noraid; it would be political suicide—but if Noraid could be shown to be linked with drug trafficking, that was something else. Maybe Kev was working against PIRA and got killed by them.

I said, "Do you reckon Kev might have come across some shit? Or maybe he was even part of it, and got fucked over?"

"I haven't got a clue, mate. Stuff like that gives me a headache." He paused. "So tell me, what do you need?"

I shrugged. "Cash."

He stopped eating my sub and got out his wallet. He handed me an ATM card and told me his number. "There's about three thousand dollars in there," he said. "It's a savings account, so you can draw out as much as you need. What about Kev's girl? What's the score?"

"She's all right, mate. I've got her."

If Pat was setting me up, at least I was sending a message that I was aware of that possibility and taking precautions.

I said, "Thanks very much for this, mate—for the ATM card, and just for being here." With friendships like this you didn't have to write a letter every week. I knew that he would help me out, but I didn't want him to think I was taking him for granted.

I said, "Look, I'm not going to get you in trouble. I won't compromise you, but there is something else I need. Is there any chance of you phoning me sometime tonight? I need to sit down and think about what I've got to do."

"About nine-thirty?"

I smiled. Then all of a sudden I had my second brainstorm of the day. "You don't know any Sinn Féin or PIRA locations in D.C.?"

"No, but I can find out. What are you thinking?"

"I need to see if there's a connection between PIRA and the people who are trying to zap me—and who maybe dropped Kev. If I can check who comes in and out of a location, well, it's a start. If it came to anything, maybe I'd go in and have a look around."

Pat demolished the last of my sub. "Be careful, mate. Don't get fucked over."

"I won't. Right, I'll stay here—I'll give you ten minutes and then I'll leave. The mobile will be switched on from nine twenty-five."

"No drama; we'll talk. Be lucky."

As he got up, he picked at the fragments of cheese and meat at the bottom of the basket.

15

I went back into the mall via Sears, found an ATM, and drew out three hundred dollars.

It was dark outside, but the shopping mall was packed. There was still a possibility that I was being watched, so I stood off and waited before picking Kelly up. Nothing looked unusual; the only thing I had to be aware of was the security cameras. The quicker I got in and out, the better.

I watched the area for ten minutes, then moved in closer. Across from the play center was a sporting goods store; I went in and became an instant basketball fan, studying all the shirts that were part of the display near the window. Kids Have Fun was crammed with kids, but I couldn't see Kelly.

I hung around the store a bit, went back to the rack, had another look, and caught sight of her. She was sitting on the floor watching a home-cinema type TV. She was there with about a dozen other kids, each with a small carton of juice. It dawned on me that the girl did nothing but eat, drink, and watch TV. It was a wonder she didn't look more like Slack Pat.

I went in, presented my identification card, and asked for my daughter. They went through their process of verification, and a few minutes later Kelly appeared with an escort.

I started to put her shoes on. "Hi, Josie, how's it going?"

She sat there sulking because I'd arrived halfway through a movie. I took that as a good sign; it showed there was a slight trace of normality coming back in. It had been a relief not having her with me for a short while, but at the same time it felt good to have her back. I didn't know quite what to make of that.

We got a taxi but had it drop us off about four blocks short of the hotel and walked in. It was our only secure area.

I opened the door. The TV was still on, telling us how great Toyota cars were. I flicked the light switch, told Kelly to stay where she was, and looked inside.

The beds weren't made and the curtains were closed, so it looked as if the maid had obeyed the sign on the door. She wouldn't have given a damn; it was less for her to clean, and she still got the same money.

More tellingly, the small pleat was still in the blanket. If I'd seen from the doorway that it had been disturbed, I'd have needed to make a very quick decision on whether to just walk away.

We went inside. Using the TV for support, I leaned to the rear of the bureau, looking into the gap between it and the wall. The match was still in place, covering the pinhead-sized pen mark. Even if they'd noticed that they'd dislodged it when checking under the chest of drawers, it was very unlikely that they'd have put it back in exactly the same position. Looking good so far.

"What are you doing, Nick?"

"I'm just checking to see if the plug is in properly. It looked like it was going to fall out."

She didn't say anything, just looked at me as if I'd had a stupidity leak. Still not looking at her, I got on my knees, ready to look at the drawer.

"Do you want some help, Nick?"

"I'd like to hear what's on the TV."

She sat down on the bed and went to work on a box of Oreos. This kid was really eating healthy.

There were three drawers in the low chest; I'd slipped the paper clip in the front left side of the middle one. I got the table lamp and shone it up and down, trying to catch the reflection of the paper clip. I did; the drawer hadn't been opened.

I got Kelly sorted out, coat off, shoes in the pockets and hung by the door. I cleaned her bed up a bit, gathering up the food wrappers and brushing away the crumbs.

"Are you hungry?" I said.

She looked at the half-empty box of Oreos. "I'm sorta stuffed, but I'm sorta still hungry."

"Without a doubt. I'll go and get some food. You can stay here. I'll let you stay up late. But don't tell anybody, it's our little secret!"

She laughed. "I won't!"

I realized that I was hungry, too. Pat hadn't left me much at SubZone.

"Same routine, OK?" I went through it all over again. "I'll put up the DO NOT DISTURB sign, and you don't open the door for anyone. Do you understand?"

"Without a doubt."

I did a double take. "You making fun of me?"

"Without a doubt."

It wasn't that busy on the street, and the rain had eased. I got more clothes for us both—jackets and coats, jeans and shirts—enough to see us through the next two appearance changes at least.

Once done, I walked over to the burger joint. As I stood in line I thought how weird this all was. One minute I'm at Vauxhall being briefed for a job, the next I'm trying to remember what flavor milk shake to buy for a child. I wondered if she'd approve of the shirts I'd got her.

On the way back I checked my watch. It was 9:20; I'd been longer than I expected. Time to turn on the phone. I waited in a shop doorway out of the drizzle.

It rang right at 9:30. I was excited, but at the same time nervous. It might be for Kev. I hit the Receive button. "Hello?"

"Hi, it's me. I've got something for you."

"Great, wait . . ." I put my finger in my other ear. I didn't want to mishear this. "Go ahead."

"It's one-twenty-six Ball Street. It's in the old part of Crystal City by the river—between the Pentagon and National Airport. Got that?"

"Yeah." I let it sink into my head. I'd been to the Pentagon before, and had used the domestic airport a couple of times. I had a rough memory of the area. "Are you going to phone me tomorrow?"

"Yeah."

"Same time?"

"Same time. Stay lucky, mate."

"Cheers."

And that was it. I turned off the power and repeated the address to myself to keep it in my head. I wasn't going to write it down. If I got lifted, I needed to be sterile.

On the way back to the hotel, I was feeling quite upbeat. Up until now I'd been in the wilderness. I didn't exactly know what I was going to do with this new information, but it was a start. I felt more in the driver's seat.

We ate and I watched some television with Kelly, but she looked more interested in talking.

"Hey, Nick, do you watch TV at home?"

"Some."

"What's your favorite show?"

"I don't know. The news, I suppose. We have different programs from you. What's your favorite?"

"Clueless."

"What's that, a detective show?"

"You moron! It's about a girl." She did a very good impression of a Valley girl.

"What does she do?"

"She goes shopping."

By 10:45 she'd fallen asleep. I got out the city guide I'd forgotten to give back at the Latham and looked for Ball Street.

I followed the river south until I saw National Airport. The target really was very close to the Pentagon, on the west bank. I had a little laugh to myself. If it was a PIRA location, they had a lot of balls; they probably drank at the same bars as the boys from the National Security Council.

There was not a lot I could do at the moment. Kelly was lying on her back, imitating a starfish. I covered her with the comforter, moved all the shit off the other bed, and got my head down. A saying from my infantry days, a lifetime ago, roared in my ears: "Whenever there is a lull in battle, sleep. You never know when you are going to get another chance." At last I was doing as I'd been told.

* * *

When I woke up it seemed like the same cartoon was on. I must have left the TV on all night. I was dying for some coffee.

I got up, wet my hair, and looked out the window. The rain had gotten a bit more intense. I went downstairs and collected enough food and drink for three people—which was just as well, seeing the amount that Kelly ate.

"Wakey wakey!" I said.

Kelly still wanted to be marine life but woke up yawning, stretching, then curling up into a ball. I went into the bathroom and started to run a bath.

She appeared in the doorway with a towel. She was starting to catch on.

While she was splashing around, I sat on the bed flicking through the news channels. There was nothing about us. There had been so many other murders in the homicide capital of the USA that we were old hat.

She came out, got dressed, and combed her hair, all without a single reminder from me. I opened an eat-from-the-pack carton of Froot Loops for her and poured in some milk, then headed for the shower.

When I reappeared, all clean and presentable, I said, "We've got to move from here today because the woman wants the room back."

Her face lit up. "Can we go home now? You said Pat was going to help us go home."

I took her coat off the hanger and slipped her shoes on. "Really soon, yes we will. But Daddy needs more time to rest. Pat will find out when it's OK," I said. "But first, we've got to do some stuff. It's really difficult for me to explain to you what's going on just now, Kelly, but it won't be long. I promise you will be home soon."

"Good, because Jenny and Ricky are missing me."

My heart missed a beat. Had I fucked up? Had there been other people in the house?

She must have read my mind. "They're my teddy bears," she explained. Her face went serious. "I miss them. And I want to go to Melissa's party."

I started patting the top of her head. She looked at me; she knew she was being patronized. I changed the subject.

"Look, I'll show you where we're going."

I got the map out. "This is where we are now, and that's where we're heading—just by the river. We'll get a taxi, find a nice hotel, and we'll make sure they've got cable so we can watch movies. If they haven't, maybe we could go to the movies."

"Can we see *Jungle 2 Jungle*?"

"Sure we can!"

What the fuck was that? Never mind; at least we'd gotten off the subject of family.

After checking out and, to my surprise, being offered a one-night rebate, I went upstairs to collect Kelly and the blue nylon sports bag. I left the USP in the toilet tank. It had only one 9mm magazine; I was carrying three .45s with the Sig.

Leaving the hotel, we turned left and immediately left again. I wanted to get out of sight of the reception desk before somebody thought of asking, "Where's his wife?"

We hailed a cab, and I asked for Pentagon City. The driver was an Asian in his sixties. He had a map on his seat but didn't bother to look at it. We seemed to be heading in the right direction. Kelly had her hat on; I thought of teasing her that she looked like Paddington Bear, but it would have taken too long to explain.

The driver asked where exactly I wanted to be dropped.

"The Metro station, please." I didn't have a clue where that was, but it sounded as good a place as any.

I gave the old boy his cash and off he drove. The whole area looked new and high rent, both shopping and residential. There was a Ritz Carlton hotel and, a few minutes away, the Pentagon. I got my bearings and led Kelly toward the mall. I wanted to visit an ATM to celebrate the start of a new financial day.

We exited and walked across the supermarket parking lot, then on toward the river. It was strange, because for the first time I felt like I was really responsible for Kelly. I still held her hand when we were crossing roads, but now it seemed natural to keep holding it on the sidewalks, too. I had to admit, it felt good to have her with me, but maybe that was only because I knew it looked natural and therefore provided ideal cover.

We walked under the concrete freeway bridge that led to downtown D.C. It was very busy. The traffic sounded like muffled thunder; I told Kelly about the scene in *Cabaret* in which Sally Bowles goes under the railway bridge to scream when things get too much for her. I didn't tell her that was what I'd been feeling like doing for the last forty-eight hours.

Past the bridge the landscape changed. It was easy to imagine what this area must have looked like maybe fifty or sixty years earlier, because it hadn't been fully developed yet. It was full of derelict railway-siding buildings, some of which had been taken over as offices, though much of the area was just fenced off into lots or used as car pounds.

I looked left and saw the elevated section of the highway disappear into the distance toward downtown Washington. A concrete wall hid all the supports, and a road ran alongside. There was no sidewalk, just a thin strip of hard ground, littered with soda cans and cigarette packs. It looked as if people parked up on the shoulders here to avoid the parking charges farther in. There were old, ramshackle buildings everywhere, but the place was still being used. On the right was the Clark Street Playhouse, a theater in what had once been a railway warehouse. The tracks were still there, but they were now rusty, and weeds were growing through. From above us came the continuous roar of traffic on the elevated highway.

We passed a scrap-metal yard, then a cement distribution plant where the boats used to come up the Potomac and dump their loads. I then saw something that was so totally out of place it was almost surreal. A late 1960s hotel, the Calypso, was still standing in defiance of progress. It was marooned in the middle of an ocean of chrome, smoked glass, and shiny brick, as if the owners had decided to give the finger to the property developers who were slowly taking over this dying area.

It was a very basic, four-story building, built in the shape of an open square; in the middle was a parking lot crammed with cars and pickups. There were no windows on the outer walls, just air conditioners sticking out of the cinder block.

We turned left; with the highway thundering away above us we walked past the hotel on my right side. We were now parallel with Ball Street, which lay behind it. Kelly hadn't said a word. I was in work mode anyway; if it weren't for the fact that I had hold of her hand, I would probably have forgotten she was with me.

As we got even with the Calypso I wiped the drizzle from my face and peered up into the gloom. On its roof was a massive satellite dish, easily three yards across. It wouldn't have looked out of place on top of the Pentagon. We turned right and right again. We were on Ball Street.

From street numbers on the map I knew that the target was going to be on my left. I kept to the right side for a better perspective.

It was still incredibly noisy; if it wasn't an aircraft taking off from the airport just the other side of the tree line, it was the continuous roar from Highway 1. "Where are we going?" Kelly had to shout to be heard above it all.

"Down there," I nodded. "I want to see if we can find a friend's office. And then we can find a nice new hotel to stay in."

"Why do we have to move around all the time?"

I was stumped on that one. I was still looking at the street numbers, not at her. "Because I get bored easily, especially if the food's no good. That one last night was crap, wasn't it?"

There was a pause, then, "What's crap?"

"It means that it's not very nice."

"It was OK to me."

"It was dirty. Let's go to a decent hotel, that's what I want to do."

"But we can stay at my house."

A jet had just left the runway and was banking hard at what appeared to be rooftop level. We watched for a while, transfixed; even Kelly was impressed.

As the roar of its engines died down I said, "Come on, let's find that office."

I kept looking forward and left, trying to judge which building it was going to be. There was a hodge-podge of styles—old factories and storage units, new two-story office buildings rubbed shoulders with parking lots and truck container dumps. In between the buildings I could just glimpse the trees that lined the Potomac maybe three hundred yards beyond.

We were in the high nineties, so I knew the PIRA office building wouldn't be far away. We walked on until we got to a new-looking, two-story office, all steel frames and exposed pipework. All the fluorescent lights were on inside. I tried to read the nameplates but couldn't make them out in the gloom without squinting hard or going closer, neither of which I wanted to do. One said UNICOM but I couldn't make out the others.

It didn't look much like the sort of Sinn Féin or PIRA offices I was used to. Cable Street in Derry, for example, was a row house on a 1920s residential street; the places in west Belfast were much the same. Had Pat got this right? In my mind I'd been expecting some old tenement. Chances were this was just a front—it would be a commercial business; people working there would be legit.

I focused on the target as we walked past, but didn't look back. You have to take in all the information the first time around.

"Nick?"

"What?"

"My feet are really wet."

I looked down. Her feet were soaked; I'd been concentrating so much on what to do next that I hadn't noticed the puddles we were walking through. I should have bought her a pair of boots at the mall.

We got to a T-intersection. Looking left, I could see that the road led down toward the river. More cars parked up on the shoulders, and even more scrapyards.

I looked right. At the end of the street was the elevated highway, and just before that, above the rooftops, I could see the dish on top of the Calypso Hotel. I was feeling good. A successful recon and somewhere to stay, and all before 11 A.M.

16

We walked into the hotel parking lot. I pointed between a pickup truck and a UPS van. "Wait under the landing, and keep out of the rain. I'll be back soon."

"Why can't I come with you, Nick? It's dark under here."

I started my puppy-training act. "No—wait . . . there. I won't be long." I disappeared before she could argue.

The hotel lobby was just one of the first-floor rooms turned into an office. Checking in was as casual as the layout. The poor Brit family story was understood a lot quicker here.

I went outside, collected Kelly, and, as we walked along the concrete and cinder block toward our new room on the second floor, I was busy thinking about what I'd have to do next. She suddenly tugged on my hand.

"Double crap!"

"What?"

"You know, like not nice. You said the other one was crap. This is double crap."

I had to agree. I even thought I could smell vomit. "No, no, wait till you get in. You see that satellite dish? We can probably get every single program in the world on that. It's not going to be crap at all."

There were two king-size beds in the room, a big TV, and the usual dark, lacquered surfaces and a few bits of furniture—a long sideboard that had seen better days, a closet that was just a rail inside an open cupboard in the corner, and one of those things that you rest your suitcase on.

I checked the bathroom and saw a little bottle of shampoo.

"See that?" I said. "Always the sign of a good hotel. I think we're in the Ritz."

I plugged in the telephone and recharger, then it was straight on with the television, flicking through the channels for a kids' program. It was part of the SOPs now.

I pulled Kelly's coat off, gave it a shake, and hung it up, then went over to the air conditioner and pressed a few buttons. I held my coat out, testing the air flow; I wanted the room to get hot. Still waiting for some reaction from the machine, I said, "What's on?"

"Power Rangers."

"Who are they?"

I knew very well what it was all about, but there was no harm in a bit of conversation. I didn't want us to be best buddies, go on vacations together, and share toothbrushes and all that sort of shit—far from it. The sooner this was sorted out, the better. But for the relationship to look normal it had to be normal, and I didn't want to get lifted because some busybody thought we didn't belong together.

I said, "Which one do you like?"

"I like Katherine. She's the pink one."

"Why's that, because of the color?"

"Because she's not a moron. She's really cool." Then she told me all about Katherine and how she was a Brit. "I like that because Daddy comes from England."

I made her change into a new pair of jeans and a sweatshirt. It took a lifetime. I thought, *Fuck parenting, it's not for me. Every moment of your time is taken up. What is the point, if you just spend all day on butler duty?*

She was finally dry and sorted out. Next to the TV was a coffeemaker and packets of milk and sugar, and I got that going. As the machine started to purr and bubble I went to the window. As I looked out past the curtain, left and right of me were the other two sides of the drab, gray concrete square; below was the parking lot, and across the road and higher up was the highway. I realized that my mood matched the view.

Rain was still falling. I could see the plumes of spray behind the trucks as they rolled along the highway. It wasn't heavy, but it was continuous, the kind that seeps into everything. I was suddenly aware of Kelly standing next to me.

"I hate this type of weather," I said. "Always have, ever since I was a teenager and joined the army. Even now, on a really wet and windy winter's day, I'll make myself a cup of tea and sit on a chair by the window and just look out and think of all the poor soldiers sitting in a hole in the middle of nowhere, freezing, soaking wet, wondering what they're doing there."

A wry smile came to my face as the coffee stopped dripping, and I looked down at Kelly. What wouldn't I give to be back on Salisbury Plain, just sitting in a soaking-wet trench, my only worry in the world how to stop being wet, cold, and hungry.

I went and lay on the bed, working out my options. Not that there were that many. Why didn't I just make a run for it? I could steal passports and try my luck at an airport, but the chances of getting away with it were slim. There were less conventional routes back. I'd heard that you could get all the way from Canada to the UK by ferry and land-hopping, a route popular with students. Or I could go south, getting into Belize or Guatemala; I'd spent years in the jungle on that border and knew how to get out. I could go to an island off Belize called San Pedro, a staging post for drug runners on their way to the east coast of Florida. From there I could get farther into the Caribbean, where I'd pick up passage on a boat.

More bizarre still, one of the guys in the Regiment had flown a single-engined Cessna from Canada to the UK. The tiny fixed-wing aircraft had no special equipment apart from an extra fuel tank in the back. The radio wasn't the right kind; he'd had to work out the antenna lengths with wire hanging from the aircraft on a brick. He wore a parachute so that if anything went wrong, he'd open the door and leap out. How I'd sort that out I didn't know, but at least I knew it could be done.

However, there was too much risk involved in all these schemes. I didn't want to spend the rest of my days in a state penitentiary, but at the same time I didn't want Kelly and me to be killed in the process of escaping. Simmonds had presented me with the best option. If I turned up in London with what he wanted, I wouldn't exactly be home and dry, but at least I'd be home. I had to stay and tough it out.

It all boiled down to my needing to see who and what was going into and out of the building on Ball Street.

"Kelly? You know what I'm going to say, don't you?"

"Without a doubt," she smiled. I'd obviously been forgiven for drying her hair and putting her into nice dry clothes.

"Ten minutes, all right?"

I closed the door, listened, heard her hook the chain, and hung the sign on the door. Farther to my left was a small open area that housed the Coke and snack machines. I bought a can, then walked back past our room toward the elevator. To the left was the fire escape, a concrete staircase leading up and down. I knew the safety regulations meant that there had to be an exit onto the roof; in the event of a fire down below, the rescue would be by helicopter.

I went as far as I could upstairs. Double fire doors led to the roof; push the bar and they'd open. There was no sign warning that the doors were alarmed, but I had to check. I looked around the doorframe but couldn't see a circuit-break alarm. I pushed the bar and the door opened. No bells.

The roof was flat, its surface covered with lumps of gravel two inches in diameter. I picked up a handful and used it to jam the doors open.

An aircraft was landing at National; I could just see its lights through the drizzle. The satellite dish was on the far corner of the roof. There was also a green aluminum shed, which I guessed was the elevator housing. A three-foot-high wall ran around the edge of the roof, hiding me from the ground, but not from the highway.

I walked across the gravel to the side facing the river. Looking down at the target building from this angle, I could see the flat roof and its air ducts. It was rectangular and looked quite large. Behind it were a vacant lot and fences that seemed to divide it into new building plots waiting to be sold. I could just make out the Potomac beyond the tree line and the end of the runway.

I walked back, stepping over a series of thick electric cables. I stopped at the elevator housing. What I wanted now was a power source. I could use batteries to power the surveillance equipment I'd be using, but I couldn't guarantee their life. I tried the door of the elevator housing, but it was locked. I had a quick look at the lock: a pin tumbler. I'd be able to defeat that easily.

Back in the room, I got out the Yellow Pages and looked for addresses of pawn shops.

Then I went into the bathroom, sat on the edge of the bath, and unloaded the .45 ammunition from the magazines into my pocket, easing the springs. It's not something that you have to do every day, but it needs to be done. The majority of weapon stoppages are magazine connected. I didn't know how long it had been left loaded; I might squeeze off the first round and the second one wouldn't feed into the chamber because the magazine spring had stuck. That's why a revolver is sometimes far better, especially if you're going to have a pistol lying about for ages and don't want to service it. A revolver is just a cylinder with six rounds in it, so you could keep it loaded all year and it wouldn't matter—as soon as you pick it up you know the thing will work. I emptied the magazines into my pocket so that I then had the ammunition, magazines, and pistol all on me.

I came out of the bathroom and wrote myself a shopping list of supplies that I was going to need and checked how much money I had. There was enough for today. I could always get more out tomorrow.

I wasn't worried about Kelly. She had loads of food and was half-asleep anyway. I turned up the heat on the air conditioner. She'd soon be drowsy.

I said, "I'm going to go and get you some coloring books and crayons and all that sort of stuff. Shall I bring back something from Mickey D's?"

"Can I have sweet and sour sauce with the fries? Can I come with you?"

"The weather's terrible. I don't want you catching a cold."

She got up and walked to the door, ready to drop the latch without me having to ask.

I went downstairs and walked to the Metro station.

17

The Washington Metro is fast and quiet, clean and efficient, everything a subway should be. The tunnels are vast and dimly lit, somehow soothing, which is maybe why passengers seem more relaxed than in London or New York and some even exchange eye contact. It's also about the only part of the capital where you won't be asked by a seventeen- or seventy-seven-year-old Vietnam vet if you can spare some change.

I got out after seven or eight stops and one transfer. The place I was looking for was just a few blocks away, but it was in a neighborhood I bet didn't feature in anybody's vacation brochure. I was used to the Washington where those who had really had. This was the part of town where those who didn't have had absolutely nothing.

The single-story building was set back from the road and looked more like a supermarket than a pawn shop, with a front that was at least fifty yards long. The whole facade was glass, with bars running vertically. The window displays were piled high with everything from drum kits to surfboards and bedding. Fluorescent-yellow posters promised everything from zero percent interest to the best gold price in town. Three armed guards controlled the doors and watched me enter.

Looking along one of the aisles to the rear, I saw a long glass showcase that also formed the counter. Behind it were more than a dozen assistants, all wearing similar red polo shirts. It seemed to be the busiest department in the shop. Then I saw all the handguns and rifles behind the glass. A sign announced that customers were welcome to test fire any weapon on the range out back.

I went to the camera department. In an ideal world, what I was looking for would be something like a security camera, with a long cable connecting the camera itself to a separate control box that also housed the videotape. I could put the camera in position on the roof, leave it where it was, and hide the control box elsewhere, maybe inside the elevator housing. That way it would be easier for me to get to it to change the tape and—if I couldn't tap into the power lines—the batteries, and all without having to disturb the camera.

Unfortunately I couldn't find anything like that. But I did find something that was almost as good: a Hi-8 VHS camera, the type favored by a lot of freelance TV journalists. Certainly I'd be able to change the lens to give me more distance. I remembered working in Bosnia and seeing guys running around with Hi-8s glued to their eyes. They all thought they were destined to strike it rich by selling the networks "bang-bang" footage.

I caught the eye of one of the assistants.

"How much for the Hi-8?" I said in my usual bad American accent.

"It's nearly new, hardly out of the packaging. Five hundred dollars."

I smirked.

"So make me an offer," he said.

"Has it got a spare battery and all the attachments for external power?"

"Of course. It's got it all. It's even got its own bag."

"Can I see it working?"

"Of course, of course."

"All right—four hundred, cash."

He did what every plumber and builder throughout the world does when discussing prices: started sucking air through his teeth. "I'll tell you what: four-fifty."

"Done. I also want a playback machine, but it can't be a VCR."

"I have exactly what you want. Follow me."

The machine he retrieved from the back of a shelf had a

hundred-dollar price tag. It looked about a hundred years old, complete with dust. He said, "I'll tell you what—save the trouble: ninety dollars and it's yours."

I nodded. "I also want some lenses."

"What kind are you after?"

"At least a two-hundred-millimeter zoom to go on this, preferably Nikon."

I worked on the basis of one millimeter of lens for every yard of distance to target. For years I had been stuck in people's roof spaces after breaking into their house and removing one of the tiles so I could take pictures of a target, and I'd learned the hard way that it's a wasted effort unless the result is good ID-able images.

He showed me a 250mm lens. "How much?"

"One-fifty." He was waiting for me to say it was too much.

"All right, one hundred fifty dollars. Done—if you throw in two four-hour tapes and an extension cord."

He seemed almost upset at the lack of a fight. "What length?"

More haggling. He was dying for it.

"The longest one you've got."

"Twenty-foot?"

"Done." He was happy now. No doubt he had a forty-foot.

I came across a Wal-Mart a couple of blocks short of the Metro. I ducked inside and wandered around, looking for the items I'd need to set up the camera.

As I moved down the aisles, I found myself doing something I always did, no matter where in the world I was: looking at cooking ingredients and cans of domestic cleaner and working out which would go with what to make chaos. Mix this stuff and that stuff, then boil it up and stir in a bit of this, and I'd have an incendiary device. Or boil all that down and scrape off the scum from around the edge of the pot, then add some of this stuff from the bakery counter and boil that up some more until I got just a sediment at the bottom, and I'd have low explosive. Twenty minutes in Safeway would be enough to buy all the ingredients for a bomb powerful enough to blow a car in half, and you'd still have change from a ten-spot.

I didn't need any of that today, however. All I was after was a two-liter plastic bottle of Coke; a pair of scissors; a roll of trash bags; a mini Maglite flashlight with a range of filters; a roll of gaffer tape; and a tool kit with screwdrivers, wrenches, and pliers—twenty-one pieces for five dollars, and an absolute rip-off; they'd last about five minutes, but that was all I'd need. That done, I grabbed some coloring books, crayons, and other bits and pieces to entertain Kelly. I also put a few more dollars in Mr. Oreo's pocket.

I entered the Metro and found a bench. Lights at the edge of the platform flash when a train's approaching; until then most locals sit chatting or reading. There was nothing else to do so I started a connect-the-dots picture in one of the coloring books and waited for the lights.

The rain had stopped at Pentagon City, though it was still overcast and the ground was wet. I decided to do a quick check of the target while I didn't have Kelly.

Cutting across the supermarket parking lot, I headed for the highway tunnel and Ball Street.

I was soon on the same side of the road and even with the building. A small concrete staircase surrounded by dense shrubbery led up to the glass doors at the front. They opened into a reception area, and then another set of doors that probably led into the office complex itself. A security camera was trained on the front doors, looking down from the right-hand corner. The windows were sealed, double-glazed units. Inside, the building on both floors seemed full of PCs and bulletin boards, the normal office environment.

I couldn't see any external alarm signs, nor any signs saying that the property was guarded. Maybe the alarm was at the rear. If not, whatever detectors there were, were probably connected to a telephone line connected directly to the police or a security firm.

I got to the end of the road, turned right, and headed back to the hotel.

The room was like a sauna. Kelly's hair was sticking up all

over the place; she had sleep in her eyes. Her face was creased and had some crumbs stuck on it. By the look of it she'd been halfway through a cookie and fallen asleep.

As I dumped all the supplies on the side she said, "Where have you been?"

"I've bought tons of stuff." I started diving into the bags and dragging things out. "I've got you some books, some coloring books, some crayons . . ."

I laid them on the bed and stepped back, waiting for some form of appreciation. Instead, she looked at me as if I were crazy.

"I've done those."

I thought a coloring book was a coloring book. I'd quite enjoyed doing my connect-the-dots. "Never mind, I've got you some sandwiches and Coke, and you're to drink as much as you can because I need the bottle for something."

"Aren't we going out to get something to eat?"

"There's some cookies in there . . ." I pointed at the bag.

"I don't want any more. I hate it in here all the time."

"We've got to stay in the hotel today. Remember, we've got people who are looking for us at the moment, and I don't want them to find us. It won't be for long."

I suddenly thought, *Shit—what if she knows her home number and starts using the phone?* While she was pouring out some Coke with both hands around the bottle that seemed as big as she was, I stretched around the back of the small cupboard between the two beds and pulled out the telephone jack.

I looked at my watch. It was 4:30; the best part of five hours to go until Pat made contact again.

I wanted to get the camera sorted out. I wanted it working at first light; I might even be able to get in an hour of filming before last light today.

Kelly got up and looked out the window, a bored, caged-up kid.

I poured myself some Coke and asked, "Do you want some more of this before I dump it out?"

She shook her head. I went into the bathroom and poured the remainder down the sink. I ripped the wrapper off and with the scissors I'd just bought I started to make a cut at the top where the bottle started to curve into the neck. I also cut at the base so I was left with a cylinder. I cut a straight line up it and pushed the resulting rectangle of plastic down flat to get rid of the curve. I cut a circle, first by trimming off the corners of the rectangle, then developing the shape. That was me, ready to burgle.

I came back into the room and checked the cords and made the camera ready for use, by battery or power lines.

"What are you doing, Nick?"

I'd been hoping she wasn't going to ask, but I should have known better by now. I had a lie all prepared. "I'm going to make a film so you can say hello to Mommy, Daddy, and Aida because you said you were bored. Here, say hello."

I put the camera to my eye.

"Hello, Mommy, Daddy, and Aida," she said into the camera. "We're in a hotel room, waiting to come home. I hope you get well soon, Daddy."

"Tell them about your new clothes," I cut in.

"Oh yes." She walked over to the wall. "This is my new blue coat. Nick got me a pink one, too. He knew my favorite colors are pink and blue."

"I'm running out of tape, Kelly. Say good-bye."

She waved. "Bye, Mommy; bye, Daddy; bye, Aida. I love you."

She came skipping over to me. "Can I see it now?"

Another lie. "I haven't got the cords to plug in to the TV. But I'm seeing Pat soon, so maybe he'll get some for me."

She went back to her glass of Coke a very happy bunny. She picked up a crayon and opened the coloring book, and was soon engrossed. Good; it meant I was able to put a tape into the camera without her seeing.

I picked up two plastic coffee cups, got the rest of the kit together, put it all in the video bag, and said, "Sorry about this, but . . ."

She looked at me and shrugged.

I made my way up to the roof. The rain was holding off—the aircraft and traffic noise wasn't.

The first thing I wanted to do was get into the elevator housing; I needed to know whether I could get direct power.

I got out my circle of plastic and put it in the crease of the green door. I pushed and turned it, making it work its way through the twists and turns of the doorframe until it hit against the lock itself. The door was there to keep people out for safety reasons, not to protect something of value, so it was a simple lock to defeat.

Once inside I turned on my mini Maglite, and the first thing I saw was a bank of four power sockets.

I looked up at the ceiling. The shed was made of panels of quarter-inch mild steel bolted onto a frame. I got the wrench and undid two of the bolts enough to lift up a bit of the roof. Then I got the power cord from the camera, pushed it through the gap, and ran it down against the wall. It didn't look out of place among all the other shit. The small gap I'd created wouldn't let in much rain, so there wouldn't be a flood that somebody had to come up and investigate. I plugged the cord into one of the sockets and hoped I'd remember there was juice coming out the other end when I started to mess around with the camera.

I kept the door open to give me some light while I prepared the camera. I got two trash bags and put one inside the other, then put the camera inside, pushing it against the plastic at the bottom until the lens just burst through. I then took the two plastic coffee cups, split them both down the sides, cut the bottoms off both, put them into one another, and then fitted them over the lens as a hood. That was going to keep off the rain but at the same time let enough light into the lens so the thing could work. I used gaffer tape to keep everything in position.

I got on the roof with the camera and plugged it in. I lay flat and looked through the viewfinder, waiting for it to spark up and show me what the lens could see. I wanted a reasonable close-up of the staircase leading up to the main door.

Once it had jumped into life I used the zoom, got it right on target, and pressed Play. I tested Stop and Rewind, then Play again. It worked. I tucked in the plastic, making sure not to dislodge the camera, pressed Record, and walked away.

18

I went and bought a cartwheel-sized pizza, which we sat down and ate in front of the television, with the cell phone plugged in, charging.

Then it was just a matter of hanging around with indigestion waiting for Pat to call and the four-hour tape to finish. It was dark now, but I wanted it to run the full four hours: one, to check that the system worked, and two, to see what the quality was like at night.

For the first time, both of us were bored. Kelly had had death by TV, death by pizza, death by Mountain Dew and Coke. She wearily picked up one of her new books and said, "Would you read to me?"

I thought, *All right, it's just a collection of stories, it won't take that long to read a couple.* I soon discovered it was one continuous adventure, with optional endings to each chapter. I was reading to her about three kids in a museum. One had gone missing—no one knew where—when the story just stopped. At the bottom of the page it said, *"Do you want to go to p. 16 and follow him through the magic tunnel, or do you want to go and see Madame Edie on p. 56, who might tell you where he is? It's your choice."*

"Where do you want to go?" I said.

"Through the tunnel."

Off we went. After about forty-five minutes and changing tack about eight times, I thought we must be getting to the end soon. It took nearly two hours to get through it. At least *she* had fun.

The room was warm and I still had all my stuff on, ready to go. I kept dozing off, waking up every half hour or so to the sound of *The Simpsons* or *Looney Tunes*. One time I woke up and looked down at my jacket. It had come undone, and my pistol was exposed. I looked across at Kelly, but she didn't even give it a second glance; maybe she was used to her dad wearing one.

I opened up a can of Mountain Dew and looked at my watch. It was only 8:15; I'd go and get the first video in about fifteen minutes, put a new tape in, and then wait for Pat's call.

When the time came I said, "I'm just popping out for five minutes to get something to drink—do you want anything?"

She looked quizzical and said, "We've got loads here."

"Yeah, but it's all warm. I'll bring some cold ones."

I went up to the roof. It was damp and drizzling now. I opened up the back of the plastic bag, pressed the Eject button, and quickly exchanged tapes. I was ready for the morning.

I came downstairs, passed our room, and got another couple of sodas. Coca-Cola shares had probably skyrocketed over the last few days.

Clueless came on, the TV series she'd told me she loved. I was amazed as I listened to her imitating all the catch-phrases. She had them down pat: "Loser . . . double loser, moron . . . whatever!" Now I knew where a lot of her sayings came from.

At last it was just three minutes to go before Pat was due to check in. There was no way I'd tell Pat where we were or that Kelly was actually with me. All I would tell him was what he needed to know, as protection for him as well as for us. I went into the bathroom, closed the door, and listened for *Clueless*. Nothing.

Right on time the phone rang.

"Hello?"

"All right, mate? Thanks for the sub!"

We both had a quiet laugh.

"Do you know what floor they're occupying?"

There was a short pause, then, "Second floor."

"OK. Any chance of more money? I need a big wad, mate. You know I'll square it away when I get back."

"I could get you about ten grand. But you're going to have

to wait a day—I won't be able to get it until tomorrow, or possibly the day after. You're welcome to it until you're sorted—and I take it you've got a way out?"

"Yeah," I lied. It was for the best. If he got lifted, he could give only false information, and they'd start combing the airports and docks instead of looking around Washington.

Then I said, "I need more contact in case I manage to find anything out about the building and things start changing rapidly. What about twelve hundred hours, eighteen hundred, and twenty-three hundred—is that OK?"

"All right, mate. Is there anything else?"

"No, mate. Be careful."

"And you. See ya!"

I turned the telephone off, went back into the bedroom, and put it back on the charger. I didn't know if Kelly had heard anything, but she was quiet and seemed uneasy.

I got the playback machine set up, pushed the tape in, and tuned in the television.

Kelly was watching intently.

"We're going to play a game," I said. "Do you fancy playing? If not, I'll just do it on my own."

"OK." It beat counting cars on the highway. "I thought you didn't have any cords."

She'd got me on that one. "I bought some when I went out."

"So why can't we see the video we made?"

I had to think quickly. "Because I've already mailed it. Sorry."

She looked at me, a little confused.

"We're going to watch this tape of a building," I went on. "It's got people going in and out of it. Now, there's going to be some famous people going in there, there's going to be people that you know, like friends of Daddy's and Mommy's, and people that I know. So what we've got to do is see how many people we can each recognize. Whoever sees the most is the winner. You want to play?"

"Yeah!"

"You've got to be really quick, because I'm going to fast-forward it. Every time you see somebody moving, you've got to tell me, then I'll stop, rewind, and we'll have a look at it."

I took some of the hotel stationery and a pencil and off we went. I had to use the button on the machine to fast-forward because there was no remote. I sat on the floor under the player by the TV and hit the fast-forward button. Kelly's eyes didn't leave the screen. I was quite pleased with the result. The quality wasn't bad at all; you could tell the difference between this and a home video, and I'd managed to get full-length pictures of the people covering about two-thirds of the screen.

"Stop, stop, stop!" she shrieked.

I rewound and had a look. Kelly had correctly spotted some movement. There were a few people entering. I didn't recognize any of them. Kelly was sure that man number three was from a pop group called Backstreet Boys.

She got into the game more and more. Everyone seemed to be famous. I logged them all, using the counter.

Two men, one with a long light coat, one with a blue coat.

People think that being a baby spy is all James Bond, sports cars, and casinos. I'd always wished the fuck it was. The reality is sheer hard work, getting information, then sitting down and working out what it is you've gathered—and then interpreting it. Two people walking up a set of stairs means shit. It's interpreting what's going on that's important—identifying them, their body language, what happened before, what you think is going to happen later on. So you log everything, in case at a later date it might be important. Give me a sports car any day.

The screen was slowly getting darker. The ambient street light was helping, but it was quite hard to see faces and we were losing color; I could tell the difference between a man and a woman and their ages, but just barely.

It came to the end of the working day and everything began to close down; people going home were throwing switches and the light dwindled. In the end there were lights only in the reception area and corridors.

I left the tape running at normal speed. What I now wanted to know was whether there was a night watchman around, but I couldn't see anyone.

Kelly was loving it. She'd seen four actors, two of the Spice

Girls, and a teacher from her school. Not bad at all. But what if she did recognize somebody? I'd have to take it with a grain of salt; after all, she was only seven. But I'd have nothing to lose in believing her.

"Do you want to do this again tomorrow?"

"Sure. I have more points than you."

"So you do. I tell you what, after all that winning I think you should lie down on the bed and take a nap."

If Kelly or I identified anybody on the tape tomorrow, it would be a bonus for me to take to Simmonds and prove a link. It would also mean that I'd definitely have to CTR—close target reconnaissance—the building and find out why they were there. I decided to go and have a closer look at the outside, and then I could plan how to make entry.

By 11 P.M. Kelly was sound asleep, still fully clothed. I put the bedspread over her, picked up the key card, and left.

To avoid the office I came out of the hotel via the emergency stairs. I got on the road by the highway, turned right, and walked past the playhouse toward the target. The traffic was quieter now, just peaks of noise instead of a constant roar. I turned right, then right again. I was on Ball Street.

It was the back I really needed to take a look at, but first I wanted to recon the front again. I wanted to see if there was a night watchman in there and get a mental picture of what it looked like inside.

I moved into a doorway across the way. If I was spotted, I'd pretend I was drunk and taking a piss. I was in deep shadow as I looked over at the target. I could see through the two sets of doors into the reception area; the lights were still on, giving a sheen to the wet concrete steps and the leaves of the bushes. I looked upstairs and saw light shining through the windows directly above the main entrance. That meant the corridor lights were on upstairs as well.

I waited around for fifteen minutes, watching for signs of movement. Was security sitting downstairs watching the TV? Was he upstairs, doing his rounds? I didn't see anything. Time to look at the rear.

I went back the way I'd come but instead of turning left went right toward the river. It was just a one-lane road with muddy mush on the sides and potholes filled with oily water that glistened in the ambient light. Using the shadows, I passed the scrap-metal yard and crossed over the railway tracks that led to the old cement depot. My footsteps made more noise than the highway now. Fences divided all the plots, secured with old chains and padlocks. I followed the road farther, looking for a point to turn and get behind the target.

The highway lights weren't strong enough to have any effect at this distance, but I could make out the mist coming from the river. I'd reached a dead end. A fence blocked the old road, and a large, muddy turning circle had been made by cars looking for a parking space and discovering what I just had. I could also see lights from the airport, beyond the woods that sloped down to the Potomac.

There was no alternative but to walk back to the abandoned railway tracks, which years ago would have been a branch of the main line. I looked left, following the tracks; they ran about two hundred yards to the rear of the target, and to their left were some old, rusted corrugated-iron buildings.

I started climbing over the wire gates where the trains would have gone through to the depot. The padlocked chains rattled under the strain. I got into some shadow and waited. There were no dogs barking, and the airport was probably closed down this late at night because it was so close to the city; all I could hear was a distant siren.

I carried on along the tracks, and soon the only noises were of my feet and breath.

To my right was the scrapyard, enclosed by a fence, with old cars piled on top of each other seven or eight high. After about a hundred yards the ground started to open up and I could see buildings. Fences made it clear what belonged to whom. The area had been cleared and flattened, ready for developers. One of those buildings beyond it was the rear of my target; on the other side I could see street lights on Ball Street and the highway. The drizzle gave them a misty, faded appearance.

I slowed down, had a quick look at the target, then started to walk across the 150 yards of newly leveled ground to a fence that was about 50 yards short of the target building.

Near the fence I found some bushes, stopped, and squatted down. The things that always give you away are shape, shine, shadow, silhouette, spacing, and movement. Forget about them and they'll get you killed.

Still on my haunches, I did nothing but sit and watch for the next few minutes. You have to give your senses a chance to adjust to a new environment. After a while my eyes began to adapt to the light and I could start to make things out. I could see that there were no windows in the back of the building, just a solid brick wall. There was, however, a four-flight steel staircase leading to the ground. This was the fire escape route for both the first and second floors. To the right of it at ground level were the meter boxes for the building's utilities.

I looked at the fire exits. If I had to make entry at some stage to find out what PIRA was up to, that was probably the way I'd go in. It depended whether they had external locks, and there was only one way to find out.

I scanned along the line of the six-foot chain-link fence, looking for a break. I couldn't see one. Grabbing the top edge of the wire, I pulled myself up, got a foot on the top, and clambered over. I crouched down again and stayed still, watching and listening for any reaction.

There was no need to rush; slow movement meant that not only did I reduce noise and the risk of being detected, I could also control my breathing and hear more around me. I used the shadows created by the building and trees, moving from one pool of darkness to the next, all the time keeping eyes on the target and the surrounding area.

Once I got close enough, I stopped at the base of two trees and stood against one of the trunks. Looking at the rear wall, I noticed a motion detector that had been fixed at a height and angle to cover people walking up the fire escape. I had no way of knowing what the detector triggered, whether an alarm, a light, or a camera, or maybe all three. I couldn't see any cameras. But I could see lights, two of them, one above each fire exit. They weren't on. Were they what the motion detector would trigger? Probably, but why wasn't there also a camera covering the rear so that security could see what had triggered the light? It didn't matter; I'd treat the detector as if it triggered everything.

I noted three wooden pallets to the right of the building by the fence. I could use those.

I looked at the doors. They had sheet steel covering them, together with an extra strip that went over the frame to prevent anyone from tampering with the gap. Close up, I could see that the locks were the pin-tumbler type. Piece of cake; I could defeat them.

A quick check of the utilities boxes and dials showed me that gas, electricity, water, and telephone were all there, all exposed and ready to be played with. I was feeling better about this all the time.

I was still worried about the possibility of a night watchman. In some circumstances, it can actually be a bonus. You can try to get him to come and open the door—and hey presto, you've got an unalarmed entry. However, if I had to go in, it would be covertly.

The parking lot was empty, which could be another indication that there was no one inside. I had to confirm it one way or another. I decided to be slightly drunk, walk up to the main entrance, and take a leak; while I was doing that, I could get a better look inside. If there was anybody in the foyer, he might come out and give me grief, or I might see him watching television in the back somewhere.

I followed the same route all the way back and reached Ball Street. I was quite damp now; the drizzle and wet rusty fences had done their work on my clothes.

I walked on the opposite side of the road toward the target. As I got nearer, I started to cross at an angle that gave me more time to see the target. Head down, conscious of the camera covering the door, I started to stumble up the steps, and about three-quarters of the way up, as soon as I was able to see into the right-hand window, I turned, opened my fly, and started pissing down onto the bushes.

Almost instantly, a man's voice roared, "Fuck you! Fuck you! Fuck you!" and there was an explosion of movement in the shrubbery. I nearly jumped out of my skin.

I took my hand straight off my cock and onto the Sig. I tried to stop pissing but I was in full flow. My jeans took the brunt.

I went for the pistol, then realized that maybe I didn't need to pull it out yet. He might be security. Maybe I could talk my way out of this.

"Fuck you! Who do you think you are? You motherfucker!"

I could hear him but still couldn't see anything. There was rustling and all sorts of shit going on, then more "Fuck you! Fuck you!" and I saw him appearing through the bushes.

"Fucking asshole, piss on me, you fuck. I'll show you! Look at me! You've pissed on me!"

He was in his mid-twenties, wearing old army boots without laces and dirty, greasy black jeans. He had a hooded, parka-type jacket that was in shit shape, grimed with muck and with the elbows hanging out. When he was about ten yards away I could also see he had a straggly excuse for a beard, a big earring in one ear, and long greasy dreadlocks. He was soaked.

The moment he saw me, his face lit up. To him I was the accidental tourist, lost at the wrong end of town. I could almost see the cogs turning; he thought he'd cracked it here, he was going to get some easy money out of this greenhorn.

"Fuck you, asshole, you owe me a new sleeping bag! Look at my clothes—you've pissed all over me, you fucking animal! Give me some money, man!"

He was certainly going for an Oscar. "Do you know who I am? Fucking piss on me, man, I'll fucking kick your ass!"

I needed to take advantage of this. I went up to the window and started banging hard. If there was security, he should come investigate. I'd just play the innocent needing protection from this madman.

I banged so hard I thought the glass would break, making sure all the time that I had my back to the camera. It sparked up the homeless guy even more because he thought I was panicking.

He started to come up the stairs. I kept on looking inside the building. There were no used ashtrays in sight, no magazines lying open on chairs, no TV on; the furniture was well arranged, the chair by the reception area was neatly under the desk. There was nothing to show that anyone was around.

Nearly on top of me now, I heard, "Fucking asshole!"

I turned, opened my jacket, and put my hand on the pistol.

He saw it and stopped in his tracks. "Ah, for fuck's sake! Fucking hell!" He backed off, started to retreat down the stairs, his eyes fixed on the pistol. "Fucking cops," he muttered.

I had to try hard not to laugh.

"Fucking cops, piss on me every fucking which way!"

I waited for him to disappear. The guy thought he had

problems—this was the second time in two days that I'd had piss all over me. I felt sorry for him, though; I thought about the amount of time he'd probably spent finding himself a snug little retreat, well concealed from predators and nicely warmed by the air-conditioning outlets and other machinery tucked underneath. Then some dickhead comes and empties his bladder all over the house.

It took me fifteen minutes to get back to the hotel. I opened the door nice and quiet. Kelly was in kid heaven, not having had to take a bath or clean up her mess, just falling asleep surrounded by candy and cookies.

I got undressed, took a shower and shaved, then stuffed the clothes into the hotel laundry bag. The duffel was getting pretty full now with dirty and bloodstained clothes. I was down to my last change. I got dressed again, tucked the pistol into my waistband, put my coat on, and set the alarm for 5:30.

20

I was half-awake anyway when the alarm went. I'd been tossing and turning all night, and now I couldn't really be bothered to get up. People must feel like this when they go to a job they really hate.

I finally got myself to my feet, went over to the window, and opened the curtains. We were just below eye level with the highway and almost in its shadow. Headlights lumbered silently toward me from out of the gloom; in the other lanes, taillights disappeared back into the darkness like slow-moving tracers. It wasn't time yet.

I let the curtain fall and turned down the heat, got the coffee machine gurgling, and went into the bathroom.

As I took a leak I looked at myself in the mirror. I looked like a scarecrow with creases on my face where I'd been lying on some crayons. I took my jacket off, turned the collar in on my polo shirt, and splashed my face in the sink.

I went back to the bedroom. The brew wasn't ready yet, and my mouth felt as if a gorilla had dumped in it. He'd certainly been in the room while we were both asleep, throwing soda cans and food everywhere. I picked up an already opened can of Mountain Dew and took a couple of flat, warm sips.

Until first light, there wasn't that much to do. I was used to this; so much of my life had been hurry up and wait. I put the chair by the window and opened the curtains again. Looking at the highway, I couldn't make out whether it was still raining or if it was just vehicle spray in the headlights that made it look that way.

By the end of a quarter hour I could begin to make out the shape of the cars as well as their headlights. It was time.

There was no need to wake Kelly; the more she slept, the easier my life would be. I checked that I had the key card and moved up to the roof.

Rain danced on the metal roof of the elevator housing. I pulled myself up and lay there getting soaked front and back as I pressed the Play button on the camera and tested the flashing light. I checked to see that I still had the correct site picture and that the lens hadn't misted up. It had. I cursed at myself because I should have put on another plastic bag to keep the moisture from getting in overnight. I started to wipe the moisture off with my cuff and suddenly felt as if I were between two worlds. Behind me roared the early morning traffic, yet to my front, toward the river, I could just about hear birds giving their early morning song. I was almost enjoying it. The moment was soon shattered when the first aircraft of the day took off and disappeared into low cloud.

Lens dry, I rechecked the camera position, made sure it was recording, and closed the trash bags.

It was now nearly 6 A.M. I went back to the room and my chair by the window, coffee in hand. I smiled as I watched a couple come out of the room next door, hand in hand. Something about them didn't quite match up. I made a bet with myself that they'd leave in separate cars.

For the hundredth time, my mind drifted to the telephone call I'd had with Kev. Pat had said that if it was PIRA, there could be a connection with drugs, Gibraltar, and the Americans. My hard drive went into freewheel, because something about the Gibraltar job had always puzzled me.

The year 1987 had been PIRA's annus horribilis, and as Detachment operators in Northern Ireland, Euan and I had done our fair share to fuck them over. At the beginning of the year they'd promised their faithful "tangible success in the war of national liberation," but it hadn't taken long for that to turn to rat shit. In February, PIRA fielded twenty-seven Sinn Féin candidates in the Irish general election, but they managed to scrape only about a thousand votes each. Few people in the South gave a damn about reunification with Northern Ireland; they were far more concerned with other issues like unemployment and the crippling level of taxation. It showed how out of touch PIRA was, and how successful the Anglo-Irish accord was proving. Ordinary people really did believe that London and Dublin could work together to bring about a long-term solution to the Troubles.

PIRA couldn't take that lying down and must have decided they needed a morale booster. Their knee-jerk reaction was the murder, on Saturday, April 25, of Lord Justice Maurice Gibson, one of the province's most senior judges. Euan and I saw firsthand the celebrations in some of PIRA's illegal drinking dens that weekend. We even had a few drinks ourselves as we hung around. The players loved what had happened. Not only had they gotten rid of one of their worst enemies, but recriminations were flying left, right, and center between London and Dublin. The Anglo-Irish accord, which had done so much to undermine PIRA's power base, was itself now in question.

However, barely had the hangovers gone away than PIRA had another disaster. Two weeks later, at Loughall in County Armagh, guys from the Regiment ambushed PIRA's East Tyrone Brigade while they were attempting to bomb a police station. From a force of 1,000 hard-core players in 1980, PIRA's strength had dwindled to fewer than 250, of which maybe 50 were members of active service units. Our successes had further cut this to 40, which meant that the operation at Loughall had wiped out one-fifth of PIRA's hardliners at a stroke. It was their biggest loss in a single action since 1921. If this continued, all of PIRA would soon be riding around in the same taxi.

The massive defeat at Loughall was followed soon afterward by a disastrous showing by Gerry Adams in the British general election. Sinn Féin's vote plummeted, with the Catholic vote switching to the moderate SDLP. Then, on October 31, during Sinn Féin's annual conference in Dublin, French Customs seized a small freighter called the *Eksund* off the coast of Brittany. On board was an early Christmas present to PIRA from Colonel Gaddafi—hundreds of AK-47s, tons of Semtex, several ground-to-air missiles, and so much ammunition it was a miracle that the ship stayed afloat.

The humiliation was complete. No wonder Gerry Adams

and PIRA wanted revenge and some sort of publicity coup to show people like Gaddafi and those Irish Americans who contributed to Noraid that they hadn't completely lost their grip.

On November 8, Remembrance Day, they planted a thirty-pound bomb with a timer at the town memorial in Enniskillen in County Fermanagh, Northern Ireland. Eleven civilians were killed in the explosion, and more than sixty were seriously injured. Outrage at the atrocity was instant and worldwide. In Dublin, thousands lined up to sign a book of condolence. In Moscow, not a place well known for its compassion, the TASS news agency denounced what it called "barbaric murders." But worst of all for PIRA, even the Irish Americans appeared to have had enough. PIRA had fucked up big-time. It had thought the bombing would be hailed as a victory in its struggle against an occupying power, but all it had done was show it up for what it really was. It might be one thing to kill "legitimate" targets like judges, policemen, and members of the security forces, but murdering innocent civilians while they were honoring their dead at a Remembrance Day service?

That was why Gibraltar had been such a puzzle to me. I could see why Adams and company would be desperate to show their diminishing group of sympathizers that they were still in business, but why risk a repeat of the international backlash they'd suffered after Enniskillen? If they bombed Gibraltar, it wouldn't be only British civilians who might end up killed. At that time of the year, hundreds of foreign tourists pack the squares and streets of the colony, many from the cruise liners that regularly dock in the harbor. And many of those, PIRA would have known full well, were American. I'd never been able to see a method to their madness.

It suddenly hit me that maybe I'd been looking down the wrong end of the telescope. PIRA were terrorists, but their presence here in Washington proved that they were also businessmen. There was no sectarian divide when it came to money, just normal competition and greed. They got together with Protestant paramilitaries on a regular basis to talk about their drug, prostitution, and extortion rackets, even to discuss demarcation lines for different taxi firms and sites for slot machines back home. They had the infrastructure, the knowledge, and the weapons to be major players in the world of crime. With cooperation from other terrorist organizations throughout the world, the possibilities were endless. If so, this was some serious shit.

Down in the parking lot the couple was having a long, lingering embrace. What was going on there was some serious shit, too. Then one final kiss and, yep, separate cars.

I wasn't expecting a phone call from Pat until noon and there were still about three hours to wait for the tape to finish recording, so there wasn't much to do apart from watch invaders from Mars and talking shoes who lived in wastebaskets. I felt uneasy. I needed to do something.

I shook Kelly. "Kelly, Kelly, wake up."

She moaned, pulling the covers back over her. I spoke gently in her ear. "I'm going downstairs to buy some stuff, OK?"

I got a very weak yes. She couldn't have cared less. I was beginning to realize she wasn't a morning person.

I used the emergency stairs again and crossed under the highway to the 7-Eleven. Inside, it looked like Fort Knox. There was a grating in the wall with a cubbyhole behind it and an Asian face glowering out and then turning back to watch a portable TV. The store was too hot and stank of cigarettes and overbrewed coffee. Every inch of wall space was plastered with signs informing the local villains CASH REGISTER HOLDS ONLY $50—EVERYTHING ELSE DEPOSITED.

I didn't really need to buy anything; we had more stuff in the room than we could eat in a year, but I wanted some time to myself, away from Kelly. I found it tiring just being around her. There was always something that needed doing, checking, or washing, and in any time that was left over I seemed to be nagging her to hurry up and get dressed.

At the magazine rack another friendly sign said, NO SPITTING OR READING THE MERCHANDISE. I picked up a *Washington Post* and a handful of magazines, some for me and some for Kelly—I didn't even bother looking at what they were—and went and put my money through the small hole in the grille. The man looked disappointed I hadn't forced him to use the machete I was sure he had under the till.

I strolled into the lobby to get breakfast. There were seven or eight people sitting around, eating, and watching a TV mounted on a wall bracket above the table with the food and drink. As I started to load up three paper plates on a tray, above me I could hear an anchorman talking about George Mitchell and his part in the Irish peace process. I listened to a couple of soundbites from Sinn Féin and the British government, both pouring scorn on the other side's statements, both claiming that they were the ones who truly wanted peace.

A woman's voice interrupted my thoughts. She was anchoring the local news, and as I poured some orange juice for Kelly I could feel my skin tingle all over. She was talking about the Browns.

I didn't dare turn around. One of the barbecue pictures could appear on screen at any moment.

The woman told viewers that police had not come up with any new leads, but the kidnapping of seven-year-old Kelly had moved forward with a computer image of the man seen leaving with her. She gave my height, build, and hair color.

There wasn't room to pour any more coffee or juice, and the tray was overflowing with food. But I didn't dare move. It felt as if every pair of eyes in the room was fixed on me. I put a bagel into the toaster and waited, drinking coffee, not looking up or around. I felt I was in a cocoon of silence, apart from the voice of the newscaster. I prayed for her to turn to a new subject. The bagel popped up. Shit. I put some spread on it. I knew people were looking at me; they had to be.

I'd run out of things to do. I took a deep breath, picked up my tray, and turned around. The noise of the room came back. No one was looking. They were too busy eating, talking, and reading the papers.

Kelly was still asleep. Good. I put her food on the side and started to munch on my Cheerios. I switched the TV on, muted it, and flicked through the channels, looking for local

news. There was nothing more about the situation on Hunting
Bear Path.

I attacked the newspaper. We were famous—well, sort of.
A small piece on page five. No pictures. A police spokesman
was reported as saying that they were reluctant to come up
with any theories until they had more concrete evidence, but
yes, the murders were being treated as drug-related. Luther
and his bunch would be pleased about that. Otherwise, there
were no new leads. I wasn't the only one in the dark.

I had to try to cut all the conjecture from my mind because
it was getting far too confusing. As the policeman said,
without information it was pointless spending time and effort
trying to think of different scenarios. I determined to focus
all my effort into: one, protecting Kelly and myself; two,
keeping the video on target to discover if there was a connection between PIRA and Kev's death; three, getting some
money from Pat so I could arrange my return to the UK; and
four, getting hold of Euan for help in dealing with Simmonds,
or, if I had nothing for him, to help me negotiate with him.

I looked over at Kelly. She was on her back with her arms
out in a star shape, dreaming she was Katherine, the pink
ranger. I felt sorry for her. She hadn't a clue what had happened to her family. Some poor bastard was going to have to
tell her one day, and after that someone would have to look
after her. I just hoped it was someone nice; maybe her grandparents, wherever they might be.

At least she was alive. Those boys must be sweating now.
They'd have to assume that Kelly had given me their descrip-
tions and that she'd overheard what all the shouting was
about. They had to be desperate to get their hands on us.

I started to wonder how I could get more information out
of her but gave up on that one. I was no psychologist; if anything, I was a candidate for seeing one.

I picked up a bike magazine and by the end had changed
loyalties from Ducati to BMW. Then I read in a fishing magazine how wonderful Lake Tahoe was for men with waders. I
was lost in a whole new world of hook sizes and rod materials
when all of a sudden there was a knock on the door.

No time to think. I pulled the Sig, checked chamber, and looked at Kelly. I thought: *We both might be dead soon.*

I put my hand over her mouth and gave her a shake. She woke up scared. I put my fingers to my mouth. It wasn't in a nice manner—it was saying: "Shut the fuck up. Don't say a fucking thing."

I called out, "One minute, one minute!" I went through and turned the shower on, came back out, then went up to the door, sounding disorganized. "Hello, who is it?"

A pause. "Housekeeping."

I looked through the peephole and saw a woman, black, mid-fifties; she had a cleaning uniform on and a cart behind her.

I couldn't see anything else, but then, if she had the police or Luther's boys on either side of her, they weren't going to be showing their faces.

I looked at her and tried to interpret what was going on from her eyes. They would soon tell me if there were ten policemen around the corner bristling with body armor and firepower.

I said, "It's OK, not today, thank you, we're sleeping."

I saw her look down and heard, "Sorry, sir, you didn't have your sign out."

"Oh, OK."

"Would you like some towels?"

"Hang on, I'm just coming out of the shower. I'll get some clothes on."

It would be natural to be wanting towels.

I put the weapon in my left hand, undid the lock, and opened the door just a fraction. The weapon was pointing through the door on the left side; if any fucker pushed her to get in, it would be the last thing he did.

I opened the door a little more, held it with my leg, and put my head in the gap. I smiled, "Ah, hiya," the gun pointing at her behind the door. I didn't put my hand out to get the towels; I didn't want someone grabbing it. I said, "I just need two big towels, that'll be fine—and have you got some more shampoo?"

She gave me what I wanted. I said, "Thank you," and she smiled back. I closed the door.

Kelly was lying on the bed openmouthed, watching my every move.

I shrugged. "Don't you just hate it when people do that?"

She started laughing. So did I. "They nearly had us that time!" I said.

Her expression changed, and she slowly shook her head. "I know you won't ever let them get me."

It was 10:30: another twenty minutes to go before I went up and changed the tapes. I picked up the one we'd been watching the night before, slapped it back into the player, and rewound it for the next session.

This time I only had to smile at her and she jumped up and went to the door, ready to drop the latch.

"While I'm out I want you to take a shower. Will you do that?"

She shrugged. "Whatever. I get all the good jobs."

I went upstairs to the roof.

The weather was still shitty.

21

There was still an hour to go before the noon call. We sat down together to watch the latest footage.

I said, "It's really important; we might see somebody we know. Then we can give the tape to Daddy and he can find out who was shouting at him. Anybody you think you might know, like Melissa's dad or the man at the grocery store, or even the men who came to see Daddy, tell me and we can have a closer look, OK?"

I started to fast-forward, stopping the tape whenever there was traffic. I logged what they looked like: male, female, black, white, Asian; and what they were wearing: black on blue, red on blue.

The game wasn't as much fun for Kelly the second time around.

"What about him?" I enthused.

"No."

"That lady?"

"No."

"You sure you've never seen this man?"

"Never!"

At last she spotted somebody she knew. I rewound the tape. "Who is he?"

"Mr. Mooner on *Fox Kids*."

"OK, I'll write that down."

Another guy started to walk up the stairs. I stopped the tape and rewound. I said, "Do you know him?"

She shook her head.

I said, "Well, I know somebody who looks exactly like him. A man I used to work with who could never remember where he left things, and one day we hid his false teeth and he had to eat soup all week!" She had a little laugh; it kept her going a bit longer.

At 11:45 we were still going through the tape and logging. I stopped at two men who were going in together.

"Do you know either of them? Because I don't. I can't think of anybody who even looks like them." I was racking my brains trying to think of another story to keep her interested.

"No, I've never seen them before."

"Oh, all right then. Just a couple more, then we'll do something else." I started to fast-forward, saw a figure coming out of the building, rewound, and played it.

She moved to the edge of the bed. "I know that man," she said.

I pressed Freeze-frame. We were looking at a black guy in his mid-thirties.

"Who is he?"

"He came to see Daddy with the other men."

I tried to sound calm. "What's his name? Do you know any of their names?"

"Can I go home and see Mommy now? You said I could go home tomorrow and now it's tomorrow."

"We have to sort this out first, Kelly. Daddy needs to know their names. He can't remember."

I was trying to do the psychology bit—but I knew more about fly-fishing now than I did about child psychology.

She shook her head.

"Daddy knew them though, didn't he?"

"Yeah. They came to see Daddy."

"Can you remember anything else about them? Were they smoking?"

"I don't remember. I don't think so."

"Did any of them have glasses?"

"I think this guy had glasses."

I looked closer at the screen. He wore thin wire frames.

"OK, were they wearing rings or anything?"

"I don't know, I didn't see."

I tried the color of the car, their shoes, their coats. Did

they talk to each other using different names? Were they American?

She was starting to get upset, but I had to know.

I said, "Kelly, are you sure this man came to see Daddy the day I found you?"

Her eyes were welling up. I'd gone too far.

"Don't cry." I put my arm around her. "It's OK. This man came with the other men, yes?"

I felt her nod.

"That's very good, because I can give this information to Daddy when I see him and that will help catch them. You see, you've helped him!"

She looked up at me. There was a slight smile under the tears.

If she was right, what we had was one of the people who killed Kev coming out of an office that was fronting for PIRA.

There was still more tape to run. I tried to sound upbeat. "OK then, let's have a look and see if we can see the other men. They were black, too, weren't they?"

"No, they were white."

"Oh yes, of course."

We went on through the tape. I came out with a possible ID of Nelson Mandela, and she saw Michael Jackson. Apart from that, jack shit.

"Can we go home now and show this to Daddy? Maybe he's better now. You said we could, if we saw anyone."

I was digging myself deeper. "No, not yet. I have to make sure that this is the man who came to see Daddy. But not long now, not long."

I lay on the bed, pretending to read the fishing magazine. *She knew who they were.* My heart was beating loud and slow. I was trying to keep to my game plan of concentrating only on the matter at hand, but I couldn't. Why would Kev be killed by people who knew him? Had it been Luther and company? It must have been. What did Kev know, or what was he involved in? Why would he tell me about his problem if he were corrupt? Was the DEA investigating PIRA and drug dealing? Maybe Kev was, and the murders were carried out by PIRA or the drug dealers because of something he had done or was about to do? But why did they know him?

Conjecture would get me nowhere. It was just a waste of time and effort. Kelly was stretched out beside me, looking at the magazine. It was a strange feeling having her head on my chest. I moved my arm around her to look at my watch. She thought I was going to cuddle her.

It was nearly time for Pat to call. I got up and switched on the mobile phone, then stood by the window, pulling a gap in the curtain, looking at the highway through the rain, deciding on my next move. I tried to think of a good RV. It wouldn't be secure to meet again at the shopping mall.

Right on time the phone rang.

"Hello?"

"Hello, mate." I could hear the traffic going past a phone booth.

"Things are happening," I said. "I need an RV."

"In two hours, is that OK?"

"Two hours. Union Station all right for you?"

"Er . . . Union—yep, no problem." He sounded spaced out.

I'd traveled through it a few times and could remember the layout. "Come in through the main entrance," I said. "Go up to the top floor, to the coffee bar facing the stairs. Buy a cup of coffee, sit down, and wait. I'll pick you up there, OK?"

There was a long, worrying pause. "Is that OK, Pat?"

"I'll be there. See ya." The line went dead.

Union Station is so grand and elegant that it should be in Paris, not here in the home of cinder block and dark wood veneer. At most major railway stations in the world you expect to find the seedier side of life, but not at Union. The ticketing, check-in, and baggage-handling areas look like part of a modern airport. There's even a first-class lounge. You don't see the trains because they're behind screens, and in any case you'd be much too distracted by the shopping mall, the food court, the coffee shops, even a multiplex cinema. More important for me, however, I'd remembered it as a big, busy location, and because of the Easter holiday I knew there'd be a big transient population of people from out of town who would know nothing of the events on Hunting Bear Path.

* * *

A cab got us to the station early. There was just under an hour to fill, so I made the most of it shopping for items I'd be needing for the reconnaissance of the PIRA office, besides the stuff I'd already bought at Wal-Mart. Now that Kelly had recognized the black guy, the only option was to get in there and have a look around.

I bought a Polaroid camera and six packs of film; a pair of cheap and nasty polyester coveralls, more rolls of gaffer's tape and Scotch tape; heavy-duty scissors that promised I could cut through a shiny new penny with them; a Leatherman, a tool that's a bit like a Swiss Army knife; running shoes; rubber gloves; batteries; Saran Wrap; a plastic bottle of orange juice with a large spout; a box of push pins; a dozen eggs; and a quartz kitchen clock, nine inches in diameter. Kelly looked at it all and raised an eyebrow, but didn't ask.

By 1:40 I had a couple of shopping bags full of gear, as well as the books and time-wasters I'd had to put in her basket to keep her involved.

I remembered the beautiful tiled floor in the entrance hall, but I'd forgotten the cathedral ceilings. In the middle was a rotunda with a newsstand and groups of tables outside. Above it, reached by a flight of stairs, was a restaurant. It was absolutely perfect for what I needed.

We were greeted at the top by a waitress.

I smiled. "Table for two, please."

I pointed to a table right at the back. "Can we have that one?"

We sat down, and I put the bags under the table. I couldn't see the main entrance, but I'd be able to see Pat heading toward the coffee shop because that was farther into the main part of the station and up a level.

The waitress came to take our drink order. I asked for two Cokes and said, "I'm ready to order now, if that's all right? We'll take a nine-inch pizza."

Kelly looked up. "Can we have extra mushrooms?"

I nodded at the waitress and she left.

Kelly smiled. "Mommy and me both like extra mushrooms.

Daddy says we're like forest pixies!" She smiled again, wanting a reaction.

"That's nice," I said. This was a conversation that needed nipping in the bud.

Kelly got stuck into her Coke, enjoying being able to watch real people for a change.

Pat was early, wearing the same clothes as a VDM—visual distinguishing mark. Either that or the fucker simply hadn't changed. As he walked past and below me, something about him didn't seem right. There was a very slight stagger in his stride, and I knew it hadn't come from drinking too much beer. I feared the worst.

I continued my checks, covering his back to protect my own.

I gave it about five minutes, got up, and said to Kelly, "I have to go to the men's room. I won't be long." On the way out I asked the waitress to keep an eye on Kelly and our bags.

Another set of doors took me into the main ticketing and train area. The place was heaving; half of the USA must have been on the move. Even the air-conditioning was finding it too much: the combination of heat and humidity from the people made it feel like a greenhouse. I joined the packed crowds slowly shuffling up to the top floor.

He was in line at the coffee shop, about three or four people ahead of him. Very hale and hearty, I went over and slapped him on the back. "Pat! What are you doing here?"

Reciprocating my big smile, he said, "I'm here to meet somebody." His pupils were as big as saucers.

"Me, too. You got time for a Mickey D's?"

"Yeah, yeah, why not?"

We started to walk beyond the coffee shop, following exit signs through automatic doors, and took the escalator up to the multistory parking garage.

Pat was a step or two above. He looked down at me, puzzled. "What the fuck's a Mickey D's?"

"McDonald's," I said, as if he should have known. But then he didn't have a seven-year-old on his case day and night. "Come on, Pat, get with the program!"

He started to do a Michael Jackson moondance.

By now we were nearly at the bus station level. I said, "If there's a drama, I'm going to the bus station area, turning right and out an exit."

"Fine. No problem!" He sounded OK but looked like shit.

The cars were on the two levels above. We walked up the bare concrete stairs, stopped at the first level, and **got** into a position that looked back the way we had come.

I didn't have time to fuck around. "Two things, mate. I've got a list here I didn't fancy reading to you over the phone." I passed it over. "I need all that stuff. And the other thing—what's the score on the money?"

He was already looking at the small notebook I'd handed him. Either he was amazed at the contents or he couldn't focus. Without looking up he said, "I got some money for you today. But fucking hell, most of it's going to be used up on this stuff. I'll be able to get you some more, probably tomorrow or the day after. Fuck me." He shook his head. "When do you want all this by?" He then started to giggle as if he'd just cracked a joke in his head and wasn't going to share it with me.

"Actually, tonight, mate. You think you can do it, or what?" I moved my head to get eye-to-eye with him.

The giggle became a laugh until he saw me looking serious. He cleared his throat and tried to switch on. "I'll do my best, mate. I'll see what I can get on this list."

"I'd really fucking appreciate it," I said. "Don't let me down, Pat. I really need your help." I hoped the urgency was going to register with him. I was still checking down the stairs. "Also at the back there"—I opened the page for him to make sure he saw it—"I've put a casual pickup—I need that to happen at 2300 tonight."

Pat was looking at the RV notes. I bent my knees to lower myself and moved his face over so I could get eye-to-eye again. "Eleven o'clock tonight, mate, eleven o'clock, OK?"

I knew Pat well enough to tell he knew it was serious. He knew he was fucked up and was trying hard to understand everything I said.

I was glad now that I'd put the details down on paper for him. He looked as if he needed all the help he could get.

"What do you drive?" I asked.

"A red Mustang." He pushed his face closer to mine. "Redder than Satan's balls!" He enjoyed the joke so much he couldn't help laughing.

"Leave via H Street." I pointed away from the rear of the station.

"See you tonight then." He smiled, moving off. From behind I could see a slight veer to the left as he walked.

I waited and checked he wasn't being followed, then went on up toward the parking level, making it look as if I were off to my car. From there I took the elevator back down to the coffee shop.

I went back toward the restaurant, stood off, and watched. Kelly was still struggling with the pizza.

"What took you so long?" she said through a mouthful of mushrooms.

"They ran out of toilet paper." I laughed as I rejoined her. She thought about it a moment and did the same.

22

As soon as we got back to the hotel I put the TV on for Kelly and dumped out the shopping bags on my bed. She asked me what I was doing.

"I'm just helping Pat. You can watch the TV if you want. You hungry?"

"No." She was right; after a pizza the size of a tank mine, it was a stupid question.

I picked up the big red-and-white-framed quartz kitchen clock and sat in the chair by the window. I broke off the frame until I was left with just the hands and clockface, with the quartz mechanics behind it. By bending it very gently, I now started to break off the plastic face. When there was just about an inch of jagged remains around the center of the hands, I finally snapped off the hour and second hands. Only the minute hand was left. I put in a new battery.

Kelly was watching. "Now what are you doing, Nick?"

"It's a trick. Once I've finished I'll show you, OK?"

"OK." She turned back to the TV, but with one eye on me.

I took the egg carton over to the wastebasket and tipped out its contents. I ripped off the top and half of the bottom so that there were just six compartments left. With Scotch tape I fashioned a small sleeve running all the way up the side of the carton, just big enough to accommodate the minute hand. I called over to Kelly, who was humming the theme to a soap. "Do you want to see what this does?"

She looked intrigued as I slotted the carton onto the minute hand.

The nightstand was about four inches below the level of the TV's controls. I positioned the clock on it so it was directly below the infrared sensor on the set and secured it in place with gaffer tape.

Kelly was taking even more interest. "What are you doing?"

"See the remote? Use it to turn the sound up."

She did.

"Now turn it down. OK, I bet you that in about fifteen minutes you can't turn the sound up." I joined her on the bed. "Both of us must sit here and not move, OK?"

"OK." She thought I was going to do something to the remote and smiled as she hid it under the pillow.

It was quite nice really, watching TV during some downtime, apart from every minute hearing, "Is it fifteen minutes yet?"

"No, only seven." By now the egg carton, attached to the minute hand, was working its way up toward the base of the TV.

When the egg carton was upright and obscuring the sensor, I said, "Go on then, try to turn the sound up."

She did, and nothing happened.

"Maybe it's the battery?" I teased.

We put a fresh battery into the remote. Still nothing. She couldn't figure it out, and I wasn't going to explain my trick.

"Magic!" I grinned.

I extracted the rest of the gear, drank some of the orange juice and rinsed out the container, made sure that all the electrical equipment had fresh batteries, and prepared everything to be packed.

It was about 10:20, and Kelly was asleep. I'd have to wake her up and tell her I was going because I didn't want her to get up and start worrying. At times I thought she was just a pain in the neck, but I did want to protect her. She looked so innocent playing starfish again. What would happen to her after all this, I wondered—presuming she survived.

I tested everything again, unplugged the mobile and put it in my pocket, and finally checked my weapon and made sure I had some cash. I picked up a half-empty pack of cookies to eat on the way.

Close to her ear, I whispered, "Kelly!"

I got no response. I shook her a bit. She stirred and I said, "I've put the TV on low so you can watch it if you want—I've got to go out for a couple of minutes."

"Yeah."

I didn't know if she understood or not. I preferred telling her this when she was half-asleep.

"Don't put the lock on this time because I'll take the key. I don't want to wake you when I come in, OK?"

I left, and went down in the elevator and onto the road. The highway traffic rumbled above me. At last, no rain, just air that smelled damp.

I turned left and walked in the opposite direction from the usual, just for one last check. I munched on the cookies as I walked past the target. All the same lights were on; nothing had changed. I wondered if the homeless bloke was underneath, waiting with a chain saw for somebody else to piss on him. I quickened my pace to meet Pat on time. I got to the highway and turned right, following the road, with the roar of traffic above me.

The road swung right, and I started to leave the highway behind. Soon there was a vacant lot on both sides, and the sound of traffic receded. I could hear my footsteps again. To my right were more car pounds. How could Washington be in such a financial mess when the city must be making a fortune on towed vehicles? To my left there were the new, jerry-built office-cum-workshops. I got to the first one, moved off the road into its shadow, and waited.

It was bizarre to be only a few hundred yards from the Pentagon and possibly right under the nose of the people who'd like to see me dead. It was also quite a thrill. It always had been. Pat had a term for it; he called it "the juice."

I heard an engine coming toward me. I looked around the corner of the building. Just one vehicle. It must be him. I pulled my pistol.

The red Mustang drew up. I was in a semicrouch fire position, aiming at the driver with my Sig until it stopped. It was Pat. I could see his Roman nose silhouetted in the ambient light from the airport.

Pistol still in hand, I walked over to the passenger door and opened it; the interior light didn't come on. I got in and closed the door gently, onto its first click only.

Pat had his hand on the handbrake and slowly released it to move off. From a distance it's very difficult to tell whether a car is stopping if you can't see brake lights. That was why Pat was using the handbrake; with no interior light coming on and no noise of a car door shutting, the pickup would have been very hard to clock.

Checking the road behind us, I said, "Turn right at the next intersection."

There was no time to fuck around; he knew it and I knew it. Pat said, "Everything's in the back, in that duffel." He'd come down from whatever high he'd been on and sounded quite embarrassed.

I leaned over and lifted out the laptop. I said, "Is the sound turned off?" When Windows 95 came up, I didn't want the Microsoft sound playing.

He made a face that let me know I was a dickhead for even asking. We both laughed; it broke the ice.

We came up to the concrete wall. As we passed the hotel I was careful not to turn my head. We turned right under the highway and pulled up at stop lights on the other side.

I said, "Go straight and turn right on Kent."

"No problem."

The area was urban and well lit. He kept checking in his rearview mirror to see if we were being followed. My eyes were fixed on the side mirror. I didn't turn and look now; neither of us wanted to appear aware.

There were a few cars behind us, but they had come from other directions. That wasn't to say they weren't following us.

I looked at Pat. His 9mm semi was snug under his right thigh, and in the footwell under his legs he had a 9mm MP5K, an excellent in-car weapon because of its compact size and rate of fire. He'd clipped on double thirty-round magazines.

"What the fuck did you bring that thing along for?"

"I didn't like the sound of your new best mate, Luther. I didn't want him and his buddies dragging me in for a little chat."

We approached another set of lights.

"Do a right to left switch here, mate. Let's see if we have any groupies."

There were one or two cars behind us. The shape of a vehicle's headlights, once it is up close, helps a lot to ID it. If the same shape is up your ass on three turns in the same direction, it's time to get out the worry beads.

Pat signaled and started to move to the right. All the other cars seemed to want straight ahead or to turn right with us; nobody was in the left-turn lane. At the last moment Pat signaled left and moved over—nothing that was aggressive or would provoke a bout of road rage, just a change of mind.

We were all held up at the light. I looked at each car in turn. Just couples or kids cruising—or so it appeared. I'd soon know if I saw them again.

We turned on the green, and nothing followed. It was now time to talk.

Pat started it off. "Your instructions were shit. You said three buildings; there were four. It's a good thing I know what I'm doing." He was waiting for praise.

"The fact is, I couldn't remember how many. The taxi was driving too fast. I can't count anyway."

We were now just cruising. Pat said, "I've been thinking. Do you want me to go in as your number two?"

That would be good. It would get the job done quicker and would mean better security and firepower if we were in trouble. But I decided against it; Pat was my only link with the outside world, and I didn't want to compromise that. I told him my reasons and he nodded his acceptance.

"Take us back to the Pentagon City Metro station, will you, mate?"

I started to prepare for the drop-off and got into acting mode again. He put his signals on, everything correct, nothing untoward, nice slow approach and into the curb outside the Metro. I got out, put my head back in through the open window. "Thanks a lot, mate, see you later." I retrieved the black nylon bag from the backseat. My mind-set was that I'd been playing baseball with him all night and now I was going home; he'd just dropped me off after a drink. I closed the door and tapped the roof a couple of times, and off he drove. I suddenly felt very alone. Had I made the right decision about Pat not coming with me? I made distance and angles before doing a circuit back to the hotel, arriving at about 11:50.

I quickly sorted out and double-checked all the stuff that Pat had given me and packed what I needed into the bag. I emptied my pockets of change and anything else that might rattle or fall out. Then I cut off most of the top end of a trash bag, put in my passport and wallet, wrapped it into a small bundle, and put it into my coat pocket.

Once I'd done that, I jumped up and down one more time to check for noise, picking up the bag and shaking that as well. "Guess what, Kelly? I'm going to go out again in a minute, but I'll be back very soon. Will you be OK?"

But she was out of it. I left the hotel and walked toward the target.

23

The bag had two handles and a long shoulder strap. I walked toward the river with it slung over my shoulder, following the same route as the previous night. Nothing had changed except that the lights from the highway were a bit brighter tonight without the mist.

At the fenced gate I used the handles of the duffel to put it on my back like a rucksack and climbed over. I'd keep it on my back now; if I was confronted, I could run and still keep the kit, or, as a last resort, draw down on them with the Sig.

I got level with the target building, with the vacant lot and fence in between. There was no sound apart from the hum of the highway. I started to pick my way through the clutter. It was muddy—not deep squelching mud, because the ground was quite hard, but I still needed to take my time to get through; I didn't want to slip and make noise, because my pal in the shrubbery might not be the only homeless person around here.

I got to the fence near the PIRA building. Using the bush as cover, I eased the bag off my shoulder and sat on it. The first leg was completed; it was time to stop, look, listen, and take everything in. I needed to be extra careful because I was on my own. Really this was a job for two people, one watching, one doing. I spent a few minutes more just tuning in. Visibility was a bit better tonight because of the stars. Looking left, the parking lot was still empty; to the right, the pallets were still where I'd seen them.

From my coat pocket I pulled out the trash bag protecting my docs. Right at the base of a bush I dug a shallow hole in the mud with my hands, threw in the bundle, and covered it over. This was my emergency cache, my hidey-hole, as Kelly would say. If I got lifted, I would be sterile, and if I got away, there would always be the chance of coming back and retrieving it.

I wiped the mud off my hands onto a small tuft of grass and started to get myself ready for the job. I gently unzipped the duffel. I got out the pair of navy blue coveralls, probably just like the ones Kev's friends had worn.

The problem with climbing over a high fence with a forty-pound bag is that you can spend more time getting stuck and making noise than actually crossing it.

I pulled the draw string from the center of my coat and put it between my teeth. Moving as near to the steel stake support as I could without breaking cover, I then lifted the bag up to shoulder height. Using my shoulders to support its weight, I tied the handles as near to the top of the fence as I could with a quick-release knot, throwing the free end of the string over the top.

Checking that my weapon was secure, I reached up, put my fingers through the chain links, and started to climb. Once on the other side I again stopped, looked, and listened; only then did I climb back up and haul the bag over the fence. I climbed down once more and then got hold of the free end of the string and pulled. The bag came free from the fence, and I took its weight. Then, squatting, I watched and listened again.

Working alone on a job takes a lot of concentration because you can't look and work at the same time, yet both have to be done. So you do one or the other; you either get on with the job or you get on with looking. Try to do both and you'll fuck up.

I stood up, put the bag on my left shoulder, and gently pulled apart the Velcro of the coveralls so that, if necessary, I could get to my weapon. Taking my time, I moved to the left side of the building.

Before I did anything, I had to defeat the motion detector. I was to the left of it, with my back against the wall. Putting the bag in my left hand, I kept my eyes on the detector high above me and started slowly edging toward it. When I got more or less as far as I estimated I could without getting spotted, I bent down and placed the bag by my feet. Everything I did from now on would happen on the near side of the bag.

Security lights that respond to movement make life much harder for people like me, but only if they cover the whole of the building. I found it strange that there was only one detector, rather than two or three overlapping each other to eliminate dead spots. I was expecting, at any moment, to be nailed by one I hadn't noticed. But whoever had installed the security system had obviously worked on the premise that only the lower fire escape door had to be covered and not the approach routes to it.

It was nearly 1 A.M., which left me just over five hours before first light. Time was against me, but I wasn't going to rush. I went the long way around to collect one of the pallets. I got both hands in between the slats of wood, heaved it up against my chest, and started to walk slowly. The ground still had a top layer of mud, and my shoes squelched as they made contact. I finally reached the wall, placed the pallet against the brickwork on my side of the bag, and went back for the second one.

I wedged the two pallets together, the bottom of the second jammed into the gap about three rungs down from the top of the first to make a ladder. I stopped, looked, and listened. The pallets had been heavy; I heard nothing apart from the sound of my lungs gagging for air through my dry throat.

I climbed up on the first pallet, and that was fine. I got up onto the second pallet and it, too, seemed stable enough. I started to climb. I'd moved just two rungs when the whole structure buckled and collapsed. I hit the ground like a bag of shit, and the two pallets slammed down onto each other with a resounding thud and clatter. *Shit. Shit. Shit.*

I was lying on my back, with one of the pallets across my legs. No one came running to investigate, no dogs started barking, no lights came on. Nothing but the noise of the traffic and me swallowing hard, trying to moisten my mouth.

Luckily everything had happened on my side of the bag. I lifted the pallet and crawled from under it, quietly cursing. This was crap. But what else could I have done—bought a ladder at the mall and carried it to the target? I moved to the corner of the building, got down on the tips of my toes and fingers, as if I were going to do a push-up, and stuck my head around toward Ball Street.

I was still annoyed with myself. I could spend all night improvising before I even got into a position to attack this motion detector. Maybe a ladder wasn't such a stupid idea; I should have gotten one and somehow tried to drop it off earlier, then pick it up en route. But it was too late now.

I stood against the wall and reevaluated. I decided to "react as the situation dictated," which was the Firm's favorite get-out clause. It simply meant they didn't know what to do. A bit like me really.

Fuck it, I was going to get Kelly. All she'd have to do was lean against the pallets; she had to be there only for about fifteen minutes and I'd be done. After that she could stay with me or I could drop her back at the hotel. I'd cross that bridge when I came to it.

I picked up the bag, retraced the route to the high fence, and, staying on the target side, dumped the bag and coveralls. Then I followed the fence along, looking for an opening to get to Ball Street. There wasn't time to do the job properly and go back all the way around. I finally found a service alley between two buildings that belonged in some film about the mafia in 1950s New York. It took me down to the road. I turned left and walked briskly to the hotel, no more than two minutes away. It was only then I realized that I didn't have the room key because I'd left it in the trash bag. I'd have to wake Kelly.

I knocked gently at first, then a bit harder. Just when I was starting to sweat, I heard "Hi, Nick." A moment or two later, the door opened.

I gave her a look of concern. "How did you know it was me? You should have waited until I answered." Then I saw the chair and the drag marks on the carpet. I smiled and gave her a pat on the head. "You looked through the peephole, didn't you, clever girl? Hey, because you're so clever, I've got a job for you. I really, really need your help. Would you like to help me?"

She looked sleepy. "What do you want me to do?"

"I'll show you when we get there. Will you come with me?"

"I guess so."

I had a brainstorm. "Do you want to do what your dad does? Because this is what Daddy does for the good guys. You can tell him all about it soon."

Her face brightened. She was a happy bunny again.

She had to more or less run to keep up with me. We got to the alley and headed down toward the vacant lot. It was dark; she was less than eager. She started dragging her feet. "Where are we going, Nick?"

"You want to play spies, don't you?" I said in an excited whisper. "Imagine you are a Power Ranger and you're going on a secret mission."

We reached the empty lot and took the same route toward the chain-link fence. I held her hand, and she kept pace; I hoped she was getting into it.

We got to the bag. I picked up the coveralls and said, "I've got to put these on because they're special spy coveralls." Her face changed when she saw them. I suddenly realized she must have made the connection with the men who'd come to see Kev. "Your Daddy wears them, too. You'd better be a spy as well; undo your coat." I turned it inside out and told her to put it back on. She liked that.

I picked up the bag and put it over my shoulder. I pointed. "Now we'll walk really slowly over there."

When we reached the pallets, I put the bag down in the same place as before. "OK?" I asked, giving her a thumbs-up.

"OK." Thumbs-up.

"See that thing up there? If that sees you, it'll go *waa-waa* and there'll be lights and all sorts, and then we've lost. So you must never go to the other side of that bag, OK?" I pointed.

"OK." We gave each other another thumbs-up.

I repositioned the pallets and showed her what I wanted her to do. I could hear her making little grunts. She had started leaning as I'd shown her and probably thought she had to make noises, doing manual work and all.

I unzipped the bag, pulled out the clock and egg carton,

and slipped the minute hand into its Scotch tape sleeve. I gently squeezed the tape onto it; it held nice and firm.

Kelly was still pushing, and I told her to rest. At least she was into it. She was watching me as I put the clock and egg carton on the ground and placed two elastic bands around my wrist.

"It's magic, watch me!"

She nodded, probably still trying to work out how I'd stopped the remote from operating the TV.

"You ready, Kelly?"

"Ready."

"Let's go!"

I climbed up slowly, trying hard to give the least possible weight and movement for Kelly to handle.

Once up, and about an arm's length from one side of the detector, I got my wrist resting on my chest so that I had a good firm support. I turned the egg carton so that its long edge was horizontal to the ground. Then gently, gently, I moved it about six inches below the motion detector, but not going any farther than its front. Once there, I rested my back against the wall and my wrists on my chest. I'd have to stay like that for about fifteen minutes.

I was waiting for the egg carton to move up against the face of the motion detector, the movement so imperceptible that the detector simply wouldn't register it—otherwise, it would have triggered every time a spider walked across its face. I just hoped Kelly wouldn't give up. I'd find out soon.

Now and again I looked down and winked at her. "Good, this, isn't it?" She looked back at me with a big smile—or so I assumed, because all I could see was an inside-out coat, a hood, and a cloud of breath.

As we both waited for the minute hand to become vertical, all of a sudden there was a single *waa!* of a dying police siren.

Shit! Shit!

It was on the road on the other side of the building. It couldn't have anything to do with us. Otherwise why just one unit, and why use the siren anyway?

I couldn't move. If I did, it would trip the device—and what for? I hadn't even seen a flashlight yet.

"Nick, Nick, did you hear that?"

"It's OK, Kelly. Just keep on pushing. It's OK, I can hear them."

What could I do? I told myself to stay calm and think.

A shout echoed around the parking lot. It had come from Ball Street, but a bit of a distance away. Other voices joined in. An argument had broken out. I couldn't make out what was being said, but there were car doors being slammed and words exchanged, then the sound of a car starting up. All I could think of was that someone had parked while I fetched Kelly. Possibly one of the couples I'd seen from Pat's car—they'd been busy getting the windows steamed up and had got caught by the police. It sounded plausible; I just made myself believe it.

The egg carton was close to vertical. I held my breath. This wasn't a science; we had a fifty-fifty chance of success, no more. If it spotted us, we'd have to get the fuck out of there PDQ and take our chances.

At last the box obscured the detector. No lights came on. With my teeth, I pulled the two thin elastic bands off my wrist; I got the first one over the top of the egg carton and around the motion detector, then pulled the back of it tight, twisted it, and wound around another loop of the band. I put the other band around to make it even tighter. The motion detector was defeated.

I slipped the clock off the box and put it in one of the deep pockets at the front of my coveralls. I clambered down and rubbed Kelly's shoulders. "Good work!"

She gave me a huge smile, still not too sure what it was all about—but hey, this was what Daddy did.

24

The next thing to attack was the alarms, which would mean neutralizing the telephone lines. One of Pat's presents was a disruption device—a black box of computer technology about eight inches by six; coming out of it were six different-colored cables with crocodile grips at the end, a combination of which I'd attach to the telephone line. When the intruder alarm inside the building was tripped, a signal should, in theory, be sent to the monitor station or the police; however, it wouldn't get there because the disruption device would have engaged all the lines.

I got close to Kelly's ear and said, "You can help me even more now." I put the clock back into the bag, and walked past the fire exit doors to the bank of utility boxes.

From the bag I pulled out another item from Pat's shopping list, a six-foot square of thick blackout material, the sort photographers use.

I winked at Kelly. "More magic," I said, "and I'll need you to tell me if it works." I was talking in a very low tone; at night, whispering can sometimes be heard as far away as normal speech. I came right up to her ear again and said, "We've got to be really quiet, OK? If you want to talk to me, just tap me on the shoulder, and then I'll look at you, and you can talk in my ear. Do you understand?"

She spoke into my ear. "Yes."

"That's great, because that's what spies do." I put on my rubber gloves.

She stood there with an earnest expression on her face but looking quite stupid with her coat inside out and the hood up.

I said, "I also want you to tap me on the shoulder if you see any of the light coming out, OK?"

"Yeah."

"Even if there's only a little bit of light coming from me, tap me on the shoulder. OK?"

"Yeah."

I went over to the bank of utilities, put the material over my shoulders, turned on the Maglite with a red filter, and got to work.

I'd used disruption devices many times. I worked with the flashlight in my mouth, and was soon dribbling. I attached the clips to the telephone line in a variety of combinations; as they bit in, a row of lights came on. The aim was to get all six red lights up; when that happened, the lines were engaged. Ten minutes was all it took.

I rested the box in between the electric and gas meters. I only hoped there wasn't an audio alarm as well as a telephone warning. I doubted it somehow, seeing as the budget had stretched to only one external detector.

I took off the blanket, wrapped it in a bundle, and handed it to Kelly. "You've got to hold that for me because I'm going to need it again in a minute. It's fun, this, isn't it?"

"Yes. But I'm cold."

"We'll be inside in a minute and it'll be all nice and warm. Don't you worry about that."

I stopped, looked, listened, then moved over to the door. The next thing was gaining entry.

The Americans are into pin tumbler locks in a big way. There are three main ways to defeat them. The first, and easiest, is just to get a duplicate key. The second is called hard keying. You get a titanium key the size of the lock, and the key has a bolthead that you whack with a hammer; the titanium key pushes in and gouges out all the soft steel. You then fit a special bar onto the bolthead, pull down, and it rips out the whole of the cylinder. Hard keying was no good for me tonight because I wanted to go in and come out without anybody knowing. I'd have to use the third option.

A lock-pick gun is a metal lock-picking device that looks like a small pistol. It has both straight and offset pick options to accommodate different locks and keyways. The "trigger" of the gun is spring-loaded; you squeeze it rapidly, and this trigger movement causes the pick to snap upward within the lock and transfers the striking force to the pins that work the lock mechanism. When the pins are properly aligned, you use a separate tension wrench to turn the lock cylinder. Bad news for people with pin tumblers, but a lock-pick gun can open most of them in less than a minute.

With the blanket over me I turned on the Maglite and put it in my mouth. I inserted the tension wrench into the bottom of the keyway opposite the pins and applied light pressure counterclockwise, in the direction I expected the lock to turn. I then inserted the pick that protruded from the front of the lock-pick gun. Once the gun and tension wrench were in place, I started squeezing the trigger rapidly. I gave it five shots but the lock didn't open, so I increased the tension adjustment and tried again. I could hear it go *clink, clink, clink* as I squeezed; again I turned the tension adjustment so that the needle would strike the pins with just enough force. One by one I heard the pins drop, and eventually the tumbler turned. I held the small tension wrench in the lock and pulled the door to take the pressure off the lock itself, because I didn't want to have too much torque on the wrench and bust it, leaving the telltale bit of metal stuck inside. I pulled the door and felt it give.

I opened it a fraction, half-expecting the sound of an alarm. Nothing. I grinned at Kelly, who was right up against the wall with me, very excited. I closed the door again to keep the light in. "When we get in, you mustn't touch anything unless I tell you, OK?" She nodded.

There's a world outside that is full of mud and shit, and there's a world inside that is clean, and if you don't want to be compromised, you don't combine the two. I took off the coveralls, turned them inside out, and deposited them in the bag. I then took off my shoes and stuck them into the bag. I put on a pair of running shoes, which meant that not only could I move quickly and silently inside but also I wouldn't be leaving a trail of mud everywhere.

I took off Kelly's coat, put it on the right way, and got her to take off her shoes and shove them in the bag.

I had one last check around the area to make sure I hadn't left anything. "We're going to go inside now, Kelly. This is going to be the first time a little girl has done spying like this—ever ever ever. But you must do what I say, OK?"

She accepted the mission.

I picked up the bag, and we moved over to the left-hand side of the door. "When I open this, just walk in a couple of steps and give me enough room to come in behind you, OK?"

"OK."

I didn't want to tell her what to do if anything went wrong, because I didn't want to get her frightened. I just wanted to make it sound as if everything I did was going to work.

"After three—one, two, three." I opened the door halfway, and she went right in. I followed, closed the door, and put the lock back on. Done: we were inside.

We followed the corridor, looking now for the staircase to the second floor. I had the bag on my left shoulder. Through glass doors at the end of the corridor I could see the front of the building. It was a large, open-office area with everything I'd have expected to see: desks, filing cabinets, and rubber plants with name tags. To the left and right of us there were other offices and a copying room. The air-conditioning was still on.

I found the stairs behind unlocked swing doors on the left of the corridor. Gently so that it didn't squeak, I pulled one of them open and let Kelly through. There was no light in the stairwell. I switched on the Maglite and shined the beam on the stairs. We climbed slowly.

Quiet as we were, the stairwell was an echo chamber, and to Kelly the red light must have made everything look scary. She said, "Nick, I don't like this!"

"Shhh! It's OK. Don't worry about it—your dad and I used to do this all the time." I grabbed her hand, and we carried on.

We got to the door. It would open toward us because it was a fire exit. I put down the bag, put my lips up to Kelly's ear, and went, "Shhh," trying to make it all exciting.

I slowly eased the door open an inch and looked into the

corridor. Same as downstairs, the lights were on and everything seemed deserted. I listened, opened the door more to let Kelly through, and pointed where I wanted her to go and stand. She was a lot happier to be in the light.

I put the bag down next to her. "Wait there a minute." I turned right, past the rest rooms and an area that housed the Coke, water, and coffee machines. Next was another photocopy room. I went to the fire-escape door, pulled it toward me, undid the latch, and checked that it would open. I already knew there was nothing on the other side to obstruct it because I'd just been fucking around below it. If there was a drama, we had an escape route.

I picked up the bag again, and we started to walk along the corridor toward the front of the building. We came to the same sort of glass doors as on the floor below, which opened up into the open area. I could see all the workstations, and around the edge there were other offices, all glass-fronted. Obviously the managers liked to keep an eye on everyone.

The windows that fronted the office block were maybe fifty feet away. Light from the street and the corridor gave the whole area an eerie glow. To the right was another glass door that led into another corridor.

I knew what I was looking for, but I didn't know where I'd find it; all I knew was that it certainly wouldn't be in this part of the building.

I looked down and smiled at Kelly. She was as happy as a clam, just as her dad would have been. Keeping well away from the windows, we walked to the other side of the open area toward the glass door.

There was all the normal office stuff: a bulletin board with targets to be reached, pictures of the salesman of the year, and a thank-you card from somebody who'd just had a baby. Most desks had a small frame with pictures of the family, and everywhere I looked there were motivational posters, shit like: WINNERS NEVER QUIT, QUITTERS NEVER WIN, or YOU CANNOT DISCOVER NEW OCEANS UNTIL YOU HAVE THE COURAGE TO LOSE SIGHT OF THE SHORE. I had to stop and read them. The only one I'd seen before was of a big pen of sheep all closed up together, and it said, EITHER LEAD, FOLLOW, OR GET OUT OF THE WAY. It was on the wall of the HQ of the SAS, and had been there for years. It seemed to me to be the only one you needed.

We went through the glass doors. The corridor was about ten feet wide, with plain white walls and not a poster or potted plant in sight—just a large fire extinguisher near the door. The sudden brightness of the lighting made me close my eyes until they adjusted. There were no more doors, but about thirty feet farther down was a T-intersection. I could see offices. We walked down to them; I put down the bag and motioned Kelly to stay with it. "Remember, don't touch a thing."

The handle on the door of each office was a large metal knob with a pin-tumbler lock in the middle. I tested each one, pulling the handle toward me so as not to make any noise, then gently trying to turn it. There were seven offices in this corridor area; all of them were locked. That was nothing special in itself; it just meant that I'd have to use the lock-pick gun on each one in turn.

I went back to the bag. Kelly was standing beside it, desperate for a job. I said, "Kelly, you've really got to help me now. I want you to stand where I tell you, and you've got to tell me if anyone's coming, all right? I've got to do exactly what I did outside and I still need your help, OK?"

I was getting nod after nod. I kept going: "It's really important; it's the most important job tonight. And we've both got to be really, really quiet, OK?"

Another nod. I moved her into position. "I want you to stand on the corner here. Your job is also to look after that bag, because there's a lot of important stuff in it. If you see anything, just tap me on the shoulder like before."

She nodded, and I got out the lock-pick gun.

I got to the first door and started to squeeze. I opened it with the tension wrench and popped my head in, made sure I couldn't see any windows, and turned on the light. It was basically just one office, quite large, about twenty feet by fifteen, a couple of telephones, a picture of the worker's wife, a couple of filing cabinets, very basic furniture. Nothing resembling what I was looking for. I didn't check the filing cabinets—the first look is nothing more than a once-over; you don't want to spend ages in one location only to find out that what you want is sitting on a desk in the room next door.

I didn't relock the door because I might have to go back in. I looked at Kelly, still at her post; I stuck my thumb up and she grinned. She had a big job to do.

I went into office number two. Exactly the same, normal office shit: the year planner with different-colored bits of tape on it, signs stating that there was a strict no-smoking policy, and individual mugs of coffee. People's offices are a reflection of themselves; that's why on a job like this it's so important that nothing be left out of place. They would notice immediately.

I continued down the corridor and went to number three. The same. Four: the same. I was starting to feel I was on a wild-goose chase.

Now for the other three offices; I crossed over the T, and as I passed Kelly she tried to look even more hard at work. I gave her another thumbs-up and went to number five.

It was a much bigger office. There were two couches facing each other with a coffee table in between and a neat arrangement of magazines; a wooden liquor cabinet, smart wooden filing cabinets, framed diplomas and all sorts of things on the wall. But nothing that looked like what I was looking for.

However, behind a large desk and leather swing chair, there was another door. I got the lock-pick gun working. Inside, I found filing cabinets, a fantastically expensive-looking leather-topped desk, and a swivel chair. On the desk was a PC. It wasn't connected to another computer, nor was it connected to a phone line. There wasn't even a telephone in the room. This could be where the key point was.

It could be a fiber-optic cable that's controlling fixed Scud launching sites in northern Iraq, or it could be just one small component in the control room of a nuclear power station, but a key point has to be protected. If it's damaged, everything else is inoperable. It might not take a hundred pounds of explosives to destroy a target; if you can identify the key point, then sometimes one blow from a two-pound hammer will do the trick. I quickly checked the remaining two offices and confirmed that this was the one I should be concentrating on.

I went back to the bag and got out the Polaroid camera. Kelly was still working on her gold star for best spy. I smiled: "I think I've found it, Kelly!"

She smiled back. She didn't have a clue what I was talking about.

I took pictures of the outer office, of what the desktop looked like, a couple of panoramic shots of the area, the coffee table in detail, including the way the magazines were lying; the way that the stuff was set on the table, a picture of all the drawers. In all I took eight shots of the inside of the first office. I now knew exactly what it had looked like when I entered, so when we left I could make sure it looked exactly the same.

I laid the Polaroids in a row on the floor against the wall by the door, just inside the office. The trash from the prints went straight into my pockets.

Waiting for the photographs to develop, I put my head around the door to check on Kelly.

I picked up the bag and brought Kelly with me into the bigger office. I said, "I want you to tell me when those pictures are all developed. Make sure you don't touch a thing, but it's really important I know when those pictures are ready. Your daddy used to do this job."

"Really?"

I closed the door behind us and jammed two wedges in place.

I remembered a job I'd once done with Kev. We'd been sent to plan the insertion of a visual and audio device into an arms dealer's house in Vancouver. This guy was selling nuclear detonators on the black market and we were assigned to recon the house, come back to the UK, and plan how to put the devices in so that a listening station set up in a nearby hotel room could find out what was happening.

Once we got into the house we took photographs of all the bits and pieces that were needed to plan and prepare our

technical attack. After a while we were just bored; it wasn't
that hard a job. We went into the bedroom, wedged the door,
and started going through his wife's closets. She was very
young, and Danish; looking at the two of them in their pictures in the living room, I'd been sure she loved her fifty-
eight-year-old grossly overweight husband: there was no way
it was his millions of dollars she was interested in. It was then
that Kev opened a drawer and discovered untold amounts of
kinky underwear.

The rest of the night was spent taking pictures of each
other with her panties over our heads. In fact, more time and
effort, planning and preparation went into getting her underwear out than into most of the rest of the job. It was while we
were tittering in the darkroom back at the embassy that Kev
had suddenly broken out in a cold sweat, convinced he'd left a
pair of panties on the bed. If he had, there was nothing we
could do about it—except imagine the overweight arms
dealer finding a pair of frillies on his pillow and thinking all
his Christmases had come at once.

I told Kelly to stay where she was, moved into the second
office, and started taking more pictures. The cleaning service hadn't been in here. The other offices had empty wastebaskets, but these two offices hadn't been touched; they
obviously did these themselves, but not every day. Even more
indication that this was a secure area. As I moved around this
small room I saw a shredder beside the filing cabinet, and that
confirmed it. What was being kept secret, however, I didn't
yet know. I put the pictures of the second room on the floor
and went back into the main office.

Looking over Kelly's shoulder, I asked, "How's it going?"

"One's nearly ready, look!"

"Great. What Daddy does also is collect the other pictures." I pointed to the ones next door on the carpet. "But one
at a time, and put them in a nice long line just here." I showed
her that I wanted them against the wall. "Can you manage
that?"

"Yeah, sure." She walked off.

I went back next door and had a quick look at the PC. It

was on but asleep. Kelly was walking in and out, carrying one picture at a time as if it were a bomb.

I pressed the Return key on the keyboard; I didn't want to touch the mouse because maybe it was positioned as a telltale. The screen came alive with Windows 95 and the Microsoft sound—which pleased me, because I'd have been struggling with any other system.

I went back to Kelly, who was still staring at the pictures in the other office.

"Look," she said, "some more are ready!"

I nodded as I delved into the bag for the disk with the sniffer program. I was not as good with computers as the sixteen-year-olds who hack into the USAF computer defense system, but I knew how to use one of these. All you have to do is insert a floppy and off it goes, rooting into passwords, infiltrating programs. There is nothing that they can't get into.

I got up and turned toward the back office. "Won't be long," I said. "Come and tell me when they're ready to look at."

Eyes glued to the pictures, she just nodded. As I walked back in, I looked at the tracks our feet had brushed in the carpet. I'd have to smooth it out again once we had finished.

I put the disk in and started it. The wonderful thing about this particular program was that you had to answer just two questions. There was a *wup!* sound and the first one came up.

Do you want to proceed with X1222? (Y)es or (N)o.

I pressed the *Y* key. Off it went again, whirring and clicking.

A progress bar came up as the machine clicked away. The next stage would take a few minutes.

I looked at the filing cabinet; it was going to be a piece of cake to get into. I went to the bag and retrieved what Pat would have called the "surreptitious entry kit" but which to me was just the pick and rakes wallet. It was a small, black leather case that contained a general assortment of tools designed for the efficient opening of most pin-tumbler, wafer, lever, and double-sided locks. Among the sixty pieces were full, half, and three-quarter rakes; diamond-tip picks and single, double, and half-double ball picks; light, medium, and heavyweight tension wrenches of various lengths and styles;

hook- and saw-type broken-key extractors, probes, feeler pick, needle pick, and double-ball rake. Don't leave home without it.

The progress bar was showing it was just halfway through a process, so I started on the filing cabinets with a feeler pick. It was a standard lock and opened easily. The contents meant nothing to me. They seemed to be spreadsheets and documents with itemized bills and invoices.

I looked at the screen. It was nearly at the end of the progress bar.

The guy who'd produced the sniffer program was a wild-partying, Ecstasy-taking eighteen-year-old whiz kid who was so into body piercing he had half of British Steel hanging out of his face. He had a shaved head—but that was only after we'd been taking the piss out of his close-cropped effort with a star dyed onto the top. The government had been spending hundreds of thousands of pounds trying to develop ways to get into computer programs only to discover, after he had got arrested on some unrelated charge, that this eighteen-year-old had come up with the greatest sniffer program ever written. His weekly unemployment suddenly started looking like a check from the National Lottery.

Wup! The progress bar was complete. Up came a little box that said: *Password: So0}Ssh1time!* Full marks to them for originality; normally it was something like a spouse's nickname, a family member's date of birth, or a license plate. Then up came *Do you wish to proceed? (Y)es or (N)o.*

Fucking right I did. I hit the *Y* key and was into the machine. I went to the bag and I got out the portable backup drive and cables and a handful of high-capacity backup disks.

I went around to the back of the machine and had a good look. I connected the drive cable and plugged it into the socket. I was going to copy everything: operating system, applications, data files, the lot.

I now had to move the mouse. I took a Polaroid but still studied it before moving it.

I selected Full System Backup, and the computer whirred into action, loading information onto the backup disks. I went back to the filing cabinets and had another mooch around, not really knowing what I was looking at, just trying to see if there was anything I recognized.

Wup! The prompt came up, telling me the sniffer software needed another instruction. It had had to work out another password and wanted to know whether to proceed.

I hit the *Y* key.

The machines whirred again. I looked at Kelly. She was sitting by the photos but playing a game with an imaginary companion. Just like her dad; give her a job to do and she'd forget it.

"Kelly, I want you to come with me. If that machine asks me a question again, I might not see it—will you look out for it?"

"OK." It wasn't as exciting a job as she'd been hoping for.

As she sat on the floor with her back against the wall, she looked up at me and said, "I have to go to the bathroom."

"Yeah, in a minute, we'll be finished soon." It was exactly as I remembered, as a kid, sitting in the car, adults not taking me seriously: "We'll be there soon, Nick, just around the corner."

She'd be all right. I said, "I'll take you in a minute."

Wup! I pressed the *Y* key.

Kelly said again, "I really, really have to go."

I couldn't think of the right words for a seven-year-old. In the end I said, "Do you want to go big toilet or little toilet?"

She looked at me blankly. What could I do? Using the rest room in a place like this is always a big no-no because of the compromise factor from noise and visible remains. What you enter with must come out with you, which was why I'd brought an orange juice bottle to piss into and Saran Wrap for anything else. I couldn't imagine getting Kelly to piss in the bottle while I held the film under her bum. That was one thing her dad could do that she couldn't.

She said, "I wanna go, I wanna go," and started crossing and uncrossing her legs. Then she stood up and was bouncing up and down on the balls of her feet.

I said, "OK, we'll go. Come on, come with me."

I didn't need this, but I had to do it. I couldn't have her shitting all over the carpet.

I took hold of her hand. I retrieved the door stops from the outer office door, gently opened it, and checked the corridor.

We moved across the open office, through the glass door, and into the fire-escape corridor. We went into the rest room and turned the light on. Poor girl, she was pulling down her trousers in such a hurry she was fumbling with her buttons. I helped her, but even so, she nearly missed the pot altogether in her rush.

I was wasting time. I had to return to the machine, and she might be there for five minutes or more. Backing away, I said, "Don't move, and don't flush the toilet afterward; I'll do all that for you. I just have to go back one minute and get the computer working. I'll be right back. Remember—shhh, be quiet!"

At that particular moment she didn't really care where I went or what I did. She was in her own heaven.

Wup! I left her and quietly ran toward the office. Once I'd got the disk copying again, I'd come back to Kelly, fish the shit out with my hand, and put it in the Saran Wrap. Then I'd keep pushing the toilet brush down the bowl to lower the level of the water by pushing it through the U bend and get some fresh water from the drinking fountain to bring the level back up again.

I got back to the office and pressed the *Y* key. Then I went to the bag to fetch the Saran Wrap.

And it was then that I heard her scream.

Fuck!

Instinctively, I pulled out my pistol and stood against the wall. I checked chamber and took the safety catch off with my thumb.

I could feel my heart beating faster as the familiar sensation of cold sweat broke out over my body. My body was getting ready for fight or flight. The screaming was from the area of the fire escape, my only way out. It looked as if I would have to fight.

25

My heart was pumping so hard it was nearly in my mouth. I'd learned long ago that fear is a good thing. If you aren't scared, you're lying—or you're mentally unstable. Everyone has fear, but as a professional you use training, experience, and knowledge to block out the emotion and help you overcome the problem.

I was still thinking it out when I heard a longer, more pitiful scream of "Nick! Help me!" The sound went through me like a knife. Images flashed through my mind of her curled up in a fetal position in the hidey-hole, of brushing her hair and playing that stupid video-watching game.

I was by the office door leading out into the corridor.

I heard a man's voice shout: "I've got her! I'll fucking kill her! Think about it. Don't make me do it!"

It was not an American voice. Or Hispanic. Or anything else I might have expected. But I knew it right off: West Belfast.

It sounded as if they were now in the main office. He started to shout more threats at me above Kelly's screams. I couldn't make out every word, and I didn't have to. I got the message.

"OK, OK! I'm going to come into your view in a minute." My voice echoed in the semidarkness.

"Fuck you! Throw your weapon into the corridor. Do it!"

Then I could hear him shouting at Kelly, "Shut the fuck up! Shut up!"

I came out of the office and stopped just short of the corridor intersection. I slid my pistol out into the main corridor.

"Put your hands on your head, walk out to the middle of

the corridor. If you do anything else, I'll fucking kill her—do you understand?"

The voice was controlled; he didn't sound like a madman.

"Yes, I'm coming out, my hands are on my head," I said. "Tell me when to move."

"Now, you fucker!"

Kelly's screams were deafening, even through the glass door.

I started to walk and, in four paces, came to the intersection. I knew that if I looked left I'd be able to see them through the door, but that wasn't the game just now. I didn't want eye-to-eye; he might overreact.

"Stop where you are, you fucker!"

I stopped. I could still hear the whimpering. I didn't say a word or turn my head.

In the movies you always hear the good guy give encouragement to the hostage. In real life it doesn't work like that; you just shut up and do what you're told.

He said, "Turn left."

I could now see them both in the shadows. Kelly had her back to me as he dragged her toward me with a weapon stuck in her shoulder area. He pushed the glass door open with his foot and came out into the light of the corridor.

As I saw him my heart dropped from beating in quick time to a slow thud. I felt as if a ten-ton weight had just been dropped on my head. It was Morgan McGear.

He was dressed very smartly in a dark-blue two-piece suit and a crisp, clean white shirt; even his shoes looked expensive. It was a far cry from the Falls Road uniform of jeans, bomber jacket, and running shoes. I couldn't see what sort of weapon he was carrying; it looked like some sort of semiautomatic.

He was watching me, checking me out. What was I doing here with a small child? He knew he had control, knew there wasn't shit I was going to do. He now had his left hand wrapped around her hair—what a pity I hadn't cut more off in the motel room—and he had the weapon stuck into her neck. This was not a meaningless gesture; he was capable of killing her.

She looked hysterical, poor kid; she was panicking big-time.

He called out, "Walk toward me—slowly. Walk now. C'mon, don't fuck with me, you shite."

Every noise in the corridor seemed to be amplified ten-fold; McGear shouting with spit flying out of his mouth, Kelly screaming. It seemed to reverberate around the whole building.

I did as he said. As I got nearer I looked at her and tried to get eye-to-eye; I wanted to comfort her, but it didn't work. Her eyes were swollen with tears, her face was soaking wet and red. Her jeans weren't even zipped up yet.

He had me within about ten feet of him, and now I looked into his eyes—and I could see that he knew he was in a position of power, but sweating a bit. His voice might have sounded confident, but his eyes gave it away. If his job was to kill us, now was his moment. With my eyes I said to him, *Just get it over and done with.* There are times when after using plans A, B, and C you must accept you're in deep shit—or shite, as this boy would say.

He snapped, "Stop!" and the echo seemed to reinforce the threat.

I looked at Kelly, still trying to get that eye-to-eye contact to say: *Everything's all right, everything's OK, you asked me to help you and I'm here.*

McGear told me to turn around. Now I knew it was really time to sweat.

He said, "On your knees, you fucker."

Facing away from him, I went down so I was sitting back on my heels; if I had the chance to react, at least from here I had some sort of springboard.

"Up!" he shouted. "Get up, get your ass up!" He knew what I was doing; this boy was good. "Kneel upright. More, more. Stay there, fuck you, think you're some fucking hard guy . . ."

He moved behind me, dragging Kelly with him. I could still hear her cries, but there was another noise now. Something else was moving; it wasn't just Kelly's moans. I didn't know what it was. I just knew that something unhealthy was going to happen. All I could do was close my eyes, grit my teeth, and wait for it.

He took a couple of labored steps toward me. I could hear Kelly getting nearer, obviously still in tow.

"Keep looking straight ahead," he said, "or I will be hurting the wee one. Do what I say or—"

Either he didn't finish his sentence or I didn't hear it. The bang on the top of my shoulders and head sent me straight down like a bag of shit.

I went into a semiconscious state. I was awake, but I knew I was fucked, like a boxer who goes down and is trying to get up to show the referee that he's all right, but he's not, he's all over the place.

I felt nailed to the floor; I looked up, but couldn't see what had done the damage. It hadn't been a pistol. It takes a decent weight to knock a person over. Whatever it was, it took me down but good.

The strange thing about the next bit was that I knew what was happening but couldn't do anything about it. I was aware of McGear pulling me over onto my back and jumping astride me, and I felt cold metal being pushed into my face and finally into my mouth. Slowly, slowly, it dawned on me that it was the pistol, and the jumble of words he was screaming became clearer and clearer: "Don't fuck with me! Don't fuck with me! Don't fuck with me!" He sounded out of control.

I could smell the fucker. He'd been drinking; there was alcohol on his breath. He reeked of aftershave and cigarettes.

He was sitting astride me with his knees on my shoulders and the pistol stuck in my mouth. He still had his left hand around Kelly's hair and had pulled her onto the floor; he was tugging her from side to side like a rag doll, either for the sheer hell of it or perhaps just to keep her screaming and make me more compliant.

All I could hear was scream, scream, scream; "Don't fuck with me!"; scream, scream, scream; "Don't fuck with me! Don't fuck with me! Think you're a fucking hard guy, do you, think you're a fucking tough guy, huh?"

Not good. I knew what they did to "hard guys." McGear once got an informer into a room for questioning; his kneecaps were drilled with a Black & Decker; he was burned by an electric fire and electrocuted in the bath. He managed to jump out a window naked but broke his back. They then dragged him into the elevator and shot him.

I felt as if I were drunk. I was aware of what was happening, but it was taking too long for the message to reach my brain.

Then the software started to kick in. I tried to see if the hammer was back on the pistol, but all I could still see were bubbles of red light in front of my eyes, and starbursts of white. All I could make out was all this screaming and ranting from him. "You bastard! I'm gonna fuck you up! Who are you?" and the screaming from Kelly. It was total confusion.

I tried again to focus my eyes, and this time it worked—I could see the position of the hammer.

The hammer was back. It was a 9mm. But what about the safety catch? It was off.

There was nothing I could do. He'd got his finger on the trigger; if I struggled, I was dead, whether he intended it or not.

He said, "You think you're fucking hard? Do you? Do you? We'll soon see who is the hard man." Then he jumped his weight up and down to crush my chest, forcing the pistol harder into my mouth.

To add to the confusion, Kelly was still screaming with terror and pain. I didn't have a clue what was expected of me; all I knew was that I had a pistol stuck in my mouth and this guy was in charge.

He started to regain his composure. The pistol was still shoved hard into my mouth, but he was beginning to ease himself to his feet. He did it by putting weight on the pistol and then against my face; as the pistol turned in my mouth, it twisted painfully up against my cheek and teeth, scraping them with the sight. And all the time he kept a grip on Kelly's hair, pulling her around all over the place.

He moved back, the pistol now aimed at my chest.

"Get back up on your knees!"

"All right, mate, OK. You got me, OK."

As I moved I saw what had taken me down. The fire extinguisher had split open the skin at the back of my head. There was blood oozing out everywhere and matting down my hair. There was nothing I could do; you just can't stop capillary bleeding.

I got back on my knees, my ass up in the air again so I wasn't resting on the heels of my feet, and I was looking at him, trying to sort myself out. He started to walk backward toward the office, keeping the weapon pointed at me.

"Come on, hard man, on your knees."

I got the hint, he wanted me to follow him.

By now Kelly was a mess. There was a small trail of my blood being wiped along the floor. Kelly must have been kneeling in it before she was moved. She had her hands on his wrist, trying to support herself. She kept on tripping up, walking on her knees, trying to pick herself up, as if she were getting dragged behind a horse. All he was interested in was moving backward with the weapon pointing at me.

He said, "Stay where the fuck you are!" and then shuffled backward past the door to the large office.

I was trying to compose myself; I knew I didn't have long to live unless I took some action.

"In there!"

I started to shuffle in.

"Walk!"

I got up and walked into the room, my back still toward him. I walked slowly toward the coffee table. I was just about to move off to the side to go around it when he said, "Stop! Turn around!"

I did as I was told. It was an unusual command because normally you want the person you're holding facing away from you so they don't know what's going on. If you can't see, it's difficult to react.

As I turned, I saw Kelly sitting on the leather swivel chair that now had been dragged to the left of the desk. McGear was standing behind her. He still had his left hand wrapped around her hair and was pulling her back onto the seat and pointing the 9mm at me.

The top half of a semiautomatic, the part of the weapon on which the fore and rear sights are mounted, is called the top-slide. It moves back when you've fired to eject the empty case, then picks up a round on its return. If it's moved back by as little as an eighth of an inch, the weapon can't fire—so if you're quick enough, you can shove your hand hard onto the front of the muzzle, push the topslide back, and the trigger won't work as long as you can keep it there. It's got to be really quick, really aggressive, but I had nothing to lose.

There was a lull—was he trying to make a decision about what to do? It was less than twenty seconds, but it seemed like forever.

Kelly kept crying and whimpering; there must have been friction burns on her knees where she had been dragged earlier. With his left hand McGear yanked her upright and said, "Shut the fuck up!" And just as he did that, we stopped having eye-to-eye contact; I knew that it was time.

I leaped forward, shouting at the top of my voice to disorient him, got my right hand and pushed it as hard as I could against the muzzle, pushing down on the topslide so I moved it back maybe half an inch.

He shouted a loud, drawn-out "Fuck!" half in anger, half in pain.

I got hold of his wrist, pulled it toward me, and pushed away with my right hand against the topslide. He tried, but it was too late for him; it didn't fire. I needed to grip my hand around the muzzle now to keep the topslide back.

As this was happening, I was pushing toward the wall—just push, push, push; he still had hold of Kelly, and she was being dragged around, screaming at the top of her voice. I shut her out of my mind, keeping my eyes on the pistol, my body bent down, pushing and pushing. I felt the air leave his body as he hit the wall. Kelly was getting in the way; I was stepping on her, he was stepping on her, and she was screaming out in pain. He must have decided he needed two hands to sort me out because, the next thing I knew, Kelly was running.

I started to head-butt in earnest. I was hitting him with my head, I was hitting him with my nose, with the side of my face. My nose was hurting and bleeding as much as his must have been, but I just kept on butting, butting, and butting, trying to do as much damage to him as possible, and, at the same time, keeping him against the wall.

He was screaming, "You fucker! You fucker! You fucker! You're dead!"

And I was doing exactly the same back, screaming, "Fuck you! Fuck you! Fuck! Fuck!"

I still had him pushed right against the wall. As I butted him, his teeth cut into my face, opening up my forehead and just below my eye. You don't notice the pain when the adrenaline is pumping. I head-butted him again and again; it wasn't going to do him much lasting damage, but that was all I could do at the moment. My hands were on the weapon and I was shouting all sorts of shit at the top of my voice to scare him and, even more, to keep me psyched.

As his head came down, I bit the first thing that came into range. I felt my teeth on the taut skin of his cheek. There was that initial resistance, and then my teeth broke into what felt like warm squid and I was ripping his face open. He screamed out even louder, but I was focused totally on what I was doing; all other thoughts went out the window and I bit, gouged, did whatever damage I could.

My teeth sank in and in. He squealed like a pig. I had a mouthful of his cheek and was ripping and tearing. I saw terror in his eyes.

By now there was blood all over the two of us; I could taste the iron tang of it, and my whole face was drenched from the cuts on my face and his, all getting mixed in with our sweat. Trying to clear my mouth, I choked some of it up into the back of my nose.

All the time, I was twisting the weapon away from me and trying to keep the topslide back. He was still pretty switched on and was squeezing the trigger, but nothing was happening—for now. His other hand was pulling at my fingers, trying to pry them off the weapon. As long as I kept my hand gripped around that topslide, I'd be all right. I kept on pushing and pushing, keeping him up against something firm so I could lean against him, because all I wanted to do was move that pistol around.

I was still biting and gnawing. I'd gone through the first

part of his cheek and kept on going. By now I was biting the top of his eyelid, I was biting his nose, everywhere I was ripping through the skin onto the bone of his jaw and skull.

I was running out of breath because the adrenaline was draining away, and pushing him against the wall had taken a lot of physical strength out of me. Then I started to choke, and I realized I had some of his skin at the back of my throat. I could hear air being sucked into the hole in his cheek as he was breathing; I could hear my own throat rattling, blocked by chunks of his skin.

I was fighting him by feel, not sight. Our blood was burning into my eyes. Everything was blurred. I didn't know where Kelly was and at this stage I didn't care. I couldn't help her until I'd helped myself.

I was still trying to get the pistol into him somewhere. I didn't give a fuck where it went—it could go into his leg, into his stomach, I didn't give a fuck, as long as I could start shooting him.

His screams increased as my finger wrapped around his on the trigger.

I turned it around, let go of the topslide, and squeezed.

The first two shots missed, but I kept on shooting. I moved it around again and got him in the hip and then the thigh. He went down.

Everything stopped. The lack of noise was absolutely deafening.

After two or three seconds I could hear Kelly's screams rebounding off the walls. At least she was still somewhere in the building. She sounded as though she was throwing a fit. All I could hear was a high-pitched continuous scream. I was too fucked up to do anything about it. I was too busy trying to cough up McGear's skin.

I'd find her later. I pulled myself up. I was in pain. The back of my neck felt as if it could no longer hold my head.

He writhed on the ground, bleeding and begging, "Don't kill me, man! Don't kill me! Don't kill me!"

I got hold of the pistol and did to him as he had done to me, jumping astride him, ramming it deep into his mouth.

For several seconds I just sat there trying to catch my

breath. McGear's body might be dying, but his eyes were alive.

"Why did you kill the family?" I said, pulling the pistol from his mouth so he could speak. "Tell me and you'll live."

He was looking at me as if he wanted to say something but didn't know what.

"Just tell me why. I need to know."

"I don't know what the fuck you mean."

I looked into his eyes and I knew he was telling the truth.

"What is on that computer?"

There was no slow reaction this time. His lip curled and he said, "Fuck you."

I jammed the weapon back into his mouth and said quietly, firmly, almost sort of fatherly, "Look at me! Look at me!"

I looked back into his eyes. No point carrying this on. He wouldn't say anything. He was too good for that.

Fuck it. I pulled the trigger.

26

I took a deep breath and wiped away the blood that had splattered onto my face when he took the round. I tried to regain some form of composure. Stop, just take that couple of seconds, take another deep breath, and try to work out what the fuck to do next.

The shots would have been heard and reported. At least, I had to plan as if they were. I could still hear Kelly screaming in the distance somewhere.

First priority was the equipment. I pushed myself up off McGear's chest and staggered back into the small office. I ripped the cable and electric cord from the PC, took the sniffer software out of the floppy drive, and put it in my top pocket. I packed everything in the bag and returned to the large office.

I went over to McGear. He looked like Kelly when she was sleeping, except this starfish had a face like a pizza and a large exit wound in the back of his head oozing gray stuff onto the plush carpet.

I picked up the bag, slung it over my left shoulder, and moved into the corridor to pick up my pistol. I had to find Kelly. Easy—I just had to follow the screams.

She was fighting with the fire-escape door, the back of her coat splattered with blood. She was right up against the door trying to manipulate the handle, but she was in such a state that her fingers couldn't do it. She was jumping from foot to foot, screaming and beating her fists against the door in frustration and fright. I came up behind her, got hold of her arm, and shook her.

"Stop it! Stop it!"

It wasn't the right thing to do. She was hysterical.

I looked into her eyes under the tears and said, "Look, people are trying to kill you. Do you understand that? Do you want to die?"

She tried to shake me off. I put my hand over her mouth and listened to her blocked-up nose fighting for oxygen. I got her face right up against mine. "These people are trying to kill you. Stop crying, do you understand me? Stop crying."

She went quiet and limp and I let go of her. "Give me your hand, Kelly."

It was like holding lettuce. I said, "Be quiet and just listen to me. You've got to listen to me, OK?" I was looking at her eyes and nodding away.

She just stared through me, tears still running down her cheeks, but she was trying to hold them back.

I pushed the fire-exit bar and cold, damp air hit my face. I couldn't see anything because my night vision was fucked. I dragged Kelly by the hand, and the clunks of our footsteps echoed down the metal stairs. I didn't give a fuck about the noise; we'd made enough already.

Running toward the fence, I slipped in the mud. Seeing me fall, Kelly let out a cry and burst into tears again. I shook her and told her to shut up.

As we got to the fence I could already hear sirens on the highway. I had to assume they were coming for us. After a moment I could hear more noise coming from the parking lot area.

"Wait here!"

I climbed up the chain-link fence with the equipment, dropped it over the other side, and jumped. They were getting closer, but I couldn't see them yet. Kelly was looking at me from the other side of the fence, bobbing up and down, hands on the wire.

"Nick—Nick . . . Don't leave me here."

I didn't even look where I was digging. My eyes were fixed on the gap between the two buildings. Coming from my right to left, flashing blue lights on the highway lit up the sky.

Kelly's whimpers turned to sobs.

I said, "We'll be all right, we'll be all right. Just stay where you are. Look at me! Look at me!" I got eye-to-eye. "Stay where you are!"

The lights and noise were now on Ball Street. I got hold of my documents and put them in my pocket.

All the vehicles had stopped, their sirens dying. The blue lights were still flashing, reflecting on Kelly's face, wet with tears.

I looked at her through the fence and whispered, "Kelly! Kelly!"

She was in a daze of fear.

"Kelly, follow me now. Do you understand? Come on!"

I started moving along the fence. She was whining and wanting her mommy. She sounded more and more desperate. As her feet slapped the ground it made her pleas sound like somebody talking in a helicopter. I said, "You've got to keep up, Kelly, you've got to keep up. Come on!"

I was moving fast. She slipped and fell into the mud. I wasn't there to pick her up this time. She lay there sobbing. "I want to go home, I want to go home so bad. Please take me home."

By now there were three police cars on the scene. We weren't even two hundred yards away yet. Very soon they would use their searchlights and spot us.

"Get up, Kelly, get up!"

The target now seemed surrounded by a haze of blue and red lights. Flashlights were already jerking in the darkness at the rear.

We carried on until we got level with the alley. The sound of sirens again filled the night.

I climbed over the fence, the bag nearly landing on top of Kelly as I let it fall. I grabbed her right hand with my left and started toward the alley.

I needed to find a car that was parked in the shadows and old enough to have no alarms.

We emerged from the alley and turned left, following a line of parked cars. I found an early nineties Chevy. I put the bag down and ordered Kelly, "Sit by this."

I opened the bag and got out the picks. Minutes later I was

in. I wired up the ignition and the engine fired. The digital clock said 3:33.

I let the engine run and put the windshield wipers and heater on full blast to clear the morning dew. I got hold of Kelly and the bag and threw them both in the back. "Lie down, Kelly, go to sleep." No argument from her on the lying down. She might have trouble sleeping, though. Perhaps for the rest of her life.

I drove to the road and turned left, nice and slow. After just a quarter of a mile I spotted flashing lights coming toward me. I got my pistol out and put it under my right thigh. If these boys stopped me, I'd have to take them on. There was no way I was going to let the fuckers take us.

I shouted back at Kelly, "Stay down, do not get up, do you understand?"

There was no reply.

"Kelly?"

I got a weak "Yes."

If I had to kill these policemen, it would be unfortunate, but when all was said and done this was the sort of thing they got paid for. I made my plan. If they stopped me, I'd wait until one or both came within range. The pistol was where my hand would naturally go, and I'd draw down on them.

The flashing blue and red came closer. I just drove on toward them. My mind-set was that I was a shift worker, on my way to earn my living. Now their lights were making me screw up my eyes so I could see beyond.

I wasn't worried. I felt very calm. Just wait and see. They sped past at more than sixty.

I looked in the rearview mirror. They hit the brakes; now I was sweating. I watched and made distance at the same time. The brake lights went off. Either they'd just been slowing down or they'd changed their minds.

I needed to dump this car before first light, which was probably the earliest the owner would discover it missing. I also had to get both Kelly and me a change of clothes, and we had to get into another hotel.

Kelly started yelling, "I want to go home! I want to go home! I want my—"

"Kelly, we are going home! But not yet!" I had to shout to cut in.

I couldn't see her, so I tilted the mirror. She was curled up with her thumb in her mouth. My mind flashed back to the times I'd found her like that and I said, quietly, "We will, don't worry."

We were following a road that seemed to parallel the Potomac, on its west side. After about half an hour I found an all-night supermarket. I parked. There were maybe twenty or thirty vehicles outside; at that time of the morning most of them probably belonged to employees.

Kelly didn't ask why we were stopping. I turned around and said, "I'm going to get us some more clothes. Do you want anything? Shall I see if they've got a deli and we'll get some sandwiches?"

She whimpered, "Don't go, don't leave me!" She looked as if she'd been slapped. Her face was bright red, with puffy eyes and wet hair stuck to her face. You don't take a beaten-up seven-year-old with blood on her clothes into a store after four in the morning.

I leaned over into the back, unzipped the bag, and took out the coveralls. I said, "I've got to leave you here. I need somebody to look after everything." I pointed to the bag. "Can you do that for me? You're a big girl now, a great spy."

She nodded reluctantly.

I started to get the coveralls on while still sitting in the car seat.

"Nick?"

"What?" I was busy fighting with a leg.

"I heard shooting. Is that man dead?"

"Which man is that?" I didn't want to turn around, didn't want to face her. "No, he's not. I think he made a mistake and thought we were someone else. He'll be OK."

I was now arching my back to get the top half on. "The police will take him to the hospital."

That was enough of that. I quickly got out of the car and poked my head back in. Before I even started to outline the routine she said, "You're coming back, aren't you? I want to go home and see Mommy."

"Definitely, I will come back, no problems, and you will see Mommy soon."

I turned the interior light on and moved the rearview mirror so I could see my face. The deep cuts on my forehead and under my eye were still wet, the plasma trying hard to get a scab going. I spat on my hand and used the cuff of the coveralls to wipe the rest of the blood off, but there wasn't much more I could do. Industrial accident.

I signaled Kelly to lock the door and lie down. She nodded and complied.

I grabbed a cart and went through the electric door. I got money from the ATM, then two sets of everything for Kelly and me, plus a washing and shaving kit and a box of baby wipes, and some painkillers for my neck. It was hurting bad now. I could look left or right only by turning my whole body. I must have looked like a robot. I threw in some Coke, chips, and cookies.

There weren't many shoppers. My cuts drew the odd glance but no stares.

I got back to the car and tapped on the window. I didn't say anything. Kelly stared up; the windows were now covered in condensation, so she had to wipe it with her sleeve. I could see she'd been crying. I pointed at the lock, and she opened it.

I was all big smiles. "Hiya, how's it going?"

There wasn't much of a reply. As I dumped all the purchases onto the passenger seat, I said, "Look, I've got a present for you." I showed her a Snickers bar. There was a reluctant smile. She took it and opened it.

I looked at the car clock. It was nearly 5 A.M. We started driving toward the Beltway, then headed west.

I saw the sign for Dulles International and slowed down for the exit. We had to dump the car soon; I had to assume that the driver was an early riser.

Kelly was lying in the back, staring at the door. Either she was in a dream world, or she had been damaged mentally by what she had seen. At the moment I didn't really care which.

We were about eight miles from Dulles. I started to keep a lookout for hotels. I saw the sign for an Economy Inn.

Absolutely perfect—but first, we had to get ourselves cleaned up.

As we continued on toward the airport I could see the wing lights of an aircraft making its approach about four miles away. I followed the signs to the economy parking, having stopped just short to check for cameras at the entrance. There weren't any; they must register on the way out. I took my ticket and parked among thousands of other cars.

"Kelly, we're going to get you dressed in some new clothes," I said.

I showed her what I'd bought, and as she was getting undressed, I got out the baby wipes and cleaned her face. "Here, let's get rid of all those tears, let's clean you all up, here you are, here's a brush." I brushed her hair—too quickly; it hurt her. "OK, let's get this sweatshirt on you. Here you go. There, you're looking good. Here's another wipe—blow your nose."

While she was doing that, I got myself changed as well, then dumped all the clothes in the passenger footwell. Kelly was still looking miserable as the shuttle took us to the terminal.

27

We walked into the departures area. The terminal was busier than I'd been expecting at this time of the morning. People were checking in all along the lines of desks, hanging around in the shops, or sitting in the cafes, reading newspapers.

I wasn't saying much to Kelly, just holding her hand as I moved along, bag on my left shoulder, looking for the Arrivals sign, then to the taxi stand. An escalator showed me the way down. We were nearly at the bottom when Kelly announced, "I need to go to the bathroom."

"You sure?" I just wanted to get out of there.

"I'm really sure."

"OK." After the last time I'd learned my lesson.

I followed signs to the rest rooms. They were to the left, near the large exit doors from international arrivals. You went in through one of two large openings in the wall and immediately came across a row of seven or eight disabled toilets, all unisex, and on either side of this were the entrances to the men's and women's rooms. I stayed outside in the main concourse, watching all the people who were waiting for the automatic doors to open and their loved ones to be disgorged.

You always know when you're being stared at. I'd been standing there a minute or two when I became aware. I looked up. It was an old woman, standing against the rail facing me on the opposite side of the channel made by the barriers, obviously waiting for somebody to come through. There was a silver-haired man with her, but her eyes were fixed on my face.

She looked away, turning her back to the exit doors, even

though people were streaming out with their carts. Every few seconds I heard a scream of joy as people were reunited.

What had she been looking at? The cuts on my face? I hoped it was just that. There was nothing I could do about it anyway. I would just shake it off, but keep an eye on her all the same.

Then I saw her start talking to her husband. She wasn't passing the time of day. Her body language looked urgent and agitated. He looked over in my direction, then back at her; he gave her a shrug that said, *"What the hell are you talking about, woman?"* She must have seen Kelly and me going into the rest rooms and said to herself, *"Where do I know those two from?"*

I wasn't going to move. I wanted to see what she was doing. The moment she started to walk away, I'd have to take action.

I could tell she was still trying to figure it out. I felt my heart pumping. I avoided eye contact, but I knew she was staring. Any moment now she'd remember the news report where she'd seen Kelly's face.

The seconds ticked by. At last Kelly came out and stood by me, a big smile on her face. "Shall we go now?" I said, grabbing her hand before she could answer.

As I turned with her for the exit, I could clearly see the woman tugging her husband's arm. She recognized us. However, the husband had now seen whoever it was they were meeting and was looking the other way.

She pulled his arm more urgently.

I wanted to run, but that would confirm it for her. We walked, and I talked crap to Kelly with the actions of a happy dad. "Look at those lights, aren't they nice? This is the airport I fly into every time I come here, have you been here before?" Kelly didn't have time to answer any of my stupid questions.

I had to fight the urge to turn around and look. I started to think, *what if?* If I got the police on me here, I was fucked. There was nowhere to go, just more of the airport, with more security than you could shake a nightstick at. My eyes were darting around. We had about thirty or forty yards to go to the exit sign. With each step I expected to hear a cop shouting for me to freeze. All I could hear was the general hubbub and the occasional squeal of greeting.

We reached the exit, turned left, and started walking downhill on a wide ramp that led down to the pickup points and the taxis. The moment we'd made that angle I started to move faster and chanced a look behind.

There was a fine drizzle in the air as we exited and looked for the stand.

Kelly said, "What's up?"

I said, "There's the taxis, let's go."

We had to wait for three other people in the line before it was our turn. I felt like a child who desperately wants a toy and cannot wait any longer. *Come on, come on!*

At last we jumped into a cab and drove off. I turned and looked behind me. Nothing. I still couldn't relax. Kelly could obviously sense the drama but didn't say another word.

I tried to block it out of my mind. Look hard enough and you'll find a positive in even the worst situation—that was what I'd always told myself. But I couldn't get a silver lining out of what had just happened. If the old woman did make the connection and told the police she had seen us heading for the taxis, it was negatives all the way.

I looked at Kelly and yawned. "I'm sleepy," I said. "What about you?"

She nodded and put her head in my lap.

I gave the driver directions. Once off the freeway we drove a few blocks, then I got him to pull in. I watched him drive away as we stood in the parking lot of the Marriott. We would walk to the Economy Inn from there.

"We're going to a hotel now," I said. "Usual story. I'll be saying a lot of things that aren't true, and all you've got to do is be quiet and look really tired, OK? If you do what you're told and it works out, we can go home." We walked toward the reception.

There was a young guy on the desk, his head buried in a textbook. We went through all the same routine, only this time I'd been beaten up during the robbery. He looked embarrassed. "All of America's not like this, you know. It's beautiful." He started talking about the Grand Canyon; after making a promise that I'd make a point of visiting it this trip, I turned and walked out.

When we got to the room, I started helping her off with her coat. As she turned so that her other arm came out of the sleeve, she asked without warning: "Are we going to see Mommy and Daddy now?"

"Not yet, we've still got things to do."

"I want my mommy, Nick. I want to go home. You promised."

"We will go soon, don't worry."

"Are you sure Mommy and Daddy and Aida will be there?"

"Of course they will be."

She didn't look convinced and sat on the edge of the bed. It was crunch time. I couldn't carry this on anymore. If we got out of this mess, I couldn't bring myself to let her be dumped on her grandparents or whoever and find out what a lying bastard I'd been all this time.

"Kelly . . ."

I sat next to her and started stroking her hair as she laid her head on my lap.

"Kelly, when you get home, Mommy, Daddy, and Aida will not be there. They've gone to heaven. Do you know what that means?"

I said it as almost a throwaway, not really wanting to get into it any deeper. I wanted her to say, "Oh, I see," and then ask me if we could have Mickey D's.

There was a pause while she thought about it. All I could hear was the hum of the air-conditioning.

Her face creased into a frown. "Is it because I didn't help Daddy?"

I felt as if somebody were stabbing me. But it wasn't too hard a question; I felt OK answering that one. "Kelly, even if you had tried to help Daddy, they still would have died."

She was crying quietly into my leg. I rubbed her back and tried to think of something to say.

I heard: "I don't want them to be dead. I want to be with them."

"But you are." I was fumbling for words.

She lifted her face and looked at me.

"You are with them. Every time you do something that you did with them means they are with you."

She was trying to work this one out. So was I.

"Every time I eat a pizza with mushrooms I think of your mommy and daddy, because I know your mommy liked them. That's why they are never far away from me—and why Mommy, Daddy, and Aida will be with you all the time."

She looked at me, waiting for more. "What do you mean?"

I had to think quickly. "I mean, every time you put plates on a table Mommy will be with you because she showed you how. Every time you catch a ball, Daddy is with you because he taught you. Every time you show someone how to do something, Aida is with you—that's because you used to show her how to do things. You see, they are always with you!"

I didn't know how good it was, but it was the best I could come up with. She was back on my leg; I could feel the heat of her tears and breath.

"But I want to *see* them. When will I see them, Nick?"

I hadn't gotten through. I didn't know who was more upset, me or Kelly. A large lump was swelling in my throat. I had gotten into something I couldn't get out of.

"They aren't coming back, Kelly. They are dead. It's not because of anything you did or didn't do. They didn't want to leave you. Sometimes things happen that even grown-ups can't fix."

She lay there listening. I looked down. Her eyes were open, staring at the wall. I stopped stroking her and put my arm around her.

People need to show sadness and loss. Maybe this was the time for Kelly to do that. If so, I wanted to reach out, not cross the street. I just didn't know if this was how you did it.

"You will be with them one day, but not for a long time. You will have children first, just like Mommy. Then your children will be sad when you die, just like you are now. They all loved you very much, Kelly. I knew your mommy and daddy for only a few years. Just think—you knew them all your life!"

I saw a small smile moving across her face. She pressed her body closer into my legs.

"I want to stay with you, Nick."

"That would be nice but it wouldn't work. I travel a lot. You have to go to school and learn how to be a grown-up."

"You can help me do that."

If only she knew. I hadn't even a garage to keep a bike in, let alone somewhere to look after a child.

Your weapon, your kit, and only then yourself—that's the order of things. I wanted to ease my magazine springs; it wasn't strictly necessary, but I felt that I needed to do it to mark the end of one phase and the beginning of a new one.

By now Kelly was sound asleep.

I plugged in the telephone to recharge it. It was my lifeline. Then I tipped all the supplies out of the bag and sorted them out. The new clothes were put to one side, and I packed the CTR stuff back into the duffel. I was pissed off about having to leave the video camera on the roof; it would be found and a connection inevitably made between us and the shooting. Plus, the videotape was lost, and that might have been of use to Simmonds—it might even have been enough to guarantee me a future.

I repacked the kit and lay back on the bed, hands behind my head. Listening to the low drone of the air-conditioning, I started to think about this whole fucking game and how people like me and McGear were the ones that got used time and time again. I was starting to feel sorry for myself. I cut it. McGear and I both had a choice; this was what we chose to do.

There were a few good things that had come out of last night's drama. At least I didn't have to worry about dumping all the blood- and piss-stained clothes that were in the blue duffel. The cops would no doubt match the blood to the Browns', but that was nothing compared with the trouble I was already in. And best of all, I had confirmed a definite connection between Kev, PIRA, the building, and whatever it was that I'd copied from that computer.

I wasn't going to attempt to get the laptop out and start messing around with it now. I was too tired; I'd make mistakes and miss things. Besides, the adrenaline had gone, and the pain across my back and neck was even more intense.

I had a hot shower and tried to shave. McGear's bite marks on my face were scabbing nicely. I left them to sort themselves out.

I dressed in jeans, sweatshirt, and running shoes and reloaded my mags. I needed rest, but I had to be ready for a quick move. The plan was to have a couple hours' sleep and something to eat, then sit down and see what was on the laptop, but it didn't work out. I tossed and turned, snatched a bit of sleep, woke up.

I turned the TV on and flicked through the channels to see if McGear was news yet. He was.

The cameras panned the front of the PIRA building, with the obligatory backdrop of police and ambulance crews, then a man faced the camera and started rattling on. I didn't bother turning the volume up; I knew the gist of what he'd be saying. I was half-expecting to see my piss-covered homeless friend describing what he had heard or seen.

Kelly was starting to toss and turn, probably with pictures of McGear in her head.

I lay there looking at her. The girl had done well, without a doubt. The last few days had been chaos for her, and I had really started to worry about it. Seven-year-old kids shouldn't be exposed to this sort of shit. Nobody should. What would happen to her? It suddenly occurred to me that I was worrying more about her than I was about myself.

I woke with the TV still on. I looked at my watch: 9:35. At noon Pat would be calling me. I hit the Off button. I wanted to start working on the laptop. I started to get up and found I could hardly move. I felt like a very senior citizen as I lifted myself off the bed, my neck as stiff as a board.

I made a racket getting the laptop out of the duffel and plugging everything in. Kelly started to wriggle around. By the time I'd got it up and running and connected to the backup drive, she was propped up on one elbow watching me. Her hair looked like an explosion. She listened for a while as I cursed the laptop for not accessing the backup drive, then said, "Why don't you just reboot and then look at the program?"

I looked at her as if to say, *You fucking smartass!* Instead, I said, "Mmm, maybe." I rebooted, and it worked. I turned around and smiled at her and got one in return.

I started to scroll through the files. Instead of the business-like file names I'd been expecting, the documents had code words like Weasel, Boy, Bruce. A lot of them turned out to be spreadsheets or invoices—I could see what they were, but I didn't know what they meant. To me, the whole forty or so pages could just as well have been in Japanese.

I then opened up the file called Guru. It was just dots and numbers across the screen. I turned to Kelly. "What's that then, smart guy?"

She looked. "I'm only seven, I don't know everything."

It was five minutes to noon. I turned the phone on and carried on flicking through the files, trying to make sense of them.

Twelve o'clock came and went.

By a quarter past, the call still hadn't come in. I was sweating. *Come on, Pat, I need to get out of the US and back to Simmonds. I have enough information—maybe. The longer I stay now, the higher the risk. Pat, I need you!*

For Slack to miss an RV there must be a major drama; even when he was high, he'd managed it before. I tried to block dark thoughts by telling myself that he'd call at the next arranged window. But as I carried on halfheartedly on the laptop, I started to feel almost physically sick. My only way out had been lost. I had that awful, sinking feeling that everything was going to go horribly wrong. I needed to do something.

I closed down the laptop and put the backup disk in my pocket. Kelly was half-buried under the covers, watching TV.

I joked, "Well, you know what I'm going to have to do in a minute, don't you?"

She jumped out of bed and threw her arms around me. "Don't go! Don't go! Stay and watch TV with me. Maybe I can come with you?"

"You can't do that, I want you to stay here."

"Please!"

What could I do? I felt her pain at being scared and alone. "OK, come with me—but you've got to do what I say."

"I will, I will!" She jumped up and went to get her coat.

"No, not yet!" I pointed to the bathroom. "First things first. Get in that bath, wash your hair, come out and I'll dry it, then you'll get changed into your new clothes, and then we'll go out. OK?"

She was trembling like a dog about to go for walkies. "Yeah, OK!" She skipped to the bathroom.

I sat down on the bed and shouted into the bathroom as I flicked through the news channels. "Kelly, make sure you brush your teeth or they'll all fall out and you won't be able to eat when you're older."

I heard, "Yeah, yeah, OK."

I found nothing more about McGear. After a while I walked into the bathroom. The toothpaste tube hadn't been squeezed. "Have you brushed your teeth?"

She nodded, looking guilty.

I said, "Well, let's have a smell." I bent down and put my nose near her mouth. "You haven't. Come on, do you know how to brush your teeth?"

"Of course I know how to brush my teeth."

"Show me then."

She picked up the toothbrush. It was way too big for her mouth, and she was brushing from side to side.

I said, "That's not the way you've been taught, is it?"

She said, "It is, too."

I slowly shook my head. I knew that she would have been taught properly. I said, "All right, we'll do it together." I put some toothpaste on the brush and made her stand in front of the mirror. I stood beside her, and she watched as I pretended to brush. Looking after kids was easy after all. It all came down to EDI: explanation, demonstration, imitation. Just that instead of doing it with a weapon to a room full of recruits, I was doing it with a seven-year-old girl. "Now with me, like this, then brush around in little circles. And let's make sure we do the backs."

And then it got silly. She started to laugh at the sight of me pretending to brush my teeth, and as she laughed, all the toothpaste sprayed from her mouth and onto the mirror. I laughed with her.

She got on with her bath and changed into her new jeans and sweatshirt. I'd also bought us matching baseball hats at the supermarket, black denim with the words Washington, D.C.

I wet my hair and washed, and we both looked sparkly clean. She put on her new blue coat and sneakers and we were all ready to go. My plan was to get to the vicinity of Pat's apartment. When he rang at six o'clock, we'd be able to meet right away.

What was I going to do with the backup disk? I decided to hide it in the room, because I was going to split my gold; if the backup stayed here and Kelly came with me and we were lifted, at least they wouldn't have the whole enchilada. The long, dark wood sideboard with the TV on top covered a third of the room; it was about two feet high and rested on little half-inch legs. I lifted one corner, gaffer-taped the disk to the underside, and positioned a couple of telltales. One last look around the room and we left.

It was drizzling and slightly colder than earlier in the morning. Kelly was on cloud nine; I gave her the same smiles and happy noises back but underneath I was sweating about Pat. As we crossed the grass to avoid the lobby, I wondered about phoning Euan. I decided not to. Not yet, anyway. I might need him later. He was a card to keep up my sleeve.

The whole area was dotted with hotels. We walked across the road to one about four hundred yards away, and I went into the lobby and ordered a taxi. Kelly waited outside under the awning.

As I came out again I said, "When we get into this taxi I'm going to put your hood up and I want you to rest against me as if you're sleepy. Remember, you promised me you'd do exactly what I said."

The taxi turned up and took us to Georgetown. Kelly leaned against me, and I got her nuzzled in on my lap with her hood up so it hid her.

We got out on Wisconsin. It was four o'clock, and everybody around us looked so normal as they chatted, strolled, enjoyed their shopping. Two hours to go before Pat rang. By five-thirty the Georgetown mall where we were sitting was quite warm and we were both feeling sleepy.

I was having a coffee, Kelly was having a milk shake, which she wasn't touching because by now she was full of burger. I looked at the display of my watch every half minute until it was five to six. Then I switched the phone on. Good battery level, good signal strength.

Six o'clock came.

Nothing.

A minute past.

Two minutes past.

I sat there almost paralyzed with disbelief. Kelly was absorbed in a comic she'd picked out for herself.

Four minutes past. This was desperate. Pat wouldn't let me down unless he couldn't help it. He knew as well as I did that on operations, if you're a minute late, you might as well be an hour or a day late, because people's lives might depend on it. The attack might have gone in, unsupported by your covering fire.

There must be a problem. A major problem.

I kept the phone switched on. Finally, at six-twenty, I said, "Come on, Kelly, we're going to visit Pat."

Now the normality stopped. There was serious shit coming down. All hope had evaporated.

28

As we came out of the mall, I flagged down a cab.

Riverwood turned out to be a well-established, upscale area, rows of weatherboarded houses with neat lawns and two European cars in the drive, and smart apartment buildings with underground parking. The shops reflected its wealth, with good bookstores, expensive-looking boutiques, and small art galleries.

I stopped the cab a block past Pat's street. I paid the driver, and he left us in the light rain. It was getting dark, a bit earlier than it should have, but the cloud cover made everything gloomy. Some cars already had their headlights on.

"Let's hope Pat's in," I said. "Otherwise we'll have to go all the way back to the hotel without saying hello!"

She looked excited about meeting him. After all, this was the man I'd said would help her go back home. I couldn't be sure if what I had said about her family had sunk in. I didn't even know if kids her age understood that death was irreversible.

Looking up the hill, I could see that Pat's street was pure Riverwood, broad and elegant, with houses and shops that had been there for years. Above the skyline one or two new apartment buildings seemed to be taking over, but even they looked very ordered, clean, and wealthy. I wasn't entirely sure which one Pat lived in, but it was easy enough to count the numbers and figure it out. We walked past, and I had a clear view into the secure rear parking lot. I saw the red Mustang, redder than Satan's balls. It was a quarter past seven. If he was there, why the fuck hadn't he phoned?

We went into a coffee shop across the way. The waft of

229

newly ground beans and the blare of rumba music inside La Colombina took me straight back to Bogotá; maybe that was why Pat had chosen to live here. We wanted a window seat, which wasn't a problem. The glass was misted up; I cleared a circle with a paper napkin and sat and watched.

Kelly was doing what she had been told, keeping quiet until I told her not to be. Anyway, *Girl!* magazine seemed the thing to shut kids up with. I checked the phone. Good signal, plenty of power.

A waitress came over to take our order. I was going to ask for food even though I didn't really want any because it would take time to prepare it, and then it would take time to eat it, and that way we could spend more time here without it looking unnatural.

"I'll take a club sandwich and a double cappuccino," I said. "And what do you want, Josie?"

Kelly beamed at the waitress. "Do you do Shirley Temples?"

"Sure we do, honey!"

It sounded like a cocktail to me, but the waitress went away quite happily to order it. Kelly returned to her magazine, and I just kept looking out the window.

The drinks arrived. When we were alone again, I said, "What is that?"

"Cherries and strawberries, mixed with Sprite."

"Sounds disgusting. Can I have a sip?"

It tasted to me like bubblegum, but it was obviously what kids liked. She was guzzling it down almost frantically.

The sandwich mountain arrived. I didn't need it, but I ate it anyway. In my days in the SAS and since, I'd learned to think of food the way an infantryman thinks of sleep: Get it down you whenever you get the chance.

Things were running their natural course in the coffee shop; it was now coming up to three-quarters of an hour that we'd been sitting there, and you can stay in a place only for so long without arousing suspicion or drowning in coffee.

Kelly made the decision for me as she spoke. "So now what are we going to do?"

I put some cash on the table. "Let's zip you up and see if Pat is home."

We went out and walked past Pat's apartment once again. The car was still there. I was desperate to know one way or another what was going on. If it was just that he didn't want to play anymore, that was fine. But I couldn't really see that; I knew that he wanted to help. There was a problem, without a doubt. But I needed it confirmed; then I could reassess and make a plan without him in it.

As we walked back down the hill, Kelly asked, "Do you actually know where Pat lives?"

"Yes I do, but I know he's not there yet. We've just walked past his place and I couldn't see him."

"Can't you phone him?"

I couldn't contact him directly; if the phone was tapped, I didn't want anyone to make the connection between us. I'd promised not to compromise him. But she'd just given me an idea all the same.

"Kelly, do you want to help me play a trick on Pat?"

"Sure!"

"OK, this is what I want you to do."

We kept on walking and started to do a circuit around the area. We practiced and practiced until she said she was ready to go. We got to a phone booth about three blocks away, an open booth attached to the wall. I brought the receiver down to Kelly's level. "Ready?"

She gave me a thumbs-up. She was excited; she thought this was great.

I dialed 911, and about three seconds later Kelly was shouting, "Yes, I've just seen a man! I've just seen a man on the second floor, eleven twenty-one Twenty-seventh Street and—and—he's got a gun and the man's shot, and—and—and he's got a gun—please help!"

I put my hand on the hook.

"Good one! Now, shall we go and see what happens next?"

I picked a different route back. This time we were going to approach from the top of the hill and walk down toward the apartment building. By now it was properly dark, and still very wet. Heads bent in the rain, we made it to

Twenty-seventh Street, turned right, and started walking slowly down the hill.

I heard its siren first, louder and louder, then the flash of its emergency lights as a police cruiser sped past us. Then I saw other blue and red lights, all flashing in the darkness in the area of the apartment.

As we got closer I made out three police cars. An unmarked car turned up, a portable light flashing on the roof, just above the driver.

We walked farther down and came to a bus stop. All I was doing was watching and waiting—much like everybody else—as a small crowd had gathered.

"Are they all coming for Pat?" Kelly asked.

I was too busy feeling depressed to answer; the sight of an ambulance arriving had poleaxed me. I stroked her head over her coat hood.

"I'll tell you about it in a minute. Just let me watch what's happening."

A quarter of an hour went by. Local TV news crews were in sight. I then saw them come out: two guys with a gurney, and on top was a corpse in a body bag. I didn't have to see the face to know who was inside. I only hoped it had been quick for him, but judging by the condition of the Browns I had a terrible feeling that it hadn't.

I said quietly, "We're going to go now, Kelly. Pat's not there tonight."

I felt as if my most treasured possession had been stolen from under my nose, and I knew that I'd never get it back. Our friendship had been rekindled after all these years, and this was the price Pat had paid for it. I felt lost and desperate, as if I'd got detached from the rest of my patrol in hostile territory, without a map, or a weapon, and no hint of which way to go. He was a true friend. I would miss the man with no ass.

As Pat was being loaded into the ambulance, I forced myself to cut away from the emotion. I turned and started to walk back down the way we'd come, to avoid the police. One of the cars had now left with its siren going and the ambulance was just about to. I imagined the crime scene people inside the apartment, putting on their coveralls and unpacking their gear. Again I tried to make myself look at the situation logically. Pat was gone; now all I had left was Euan.

We took the first left to get off the main drag, and I listened as the ambulance siren twice went off to maneuver through traffic. We kept going along the road. It wasn't a main thoroughfare; it was residential on both sides, large houses with wide stone staircases leading up to the front doors.

I had Kelly's hand. We were walking without talking.

Feelings about Pat had no place in my mind at the moment. What mattered was what information about us he could have given to whoever had zapped him. PIRA or Luther and Co., who could tell? It had to be one or the other. If it was connected with me, of course. Fuck knows what else he could have been up to. However, I had to work on the basis that whoever killed him wanted to know where we were. All Pat knew was the phone number, and that I was going into the PIRA office. OPSEC—operational security—might have saved our lives.

I was thinking so hard that at first the voice didn't really register. Then I thought it was Kelly, so I was going to give her hand a bit of a squeeze and tell her to be quiet and let me think. But then it spoke again, a man's voice, low, resolute, and this time there was no mistaking the words.

"Freeze. If you move, I'll kill you. Stay exactly where you are. Do not move."

It wasn't a druggy voice, it wasn't a young nervous voice; it was a voice that was in total control.

29

I kept my hands where they were.

Kelly flung her arms around my waist.

"It's OK, it's all right. They aren't going to hurt you," I lied like a cheap watch.

His footsteps moved from behind me and to the left. He must have come from the service alley that ran behind the houses we'd just passed.

He said, "You have two choices. Get smart by keeping still. Get dead by moving." The voice was late twenties, early thirties, precise, well drilled.

It was pointless trying to draw on him. He would kill me the instant I made a move.

I decided to take choice one.

More footsteps came from the other side, and somebody was tugging Kelly away. She cried out, "Nick! Nick!" but I couldn't help. Her grip was no match for theirs. She was dragged behind me and out of sight. I still couldn't see anything of the guys who'd caught us. I made myself calm down and accept what was happening.

The voice started to give me commands in the same no-nonsense, almost pleasant voice. He said, "I want you to raise your hands slowly, and put them on top of your head. Do that now."

When I'd complied, he said, "Now turn around."

I turned and saw a short, dark-haired man aiming a pistol at me in a very professional manner. He was standing about ten yards away at the entrance to the alley. He was breathing heavily, probably after running around the streets to find us both. He was wearing a suit, and I saw Velcro. I now knew who had gotten to Pat.

"Walk toward me. Do it now."

I couldn't see Kelly. She must have already been taken down the alley. They had got her at last. I pictured Aida's savaged little body as I came toward him.

"Stop. Turn left." Very low, very calm and confident. As he said it, I heard a car pull up to my right, and out of the corner of my eye I could see it was the blue Caprice from the first motel.

"Walk."

I moved into the alley. Still no sign of Kelly.

I heard, "Get on your knees."

I knelt down. I'd never been particularly worried about dying; we've all got to check out sometime. When it did happen I just wanted it to be nice and quick. I'd always hoped there was an afterlife, but not as reincarnation back on Earth. I'd hate to find myself back here as something low down the food chain. But I wouldn't mind a spiritual thing where you just become aware of everything from the truth about the creation of humankind to the recipe for Coca-Cola. I'd always known I was going to die early, but this was just a bit too early.

Nothing was happening and nothing was said. Then what must have been that Caprice drove into the alley behind me, its headlights illuminating the rears of the houses. Each had facing garages and three or four cars parked along the sides of the alley. I could see my kneeling shadow against the wet asphalt.

The engine was still running, and I heard the doors being opened. There was radio traffic from a different voice; this one had an accent that should have been selling hot dogs in New York. He was giving a location. "Affirmative, we're in the service road for Dent and Avon. We are on the south side. You'll see our lights. Affirmative, we have both of them."

I stayed on my knees with my hands on my head in the rain while we waited for the others to arrive. I heard footsteps coming toward me from the car. I clenched my teeth and closed my eyes, expecting to be given the good news. They walked slightly past me to my right and stopped.

I didn't hear the second one come up behind me. I just felt a heavy hand grip my own firmly on my head as the other felt for my weapon. The hand pulled out the Sig, and in front of my face I watched him check the safety catch as he released his grip on my hands and, in the same movement, produced a clear plastic bag. I could smell coffee on his slightly labored breath.

Nothing happened for a moment or two, apart from the rustling of the bag behind me. Into view on my right came a man who looked a bit like a fashion seeker, dressed in a black suit with a mandarin jacket. Fuck me, it was Mr. Armani. He was maybe late twenties, very clean-cut, and dark and smooth. He probably glided over the ground so his shoes never got wet. He was covering me.

I heard Kelly crying in the background. She must have been in the car. Fuck knows how she got there, but at least I knew where she was. The man behind me continued with the search and placed my stuff in the bag.

The hot-dog seller was being quite good with her; he didn't sound too aggressive or rough. Maybe he had kids of his own. "It's OK, it's OK," he said. "What's your name?"

I couldn't hear her reply, but I heard him say, "No, little lady, I don't think your name's Josie, I think your name is Kelly."

Good one, mate, at least you tried!

Car lights stopped on the main road about 150 yards farther down, at the end of the alley. Then the red lights of a car in reverse were coming toward me.

By now all my stuff was in the plastic bag and being held by whoever was behind me. I was still on my knees, hands on head, with Mr. Armani hovering to my right.

There were noises of more people behind me. Hopefully they were passersby who would report us. But to whom? My hopes collapsed as I heard the driver get out of the Caprice and start to speak.

"That's OK, folks, everything's under control. There's nothing to see here."

I was confused. How could they just move people on—unless they were law enforcement? Maybe there was a glimmer of hope; maybe I'd be able to talk my way out of this one. I still had the backup disk hidden. Maybe I could bargain with it.

The reversing car stopped about five yards away and three people got out—the driver from the left-hand side, and two out of the back. At first they were in shadow and I couldn't see their faces, but then one walked into the glare of the other car's headlights. And then I knew I was really in for it.

Luther was looking a little the worse for wear, and he wasn't blowing me kisses. He looked like a pissed-off devil with a large gauze dressing. He was still in a suit, but he wouldn't be wearing a tie for a while. I could tell by the smile on his face that he had a few tricks saved up for me. I guess I'd earned them.

He walked toward me. I thought he was going to make a point. I closed my eyes and got ready to take the hit, but he walked straight past. That scared me even more.

Luther started to talk as he got to the car. "Hi, Kelly, remember me? My name's Luther."

There were some mumblings in reply. I was straining to hear the conversation, but only the adult voice was audible.

"Don't you remember me? I came to pick your daddy up for work a couple of times. You have to come with me now, because I have been sent to look after you."

I could hear protests from the car.

"No, he's not dead. He wants me to collect you. Now come on, move it, you little bitch!"

Kelly screamed, "Nick, help! I don't want to go!" She sounded terrified.

Luther walked back to his car with her. He had his arm around her tight to stop her from bucking and kicking. It was all over in a few seconds. Once Kelly was secure in the back of the car, all three drove off. I felt as if I'd been taken down by the fire extinguisher again.

"Get up." My hands were still on my head, and I felt

someone's hand grip onto my right triceps and lift me up. I heard the car behind me move.

I looked to my right. The short guy had hold of me with his left hand; in his right he had the plastic bag with Kev's mobile, my weapon, wallet, passport, ATM card, and loose change. He turned me around to face the car, which had just finished parallel parking in the road, pointing toward the right. Mr. Armani had me covered.

I'd stayed calm so far. But I had to get out of this shit now. I was going to be killed, it was as easy as that. The engine was running, and I had about ten yards in which to do something. Whatever I did, there would have to be a lot of speed, aggression, and surprise. And it must work the first time; if not, I was dead.

The guy who was holding me was right-handed or he wouldn't be dragging me along with his left, and therefore, if I started fucking around, he would have to drop the bag and draw his pistol. If I was wrong about that, I would soon be dying. But I was dead anyway, so fuck it—why not go for it?

There were about three yards left between me and the car. By now Mr. Armani had glided to the rear door to open it and, as his eyes glanced down for the door handle, I knew it was time.

YAAAAAAHHHHHH!!!

Screaming at the top of my lungs, I brought my right hand down hard, half-turned my hips, and hit his left shoulder as hard as I could.

I had surprise on my side. All three now had to take in what was going on and make an assessment. It would take them little more than a second to turn that assessment into reaction.

As I hit him, I started to push in an attempt to spin him to his left so that his right side would come toward me. We were both screaming now. He'd already made his assessment. He dropped the bag and was going for his weapon.

I knew that for him also it was happening in slow motion. I could see the saliva spray out of his mouth as he shouted a warning to the others. There was nothing to worry about with the other two at the moment; if they were quicker than me, knowing about it wouldn't make it any better.

Looking down on his belt, I could see the pistol moving slowly toward me as he spun around. Nothing else mattered. I kept my eyes on it. I heard the other two screaming. We were all at it.

The Colt .45 is a single-action weapon, which means that all the trigger does is release the hammer. To cock the hammer in the first place and chamber the first round, you must first rack back the topslide by pinching in with the fingers and thumb of the left hand against its serrations, pulling it back firmly to the rear, and releasing. The pistol can be carried "cocked and locked"—hammer back and safety on, with a round in the breech. The Colt has both a manual safety and a grip safety. Even if the manual safety is off, your hand must be firm enough on the grip to keep the grip safety depressed or the weapon won't fire.

I grabbed the pistol with my left hand, I didn't care where. At the same time I brought my right hand down, with four fingers together and my thumb stretched out to present a big recess for the weapon. I pushed onto it with the web of my hand, taking the manual safety catch off with my thumb and using the web of my hand to release the grip safety by holding the weapon correctly. I couldn't see if the hammer was back. And I had no way of knowing if the weapon had a round in the chamber. With my left hand, I racked the topslide back to cock it. It had already been cocked. A brass round spun out of the ejection port, glinting as it tumbled in the street lights. It didn't matter losing one round; at least I wouldn't get a dead man's click.

I knew the first threat was Mr. Armani. He had a weapon in his hand.

I kept turning in the direction the shoulder hit had taken me, and as I did I came up into the aim, firing low because these fuckers wore armor. Armani went down. I didn't know if he was dead.

I kept on spinning and dropped the short guy, moved forward, and looked at the driver. He was still in his seat, but in a crouched position, screaming and writhing.

I ran to his side of the car, pointing the pistol. "Move over! Move over! Move over!"

I pulled the door open and, keeping the pistol on him, kicked him with my right foot. I wasn't going to start dragging him out; it would take too long. I just wanted to get in the car and go. I shoved the muzzle into his cheek and pulled out his weapon, kept it, and threw mine out—I didn't know how many rounds were left.

The injury was to his upper right arm. There was a small entry hole in the material, but not much blood around the site. He must have taken one of the rounds aimed at Armani as I spun around. His hand, however, was red and dripping from where blood was coursing down his arm. The .45 round is big and heavy and doesn't fuck about. The massive exit wound would have blown away most of the underside of his arm. I would be having no problems from this guy.

As I drove off I screamed at him, "Where are they going? Where are they going?"

His answer was half a cry, half a shout. "Fuck you! Fuck you!" His dark-gray suit was turning brown with blood.

I jabbed his leg hard with the pistol. "Where are they going?"

We were on a narrow residential road. I tore off both side mirrors in the process of turning to question him. He told me to fuck off again, so I fired. I could feel the air pressure change as the gases left the barrel, and then the smell of cordite filled the air. There was an explosion of material and flesh as the round plowed a twelve-inch furrow along and down into his leg. He howled like a stuck pig.

I didn't know where I was heading. The driver's screams quickly subsided, but he kept thrashing about. His convulsions left him on his knees in the footwell, with his head on the seat. He was starting to go into shock. He was probably wishing he did sell hot dogs in New York.

"Where are they going?" I demanded again. I didn't want him to pass out before I got the information.

"They're heading south," he moaned. "Route ninety-five south."

We were speeding on the elevated section of the highway that led to the interstate.

I looked across. "Who are you?"

His face screwed up in pain as he fought for breath. He didn't reply. I hit him on the temple with the pistol. He gave a low moan and moved his fingers sluggishly from his leg to his head. We passed the Pentagon, then I saw the sign for the Calypso Hotel. It seemed like a bad dream.

"Who are you? Tell me why you're after me!"

I could barely hear his reply. His mouth was dribbling blood, and he was finding it hard to breathe.

"Let me go, man. Just leave me here and I'll tell you."

No way was I falling for that one.

"You're going to die soon. Tell me and I'll help you. Why are you trying to kill us? Who are you?"

His head lolled. He didn't reply because he couldn't.

I found them just short of the Beltway, in the middle of the three lanes. It was easy to pick them out in my headlights. I could see they were still three up; one in the front, two in the back. No sign of Kelly, but there was enough space between the two in the back to have another body between them. She was only a little fucker; her head wouldn't be showing.

I couldn't do anything on the freeway, so now was the time to calm down and get my head around the next plan. What was I going to do? Whatever it was, it had to be soon, because I didn't know their destination, and I-95 goes all the way to Florida. Much nearer, however, about thirty minutes away, was Quantico, the FBI and DEA academy. It was starting to make sense. Luther and the other guy coming to the house, both knowing Kev; they were all the same group. But why would they kill Kev? And if they were the killers, what connection then did "bad DEA" have with my "friends over the water"? Was there something happening here between these two groups that Kev had discovered and got fucked over for?

I thought again of Florida and it gave me an idea. I tucked it away for later.

I looked down at the driver. He was in shitty shape, still losing blood. He was sitting in a pool of it because the rubber mat in the footwell stopped the carpet from soaking it up. I could see his face as the lights from the opposite side of the freeway hit us now and again; all the agitation had drained from it and he looked ashen, like an old fish; life was slowly going out of his eyes, which were staring into space. He was going to die soon. Tough shit.

I reached over, flipped open his jacket, and took the two magazines that were in a holder on his shoulder holster. He was oblivious to what I was doing; he was in his own place now, perhaps reflecting on his life before he died.

I had surveillance on the target car. My wipers were on high-speed as the trucks and cars splashed more water onto the windshield than the rain itself. I put the defroster on full blast. The driver's leaking blood and my own sweating body were misting the car up big-time.

A freeway was perfect for my purposes; I could just drive along and even allow a bit of distance to develop to the point of letting another car get in between me and the target. As an exit came up I'd just get a little bit closer; if he was going to turn off, I could then fall in naturally and come up behind him.

After about another five minutes I saw a sign saying LORTON 1 MILE. They started to indicate that they were getting into the right lane to make the exit. They weren't going to Quantico after all. This would be the time to hit them. I glanced down, changed mags, and checked chamber.

As I came across to get into the right lane, I realized for the first time that we were driving through heavily wooded terrain. The tires throbbed rhythmically as they hit the joints in the concrete freeway.

By now the driver had slumped completely into the footwell, with his back against the door. It was only the body armor under his shirt that gave him posture. He was dead.

I was now in the exit lane, just twenty yards behind them, close enough to be on top of them, but far enough away so that if they looked behind, they'd just see headlights. Nobody turned their head; they didn't seem to be aware of me. I started to take deep breaths and spark myself up.

The Lorton exit ramp went slightly uphill with a gentle curve to the right. The tall trees on each side gave the impression of a tunnel. I planned to do it at the first intersection. My brain was in overdrive, getting me into a mind-set, trying to take the fear away.

I could see traffic lights in the middle distance and put my foot on the gas to close up even more. Their brake lights came on, then their right turn signal. A truck thundered past from left to right. It looked like it was a wide major road ahead. The car started its right turn. Pushing myself back into the seat, I put my foot down hard on the accelerator and braced my arms on the steering wheel.

I must have been doing about forty-five and still accelerating as I drew level and yanked the wheel hard to the right. My right fender hit the front of theirs. There was a massive jolt. My air bag exploded as the car slewed around into the main drag. The other car spun sideways. I heard glass shattering and the screech of tortured rubber.

The moment the vehicle came to a halt I jabbed at the seatbelt release and opened the door. The air felt freezing. At first all I could hear was the hiss of the radiator and the *ping ping ping* warning that the door was open and the lights on; then came the sound of muffled shouts from inside the other vehicle.

The first priority was the driver. The car had to be immobilized. He was still fighting his seat belt. I fired through the windshield. I didn't know where I hit him, but he was down. As I looked into the back I could see Kelly, or at least her shape. She was low down in the footwell, hands over her ears.

Luther was getting his first rounds off at me. His door was half open, and he was starting to roll out. I'd have been doing the same because a car draws fire—so you need to get out of the way. As he rolled I kept on firing, just below the level of the door. He screamed. I'd got him. I couldn't tell whether it was a direct hit or the splash of the round off the asphalt, but it didn't matter, the effect was the same.

I moved from behind the hood of my car to take on the third guy. He was out now but had had a change of heart. He put his hands up and yelled, "Don't do it, don't do it!" His eyes were like saucers. I double-tapped him in the head.

Kelly was still curled up in a ball in the footwell. She wasn't going anywhere.

I searched the two bodies for wallets and magazines. I left Luther for last.

He was on the ground behind his car, hands clutched to his chest. "Help me . . . help me . . . please . . ."

He'd taken a round in the armpit as he rolled on the ground, and it must have continued on into his chest cavity. I thought of Kev, Marsha, and Aida and kicked. He opened his mouth to scream, but all that came out was a gurgle. He was on his way out. Good. Let it happen slowly.

I ran back for Kelly and lifted her out of her hiding place. I had to shout at her above her screams. "It's OK, Kelly. I'm here, it's OK."

I held her tight in my arms. She was nearly deafening me.

"It's all over now! It's OK!"

It wasn't.

The police would be here soon. I looked around. The intersection was with a main road, two lanes in each direction. To my left and downhill was I-95, crossing the road by a bridge, with a Texaco gas station about four hundred yards away on the other side of it on the right. Uphill and about the same distance away a Best Western hotel cut the skyline.

Lights were coming from the exit road toward us. Luther was lying there softly moaning to himself. He wasn't dead, but it wouldn't be long. The lights came closer.

Kelly was still hysterical. Grabbing her to conceal my pistol, I went behind the two cars. The lights were nearly level with us. I moved out and waved the vehicle down.

The good Samaritans were in a Toyota Previa, man and woman in the front, two kids in the back. I played the traumatized victim for all I was worth, shouting, "Help! Help!" as I rushed to the driver's side. The woman was at the wheel; she opened her door. "Oh my God, oh my God!" Her husband already had his cell phone out to call for an ambulance.

I put the safety catch on and held the gun against her face. "Everybody out now! Get out, get out now!" My other arm was windmilling like a madman's. Hopefully they'd think I was one. "Get out! I'll fucking kill you! Get out!"

The one thing I did know about families is that no one will

risk theirs. The husband started to lose it. "Please don't, please don't!" Then he started to cry.

Kelly had quietened down, listening to my act.

It was the mother who kept her cool. "OK, we are getting out. Dean, get the kids out. Out!"

Dean got his act together. I yelled at him, "Throw your wallet back inside!"

I pushed Kelly through the sliding door, slammed it shut, ran around to the driver's side, climbed up, and we were off.

I wanted to get away from the initial danger area, then sort myself out. The freeway was out because it would be too easy for the police to pick me up. I drove up onto the intersection and turned left under the bridge, past the garage. The road became a normal two-lane highway, and I put my foot down.

This was no time to be explaining stuff to Kelly. She was curled up in the backseat, sobbing. My adrenaline rush was slowing down, but my face was soaked with sweat and I was lathering up. I took deep breaths, trying to get more oxygen into my body and calm everything down. I felt unbelievably angry with myself for losing control back there. I should have killed Luther right off the bat, not fucked around.

I realized we were heading south, away from the airport. I'd have to stop and get my shit together instead of just running in a blind panic. I pulled over and checked the road atlas. Kelly didn't look good, but I didn't have too much of a clue what to say to comfort her. "It's OK now," I tried. "I told you I was going to look after you, didn't I?"

She looked up at me and nodded, her bottom lip quivering.

I made a decision. *Fuck it, let's just go straight to the hotel, get the backup disk, and clear out.* I swung the Previa around in a U-turn, heading for the freeway. We stayed on it until we hit the Beltway.

Blue lights flickered toward us. There must have been ten of them. I wasn't worried. Even if they did ID me, they'd have to get across the median.

It took us just under an hour to get to the Economy Inn. We drove straight into the parking lot, and I told Kelly to wait where she was. If she did hear me, there was no reaction. I tried again and got a nod.

I went upstairs, got out my pistol, and went inside. I pulled the bureau onto its side, the TV crashing onto the floor, and ripped the disk away from the tape. If Luther and company were connected with PIRA, they must know I had a disk—they had to assume it, anyway. Retrieving the black bag, I went into the bathroom and threw two hand towels into the bath and ran the water. While that was happening I got the plastic laundry bag from the drawer. I put in the wet towels and some soap. I walked out of the room, keeping the DO NOT DISTURB sign on the handle.

Kelly was still curled up in the backseat. We drove straight down the road to the Marriott.

30

I parked up alongside a line of cars and pickup trucks and grabbed the towels. The moment I opened the door, Kelly ambushed me, throwing her arms around my neck and clinging hard. Her whole body was shaking.

I lifted her head off my shoulder. Blood from the guy I'd head-jobbed had gone all over my jacket, and now some of it was on her face, too, mixing with her tears. I whispered in her ear, "It's OK now, Kelly, really it is—it's all over."

She held on even harder. Her tears were warm and wet on my neck.

I said, "I've got to go and get another car, so I want you to stay here. I won't be long."

I started to lift her away from me to put her back on the seat but she resisted, burying her face into my shoulder. I could feel the heat of her breath through the material of my jacket.

I put my hand on the back of her head and rocked gently. For a moment I didn't know who was clinging to whom. The idea of what was happening and who might be behind it scared me shitless. I had to confirm what Luther had said, and now was as bad a time as any. "Kelly, do you know Luther? Was it true what he said about him coming to pick up Daddy?"

I could feel her head nod slowly against my shoulder.

"I'll never leave you alone again, Kelly. Let's just clean ourselves up a bit, shall we?"

I tried to sound happy as I used one of the wet hand towels to wipe her face. "If you're going to come with me, I'd better give you a really important job. I want you to look after the bag while I go and get a car, OK?"

"OK."

As she dried herself I checked the wallets. Just over two hundred dollars in all.

The parking lot surrounded the whole hotel and was lit only by borrowed light from the street. The area dividers that made it easier for people to find their cars were waist-high bushes and shrubs, with small trees around the main perimeter. There was plenty of shadow.

I positioned Kelly in a clump of shrubbery with the bag. "Don't come out until I stop the car and get out to fetch the bag, OK?"

"Will I be able to see you?" she whispered as she put her hood up. Her coat was already wet from the leaves. "I want to see you."

I had my eye on a family-size Dodge among the long lines of cars. I said, "See that big blue car over there? That's the one I'm going to pick up." I didn't actually want to tell her I was going to steal it, which seemed crazy after what had just happened.

It took about five minutes to break in. The vehicle started immediately. I put the windshield wipers and defroster on high, rubbing the inside of the screen with my sleeve. I backed up to the bushes, stopped, and got out. Kelly climbed into the front with a big smile, and we started off. I stopped. "Seat belt!"

She put it on.

We headed south on I-95. About twenty miles before the Lorton exit we came across temporary traffic signs warning us that the junction was closed off. As we crossed the bridge, I looked down to my right and got a bird's-eye view of the shooting. Police cars dotted the area, red and blue lights flashing. I didn't slow down with the rest of the traffic to take a closer look.

The gas gauge showed three-quarters full, so we could gain a decent distance before refueling. I turned on the radio, surfing the channels to find some news.

There was quite a lot of traffic, which was good because it made us just one of many, but the highway itself was mesmerizingly boring. The only variant was that sometimes it was two lanes, then three, then back to two. At least it had stopped raining.

After a hundred miles or so I was exhausted and my eyes were starting to sting. I stopped for gas just over the Virginia–North Carolina border and continued on south. Kelly was asleep in the back.

By 1 A.M. we had traveled about 170 miles, but at least the speed limit was higher now, up from sixty miles an hour to seventy. I kept seeing large billboards featuring a cartoon of a Mexican, advertising a place called South of the Border. That would be our next stop—in two hundred miles' time.

We crossed into South Carolina at about 5 A.M. South of the Border, just a mile or two farther down the road, turned out to be a mixture of service area and amusement park. It was probably a great hit with families going to and from the beaches of North and South Carolina. It covered a huge area and included beachwear shops, grocery stores, drugstores, even a bar with dancing. It looked as if it was still open, judging by the number of cars parked outside.

I started to fill up with gas. The weather was only a little bit warmer than in D.C., but I could hear the crickets; it definitely felt like I was going south. I was still standing there watching the numbers spin on the pump when a brand-new four-wheel-drive Cherokee rolled up. Rap music blared out as the doors opened. Inside were four white college-age kids, two boys and two girls.

Kelly had already been awoken by the strong white light under the filling station's canopy and now took an interest in the mobile disco. I motioned with my hand through the window to ask her if she wanted a drink. She nodded, rubbing her eyes.

I went inside, picked up some drinks and sandwiches, and went up to the counter. The cashier, a guy in his late fifties, started totaling up my stuff.

The two girls came in, followed by one of the boys. Both girls had dyed-blond shoulder-length hair. The lad was skinny, pimply, and had an unsuccessful attempt at a goatee.

The cashier winked and said quietly, "Love is blind." I smiled in agreement.

The girls were talking to each other, making more noise than the music system. Maybe they'd blown their eardrums. I looked outside at the other boy filling up. All were in the same uniform: baggy T-shirts and shorts. They looked as if they'd been to the beach. You could tell they had money—Daddy's money.

They lined up behind me. One of the girls was going to pay. "That was a totally cool day," she shouted. I was meeting a real-life member of the cast of *Clueless*. By the sound of the conversation their parents were total assholes who never gave them enough money, even though they were loaded and could easily afford it.

The cashier gave me my change and leaned over to me. "Maybe getting a job would help!" His eyes twinkled.

I grinned back and started to pick up my stuff from the counter. The girl came up to pay and opened her purse. Clueless Two, still behind me with the boy, was pissed off by the cashier's comment, and at me for agreeing. "Look at that face, guys!" she stage-whispered behind my back. "What's bitten you, mister?" The lad guffawed.

Daddy was very generous by the look of it, no matter what she said. I saw a wad of cash and enough cards for a bridge tournament. The other two were holding the beers they'd gotten from the fridge and were giggling. I left.

Our vehicles were facing each other at the pumps. Sitting in the front of the Cherokee was the fourth member of the group, who'd finished filling up and was now air-drumming along to whatever shit was on the CD.

Kelly was stretched out across the backseat. I went over to her window and tapped. Kelly sat up, startled, and I held out her Coke.

The other three were now coming out of the shop. Clueless Two was still pissed off. As they got in their car I heard one of the girls shriek, "Fucking asshole," and they closed the doors to gales of laughter.

I got into the Dodge and drove over to the air pump. The story was now being told to the driver, and I could see them all getting worked up about it. The boys had to show how hard they were, and the girls didn't like being shown up in front of their beaus. There was a lot of chemistry driving out of the garage.

As the Cherokee rolled away from the pumps, it caught me in its headlights, chatting away with Kelly as I checked the tires. They slowed right down and looked at us. Clueless One must have made a crack about my appearance, because they all laughed and the driver gave me the finger to make him look good, then zoomed off into the night.

I gave it about a minute, backed out, and followed.

I didn't want to do it on the highway unless I had to. Sooner or later I knew they'd turn off the main drag so they could drink those beers out of sight of highway cops and maybe spread a couple of blankets on the ground.

After just five miles we followed the big Jeep onto a pot-holed road that seemed to go through the middle of nowhere.

"Kelly, see that car ahead? I have to stop and ask them something. I want you to stay in the car, OK?"

"OK." She was more interested in the Coke.

I didn't want to force them off the road or do anything drastic. It had to look natural in case another car drove past.

We passed a roadside store that was closed, then a large truck stop, then a trailer park and a big stretch of dark nothingness, then an isolated house. I was beginning to think I'd fucked up when at last it happened. I saw a stop sign four hundred yards ahead; accelerating, I got a bit closer and checked for other car lights.

I drove up on their left-hand side. Beeping my horn, I waved at them with the road map and gave a big smile. They all looked over, and as I turned the interior light on they saw first me, then Kelly in the back half-asleep. They looked worried, then recognized me as the asshole from the gas station. Jokes were exchanged, and their beer cans came back up to their mouths from their hiding places.

I got out. The crickets were louder out here than at the filling station. I kept looking at them, smiling. The map was for Washington, D.C., but they couldn't see that, and by the time they did, it would be too late.

The driver was making a comment to the rest, probably proposing driving off as soon as I got to the door.

I said, "Hiya! Can you help me? I'm trying to get to Raleigh"—which was a place I'd seen signs for on the freeway, way back in North Carolina.

As the electric window rolled down farther, I could hear whispered giggles from the backseat ordering the driver to tell me to fuck off. I could see he had other ideas, maybe to send me anywhere but Raleigh. "Sure, man, I'll show you."

I offered the map through the open window. "I don't know how I got lost. I must have taken the wrong exit after I got gas."

He didn't need the map. He started to give directions, pointing down the road. "Hey, man, just turn left and go for about twenty miles until you see . . ." The girls were liking this one, working hard to stifle their sniggers.

I got hold of his head with my left hand, pulled my pistol up, and stuck it into the young flesh of his cheek.

"Oh shit, he's got a gun, he's got a gun!"

The other three went silent, but the driver's mouth went into freewheel. "I'm sorry, man, it was a joke, just a joke. We're drunk, man. It's the bitch in the back who started it. I've got nothing against you, man."

I couldn't even be bothered to answer him. I shouted into the back, "Throw your purses out! Now!"

My Southern drawl was quite good, I thought. I just hoped I was looking scary enough. The girls passed over their handbags. By now the driver was trembling, and quiet tears rolled down his cheeks. The girls huddled together.

I looked at the front passenger. "You."

He looked at me as if he were one of a hundred I could be talking to.

"Yes, you. Give me your money, out this window." It took all of two seconds for him to comply.

It was the driver's turn. He beat his pal's record. I reached in, took the keys, and put them in my pocket. He didn't seem too clever now. I had another look around for lights. All clear. The pistol was still against the driver's skin. I said quietly into his ear, "I'm going to kill you now."

Everyone else heard it and wanted nothing to do with him. I said, "Say whatever prayer you need to say, and be quick."

He didn't pray, he begged. "Please don't kill me, man, please don't."

I looked down and saw that his shorts, made of gray sweatshirt material, were rather darker now. Daddy would not be impressed with the stains on his nice beige leather.

I was quite enjoying it, but knew I had to get going. I stepped back and picked everything off the road. I glanced at Clueless Two. She looked like she'd swallowed a wasp. "What's bitten you?" I said.

I got in the car, did a one-eighty, and drove off.

Kelly said, "How come you made those people give you their money?" She sounded confused.

"Because we need loads of money, and we're much nicer than they are, so they wanted us to have it."

I looked at her in the rearview mirror. She knew damned well I was lying.

I said, "You want a job?"

"Like what?"

"Count this money."

She opened up the bags and wallets and piled all the bills in her lap.

"At least a million dollars," she said at length.

"Maybe count it once more to check."

Five minutes later I got the more realistic figure of $336. The clueless girls were wrong. Daddy was a diamond.

We started seeing signs for Florence. That would do me fine. The town was about sixty miles away, and it was about five-twenty in the morning. It would be getting light by sevenish, and if possible I wanted to be in a town before dawn. I'd dump the Dodge, and we'd have to find some other form of transport. We had to get to Florida if I was to get the help I needed.

About ten miles short, I saw a sign for a tourist information area. I pulled in and took a free map of the town and surrounding area. Kelly was half-awake as we parked. I opened the door and got out. The birds were singing, and I could just make out first light. There was a little nip in the air, but you could tell it was going to be a nice warm day. It felt great to have a stretch. I stank of sweat and had a layer of grease on my skin; my eyes were stinging and no doubt bloodshot and swollen from lack of sleep. The pain in my neck still made me walk as if I had a plank of wood strapped to my back.

The map showed a train station in the town; not necessarily helpful, but it was a start. I got back into the car and started to get the bags and wallets together to dump. All were expensive leather. A couple were even monogrammed. Inside one of them I found coke and a lump of pot in a plastic bag. The spoiled brats had obviously been on spring break, college kids using up all their hormones before the end of the semester. Mom and Dad worked their asses off and provided for these kids and they thought the world owed them a living. Fuck 'em, I was glad I'd robbed them. I laughed; they were probably still sitting there blaming each other, trying to think of a way of getting piss stains off leather upholstery. There was a good chance they'd be too embarrassed to even report it. I dumped everything in the trash cans.

We drove toward the train station. It looked as if the town center were terminally ill, but big efforts had been made to keep the patient alive; the old historical part had been rejuvenated, but it seemed that every store sold candles, perfumed soap, and potpourri. There was nothing there for real people, no life in it at all.

We got to the station, which could have been any station in any town, full of the homeless who stay there because it's warm. It reeked of bodies and decay. Drunks were sprawled on benches that nobody in their right mind would go near for fear of getting their head bitten off.

I looked at the departure signs. It seemed we could get to De Land by train, with a bus transfer to Daytona Beach. It was just before six; the train would be arriving at seven.

The ticket office was already open and looked as if it had been modeled on an urban 7-Eleven, wire mesh everywhere, painted white but chipped. I could just about see the large face behind it that was demanding to know where I wanted to go.

An hour later we got on the train, found our seats, and collapsed. Our car was no more than half full. Kelly cuddled into me, dog-tired.

"Nick?"

"What?"

I was busy looking at the other passengers. They all looked like me, frazzled grown-ups looking after kids.

"Where are we going?"

"To see a friend."

"Who's that?" She sounded happy at the idea. Probably she was fed up with my company.

"He lives near the beach. His name is Frankie."

"Are we going on vacation with him?"

"No, Frankie's not that kind of friend."

I decided to keep the conversation going, as she would be asleep in no time at all. The rhythmic sounds and motion of the train would soon send her off.

"Who is your best friend? Is it Melissa?"

"Yes."

"How come she's your *best* friend?"

"Uh—we ride bikes together, and go to each other's houses a lot. We have secrets."

"What kind of secrets do you have?"

"Silly, that would be telling! Who's *your* best friend?"

That was easy, but I wasn't going to say his name. If we were lifted again, I would hate it if he was mentioned and put in danger. The sun was starting to burn through the windows; I leaned across her and pulled down the blind.

"My best friend is called . . . David." It was about as far away from Euan as I could think of. "Just like you and Melissa, we tell each other things that no one else knows. In fact, he has a daughter who's just a little bit older than you. No one else knows about her apart from David and me—and now you!"

There was no reply. It seemed she was starting to doze off. I continued anyway, I didn't know why. "We've known each other since we were seventeen, and we've been friends ever since." I started to stroke her hair. I was going to talk more but found it really hard to tell her. I couldn't put it into

words. Euan and I were just there for each other and always
had been. That was it, really. I just didn't have the tools to
describe it.

31

Frank de Sabatino had been crossed off the Christmas-card list of LCN—La Cosa Nostra—in Miami and for his own protection had been sent over to the UK as part of the federal witness protection program. I had been one of the team charged with looking after him for the three months he spent in Wales before returning to the US. I remembered Frankie as about five-foot-five and seedy; he had very black, tight, curly hair that looked as if it had been permed in the style of a 1970s pop star.

The FBI had been investigating LCN in South Florida—they don't use the word "Mafia"—and had discovered that de Sabatino, a thirty-four-year-old computer nerd who worked for one of the major players, had been skimming off hundreds of thousands of dollars from their drug operations. The government agents coerced de Sabatino into gathering evidence for the prosecution. He had no choice—if he were arrested, LCN would be told what he'd been up to. LCN members in prison would have done the rest. Pat had had a good relationship with him during the job, and we'd later joked that maybe that was why he'd got out right afterward. I now knew that Pat had liked to sample the goods a bit too much.

Frankie's clothing had been anything but low profile; to him, "subdued" meant a pale orange shirt with purple pants and alligator skin cowboy boots. Whatever he was wearing, his fat would push up against his shirt. The last I'd heard of him, he'd been given a new identity after the trial and, very surprisingly, had opted to stay in the States—and, even more weird, in Florida. Maybe the shirt selection wasn't so good elsewhere.

I'd thought again about calling Euan, but what could he do for me at the moment? I decided against it; better not use up all my resources at once. Frankie would help decrypt the PIRA stuff, then Euan could help me once I was back in the UK.

We got to De Land station just before 2 P.M. The bus was waiting to take us to the coast. After so many hours of air-conditioning on the train, the Florida afternoon hit me as if I'd opened the door of a blast furnace. Both of us were blinking like bats under the clear, oppressive sky. We were surrounded by people wearing tans and summer clothes. The electronic information scroll at the station told us it was ninety-one degrees. We boarded the hot bus, sat down, and waited for the PVC to stick to our backs as we chugged along the highway to the Daytona Beach bus depot.

It was an uneventful trip. Occasionally from behind us would come the sound of rolling thunder, and a blur of chrome, leather, and sawed-off denim would flash past with the distinctive, explosive bubbling gurgle of a Harley-Davidson. I'd forgotten Daytona Beach was a mecca for bikers. From the bus window, the roadside diners looked black with them.

Two hours later we trundled across the bridge over the inland waterway into downtown Daytona Beach. We peeled ourselves off the seats, and I reclaimed our bag. The first thing I did was buy us two fresh-squeezed orange juices, and as we walked from the shelter of the bus depot I could feel the sunlight burning through my shirt.

At the taxi stand I asked the driver to take us to an ordinary hotel.

"What kind of ordinary?" he asked.

"Cheap."

The driver was Latino. Gloria Estefan blasted out of the cassette player; he had a little statue of the Virgin Mary on the dashboard, a picture of his kids hanging off the mirror, and he was wearing a big, loud, flowery shirt de Sabatino would have died for. I rolled my window down and let the breeze hit my face. We turned onto Atlantic Avenue, and I found myself staring at a massive white ribbon of hard-packed sand that stretched to infinity. We drove past diners, beachwear and biker stores, Chinese restaurants, oyster houses, 7-Elevens, parking lots, tacky hotels, then more diners and beachwear stores.

The whole place was built for vacations. Everywhere I turned I saw hotels with brightly colored murals. Nearly all had signs saying SPRING BREAKERS WELCOME. There was even a cheerleaders convention going on; I could see scores of girls in skimpy outfits strutting their stuff on a ballfield outside the convention center. Maybe Frankie was there, sitting in a corner, ogling.

"Are we there yet?" Kelly asked.

The driver said, "Two more blocks on the left."

I saw all the usual chain hotels, and then ours—the Castaway Hotel.

Standing on the sidewalk outside, listening to Gloria's singing disappearing into the distance, I looked at Kelly and said, "Yeah, I know—crap."

She grinned. "Triple-decker crap with cheese."

Maybe, but it looked perfect for us. What was more, it was only twenty-four dollars a night, though I could already tell from the outside that we'd get only twenty-four bucks' worth.

I came out with the same old story, plus us being determined still to have our Disney vacation. I didn't think the woman at the desk believed a word I was saying, but she just didn't care, as long as I gave her the cash that went into the front pocket of her dirty black jeans.

Our room was a small box with a pane of glass in one wall. The floor had a layer of dust that it would have been a shame to clean, and the heat bouncing off the cinder block made it feel like the black hole of Calcutta.

"Once the air-conditioning is on it'll be OK," I said.

"What air-conditioning?" Kelly asked, looking at the bare walls.

She flopped onto the bed. I could swear I heard a thousand bedbugs scream.

"Can we go to the beach?"

I was thinking the same, but the first priority, as ever, was the kit.

"We'll go out soon. Do you want to help me sort every-thing out first?"

She seemed happy at the suggestion. I gave her the .45 magazines from the Lorton exit shooting. "Can you take the bullets out and put them in there?" I pointed to the side pocket of the bag. The mags didn't fit into my Sig, but the rounds were the same.

"Sure." She looked really pleased.

I didn't show her how to do it because I wanted to keep her busy. I hid the backup disk inside the bed, using one of the screwdrivers to rip the mattress lining. I got the washing kit out, had a shower and a shave. The scabs were a dark color now and hard. I got dressed in my new jeans and gray T-shirt. Then I got Kelly cleaned up too.

It was 4:45. She was still getting dressed in black pants and a green pullover as I leaned over to the cabinet between the two beds and pulled out the telephone book.

"What's this?" I pointed a thumb at the TV.

"The Big Bad Beetleborgs."

"The who?"

She started to explain but I wasn't really listening; I just nodded and agreed and read the phone book.

I was looking for the surname De Niro. It was a crazy name for him to have chosen, but I remembered that was what he'd renamed himself: Al De Niro. For somebody who was sup-posed to spend his life keeping a low profile it wasn't exactly the most secure, but he was Al and Bob's biggest fan. The only reason he'd got involved in the drug scene in the first place was that he'd seen Al Pacino in *Scarface*. His whole life had been a fantasy. He knew all the dialogue from their films; he'd even entertained us in Wales with passable impressions. Sad, but true.

There was no listing under De Niro, A. I tried directory as-sistance. They couldn't help, either. The next step would be to start phoning all around the state or to get a private eye on it with some story, but that was going to take a lot of time and money.

Scratching my butt until I realized Kelly was watching, I walked over to the curtains, and pulled them back. We were two bats in the bat cave again, exposed to the deadly sunlight. Craning my neck around to the left, I could just about see the oceanview I'd paid an extra five dollars for. People were strewn all over the beach; there was a young couple who couldn't keep their hands off each other, and families, some with tans and others like us, the lily-white ones, who looked like uncooked french fries. Maybe they'd come on the same train.

I turned to Kelly. She was happy enough that the Beetle-borgs had saved the world again, but looked bored. "What are we going to do now?" she said.

"I've got to find my friend, but I'm not sure where he lives. I'm just wondering how to go about it."

"The computer geek you told me about?"

I nodded.

All very nonchalant, she said, "Why don't you try the Net?" She wasn't even looking at me; she was now back to watching the shit on the TV. Of course—the bloke is a computer freak, there's no way he's not going to be on the Internet, probably surfing the porn pages for pictures of naked teenagers. It was as good a starting point as any. Better than my private eye idea, anyway.

I walked over to the bag. "You can use the Net, can you?"

"Sure. We do it at school."

I started to get the laptop out, feeling quite excited about this girl's genius.

I suddenly realized that even if there was an internal modem and Internet software on the laptop, it would be no good to me. I didn't have any credit cards I could use to register with, and I couldn't use the stolen ones because they'd need a billing address. I put the laptop on the bed.

"Good idea," I said, "but I can't do it on this machine."

Still looking at the TV, she was now drinking a warm Minute Maid that had been in the bag, using both hands on the carton so she didn't have to tilt her head and miss anything. She said, "We'll just have to go to a cyber cafe—when Melissa's phone was out of order, her mommy used to go to the cyber cafe for her e-mail."

"Oh, did she?"

* * *

Cybercino was a coffee shop with croissants, doughnuts, and
sandwiches, with the addition of office dividers to create
small cubicles. In each was a PC, with a little table for food
and drink. Pinned on the dividers were notices about session
times, how to log on, and little business cards advertising
various sites.

I bought coffee, doughnuts, and a Coke and tried to log on.
In the end I handed the controls to a more skilled pilot. Kelly
zoomed off into cyberspace as if it were her own backyard.

"Is he on AOL, MSN, CompuServe, or what?" she
demanded.

I didn't have a clue.

She shrugged. "We'll use a search engine."

Less than a minute later we were visiting a site called Info-
Space. Kelly hit the e-mail icon and a dialogue box appeared.

"Last name?"

I spelled out De Niro.

"First name?"

"Al."

"City?"

"Better leave that blank. Just put Florida. He might have
moved."

She hit Search, and moments later, up came his e-mail address. I couldn't believe it. There was even a Send Mail icon,
which she hit.

I sent a message saying I wanted to contact Al De Niro—
or anyone who was a Pacino/De Niro fan and knew "Nicky
Two" from the UK. That was the nickname de Sabatino had
given me. There were three Nicks on the team. I was the
second one he'd come in contact with. When we met he
would do his *Godfather* thing, holding out his arms, saying,
"Heyyy, Nicky Two" as he gave me a kiss and a hug. Thankfully, he did that to everyone.

The cafe would open the next day at 10 A.M. Our session
fee included the use of the Cybercino address, so I signed off
by saying that I would log on at 10:15 tomorrow morning to
retrieve any messages. The risk that his e-mail was being

monitored and somebody could make a connection with "Nicky Two" was minimal.

By now I was hungry for more than doughnuts, and so was Kelly. We walked back toward the main strip and stopped at our favorite restaurant. We ordered to go and ate our Big Macs on the walk back. The temperature was still in the seventies, even at this time of the evening.

"Can't we play miniature golf?" Kelly said. She pointed to what looked like a cross between Disneyland and St. Andrews, with trees, waterfalls, a pirate ship, all made to look like a floodlit Treasure Island.

I actually enjoyed it. There was no danger, and the pressure release was tremendous, even though Kelly was cheating. She started to putt on the eleventh hole. A dragon behind us was blowing out water rather than fire from its cave.

"Nick?"

"What?" I was busy working out how to negotiate the ninety-degree angle I needed to hole the ball.

"Can we see your friend, what's his name—David?"

"Maybe some day." I swung, and it didn't work. I was stuck on the water obstacle.

"Do you have any sisters or brothers?"

Where was this going? "Yes, I have."

"How many?"

I marked my card after six attempts on a par three hole.

"Three brothers." I decided to cut the interrogation. "They are called . . . John, Joe, and Jim."

"Oh. How old are they?"

She got me on that one. I didn't even know where they lived, let alone how old they were. "I don't know really."

"Why not?"

I found it hard to explain because I really didn't know the answer.

"Because." I positioned the ball for her to putt. "Come on or we'll hold everyone up."

On the way back I felt strangely close to her, and that worried me. She seemed to have latched on to me as a stand-in parent and we'd been together only six days. I couldn't take the place of Kev and Marsha, even if I wanted to. The prospect was too scary.

Next day. It was ice cream for breakfast, then we logged on at ten-fifteen. There was a message waiting for us, telling us to visit a certain chat room. Kelly hit a few keys and there we were. De Sabatino was waiting for us, or at least someone called Big Al was. A dialogue box invited us to a private room for a one-on-one; thank goodness Kelly was there to do the navigating.

I got right down to it. Kelly typed with two fingers: *I need your help.*

What do you want?

I've got something here that I need you to decode or translate—I'm not entirely sure what it is, but I know you'll be able to do it.

What is it? Work?

I needed to get him hooked. For him, half the point of stealing all that money had been the sheer kick of doing it— "the juice." Thinking about it now, Pat had probably got the term from Big Al in the first place. This guy enjoyed putting one over on the big boys; he needed to be involved, to be part of something, and I knew that if I used the right bait, he'd come and see me.

I spoke and she typed: *I'm not going to tell you! Believe me, it's good. If you want to look, you'll have to see me. I'm in Daytona.* And then I started to lie. *Other people say it's impossible. I thought of you.*

He came back at once: *What format?* I'd got him.

I told him all the details.

He said, *Can't see you until 9 tonight. Outside Boot Hill Saloon, Main Street.*

I'll be there.

Big Al came back: *Yeehaa! Yeehaa!*

There was nothing changed about him, then. Kelly logged off, and we paid the twelve dollars. About a hundredth of what a private eye would have cost me.

* * *

Now we had hours to kill. We bought sunglasses, and I also got Kelly a fashionable pair of shorts, a T-shirt, and sandals. I had to stay as I was, wearing my shirt over my pants to cover my pistol. The only addition was a bandanna to cover the cut on my forehead. Chrome aviators covered the lower one.

With the wind on our faces, we sauntered along the beach. It was that time of day when the restaurants were starting to fill up with people wanting early lunches.

Back at the hotel I made some calls to check flights out of the country. If the stuff Big Al decrypted for me seemed to be what Simmonds needed, Kelly and I were out of here. I knew Big Al would have the contacts and resources to get passports for our exit, even money.

We had lunch, followed by eighteen holes with the pirates—I let her win—and then it was time to start getting ready for the meet.

At about 7:30 the sun started to go down and the street neon came on. Suddenly it was another world, with music pumping out of the stores and the kids now driving up and down the strip faster than the legal ten miles an hour.

I didn't know what it was, the weather maybe, but I felt detached from the situation I was in. It was just the two of us, we were having fun, eating ice cream and walking around looking in shops. Kelly was doing usual kid things, even to the point of spotting something in a store window and doing the "Look at that!" act as in, Hint, hint, are you going to buy it for me? I found myself acting the parent, saying, "No, I think we've had enough for today."

I did worry about her. I felt she should be more upset, shouldn't really be taking it so well. Maybe she hadn't understood what I'd said to her about her family; maybe her subconscious was putting a lid on it. At the moment, however, that was exactly what I needed: a child looking and behaving normally.

We stopped outside a toy store. She asked for a ring in the window that glowed in the dark. I lied and said I had no money left.

"Couldn't you steal it for me?" she said.

She was getting into this on-the-run thing too much. We had a serious talk about right and wrong.

It was about a quarter of nine by now; we'd had a pizza, and at that time of night on vacation, the next thing you should always have is a Häagen Dazs. Afterward, we started to wander to the RV with Big Al. We squeezed past ranks of parked motorcycles and jostling crowds, most wearing T-shirts with bike slogans.

I got us into a position from which I could see both approaches to the Boot Hill Saloon from the old graveyard on the other side of the street. It was all that remained of the original town, the only thing that couldn't be ripped apart and have a hotel built on it. As bikers parked and opened the doors, loud rock and roll thundered from the bar. It collided head-on with the Latin and rap that were blaring from the vehicles cruising up and down; it was that body-fluid time of night, and groups of breakers were hanging out of Jeeps and pickups with banks of six or seven speakers in the back. Some even had electric blue lights fitted under the car; as they drove past, they looked like hovering spaceships playing music from Mars. I thought about our friends in the Cherokee. I wondered if they'd gotten home yet.

Kelly and I just waited, eating our ice cream and sitting on a bank next to Mrs. J. Mostyn, who went to Our Savior on July 16, 1924, God rest her soul.

32

Main Street wasn't in fact the main drag but a road that led from the sea to a bridge over the inland waterway. Daytona has a bike week each year, and this was the street on which the thousands of bikers descended. It was a one-theme street, and that theme was Harleys. If it wasn't a bike bar, it was a store selling spare parts, helmets, or leather goods. And even when the convention wasn't on, bikes with helmets on the seats were lined up by the dozen outside bars with names like Dirty Harry's or Froggie's, where there was even a bike made of dusty bones in the window.

I could spot Big Al a mile away as he shambled toward us from the direction of the bridge. He was wearing a blue, white, and yellow Hawaiian shirt and pale pink pants, both straining against a body that was even fatter than I remembered; his outfit was set off by white shoes and the same shaggy hairstyle. He looked like an out-of-work extra from *Miami Vice*. In his left hand he carried a briefcase, which was a good sign; he'd brought the tools of his trade with him. He ducked into the Main Street Cigar Store and emerged chomping on a huge corona.

He stopped outside the Boot Hill Saloon, Harleys all around him. He put his briefcase down between his feet and stood there sucking his cigar as if he owned the place. Behind him was an enormous mural of a biker on the beach, covering an entire wall of the saloon. A board announced NO COLORS, CLUB PATCHES, OR INSIGNIAS.

I nudged Kelly: "See that man over there?"

"Which one?"

"The one with that really big flowery shirt on, the big fat man."

"You mean the geekazoid?"

"What?"

"It's like a double geek."

"Whatever." I grinned. "He's the man we're going to see."

She said, "Why didn't we wait over there for him?"

"No, no—what you do is 'stand off' and watch. See what I'm doing? I'm looking up and down the road, just to make sure there's no bad guys following him. Then I know we're safe. What do you think? Think it's OK?"

All of a sudden she'd become very important. She looked up and down and said, "All clear." She didn't have a clue what she was looking for.

"Come on then, give me your hand. We've got to be careful with these cars driving so fast."

We left Mrs. Mostyn and stopped at the curb. I said, "When we go and meet him, I might have to do something that looks funny, but actually it's not—we do it all the time. He understands it."

As we dodged through the traffic she said, "OK." After what she had seen lately this would be kindergarten stuff.

We got closer; he was certainly looking older. He recognized me from twenty yards away and was suddenly starring in *The Godfather* again. Cigar in his right hand, arms thrown out wide, head cocked to one side, he growled, "Aaaggghh! It's Nicky Two!" He had a smile on his face the size of half a watermelon. It was probably shit living in hiding; at last he had somebody from the past he could talk freely with.

He jammed the cigar back into his mouth, picked up his briefcase in his right hand, and walked toward us, his fat thighs rubbing together. "Hey! Nicky! How's it going!" He beamed and started pumping my hand, at the same time studying Kelly. He stank of flowery aftershave. "And who's this pretty little lady, then?" He bent down to greet her and I felt a slight twinge of wariness. Maybe the charm was genuine, but for some reason it made me feel a bit revolted.

I said, "This is Kelly, one of my friend's daughters. I'm looking after her for a while."

I very much doubted he knew what had been going on up north. He certainly didn't know Kev.

Still bending down and shaking her hand for a bit too long, he said, "Welcome to the Sunshine State! It's great here—we've got Seaworld, Disney World, everything to make a little lady happy!"

He stood up and said, slightly out of breath, "Where are we going?" He pointed hopefully and said, "Main Street Pier? Shrimp?"

I shook my head. "No, we'll go back to our hotel. I've got all the gear there I want you to have a look at. Follow me."

I held Kelly's hand in my left and got him on the right. As we walked we made small talk about how wonderful it was to see each other again, but he knew very well that this meeting wasn't casual—and he liked it. He got off on this sort of stuff, just like Al and Bob.

We turned right and then took the first left, which was into a parking area behind the shops. I looked at Kelly and nodded to show everything was fine, then let go of her hand. Big Al was still jabbering away. I grabbed his left arm with both hands and used his own momentum to turn him against the wall. He hit it with quite a bounce. I pushed him into the doorway of a restaurant's fire exit.

"It's cool, I'm cool." Big Al was keeping a low voice. He knew the score.

Just looking at him, it was obvious he couldn't conceal as much as a playing card under his clothes, let alone a weapon, the material was stretched so tight against his skin. However, I ran my hand down the back of his spine in case he had something concealed in the lumbar region; the natural curve makes it a wonderful place to hide odds and ends, and Big Al's was curvier than most. I continued frisking him.

He looked down at Kelly, who was watching everything. He winked. "I suppose you've seen him do this all the time?"

"My daddy does it, too, in heaven."

His answer was quick. "Ah, OK, yeah, smart kid, smart kid." He looked at her and tried to work that one out.

Then came the bit that he probably enjoyed most, me running my hand up his pant legs. I checked thoroughly at the top. I said, "You know I need to look in your briefcase now, don't you?"

"Yeah, sure." He opened it up; I found two cigars in tubes, and all his work tools—floppy disks, a backup drive and disks, cables, wires, all sorts of shit. I had a quick feel around to make sure there wasn't a secret panel.

I was happy. He was also. In fact, he probably had a hard-on.

I said, "Right, let's go."

"Let's get some ice cream on the way," he suggested.

We waved down a cab. Kelly and I got in the back and he squeezed in the front, resting a pint of Ben & Jerry's on his briefcase.

We got to the hotel and went to the room. His body language was excited, probably because he thought it was like the old days, all spies and shit, and the cheapness of the room only made it all the more exhilarating for him. He put his briefcase on one of the beds, opened it up, and started taking out all his gizmos. He fished, "So what are you up to these days?"

I didn't reply.

Kelly and I were sitting on the bed, not really doing much except watching what was going on. Kelly started to take quite an interest.

"You got any games?" she said.

I thought de Sabatino would look at her in disgust: I'm a technician, I don't have games. But he went, "Yeah, loads! Maybe, if we get time, we can sit down and play a few. What ones do you like?"

They went off on a tangent about Quake and Third Dimension. I cut in and said, "So what do you do with yourself nowadays?"

"I just teach people how to work these things." He pointed at the laptop. "Also, I do a bit of work for a couple of private eyes down here, getting into bank accounts, that sort of thing. It's pretty low-key but it suits me—I have to keep my head down."

Almost choking on Kouros cologne and looking at his

choice of clothes, I wondered what his idea of high profile would be.

Without a reply to his original question, he seemed to feel compelled to fill the silence. He started sniggering and said, "Still managed to tuck away a few hundred thou! So, plus the resettlement, things ain't too bad."

He was fiddling about, attaching more cables to the laptop; God knows what he was doing, so I let him get on with it. He tried again. "What about you? Same old thing?"

"Yeah, same sort of stuff. Bit of this, bit of that."

Now sitting at the table with his back to me, he was concentrating on the laptop. "You still being a—what did you call it—a baby spy?"

"I do that a bit."

"You working now, are you?"

"Yeah, I'm working."

He laughed. "You lying sonofabitch!" He looked at Kelly and said, "Oops! Do you learn French at school?" He turned back to me and said, "You wouldn't need me if you were, you'd be getting somebody else to do it. You can't bullshit Big Al!" He looked at Kelly and said, *"Français!"* Then he looked back at me and said, "You still married?"

The Microsoft sound chimed as Windows 95 opened on his machine.

"Divorced about three years ago," I said. "I haven't heard from her for about two years. I think she's living up in Scotland or somewhere, I don't know."

I suddenly realized that Kelly was hanging on my every word.

He winked at her. "Just like me—young, free, and single! Yeah!" Big Al was one of life's really sad fucks; I was probably the nearest thing he had to a friend.

I handed him the backup disk, and it was soon humming in the drive. It wouldn't be long before I got a few answers. By now there was a pall of cigar smoke filling the top quarter of the room. Between that, the Kouros, and the lack of air-conditioning, the room was close to unbearable. It was just as well we'd be moving from here the moment Big Al left. I checked outside by moving the curtain, then opened the window.

The first batch of documents came up on the screen, and I looked over his shoulder as he tapped away in the semidarkness. I pointed at one of the spreadsheets. "This is where I've got a problem. I haven't got a clue what that means. Any idea?"

"I'll tell you what we have here, Nicky." His eyes never left the screen. "These are shipment and payment records—of what, I don't know." As he pointed to the screen, his finger touched it and squidged the liquid underneath. "Never touch the screen!" he scolded himself as if he were telling off one of his students. He was really getting into this.

"See these here?" His voice had changed from that of a no-hoper to someone who knew his stuff.

I looked at columns headed by groups of initials like MO'N, JC, LN. He said, "They refer to shipments. They're telling you what's going where, and to who."

He started to scroll down the pages, confirming it to himself. As he was looking through he nodded emphatically. "These are definitely shipments and payments. How did you get into this, anyway? You're not exactly the world's greatest hacker, and there's no way these files weren't password-protected."

"I had a sniffer program."

"Wow! Which one do you have?" The computer nerd was coming back.

"Mexy twenty-one," I lied.

"That's shit! Oops, garbage! There are sniffers now that do it at three times the speed." He looked down at Kelly. "That's the problem with the Brits. They're still in the Steam Age."

He was now out of the spreadsheets and looking at more file names.

I said, "This is another group of files I was having problems with. Can you decrypt them?"

"I don't understand," he said. "Which files are you having trouble with?"

"Well, they're in code or something—just a lot of random letters and numbers. Any chance of you figuring it out?" He made me feel like a six-year-old child having to ask to have his shoelaces tied.

He scrolled down the file names. "You mean these GIFs?" he said. "They're graphics files, that's all. You just need a graphics program to read them."

He tapped a few keys, found what he was looking for, and selected one of the files. "They're scans of photographs," he said.

He leaned over and pulled open the pint of ice cream, reached for one of the plastic spoons, and started to dig in. He threw a spoon to Kelly and said, "You'd better get in here before Uncle Al finishes it all."

The first picture was now on the screen. It was a grainy black and white of two people standing at the top of a flight of steps that led to a grand old building. I knew both men very well. Seamus Macauley and Liam Fernahan were "businessmen" who fronted a lot of fund-raising and other operations for PIRA. They were good at the game, once even getting a project backed by the British government to finance revitalization in Northern Ireland's cities. The whole scheme was designed to provide local employment. They convinced Westminster that if a community was responsible for its own rebuilding, there would be less chance of them then wanting to go and blow it up. But what the government didn't know was that the contractors could only employ people that PIRA wanted to work; those people were still claiming unemployment and social benefits, and PIRA was getting a kickback from letting them work on the sites illegally, so it was costing the government twice as much—and, of course, the businessmen got their cut as well. And if the government's paying, why not blow more up and rebuild?

Without a doubt, PIRA had come a long way from the days of rattling its tin cups in West Belfast, Liverpool, and Boston. So much so that the Northern Ireland Office had established a Terrorist Finance Unit as a countermeasure in 1988, staffed by specialists in accounting, law, taxes, and computing. Euan and I had done a lot of work with them.

Big Al now opened and viewed a series of shots of Macauley and Fernahan shaking hands with two other men, then walking down the steps and getting into a Mercedes. One of them was the late Mr. Morgan McGear, looking very smart in a suit I was familiar with. The fourth man I had no idea about.

The photography was covert: I could see the darkness around the edge of the frames where they hadn't gotten the aperture right, but it was good enough for me to tell, by the cars parked in the background, that they were on the Continent.

I said, "Let's see the next one."

De Sabatino could tell that I recognized something or someone; he was looking at me, dying to know what, wanting to get in on the act. He'd had five years on the back burner, and now was his chance for a comeback.

I wasn't going to tell him jack shit. "Let's push on."

There was another group of pictures that he opened and viewed, but these meant nothing at all to me.

Big Al looked at them. The big half watermelon was back on his face. "Now I know what all those spreadsheets refer to."

"What's that?"

"*¡Está es la coca, señor!* Hey, I know this guy. He works for the cartels."

I was looking at a really smart-looking Latino in his early forties getting out of a car. I could tell by the surroundings that it was in the United States. "That's Raoul Martinez," he said. "He's part of the Colombian trade delegation."

This was getting more interesting by the minute. PIRA always claimed no association with drug trafficking, but the profits were too great for it to ignore. What I had in front of me now was close to admissible evidence of its direct involvement with the cartels. But that still didn't help me with my problem.

He looked through the pictures. "You'll see Raoul with somebody else in a minute, I guarantee it." He flicked through a couple more. "There you are: big bad Sal."

This other character was about the same age but much taller; he'd probably been a weight lifter at some stage, then ballooned out to maybe three hundred pounds. Sal was a big old boy, and very bald.

De Sabatino said, "Martinez is never without him. We

used to do a lot of business with them in the old days. A nice man, a family man. We used to run cocaine up the East Coast, all the way to the Canadian border. We needed things evened out to ease the route—these guys did the necessary, and everybody was making money. Yeah, these fellas, they're all right."

As we went through more picture files, I saw both men eating in a restaurant with another bloke, a Caucasian.

Big Al said, "I haven't got a clue who he is."

I was looking over de Sabatino's shoulder, concentrating hard on the screen.

Kelly perked up. "Nick?"

"In a minute." I turned my head to Big Al. "Absolutely no idea?"

"Not a clue."

"Nick?"

I cut in. "Not now, Kelly."

Kelly butted in again. "Nick, Nick!"

"Go back to the—"

"Nick, Nick! I know who that man is."

I looked at her. "Which man?"

"The one that was in the picture." She grinned. "You don't know who he is—but I do."

"This one?" I pointed at Martinez.

"No, the one before."

Big Al scrolled back. "Him! That one there!"

It was the white guy who was sitting with Raoul and big bad Sal.

I said, "You're sure?"

"I'm totally sure."

"Who is he?" After our experience with the video I expected her to nominate anyone from Clint Eastwood to Brad Pitt.

"It's Daddy's boss."

There was a long, palpable silence as I let it sink in. Big Al was sucking air through his teeth. "What do you mean, Daddy's boss?" I said.

"He came to our house once for dinner."

"Do you remember his name?"

"No. I just came down for some water and he and a lady were eating with Mommy and Daddy in the dining room. Daddy let me say hello and he said, 'Big smile, Kelly, this is my boss!' " It was a good imitation of Kev, and I saw a flicker of sadness in her eyes.

Big Al joined the conversation in nerd mode. "Whoa! There you go! So who's your daddy?"

I swung around. "Shut up!" And so she couldn't hear it, I muttered angrily, "I turned up at her parents' house a week ago. Everybody was dead. He was in the DEA, killed by people he knew."

I pushed him off his seat and sat down with Kelly on my knee so she had a better view of the screen. "Are you definitely sure he's Daddy's boss?"

"I'm sure—Daddy told me. The next day Mommy and me made jokes about his mustache because he looked like a cowboy."

He did; he looked like a Marlboro man. As she pointed, her finger touched the screen, and Daddy's boss was distorted. Having Kelly in my arms and seeing someone who might have been responsible for her father's death made me want to do the same to him in person.

I looked at Big Al. "Let's go back through all the photos."

Big Al sat down and scrolled back through the files to the pictures of Macauley and Fernahan with McGear. "Do you know these people?" Kelly answered with a no, but I wasn't really listening to her now. I was in my own world. I'd noticed two other cars parked on the other side of the road. I looked hard at the license plates, and then I knew where the pictures had been taken.

"Gibraltar." I couldn't help mouthing it aloud.

Big Al pointed to Macauley and his mates. "Are these terrorists from Ireland?"

"Sort of."

There was a gap while I tried to work this one out.

Big Al spoke up. "It's obvious to me what's going on."

"What's that?"

"Well, these Irish guys were buying cocaine from the Colombians. It came by the normal route to the Florida

Keys, then the Caribbean and North Africa. They then used Gibraltar as the jump-off point for the rest of Europe. They made fortunes, and at the same time we took our cut for letting them move it through South Florida. All of a sudden, though, at the end of 'eighty-seven, it stopped going through Gibraltar."

"Why was that?" I was finding it hard to stay calm.

Big Al shrugged. "Some big hullaballoo with the locals. I think they now run it from South Africa instead, into the west coast of Spain, something like that. They're linked with some other terrorists up there."

"ETA?"

"Search me. Some bunch of terrorists or freedom fighters. Call them what you like, to me they're all just dealers. Anyway, they help the Irish now. No doubt old Raoul organized things Stateside with Daddy's boss to ensure that the route stayed open for the Irish, because otherwise the Colombians would have given it to someone else."

"You make it sound like allocating air routes or something."

Big Al shrugged again. "Of course. It's business." He spoke as if all this stuff was common knowledge. It was news to me.

So who the fuck was PIRA talking to in Gibraltar? Was the PIRA there in an attempt to keep the drug trafficking going? It came back to me that in September 1988, Sir Peter Terry, who'd been instrumental in pressing for a crackdown on drug smuggling and who'd been governor of Gibraltar until earlier that year, had narrowly survived an assassination attempt at his home in Staffordshire. A gunman who'd never been caught had given him the good news with twenty rounds from an AK-47—something, as it happened, that Mr. McGear was not unaccustomed to doing. Maybe the fourth man in the photograph was getting a similar warning? And was there some sort of connection between the ending of the drug runs and the shooting of PIRA players in Gibraltar just a few months later?

Whatever, it confirmed that there were some strange things going on with some members of the DEA, including Kev's boss. Maybe they were getting a cut of the action from PIRA and Kev found out?

Big Al sucked through his teeth once more. "You've got a brilliant package here, man. So which one are you going to blackmail?"

"Blackmail?"

"Nicky, you've got a senior figure in the DEA talking with big-cheese cartel members, your terrorist fellas, and Gibraltar government, law enforcement, whoever. You're not trying to tell me these pictures aren't for the purpose of blackmail? Get real. If it's not you who's going to use them, whoever took these photographs is certainly intending to."

33

We went through all the pictures one more time. Kelly didn't recognize any more of the people.

I asked de Sabatino if there was any way we could enhance the photography.

"What's the point? You seem to know everybody." He was right. I just wanted Kelly to look at "Daddy's boss" more closely.

There was silence for about three minutes as we just kept on flicking through.

"What else do you know about Gibraltar?" I asked.

"Not much. What more do you want?" His second cigar was well on its way, and Kelly was waving away the smoke. "It's common sense—if you've got enough money, do a deal with the Colombians and get the goods into Europe. Every other bunch of badasses is doing it, so why not your Irish guys?"

Big Al was looking at me as if what we'd stumbled across was very mundane. And I had to admit, it didn't seem enough for Kev and his family to have been murdered for.

There was too much silence; Big Al had to inject something. "Whatever, someone is definitely in the blackmail biz."

I wasn't so sure. Maybe it was some kind of insurance for PIRA. If Kev's boss or the Gibraltarians decided not to play anymore, maybe this was what would keep them in the game.

I looked at Kelly. "Can you do us a favor? Will you go and get some cans of soda?"

She looked happy to get out of the smoke. I followed her to the door, gave her a handful of coins, and pulled the curtain so I could see the machines. The landing was clear; I watched

Kelly until she reached the dispenser, then I sat down on the bed. Big Al was still playing with the laptop.

I pointed at the screen. "First Kev is killed. Now we've got Daddy's boss mixing with the cartels. It's reasonable to assume that what we've got here is corruption within the DEA, involving drug shipments via Florida to Irish terrorists who've been getting it into Europe via Gibraltar. Only now it seems there were some problems for them in late 'eighty-seven."

Big Al wasn't really listening. The thought of a corrupt DEA officer had taken him to another planet. "Way to go! You gonna nail the bastard?"

"I don't know what I'm going to do."

"Fucking nail him, Nicky! I hate cops! I hate the DEA! I have to live like a fucking hermit—federal witness protection program, kiss my ass!"

I was worried that five years of frustration were about to explode out of him. I had no time for that. "Frankie, I need a car."

He wasn't listening. "They used me, then they just fucked me over . . ."

"I need a car."

He looked at Kelly as she returned with a selection of soda cans, then slowly came back to earth. "Sure, OK, for how long?"

"Two days, maybe three. And I need some money."

"When do you want it by?"

"Now."

Big Al was weird and a sad fuck, too soft and stupid to be in this sort of world, but I felt sorry for him. Me turning up must have been the best thing that had happened to him in years. Life must be shit with no friends, and always worrying about being hit. But that was how mine was going to be if I didn't get this stuff back to Simmonds.

Big Al used the room phone to call a car rental agency. It would take about an hour to deliver a vehicle, so the three of us strolled to an ATM. He drew out twelve hundred dollars from four different accounts. "You never know when you're going to need *mucho dinero* in a hurry!" He grinned. Maybe he wasn't so stupid after all.

Back in the room, waiting for the car, I could sense there was more to come from him. He'd definitely been brooding on something for the last half hour.

"Would you like to make some money, Nicky—real money?"

I was checking my bag to make sure I hadn't left anything.

"Why's that? Are you going to give me some?"

"In a way." He came and stood by me as I zipped the bag closed.

"On those files there are some account numbers stuffed with narco-dollars. Give me two minutes to access what I need and then I can hack in. I could do it in my sleep." He put an arm around me. "Nicky, two minutes on my laptop and we could be talking serious enrichment. What do you say?" His head was nodding at a thousand rpm, his eyes never leaving mine.

I let him sweat a bit. "How do I know that you'll pay me my half?" I thought I'd let him know how much I wanted.

"I can transfer it anywhere you want. And don't worry, once I've moved it they'll never know where it's gone."

I had to smile. The one thing Frank de Sabatino was good at was hiding money. "C'mon, Nicky Two, let's do it!" He had his arms wide open and was looking at me like a child who'd done wrong.

I gave him the time he needed with the laptop and wrote down the account number for him to transfer my share to. Fuck it, Kelly was going to need money for school and stuff, and I wanted a payback for working against these people for so many years. It felt good and anyway it was just business.

He finished. There was a serious, down-to-work look on his face. "Where are you going now?" he asked.

"I'm not going to tell you; you know the score. People I've been in contact with are now dead, and I don't want that to happen to you."

"Bullshit!" He looked at Kelly and shrugged his shoulders. "You just don't want me to know in case I go blurting off to somebody."

"That's not the case," I said, though in fact it was. "If you did that, or didn't send the money, you know what I'd do."

He raised an eyebrow.

I looked at him and smiled. "I'd make sure the right people know where you are."

The color drained from his face for a while, then back came the watermelon. He shook his head. "I may have been out of the loop for a while, but I see nothing has changed."

The telephone rang. A blue Nissan was waiting outside the lobby. Big Al signed for it and gave me a copy of the agreement for when I dropped it off. Kelly and I got in; Big Al stayed on the sidewalk with his briefcase. I pressed the switch to open the windows.

"Listen, Frankie, I'll e-mail you to let you know where the car's been dropped off, OK?"

He nodded. It was sinking in that he was about to lose us.

"Do you want a lift anywhere?"

"No, I've got work to do. By the morning we could be seriously rich."

We shook hands through the open window. Al smiled at Kelly and said, "Make sure you come and visit Uncle Al in about ten years' time, little lady. I'll buy the ice cream!"

We set off slowly down the strip. It was still packed. There was so much neon the street lighting was superfluous.

Kelly was in the back, staring out the window, then gazing into space, lost in her own little world. I didn't tell her that ahead of us lay a seven-hundred-mile drive.

Soon Daytona Beach was behind us and we were back on the long, open road. As I drove, I mulled over Kev's words again: *You won't believe the stuff I've got here. Your friends over the water are busy!* And he'd also said: *I've just got the ball rolling on something, but I'd be interested to know what you think.* Did that mean he'd spoken to his boss? Had his boss then got him zapped? But there was no way Kev would have been talking to anyone in the DEA if he suspected corruption. So who the fuck did he call?

I now had some valuable material from the PIRA office, a lot of which I didn't understand, but maybe Kev had had more. The more information I got hold of, the better it was going to be for me when I got it to Simmonds, and that was why we were going back to Washington, D.C.

Once on the interstate I put the car into cruise control and my mind into neutral.

We drove through the night, stopping only to refuel. I bought cans of Coke to keep the caffeine levels up as we drove and in case Kelly woke up.

At first light I could begin to make out changes in the terrain, proof that we were moving north into a more temperate climate. Then the sun came up, a big burning ball to my right, and my eyes started to sting.

We stopped at another gas station. This time Kelly stirred. "Where are we?" she yawned.

"I don't know."

"Well, where are we going?"

"It's a surprise."

"Were you really married?" she asked.

"It seems so long ago I can hardly remember."

I looked in the mirror. She'd slumped back down, too tired to pursue it.

I wanted to have one last look at Kev's place to see what he had, and I wanted to do it at last light tonight. I knew there'd be a secure area somewhere in the house—exactly where, we'd have to find out. Then I wanted to be out of the D.C. area again before first light. Big Al didn't know it yet, but he was going to get his ass into gear and help us get out of the US. If he didn't do it voluntarily, I'd be giving him a jump-start.

By midmorning Kelly was wide awake, reading a comic book I'd gotten her at the last stop. She was lying in the back, shoes off, totally absorbed. We hadn't talked. We were in a world of empty candy wrappers, Styrofoam coffee cups, potato chip bags, and cans of Coke with bits of chip floating in them.

"Kelly?"

"Mm?"

"You know in your house, Daddy had the hidey-holes for you and Aida?"

"Uh-huh."

"Well, do you know if Daddy had any hidey-holes for important things like money, or where Mommy would keep her rings? Did he have a special place where they'd put stuff?"

"Sure."

Busying myself with the cruise control, I said, "Oh, and where is that then?"

"In his study."

Which made sense. But that was the room that had been torn apart already.

"Where is it exactly?"

"In the wall."

"Whereabouts?"

"In the wall! I just saw Daddy doing it once. We're not allowed in there, but the door was open and we'd just come in from school and we saw Daddy putting something in there. We were standing right by the door and he didn't know."

"Is it behind the picture?" I asked, though there was no way he'd be that obvious.

"No, it's behind the wood."

"The wood?"

"Yeah."

"Would you be able to show me?"

"Is that where we're going?" She suddenly sat bolt upright. "I want Jenny and Ricky!"

"We can't see them when we get there because they'll be busy."

She looked at me as if I was nuts. "They're my teddies, I told you! They're in my bedroom. Can I get them? They need me."

I felt like a right dickhead. "Of course you can. As long as you're quiet." I knew there was more to come.

"Can I tell Melissa I'm sorry I missed the sleepover?"

"We won't have time."

She sat back in her seat, brooding.

"But you're going to phone her mother?"

I nodded.

* * *

I started to see signs for Washington, D.C. We'd been on the road for nearly eighteen hours. My eyes were smarting worse than ever, despite the air conditioner being on full blast. We'd get there in two hours, but we'd still have most of the afternoon to kill before last light. I pulled in at a rest area and tried to sleep. It could be a busy night.

It was about six in the evening as we approached the Lorton exit. For once it wasn't raining, just overcast. Only about forty-five minutes to go.

I couldn't see Kelly in the mirror. She was hunkered down in the seat again.

"Are you awake?"

"I'm tired, Nick. Are we there yet?"

"I'm not going to tell you. It's going to be a surprise. Just keep down; I don't want you to sit up."

I drove onto Hunting Bear Path, negotiating the speed bumps ultracautiously so I could have a good look around. Everything seemed quite normal. I could see the back of Kev's garage, but I couldn't see the front of the house yet.

When I got up level, the driveway was finally exposed. Parked outside the front door was a cop car. No problem; just look ahead, act normal.

I drove on, checking in the rearview mirror. The car's sidelights were on and there were two cops inside. The house hadn't been boarded up yet, but it was cordoned off with yellow tape.

I drove straight on; I couldn't tell if they were looking at me. Even if they did a plate check as I drove past, it wouldn't matter. They'd come up with only Big Al. If I was compromised, I'd run for it and leave Kelly here. Maybe the police would be good guys and look after her. At least that would be the logical thing to do, but there was a conflict. I'd promised that I wouldn't leave her; that promise shouldn't mean much, but it did.

I went down to the bottom of the road and turned right to get out of sight as quickly as possible, then drove a big square to get back in behind them. I reached the small parade of shops. The parking lot was about a quarter full, so we could pull in without attracting attention.

Kelly shrieked, "We're at the stores!"

"That's right, but we can't buy anything because I haven't much money left. But we can go to the house."

"Yesss! Can I get my Pollypockets and Yak-backs from my bedroom, too?"

"Of course you can." I didn't have any idea what she was going on about.

I went around to the back, opened up the trunk and got out the bag, then opened her door. I threw the bag beside her and leaned in.

"Are we going to my house now?"

I started to sort out the kit I'd be needing.

"Yes. I want you to help me because I want you to show me Daddy's hidey-hole. Can you do that? It's important; he wanted me to check something. We've got to sneak in because the cops are outside. Are you going to do everything that I say?"

"Yeah, I'll do that! Can I get Pocahontas, too?"

"Yep."

I didn't give a fuck; I'd have nodded and agreed to anything as long as she showed me the cache.

"You ready? Let's put your hood up." It was dark and cloudy, and thankfully the road wasn't exactly built for pedestrians. We shouldn't encounter any Melissas en route.

With the bag slung over my shoulder, I held her hand and we set off toward the house. It was nearly seven o'clock, and the street lights were on. My plan was to work our way to the back of the house so I could have a look at it and prepare to go in.

We started to walk over the vacant lot to the rear of the house, past trailers and stockpiles of girders and building materials. The mud was so treacherous in places I thought we'd lose our shoes.

Kelly was almost beside herself with excitement but fighting it hard. "That's where my friend Candice lives!" She pointed to a house. "I helped her with their yard sale. We got twenty whole dollars!"

"Shhh!" Smiling, I said slowly, "We've got to be very, very quiet or the policemen will get us."

There was a look of confusion on her face. "Nick?"

What now? "Yes, Kelly."

"Why are we hiding from the police? Aren't they good guys?"

I suppose I should have anticipated that one. What could I say? She wouldn't have understood any of the 101 reasons why we'd be up to our necks in shit if the police caught us. Even if I did have a spare couple of hours to explain them to her. Nor did I want to undermine forever her confidence in the authorities at this early stage in her life. So I lied.

"I don't think they're real cops; I think they're just dressed up like cops. They might be friends of the men who came to see Daddy." It didn't take long for that to register.

Finally we were standing in the shadow of the neighbor's garage. I put the bag down and watched and listened. The engine of the cruiser was idling. They were less than twenty yards away on the other side of the target. I could hear a little of their radio traffic, but I couldn't make out what was being said. Now and again a car drove past, braked for the speed bumps, rattled over them, and accelerated away.

Lights were on in some of the houses, so I could see into the rooms. It had always given me a strange sort of kick doing this, like my own private viewing of a nature documentary: human beings in their natural habitat. As young soldiers in the late seventies in Northern Ireland, part of our job was to "lurk"—hang around in the shadows, watching and listening, hoping to catch a glimpse of someone with a weapon. It was amazing what you'd see people doing in their cars or living rooms, and slightly less amazing what they'd be up to in their bedrooms. Sometimes we'd watch for hours on end, all in the line of duty. I really enjoyed it. Here, people were just doing dishes or watching TV, probably worrying about the effect of multiple murders on real estate prices.

There were no motion-detector lights at the back of the house, just standard ones with an on/off switch by the patio doors. I remembered switching them on for a barbecue.

I stroked Kelly's hair and looked down and smiled. Then,

really slowly, I started to unzip the bag and get out what I needed. I put my mouth right to her ear and whispered, "I want you to stay here. It's really important that you look after this kit. You'll see me over there, OK?"

She nodded. Off I went.

I reached the patio doors. First things first: make sure they're locked. They were. I got my Maglite and checked to see if there were any bolts at the top and bottom of the frame. It's no good defeating a lock if there are also bolts across; that's one of the reasons why you try to attack a building at the point of last exit, because you know they can't be bolted again from the outside.

Normally the next thing to do would be to look for the spare key—why spend an hour with the lock-picking kit if there's one hidden only a few feet away? Some people still leave theirs dangling on a string on the other side of the mailbox, or on the inside of a pet door. Others leave it under a trash can or just behind a little pile of rocks by the door. If a key is going to be left, it will nearly always be somewhere on the normal approach to the door. But this was Kev's house: I wouldn't find spare keys lying around. I put the photographer's blanket over my head and shoulders and, with the Maglite in my mouth, got to work with the lock-pick gun.

I opened the doors gently, moved the curtain aside, and looked inside the living room. The first thing I noticed was that all the curtains and shutters were closed, which was good for me because, once inside, we'd have cover. The second thing that hit me was an overpowering smell of chemicals.

34

I tiptoed back to Kelly and whispered, "Come on, then!"

Our shoes were caked with mud, so we took them off on the concrete step and put them in the bag. Then we went inside and I pulled the doors closed.

I held the Maglite with my middle finger and forefinger over the lens to block most of the light and kept it close to the floor so we could see our way through the living room. The carpet and underlay had been taken up, and all the furniture was pushed to one side. All that was left were the particleboard sheets that the builders had used instead of floorboards. Someone had done a good job of scrubbing the brown stains under where Kev had been lying, which explained the chemical smell. The Murder Mop people had been in; once forensics finished, it was up to the commercial companies to clear away the mess.

We reached the door that led into the front hall. Kelly stood still, an old hand at all this stuff now. I got on my knees, eased the door ajar, and looked through. The front door was closed but light from the streetlamps shone through the stained-glass flower set into the window above it. I switched off the flashlight and stationed Kelly by the bag in the hallway.

I stopped and listened, and generally tuned in. The engine was still idling.

I felt Kelly pulling my jacket.

"Nick?"

"Shhh!"

"What happened to the rug—and what's that horrible smell?"

289

I turned around and half-crouched down. I put my finger to her lips and said, "We'll talk about it later."

There was a *beep beep beep* from the police car's radio. The guys inside were probably drinking coffee, pissed off to be on duty all night. Some radio traffic came on the net. Whoever was Control sounded like Hitler with a dress on.

Indicating that Kelly should stay where she was, I moved across to the study and gently opened the door. I went back, picked up the bag, and guided Kelly into the room, propping the door open with the bag to let the light come through from the hall.

Everything looked very much the same as before except that the things that had been strewn all over the place had now been arranged in a neat line along one wall. The PC was still on its side on the desk, the printer and scanner in position on the floor. They had all been dusted for prints.

I took the photographer's material and a box of tacks from the bag and lifted the chair near to the window. Taking my time, I climbed up and pinned the fabric along the top and down the sides of the entire wooden window frame. I could now close the door and put the flashlight on.

I went over to Kelly. Even above the reek of solvents and cleaners I got a waft of greasy hair, Coca-Cola, bubblegum, and chocolate. I whispered into her ear, "Where is it? Just point."

I shone the flashlight all around the walls, and she pointed at the baseboard behind the door. This was good; nothing there seemed to have been disturbed.

I immediately started prying the wooden strip away from the wall with a screwdriver. A vehicle passed the house, and I heard laughter from the police car—probably at Control's expense. They'd be there solely to deter people from coming around and being nosy. Chances were, the place would be knocked down soon; who'd want to buy a house in which a family had been murdered? Maybe it would be turned into a memorial park or something.

I kept Kelly right next to me; I wanted to keep her reassured. She was interested in what was happening, so I smiled at her now and again to show that everything was fine.

With a small creak the section of board started to give way. I pulled it right off and put it to one side. Then I bent down again and shone the flashlight inside. The beam glinted on metal. What looked like a gun safety box, about eighteen inches square, was recessed into the wall. It was going to need decoding. It could take hours.

I got out the black wallet and set to work, trying to remember to grin at Kelly and let her know it wouldn't be long, but I could see she was getting restless. Ten minutes went by. Fifteen. Twenty. Finally it was all too much for her. In a loud whisper she said crossly, "What about my teddies?"

"Shhh!" I put my finger to her lips again. What I meant was *Fuck the teddies—we'll get them later on.* I continued decoding.

There was a pause; then, no longer a whisper: "But you said!"

It had to be stopped right there and then. Obviously, being Mr. Smiley wasn't working. I turned to Kelly and hissed, "We'll do it in a minute. Now shut up!"

She was taken aback, but it worked.

I was luckier than I might have been with the decoding. I'd just finished, had put the tools away, and was opening the box when I heard a low moan from her. "I don't like it here, Nick. It's all changed."

I turned around, grabbed her, and covered her mouth with my hand. "For Christ's sake shut up!" It wasn't what she expected, but I didn't have time to explain.

With my hand still clamped hard over her mouth, I picked her up and slowly walked to the window. I listened, waited, but there was nothing. Just a bit of banter and laughing, and the crackle of the radio.

As I turned back, however, I heard a short, sharp metallic dragging sound.

Then, for a split second, nothing.

Then, as Kev's pewter tankard of pens and pencils fell from the desk and hit the bare floor, there was a resounding crash. The noise went on as bits and pieces scattered in all directions. As I'd turned, Kelly's coat must have caught on the sharp points of the pencils and dragged the tankard off the table.

I knew the noise was magnified twenty times in my head, but I also knew they would have heard it.

Kelly chose that moment to start to lose it, but there was no time to worry about that. I just left her where she was, went to the doorway, and listened to the sound of car doors opening.

Pulling the pistol from my jeans and checking chamber, I moved out of the study. Three strides got me across the hall and into the kitchen. I closed the door behind me, took a couple of deep breaths, and waited.

The front door opened; I could hear both of them in the hallway. There was a click, and light spilled under the kitchen door.

Then footsteps, and I could hear nervous breathing on the other side, and the jangle of keys on a belt.

I heard the study door opening. Then a half-shouted, half-whispered, "Melvin, Melvin—in here!"

"Yo!"

I knew it was my time. I brought the pistol up into the fire position, put my hand on the doorknob and gently twisted. I moved into the hallway.

Melvin was in the study doorway, his back toward me. He was young and of medium build. I took a couple of big strides, grabbed him across the forehead with my left hand, yanked his head back, and rammed the pistol muzzle into his neck. In a very controlled voice that had nothing to do with the way I was feeling, I said, "Drop your weapon, Melvin. Don't fuck around with me. Drop it now."

Melvin's arm came down to his side and he let the gun fall to the floor.

I couldn't see if the other one had his pistol out or not. It was still dark in the study. Their flashlight was no help. Melvin and I blocked out most of the hallway light. I was hoping that he'd already reholstered, because part of their training would be not to scare kids. As far as he was concerned, Kelly had been just a kid there on her own.

Melvin and I were in the doorway. I shouted, "Put the lights on, Kelly—do it now!"

Nothing happened.

"Kelly, turn the lights on." I heard small footsteps coming toward us. There was a click, and the lights came on.

"Now wait there." I could see her eyes were swollen and red.

Inside the room stood Michelin Man. He must have weighed around 250 pounds, and by the looks of him, he had only a couple of years to go before retirement. He was holstered, but his hand was down by his pistol.

I said, "Don't do it! Tell him, Melvin." I prodded his neck.

Melvin went, "I'm fucked, Ron."

"Ron, don't start messing around. This is not the one to do it for. It's not worth it, not just for this."

I could see that Ron was on top of it. He was thinking about his wife, his mortgage, and the chances of ever seeing another bag of doughnuts.

Melvin's radio sparked up. Control snapped, "Unit Sixty-two, Unit Sixty-two. Do you copy?" It sounded like a demand, not a request. It must have been great to be married to her.

"That's you, isn't it, Melvin?" I said.

"Yes, sir, that's us."

"Melvin, tell them you're OK." I jabbed the pistol a little harder into his neck to underline the point. "The safety catch is off, Melvin. I've got my finger on the trigger. Just tell them everything's OK. It ain't worth it, mate."

Ron blurted, "I'll do it."

Another demand: "Unit Sixty-two, respond."

I said, "Put your right hand up and answer with your left. Kelly, be very quiet, OK?"

She nodded. Ron pressed his radio. "Hello, Control. We've checked. Everything's fine."

"Roger, Unit Sixty-two, your report timed at twenty-two thirteen."

Ron clicked off.

Kelly immediately went back into crying mode and sank to the floor. I was stuck in the doorway with a pistol to Melvin's neck, and Ron, who still had a weapon in his holster, was facing me from the middle of the room.

"When all's said and done, Ron, if you don't play the game, Melvin's going to die—and then you're going to die. Do you understand me?"

Ron nodded.

"OK, Ron, let's see you turn around."

He did.

"Get on your knees."

He did. He was about four feet from Kelly, but as long as she stayed still she wasn't in the line of fire.

Melvin was sweating big-time. My hand was slipping on his forehead. There were even droplets running down the top-slide. His shirt was so wet I could make out the shape of his body armor underneath.

I said, "With your left hand, Ron, I want you to lift out your pistol. Very slow, and use just your thumb and forefinger. Then I want you to move it to your left-hand side and drop it. Do you understand me, Ron?"

Ron nodded.

I said, "Tell him, Melvin, tell him not to fuck around."

"Listen to the man, Ron."

Ron gently removed his pistol from its holster and dropped it on the floor.

"What I want you to do now, with your left hand, is get hold of your handcuffs, and I want you to drop them just behind you. Understand?"

Ron complied. I turned my attention to Melvin, who was starting to tremble. I spoke quietly in his ear. "Don't worry about it, you're going to live. You'll be talking to your grandchildren about this. Just do exactly what I say. Understand?"

He nodded.

I turned to Ron and said, "Now lie down, Ron. Facedown on the floor."

Ron spreadeagled himself and was now under control. I said, "What I'm going to do next, Melvin, is take one step back, and this pistol is going to leave your neck—but it's still going to be pointing at your head, so don't get any ideas. Once I've stepped back, I'm then going to tell you to kneel down—do you understand me?"

He nodded, and I took a swift step backward. I wanted to

be out of arm's reach from him right away; I didn't want him doing some kind of heroic pirouette to grab the gun or knock it out of the way.

"OK, kneel down, then lie down. Just like Ron. Now put your hand next to Ron's."

I now had both of them lying facedown, forearms together. I moved behind them, picked up the handcuffs, and with the pistol stuck in Melvin's ear, I locked his left wrist to Ron's right. I then took Melvin's handcuffs from their holster, stepped back, and said, "I want you to arch your bodies and move your free hands around so they're together as well. Both understand me? Believe me, boys, I want to get this over and done with; I just want out of here."

I finished the job. They weren't going anywhere. I took their wallets and threw them into the bag. I took Melvin's radio and kept it with me, and took the battery out of Ron's and threw it into the bag. At the same time, I grabbed the roll of gaffer tape. I started with their legs, then used the tape to bind their heads together as well. I put a final strip around their necks, and another around their mouths. I checked that both were breathing through their noses, then dragged them into the hallway—no small job, but I didn't want them to see what I was going to do next.

I looked at Kelly, pressed against the study wall. She looked pathetic. This must have been terrible for her. She'd been looking forward so much to coming home, only to find it wasn't the place she'd been expecting. It wasn't only that her family was missing; everything that was familiar to her was drenched in chemicals, shoved to one side, or simply not there.

I heard myself saying, "Why don't you go and see if your teddies are there."

She turned and ran. I heard her rattling up the now uncarpeted stairs.

I went into the study, crouched down by the baseboard, and, at last, was able to open the gun box. There was nothing inside but a lone floppy disk.

I put the chair back by the desk and lifted up the PC. I soon had it working. There was no password protection, probably deliberately. If anything happened to Kev, he'd want the whole world to read what was on the disk.

I clicked open various files but found nothing interesting. Then I found one called Flavius; I knew I'd hit pay dirt. It was the code name of the Gibraltar operation.

I started reading. Kev had found out pretty much what Big Al had told me—that PIRA's connection with the cartels originated when it started running drugs for the Colombians up through North Africa and into Gibraltar for distribution in Spain and the rest of Europe. PIRA was good at the job, and the cartels paid well.

After a while, PIRA had also begun to use the drug trade to raise some of its own money, funds collected by Noraid in the USA. Big sums were involved; Kev's figures showed that Sinn Féin had been netting more than $1,000,000 a year.

These donations had been invested in narcotics, transported to Europe, and then bartered for arms and explosives in the old Eastern-bloc countries. It was a business marriage made in heaven; PIRA had the drugs, the East Europeans had the weapons. The downfall of the USSR and the rise of the Russian mafia couldn't have been better timed.

I had to get back into work mode. I couldn't just sit there reading. I was in a house with two policemen and one pissed-off little girl. I ejected the floppy disk and put it in my coat pocket.

The controller from hell came back on the net. "Unit Sixty-two, do you copy?"

Shit.

I went into the hall. "Ron, time to speak up."

Ron looked at me, and I knew he was going to fuck with me. His face was a picture of defiance. I moved over to them and pulled the tape off their mouths. Ron was the first to talk: "You answer it, because we can't. You won't kill us, not for that."

Control went up an octave. "Unit Sixty-two!"

Ron had a point.

"Kelly! Kelly! Where are you?"

"Coming—I just found Ricky."

I stepped back over my two new friends toward Kelly, who

was coming down the stairs. There was no time to be sympathetic or nice. "Get your coat and shoes on—quick!"

I got all the stuff together, put my running shoes on, and checked that Ron and Melvin weren't choking to death on the gaffer tape. Both looked quite happy with themselves but were still thinking of a good excuse for why they were in this state in the first place.

We left the same way we'd come. I was gripping Kelly's hand, more or less dragging her along, keeping an eagle eye on Jenny and Ricky. I didn't want the neighbors hearing screams for lost teddies.

As we drove, bursts of light from the streetlamps strobed into the back of the car, and I could see Kelly in the rearview mirror. She was looking miserable, her eyes puffy and wet. She had every right to be sad. She was bright enough to realize that this was probably the last time she'd ever be here. This wasn't her home anymore. Now she was the same as me. Neither of us had one.

35

I hit the Dulles Airport access road and headed for economy

I hit the Dulles Airport access road and headed for economy parking. I allowed myself a wry smile; if this kept up, it would soon be full of my stolen cars. I could hear the light patter of rain on the roof as we parked.

Ron and Melvin might have made a connection between me and the car because of the drive-by. If they were back in circulation by now, they might be able to track us down. There was not a lot I could do about it but just sit tight and hope that the mass of cars and the rain would conceal us, because it was far too early for a child to be moving around an airport with an adult man with scabs on his face.

I turned around in the seat and said, "Are you all right, Kelly? I'm sorry I had to shout, but it was really important to get out quick."

She was looking down at one of the teddies, picking its fur, pouting.

I said, "You're not a bad girl and I'm sorry that I told you off. I didn't really mean it, I was just getting excited."

She nodded slowly, still playing with her furry friend.

"Do you want to come to England?"

She looked up. She didn't say anything, but I took it as a yes.

"That's good, because I would like you to come, too. You've been a really good girl, you always do what I say. Do you want to help me again?"

She shrugged. I leaned over and picked up the other teddy and rubbed its face against her cheek. "We'll get Jenny and Ricky to help me as well. How about that?"

She gave a reluctant nod.

"First of all, we've got to sort out the bag."

I got into the backseat and put the duffel between us, opening it up. "What do you think we should take out then?"

I knew exactly what we were going to take out: the blanket and washing kit, because they were the only things I needed now. I said, "What do you reckon? Is that all?" She nodded and agreed as if she'd packed it herself.

I put everything else into the trunk. The rain was coming down more heavily. I sat with her again and pulled out the blanket. "We have to wait here for the next couple of hours. It's too early to go to the airport yet. You can take a nap if you like."

I folded up the bag and made a pillow. "There, that's better—cuddle Jenny and Ricky."

She looked at me and smiled. We were mates again.

"Are you going away again, Nick?"

For once I was staying put. "No, I'm going to do some work. You just go to sleep. I'm not going anywhere." I got out and sat in the front again. I rested the laptop on my knees and lifted the screen. I checked that the keys were in the ignition and I could easily grab the steering wheel. I had to be ready to move at once if we got spotted.

I pressed the On switch, and as the screen lit up it cast a glow through the inside of the car. I inserted Kev's floppy disk. I was desperate to read the rest of his report, but first I downloaded everything onto the laptop. As I waited, I said quietly, "Kelly?" There was no reply. The gentle rhythm of the rain had done its job.

I began reading where I'd left off. Gibraltar had always been a center for international drug trafficking, money laundering, and smuggling, but it seemed that in 1987, Spain not only still wanted Gib back, it also wanted the Brits to clean it up. Thatcher's government told the Gibraltarians to sort it out, but the high-powered speedboats still ran drugs from North Africa. The Brits threatened direct control of the colony if the trafficking didn't stop and, at the same time, ordered a highly illegal operation against police and government officials they suspected of involvement. The boys taking the hush money got the hint and suddenly ceased doing business with PIRA and everyone else.

My eyes were racing ahead of my brain.

The closure of the Gibraltar route was all well and good for the war against corruption, but the Colombians were very pissed off. A major trade artery had been clamped, and they wanted it reopened. According to Kev's findings, they'd decided a show of strength was required. They wanted Gibraltar bombed as a warning that the local officials should start cooperating again, and they ordered PIRA to carry it out.

PIRA had a problem with this. It wanted the route reopened as much as the Colombians did, but, after the debacle of Enniskillen, it couldn't run the risk of killing non-UK civilians and invoking even greater international condemnation. PIRA had refused to do it.

From evidence that Kev had gathered, the cartels' reply to PIRA was blunt: either you bomb Gibraltar or we shift our drug business to the other side—the Protestant UVF. For PIRA, not a good day out.

PIRA's head honchos came up with a solution, and as I read on, I couldn't help but admire it. "Mad Danny" McCann had already been kicked out of PIRA and was reinstated against Gerry Adams's wishes. Mairead Farrell, after the death of her boyfriend, had become too fanatical for her own good—"a bit of a social hand grenade," Simmonds had said of her. PIRA's plan was to send to Gibraltar two players they'd be happy to see the back of, together with Sean Savage, who had the misfortune to be part of the same Active Service Unit.

The team had the technology and Semtex for the bomb but were told that the explosives were to stay behind in Spain until it had finished its recons and rehearsals. The team was told to take it in once the blocking car was in position, to guarantee the correct placement of the bomb. PIRA then gave the three players bad passports and leaked information to London. They wanted the Brits to react and stop the bombing so that when the three were arrested they could claim to the cartels that they'd given it their best shot.

We'd been duly told about the ASU, but we'd also been

briefed that there would be no blocking car and that the bomb would be detonated by a handheld device. These last two pieces of intelligence meant that McCann, Farrell, and Savage had never stood a chance. They were dead from the moment we thought the bomb was in position and armed, because at some stage one of them was bound to make a hand movement that would be construed as an attempt to detonate the device. I certainly wouldn't have taken the chance that Savage was only going for his packet of mints, and Euan obviously didn't when he initiated the contact with McCann and Farrell. In Pat's immortal words: Better to be tried by twelve than carried by six.

A dialogue box came up on the screen telling me that I was running short of power and needed to plug into another power source. Fuck! I wanted to read more. I got back to the screen and read as fast as I could to get the general idea.

Even though there hadn't been a bomb, the cartels had accepted that their Irish lackies were playing ball. After all, three of their people had been killed in the process. PIRA kept the trade with the Colombians, even though, as Big Al had said, it was thereafter routed through South Africa, then Spain.

PIRA was in seventh heaven. It had gotten rid of two troublemakers, not quite in the way that it had intended, but three martyrs had been created, with the result that PIRA's cause at home was strengthened, and even more dollars rolled into the coffers.

It was only the Brits who appeared to have been left with egg on their faces, but even so, no matter how much the international community publicly condemned the shootings, in secret most heads of state admired Thatcher's muscular stand against terrorism.

Fuck it. Another box came up and told me to plug into an external power source. I switched off the laptop and packed it away, full of frustration. I wanted to know more. At the same time I was on a high. If we made it back to the UK with this stuff, I'd have cracked it with Simmonds.

It was 3:30 A.M. There was nothing to do but wait for three

hours or so until the first wave of aircraft started to arrive and depart, creating enough activity for us to blend in.

I let the backrest down a bit and tried to get my neck into a comfortable position, but I couldn't relax. My mind was racing. The whole operation in Gibraltar had been a setup so that PIRA and the Colombians could keep making money. That was one thing, but where did Kev and I fit into the scheme of things? I lay there and listened to the patter of rain.

For Euan and me it had all started on March 3, less than a week before the shootings. We were both on different jobs and had got lifted off and sent to Lisburn, HQ of the British army in Northern Ireland. From there it was a quick move by Puma to Stirling Lines in Hereford, England, the home of the Special Air Service.

We were taken straight to regimental headquarters, and the moment I saw the china cups and cookies outside the briefing room I knew that something big was in the offing. Last time that had happened, the prime minister had been here.

The room was in semidarkness and packed. There was a large screen at the back of a stage and tiered seats so that everyone got a good view.

We were looking for somewhere to sit when I heard, "Oi, over here, dickspot!"

Kev and Slack Pat were sitting drinking tea. With them were the other two members of their four-man team, Geoff and Steve. All were from A Squadron, doing their six months on the counterterrorist team.

Euan turned to Kev and said, "Know what this job is about?"

"We're off to Gib, mate. PIRA's planning a bomb."

The commanding officer got up on the stage and the room fell silent. "Two problems," he said. "Number one, a shortage of time. You leave immediately after this briefing. Number two, shortage of solid intelligence. However, Joint Operations Committee wants the Regiment to deploy. You will get as much information as we know now, and as it comes in during your flight and once on the ground."

I thought, *What the fuck are Euan and I doing here? Surely*

it would be illegal for us to work outside Northern Ireland? I
kept my mouth shut; if I started querying the decision, they
might send me back and I'd miss out.

I looked around and saw members of RHQ, the operations officer, and the world's supply of intelligence corps. The
final member of the team was an ammunitions technical
officer, a bomb disposal expert on attachment to the counterterrorism team.

Someone I had never seen before moved toward the stage,
a tea cup in one hand, a cookie in the other. He stood to the
right-hand side of the stage by the lectern. There was an
overnight bag by his feet.

"My name is Simmonds, and I run the Northern Ireland
desk for the intelligence service from London. The people
behind you are a mix of service and military intelligence officers. First, a very brief outline of the events that have brought
us all here today."

Judging by the bag, it looked as if he would be coming with
us. The lights were dimmed, and a slide projector lit the
screen behind him.

"Last year," he said, "we learned that a PIRA team had
based itself in southern Spain. We intercepted mail going to
the homes of known players from Spain and found a postcard
from Sean Savage in the Costa del Sol."

A slide came up on the screen. "Our Sean," Simmonds said
with a half smile, "told Mummy and Daddy he was working
abroad. It rang a few alarm bells when we read it, because the
work young Savage is best at is bomb making."

Was he making a joke? No, he didn't look the sort.

"Then in November two men went through Madrid airport
on their way from Malaga to Dublin. They carried Irish passports, and in a routine check the Spanish sent the details
to Madrid, who, in turn, passed them with photographs to
London. It turned out that both passports were false."

I thought to myself, *Stupid timing by them, really*. Terrorist
incidents in Northern Ireland tended to decrease in the
summer months when PIRA members took their wives and
kids to the Mediterranean for a fortnight of sun and sand. The
funny thing was that the RUC—Royal Ulster Constabulary—

also took their vacations in the same places, and they'd all bump into each other in the bars. These two characters had drawn attention to themselves; if they'd passed through Malaga airport during the tourist season, they might have gotten away with it.

It turned out that one of the passport holders was Sean Savage, but it was the identity of the second man that had made everybody concerned.

Simmonds showed his next slide. "Daniel Martin McCann. I'm sure you know more about him than I do." He gave a no-fucking-way sort of smile.

"Mad Danny" had really earned his name. Linked to twenty-six killings, he had been lifted often, but had been put away for only two years.

To British intelligence, Simmonds said, the combination of McCann and Savage on the Costa del Sol could mean only one of two things: either PIRA was going to attack a British target on the Spanish mainland, or there was going to be an attack on Gibraltar. "One thing's for sure," he said. "They weren't there to top off their suntans."

At last there was a round of laughter. I could see Simmonds liked that, as if he'd practiced his one-liners so the timing was just right. Despite that, I was warming to the man. It wasn't that often you got people making jokes at a briefing as important as this one.

The slide changed again to a street map of Gibraltar. I was listening to Simmonds but at the same time thinking of my infantry posting there in the 1970s. I'd had a whale of a time.

"Gibraltar is a soft target," Simmonds said. "There are several potential locations for a bomb, such as the Governor's residence or the law courts, but our threat assessment is that the most likely target will be the garrison regiment, the Royal Anglians. Every Tuesday morning the band of the First Battalion parades for the changing of the guard ceremony. We think the most likely site for a bomb is a square that the band marches into after the parade. A bomb could easily be concealed in a car there."

He might have added that from a bomber's point of view it

would be a near-perfect location. Because of the confined area, the blast would be tamped and therefore more effective.

"Following this assessment we stopped the ceremony on December 11. The local media reported that the Governor's guardhouse needed urgent redecoration"—slight smile—"In fact, we needed time while we gathered more intelligence to stop it needing rebuilding."

Not as good as his last one, but there were still a few sub-dued laughs.

"The local police were then reinforced by plainclothes officers from the UK, and their surveillance paid off. When the ceremony resumed on February 23, a woman, ostensibly taking a vacation on the Costa del Sol, made a trip to the Rock and photographed the parade. She was covertly checked and was found to be traveling on a stolen Irish passport.

"The following week she was there again, only this time she tagged along behind the bandsmen as they marched to the square. Even my shortsighted mother-in-law could have worked out that she was doing recon for the arrival of an Active Service Unit."

There was loud laughter. He'd done it again. I wasn't too sure if we were all laughing at his jokes or at the fact that he kept on telling them. Who the fuck was this man? This should have been one of the most serious briefings ever. Either he just didn't give a fuck or he was so powerful no one was going to say a word against him. Whatever, I could already tell his presence in Gibraltar would be a real bonus.

Simmonds stopped smiling. "Our intelligence tells us that the bombing is to take place sometime this week. However, there is no sign that either McCann or Savage is getting ready to leave Belfast."

He wasn't wrong. I had seen both of them, stinking drunk, outside a bar on the Falls Road just the night before. They didn't look that ready to me. It should take them quite a while to prepare for this one—or maybe this was part of the preparation, having their last night out before work started.

"This is where we have a few problems," he went on. He was working now without his notes. Did that mean no more one-liners? Certainly, there was more of an edge to his voice.

"What are we to do with these people? If we try to move in on them too early, that would only leave other PIRA teams free to go ahead with the bombing. In any case, if the ASU travels through Malaga airport and remains on Spanish territory until the last minute, there is no guarantee that the Spanish courts will hand them over, not only because of the dispute with the UK on the question of whom Gibraltar belongs to—but because the case against them could only be based on conspiracy, which is pretty flimsy.

"So, gentlemen, we must arrest them in Gibraltar." The screen went blank; there was only the light from the lectern shining on his face. "And this throws up three options. The first is to arrest them as they cross the border from Spain. Easier said than done; there's no guarantee we'll know what kind of vehicle they're in. There would be only about ten to fifteen seconds in which to make a positive identification and effect an arrest—not an easy thing to do, especially if they are sitting in a car and probably armed.

"The second option is to arrest the team members once they're in the area of the square, but again this depends on advance warning and positive identification, and their all being together with the device. At the present time, therefore, we are going for the third option, and that's why we are all here."

He took a sip of his tea and asked for the lights to come back on.

He looked around for each group as he talked.

"The Security Service will place surveillance teams to trigger the PIRA team into Gibraltar. The two soldiers who have just arrived from Northern Ireland"—Euan caught my eye—that was him and me—"must give positive IDs on the terrorists before the civil authorities will hand over the operation to the military. You two will not, repeat, not, conduct any arrest or contact action. You understand the reasons why? The four men from your counterterrorist team will make a hard arrest *only after* they have planted the device.

"Once arrested," Simmonds went on, "they are to be handed over to the civil authorities. Of course, the normal protection will be given to the team from any court appearance."

He managed a smile. "I think that's enough, gentlemen."

He looked at the commanding officer. "Francis, I understand we fly to RAF Lyneham in ten minutes to link up with the Hercules?"

Just over three hours later I was sitting in a C-130 with Euan, who was busy worrying about a black mark on his new sneakers. Kev was checking the weapon bundles and ammunition and, more important as far as I was concerned, the medical packs. If I got dropped, I wanted fluid put into me as soon as possible.

We landed at about 11:30 P.M. on Thursday, March 3. Gibraltar was still awake; lights were on everywhere. We moved off to the military area, where trucks were waiting with our advance party to get us away quickly and without fuss.

Our FOB—Field Operations Base—was in HMS *Rooke*, the Royal Navy shore base. We had requisitioned half a dozen rooms in the accommodation block and turned them into living space, with our own cooking area and ops room. Wires trailed everywhere, telephones were ringing, signalers ran around in tracksuits or jeans, testing radios and satellite communications links.

Over the din Simmonds said, "Intelligence suggests there could be a third member of the team, probably its commander. Her name is Mairead Farrell. We'll have pictures within the hour, but here's some background for you. She's a particularly nasty piece of work: middle class, thirty-one, ex–convent schoolgirl."

He grinned, then told us more about her. She'd served ten years in prison for planting a bomb in the Conway Hotel, Belfast, in 1976, but as soon as she was released she reported straight back to PIRA for duty. There was a slight smile on his face as he explained that her lover, unbelievably named Brendan Burns, had blown himself up recently.

The meeting broke up, and a signaler came over and started handing out street maps. "They've already been spotted up by Intelligence," he said.

As we started to look at their handiwork he went on. "The main routes from the border to the square are marked in detail, the rest of the town fairly well, and of the outlying areas, just major points."

I looked at it. Fucking hell! There were about a hundred coordinates to learn before the ASU came over the border. I didn't know what was tougher—the PIRA team or the homework.

"Any questions, lads?"

Kev said, "Yeah, three. Where do we sleep, where's the toilet, and has somebody got some coffee on?"

In the morning, we picked up our weapons and ammunition and went onto the range. The four on the counterterrorism team had their own pistols. The ones Euan and I had were borrowed—our own were still in Derry. Not that it mattered much; people think that blokes in the SAS are very particular about their weapons, but we aren't. So long as you know that when you pull the trigger it will fire the first time and the rounds will hit the target you're aiming at, you're happy.

Once at the range, people did their own thing. The other four just wanted to know that their mags were working OK and that the pistols had no defects after being bundled up. We wanted to do the same, but also to find out the behavior of our new weapons at different ranges. After firing off all the mags in quick succession to make sure everything worked, we then fired at five, ten, fifteen, twenty, and twenty-five yards. Good, slow, aimed shots, always aiming at the same point and checking where the rounds fell at each range. That way we knew where to aim at fifteen yards, for example, and that was at the top of the target's torso. Because of the distance, quite a lot for a pistol, the rounds would fall lower into the bottom of his chest and take him down. Every weapon is different, so it took an hour to be confident.

Once finished we didn't strip the weapons to clean them. Why do that when we knew they worked perfectly? We just got a brush into the area that feeds the round into the barrel and got the carbon off.

Next job was getting on the ground to learn the spots system, at the same time checking our radios and finding out if there were any dead areas. We were still running around doing that when, at 2 P.M., Alpha came up on the net. "Hello, all stations, return to this location immediately."

Simmonds was already in the briefing area when we arrived, looking like a man under pressure. Like the rest of us, he'd probably had very little sleep. There was two days' growth on his chin, and he was having a bad hair day. Something was definitely going on; there was a lot more noise and bustle from the machines and men in the background. He had about twenty bits of paper in his hand. The intelligence boys were giving him more as he talked, and they distributed copies of the rules of engagement to us. The operation, I saw, was now called Flavius.

"Just about an hour and a half ago," he said, "Savage and McCann passed through Immigration at Malaga airport. They were on a flight from Paris. Farrell met them. We have no idea how she got there. The team is complete. There is just one little problem—the Spanish lost them as they got into a taxi. Triggers are now being placed on the border crossing as a precaution. I have no reason to believe that the attack will not take place as planned."

He paused and looked at each of us in turn. "I've just become aware of two very critical pieces of information. First, the players will not be using a blocking car to reserve a parking space in the target area. A blocking car would mean making two trips across the border, and the intelligence is that they're not prepared to take the risk. The PIRA vehicle, when it arrives, should therefore be perceived as the real thing.

"Second, the detonation of the bomb will be by a handheld remote control initiation device: they want to be sure that the bomb goes off at exactly the right moment. Remember, gentlemen, any one of the team, or all of them, could be in possession of that device. That bomb must not detonate. There could be hundreds of lives at risk."

I was awoken by the noise of engines in reverse and wheels on the tarmac. It was just after 6 A.M. I had been asleep for three hours. It was still dark; the rain had eased quite a bit. I leaned over to the back. "Kelly, Kelly, time to wake up." As I shook her there was a gentle moan. She sat up, rubbing her eyes.

With the cuff of my coat I started to tidy her up. I didn't want her walking into the airport looking wrecked. I wanted us as spruce and happy as Donny and Marie Osmond on Prozac.

We got out of the car with the bag and I locked up, after checking inside to make sure that there wasn't anything attractive to see. The last thing I needed now was a parking lot attendant taking an interest in my lock-picking kit. We walked over to the bus stop and waited for the shuttle to take us to departures.

The terminal looked just like any airport at that time of the morning. The check-in desks were already quite busy with business fliers. A handful of people, mostly student types, looked as though they were waiting for flights that they'd gotten there much too early for. Cleaners with floor waxers trudged across the tiled floors like zombies.

I picked up a free airport magazine from the rack at the top of the escalator. Looking at the flight guide, I saw that the first possible departure to the UK was at just after five o'clock in the afternoon. It was going to be a long wait.

I looked at Kelly; we both could do with a decent wash. We went down the escalator to the international arrivals area on the lower level. I put some money in a machine and got a couple of travel kits to supplement our washing kit and went into one of the handicap-accessible toilets.

I shaved as Kelly washed her face. I scraped the dirt off her boots with toilet paper and generally cleaned her up, combed her hair, and put it in an elastic band at the back so it didn't look so greasy. After half an hour we were looking fairly respectable. The scabs on my face were healing. No Prozac, but we'd pass muster.

I picked up the bag. "You ready?"

"Are we going to England now?"

"Just one thing left to do. Follow me." I pulled at the stubby ponytail that made her look like a four-foot-tall cheerleader. She acted annoyed, but I could tell she liked the attention.

We went back up the escalator and walked around the edge

of the terminal. I pretended to be studying the aircraft out on the tarmac. In fact, there were two quite different things I was looking for. "I need to mail something," I said, spotting the FedEx box.

I used the credit card details on the car rental agreement to fill out the mailing label. Fuck it—Big Al could pay for a few things now that he was rich.

Kelly was watching every movement. "Who are you writing?"

"I'm sending something to England in case we are stopped." I showed her the floppy disk and backup disk.

"Who are you sending it to?" She got more like her dad every day.

"Don't be so nosy."

I put them in the envelope, sealed it, and entered the delivery details. In the past we'd used the FedEx system to send the Firm photos from abroad that we'd taken of a target and developed in a hotel room, or other highly sensitive material. It saved getting caught with them in our possession. Nowadays, however, the system was obsolete; with digital cameras you can take pictures, plug in your cellular mobile, dial up the UK, and transmit.

We continued walking around the edge of the terminal. I found the power outlet I was looking for at the end of a row of black plastic seats where two students were snoring. I pointed to the last two spaces. "Let's sit down here. I want to look at the laptop."

I got it plugged in. Kelly decided she wanted something to eat. "Give me five minutes," I said.

From what I'd read earlier, I understood Gibraltar was a setup, but it still didn't explain what Kev had to do with it. It soon became clearer.

In the late 1980s the Bush administration had been under pressure from Thatcher to do something about Noraid fund-raising for PIRA. With so many millions of Irish American votes on the line, however, it was a tricky call. A deal was struck: if the Brits could expose the fact that Noraid money was being used to buy drugs, it would help discredit PIRA in the USA and Bush could then take action. After all, who would complain about a US administration fighting the spread of dangerous narcotics?

When the British intelligence service started to gather data about PIRA's drug connections with Gibraltar, it seemed to present a window of opportunity. After the events of March 6, however, the window was slammed shut. Those votes were too important.

By the early 1990s the US had a new administration—and the UK a new prime minister. In Northern Ireland, the peace process began. The US was told—and the message was delivered at the highest level—that unless it put pressure on PIRA to come to the peace table, the UK would expose what was happening to Noraid funds raised in America. The failure to fight the drug war in its own backyard, by a power that preached so readily to others, would be a serious embarrassment.

Another deal was sorted out. Clinton allowed Gerry Adams into the USA in 1995, a move that was not only good for the Irish American vote but which made Clinton look like the prince of peacemakers. He also appeared to be snubbing John Major's stand against PIRA, but the British didn't mind; they knew the agenda. Behind closed doors, Gerry Adams was told that if PIRA didn't let the peace process happen, the US would come down on them like a ton of steaming shit.

A ceasefire was indeed declared. It seemed that the years of covert talks that had gone nowhere were finally at an end; it was now time to talk for real. Clinton and the British government would be seen as peace brokers, and PIRA would have a say in the way the deal was shaped.

On February 12, 1996, however, a massive bomb exploded at London's newest business center, Canary Wharf, killing two and causing hundreds of millions of dollars of damage. The ceasefire was broken. It was back to business as usual.

But it didn't end there. Kev had also discovered that PIRA had been trying to blackmail certain Gibraltarian officials, with some success. It seemed Gibraltar was still the key to Europe. Spain was far too much of a risk. They had also targeted some important personalities in the US so they could continue to operate their drug business with impunity. One of the victims was high up in the DEA. Kev's problem was, he didn't know who.

I did; I had the photograph of his boss.

And now I knew why McGear, Fernahan, and Macauley had been in Gibraltar. Whoever the official was, they'd been there to give him a final warning and to try to blackmail him with the shipment documents and photographs to get the routes open again.

I had to get back to the UK. I had to see Simmonds.

At ten o'clock we went back down the escalator to international arrivals. I needed passports—British or American, I didn't care. I scanned the international flights on the monitor. Chances were we were going to end up with American documents rather than British, purely because of the number of families streaming back from spring vacation.

Just like before, there were people on both sides of the railings, waiting with their cameras and flowers. Kelly and I sat on the PVC seats near the domestic carousels on the other side of the international gates. I had my arm around her as if I were cuddling her and chatting away. In fact, I was talking her through some of the finer points of theft.

"Do you think you can do it?"

We sat and watched the first wave of domestic arrivals come, stand around, then leave when they collected their luggage.

I spotted a potential family. "That's the sort of thing we're looking for, but they're two boys." I smiled. "You want to be a boy for the day?"

"No way—boys stink!"

I put my nose into my sweatshirt. I agreed. "OK, we'll wait."

A flight arrived from Frankfurt; this time we struck gold. The parents were late thirties, the kids were about ten or eleven, a girl and a boy; the mother was carrying a clear plastic handbag with white mesh so you could check everything was where it should be. I couldn't believe our luck. "See them? That's what we want. Let's go, shall we?"

There was a slightly hesitant "Yeahhh." She didn't sound too keen now. Should I let her do this? I could stop it right now. As they walked toward the rest rooms I had to make a decision. *Fuck it. Let's carry on and get this done.*

"She's going in with her daughter," I said. "Make sure nobody's behind you. Remember, I'll be waiting."

We followed casually. The husband had left with the boy, perhaps to visit one of the vending machines or to wait for their bags.

Mother and daughter went in via the ladies' entrance, chatting and giggling. The mother had the bag over her shoulder. We entered via the men's on the right of the handicap toilets, and immediately went into one of the large stalls.

"I'll be in this one here, OK, Kelly?"

"OK."

"Remember what you have to do?"

I got a big, positive nod.

"Off you go then." I closed the door and held it in place. The stalls were large enough for a wheelchair to maneuver in. The slightest sound seemed to echo. The floors were wet and smelled of bleach. The timesheet on the back of the door showed the place had been cleaned only fifteen minutes ago.

My heart was pumping so hard I could feel it underneath my shirt; I was even starting to hyperventilate. My whole future pivoted on the actions of a seven-year-old girl. She had to slip her hand under the stall, grab the handbag, put it under her coat, and walk away without looking back. Not difficult—just majorly flawed. But without passports we couldn't get out of the country; it was as simple as that. I had decided there was no way I could go back to Big Al's. Besides the risk of the journey, I couldn't trust him, because I had no idea what he'd been doing since I left him. It was just too fucking complicated. We needed to get out of this country, and now.

I was shaken from my thoughts by a sudden *knock, knock, knock* and a nervous "Nickkk!"

I opened the door quickly, didn't even look, and in she ran. I closed and locked it, picked her up, and carried her over to the toilet.

I put the lid down and we sat together. I smiled and whispered, "Well done!" She looked both excited and scared. I was just scared, because I knew that at any minute all hell would break loose.

And then it came. The mother was running out of the rest room, shouting, "My bag! My bag's been stolen! Where's Louise? Louise!"

Louise came out and started to cry. "Oh, Mom, what's happened?"

I could hear both of them running off, yelling. Now was not the time to get out. People would be looking; attention would be focused. Let's just sit tight and look at the passports.

We'd just robbed Mrs. Sarah Glazar and family. Fine, except that Mr. Glazar didn't look at all like Mr. Stone. Never mind, I could do something about that later on. But the names of both kids were entered on each of their parents' passports, and that was a problem.

I pulled out the cash and her reading glasses. The toilet tank was a sealed unit behind the wall. There was nowhere to hide the bag. I got up, told Kelly to stand, and listened at the door.

The woman had found a policeman. I imagined the scene outside. A little crowd would have gathered around. The cop would be making notes, radioing Control, maybe checking the other stalls. I broke into a sweat.

I stood at the door and waited for what seemed like an hour. Kelly tiptoed exaggeratedly toward me; I bent down and she whispered in my ear, "Is it all right yet?"

"Almost."

Then I heard a banging noise, and knocking. Somebody was pushing back the doors in the vacant stalls and knocking on the doors of the others. They were looking for the thief or, more likely, to see if the bag had been dumped once the money had been taken. They'd be at our stall any second.

I didn't have time to think. "Kelly, you must talk if they knock. I want you to—"

Knock, knock, knock.

It sounded like the slam of a cell door.

A male voice shouted, "Hello, police—anyone in there?" He tried to turn the handle.

I quickly moved Kelly back to the toilet and whispered in her ear. "Say you will be out soon."

She shouted, "I'll be out in a minute."

There was no reply, just the same thing happening at the next stall. The danger had passed, or so I hoped.

All that was left to do was dump my pistol and mags. That was easy. I slipped them into Sarah's bag and crushed it into a package that would fit in a trash can.

It was an hour before I decided it was safe to leave. I turned to Kelly. "Your name is Louise now, OK? Louise Glazar."

"OK."

She didn't seem fussed at all.

"Louise, when we leave here in a minute I want you to be really happy and I want you to hold my hand." With that I picked up the bag. "OK, we're off!"

"To England?"

"Of course! But first of all we've got to get on the plane. By the way, you were great—well done!"

We got into the departures area at 11:30 A.M. Still several hours to go before the first possible flight, British Airways flight 216 to Heathrow at 5:10.

I went to a phone and, using the numbers in the airport magazine, called each airline in turn to check seat availability. The British Airways flight was fully booked. So was United Airways 918 at 6:10, the BA at 6:10, and the United at 6:40. I eventually managed to find two spare seats on a flight with Virgin at 6:45, and gave all the details of Mr. Glazar, who was on his way to the airport right now. Payment was courtesy of the details for Big Al's plastic on the car rental form.

I wandered past the Virgin desk and found it didn't open until 1:30 P.M. One and a half hours to sit and sweat.

Christian Glazar was a little older than me, and his shoulder-length hair was starting to go gray. My hair was just below the ear, and brown. Thankfully, his passport was four years old.

To the delight of Kelly and the terminal's barbershop owner, I underwent a number one crew cut, coming out looking like a US Marine.

We then went into the travel store and bought a pack of painkillers that claimed to be the answer to female pains. Judging by the list of ingredients, they were certainly the answer for me.

All the time, I kept hoping that the police had assumed the motive for the theft was money and had left it to the Glazars to report the cards and passports missing rather than pursuing the matter further. I didn't want to turn up at the ticket sales desk and be jumped on by several hundred pounds of cop.

Still thirty minutes to go before we could check in. One more thing to do.

"Kelly, we have to go to the bathroom up here for a while."

"I don't need to go."

"It's for me to get into my disguise. Come and see."

We went to the handicap toilet in departures and closed the door. I took out Sarah's glasses. They were gold-framed and had lenses as thick as the bottom of Coke bottles. I tried them on. The frames weren't big enough but they looked OK. I turned to Kelly and crossed my eyes. Then I had to stop her laughing.

I took the painkillers out of the duffel. "I'm going to swallow these and they're going to make me ill. But it's for a reason, OK?"

She wasn't quite sure.

I took six capsules and waited. The hot flashes started, then the cold sweats. I put my hands up to show it was OK as the contents of my stomach flew out of my mouth into the toilet bowl.

Kelly watched in amazement as I rinsed out my mouth in the basin. I looked at myself in the mirror. Just as I'd hoped, I looked as pale and clammy as I felt. I took two more.

There were few customers at the long line of check-in desks and only one woman on duty at Virgin Atlantic ticket sales. She was writing something so her head was down as we approached. She was in her mid-twenties and beautiful, with relaxed hair pulled back in a bun.

"Hello, the name's Glazar." Because of the vomiting my voice was lower and coarse. "There should be two tickets for me." I tried to look disorganized and flustered. "Hopefully, my brother-in-law has booked them?" My eyes looked to the sky in hope.

"Sure, do you have a reference number?"

"Sorry, he didn't give me one. Just Glazar, Christian Glazar."

She tapped that out and said, "That's fine, Mr. Glazar, two tickets for you and Louise. How many bags are you checking in?"

I had the laptop on my shoulder and the duffel in my hand. I dithered, as if working out if I'd need the laptop on the flight. "Just this one." I put the bag on the scale. It didn't weigh much, but it was bulked up respectably with the blanket.

"Could I see your passport, please?"

I looked in all my pockets without apparent success. I didn't want to produce Glazar's documents right away. "Look, I know we were lucky to get seats at all, but is it possible to make sure we're sitting together?" I leaned a little closer and half-whispered, "Louise hates flying."

Kelly and I exchanged glances. "Everything's going to be OK," I told her. My voice dropped again. "We're on a bit of a mercy mission."

I looked down at Kelly and back at the woman, my face pained. "Her grandmother's . . ." I let it hang, as if the rest of the sentence would be too terrible for a little girl's ears.

"I'll see what I can do, sir."

She was hitting the keys of her PC at such a speed it looked as if she were bluffing. I put the passport on top of the counter. She looked up and smiled. "No problem, Mr. Glazar."

"That's marvelous." But I still wanted to keep the conversation going. "I wonder, would it be possible for us to use one of your lounges? It's just that, after my chemotherapy, I tire very easily. We've been rushing around today and I don't feel too good. I only have to knock myself and I start bleeding."

She looked at my scabs and pale complexion and understood. There was a pause, then she said, "My mother went through chemo for cancer of the liver. The therapy worked; after all that pain she came through."

I thanked her for her concern and her message of support. *Now just get me into the lounge, out of the fucking way!*

"Let me find out." Smiling at Kelly, she picked up the phone and spoke. After several seconds of weird airline vocabulary she looked at me and nodded. "That's fine, sir. We share facilities with United. I'll fill out an invitation."

I thanked her as she reached for the passport. I hoped that by now she knew me so well it was just a formality. She flicked it open; I turned away and talked to Kelly, telling her how exciting it was going to be, flying to see Grandma.

I heard, "You'll be boarding at about five-thirty." I looked up, all smiles.

"Go to Gate C. A shuttle will take you to the lounge. You both have a pleasant flight."

"Thank you so much. Come on then, Louise, we've got a plane to catch!" I let Kelly walk on a few steps, then turned and said, "I just hope Grandma can wait for us." She nodded knowingly.

All I wanted to do now was get through Customs. First hurdle was security. Kelly went through first, and I followed. No alarms. I had to open up the laptop and switch it on to prove it worked, but I'd been expecting that. All the Flavius files were now in a folder called Games.

We went straight to Gate C, walked through, and got on the shuttle bus. There was a five-minute wait while the bus filled up, then the doors closed, the hydraulics lowered, and we drove about half a mile across the tarmac to the departures lounge proper.

The area was plush and busy. I heard a lot of British accents, mixed in with snatches of German and French. Kelly and I headed for the United lounge, via a detour to the candy stall.

We sat quietly with a large cappuccino and a Coke. Unfortunately, the downtime just gave me a while to think about whether I'd made any mistakes.

A security man walked into the reception area and talked to the people at the desk. My heart beat faster. We were so close to the aircraft on the other side of the glass that I felt I could reach out and touch them. I could almost smell the aviation fuel.

I told myself to calm down. If they'd wanted us, they would have found us by now.

But, in truth, so many things could still go wrong that one of them almost certainly would. I was still sweating away. My head was glistening. And I didn't know if it was the capsules or my worrying, but I was starting to feel weak.

"Nick, am I Louise all day today or just for now?"

I pretended to think about it. "The whole day. You're Louise Glazar all day."

"Why?"

"Because they won't let us go to England unless we use another name."

I got a smiling, thoughtful nod.

I said, "Do you want to know something else?"

"What?"

"If I call you Louise, you have to call me Daddy. But just for today."

I wasn't sure what kind of reaction that would get, but she just shrugged. "Whatever." Maybe that was what she wanted now.

The next three hours were grim, but at least we were out of the way. If I'd had any heart problems, I would probably have died, the blood was coursing through me so fast and hard. I could hear it pumping in my ears.

I kept saying to myself: *You're here now, there's nothing you can do about it; accept it. Just get on that fucking aircraft!*

I looked at Kelly. "You all right, Louise?"

"Yeah, I'm all right, Daddy." She had a big smile now. I just hoped she kept it.

I watched the receptionist move to the microphone. She announced our flight and told us that she had really enjoyed having us stay in the lounge.

There were about a dozen others who stood up and started to sort themselves out, folding papers and zipping up bags.

I got to my feet and stretched. "Louise?"

"Yeah?"

"Let's go to England!"

We walked toward the gate, father and daughter, hand in hand, chatting about nothing. My theory went: if I talked with her, they wouldn't talk to us.

Four or five people were ahead of us in line—like us, families with young children. Passports were being checked by a young Latino; he had an ID card on a chain around his neck, but we were too far way yet for me to make out what it said. Was he airline security or airport security?

Two uniformed security men came up and stood behind him, talking to each other. It was the kind of chat that looked so casual it probably wasn't. I used my sleeve to mop sweat from the side of my face.

Both of the uniformed men were armed. The black one cracked a joke as the white one laughed and looked around. Kelly and I shuffled forward.

I held her beside me, the protective parent anxious in a crowd. The laptop was over my shoulder. Kelly held a teddy bear under each arm.

We moved three steps forward; another wait, then it was our turn with the Latino.

I wanted to make it all very easy for him. Smiling, I handed him the boarding passes and the passport. I was convinced the uniformed guys were looking at me. I went into boxer mode: everything was focused on the Latino; everything else was in the distance, muffled, distorted, peripheral. A bead of sweat fell down my cheek, and I knew he'd noticed it. I knew he could see my chest heaving up and down.

Kelly was just behind and to the right of me. I looked at her and smiled.

"Sir?"

I silently exhaled in preparation and looked back at him.

"Just the passport, sir." He handed me back the boarding passes. I grinned, the inexperienced dickhead traveler.

He flicked through the pages of the passport, stopping at Glazar's photograph. He glanced at me, then back at the passport.

I'm in deep shit.

I let him see I was reading his thoughts. "Male meno-
pause," I grinned, rubbing my hand over what was left of my
hair. My scalp was drenched. "The Bruce Willis look!"

The fucker didn't laugh. He was making up his mind. He
closed the passport and tapped it in his hand. "Have a
pleasant flight, sir."

I went to give him a nod, but he was already paying attention to the people behind me.

We moved two paces toward the women from Virgin and
handed them our boarding passes. The two security men
didn't budge.

We started to walk onto the airbridge; I felt as if I'd been
trying to run through waist-high water and was suddenly on
the shoreline.

The Latino still worried me. I thought about him all the
way onto the aircraft. It was only when I'd found our seats,
put the laptop in the overhead locker, settled down, and
picked up the in-flight magazine that I took a deep breath and
let it out very, very slowly. It wasn't a sigh of relief; I was
boosting the oxygen levels in my blood. No, the fucker wasn't
happy. His suspicions had been aroused, but he hadn't asked
any questions, hadn't even asked my name. We might be on
the shoreline, but it was far from being dry land.

The aircraft was still filling up. I kept taking deep breaths
to try to control my pulse rate.

Officials were moving in and out of the aircraft with mani-
fests. Every time it happened I was expecting to see the two
security guys in tow. There was only one entrance, only one
exit. There was nowhere to run. As I worked through the scenarios in my mind, I just had to accept that the die was cast. I
was a passenger now, and for a fleeting second I had the same
feeling that I'd always had on any aircraft, military or
civilian—I was in the hands of others and powerless to decide
my own destiny. I hated it.

People were still filing on. I nearly burst out in nervous
laughter as the speakers played Gloria Gaynor's "I Will Survive." I looked at Kelly and winked. She thought it was great,
sitting there trying to strap in her teddy bears.

One of the male flight attendants came down our aisle, still wearing his Virgin uniform, not yet in shirtsleeves. He came down to our row of seats and stopped. Judging by his line of sight, he seemed to be checking our seat belts. It was too early for that, surely? I nodded and smiled. He turned back and disappeared into the galley.

I watched the entrance, expecting the worst. One of the female flight attendants poked her head out and looked directly at me. Kelly's teddy bears were suddenly very interesting.

I could feel tingling in my feet. My stomach tightened. I looked up again. She was gone.

The male attendant came out again, carrying a garbage bag. He approached us again, stopped, and squatted down in the aisle next to Kelly. He said, "Hiya!"

"Hello!"

He put his hand into the bag; I waited for him to bring out the .45. Good ploy, letting me think he's a member of the crew doing something for the kid.

He pulled out a little nylon daysack. Splattered all over the back was the Virgin logo and the words KIDS WITH ALTITUDE. "We forgot to give you one of these," he said. I nearly hugged him.

"Thank you very much!" I grinned like an asylum inmate, my eyes one hundred percent larger through the lenses of Sarah's glasses. "Thank you so much!"

He did his best not to look at me, as if I were indeed some sort of weirdo, then offered us a drink before takeoff. I was dying for a beer, but I might have to start performing on the other side and, anyway, I just wanted to lean back and rest. We each ordered an orange juice instead.

Sharing the in-flight guide with Kelly, I said, "What film are you going to watch, Louise?"

"Clueless," she grinned.

"Whatever," I said.

Twenty minutes later, right on schedule, the aircraft finally lifted off from the runway. Suddenly I didn't mind being in a pilot's hands after all.

36

We went through all the nonsense of the introduction by the captain, how wonderful it was to have us on board, and when we were going to be fed. My body heat was starting to dry out my sweat-drenched shirt. Even my socks had been wet. I looked over at Kelly. She had a sad face on. I nudged her with my arm. "You OK?"

"I guess. I couldn't even tell Melissa I'm going to England."

I knew how to get out of this type of thing now. "Well, all you have to do is think good things about Melissa and that will make you feel happy." I was waiting for her reply. I knew the sort of thing it was going to be.

"Do you think about David? What do you remember about David?"

Easy; I was prepared. "Well, nearly twelve years ago, we were rebuilding his house together and it needed a new wooden floor."

She was enjoying this, stories at bedtime. She certainly looked as if she would go to sleep soon, cuddling up to me. I continued telling her how we'd both swiped a squash court floor from one of the HQ Security Forces bases in Northern Ireland. We were there at three o'clock in the morning with spades, hammers, and chisels. We put the boards in a van and brought them over to his Welsh cottage. After all, HM Government spent all that time and money training us to break in and steal things. Why not use it for ourselves? The next three days had been spent laying the hallway and kitchen of the house near Brecon with his nice new flooring.

I grinned down at her for a reaction, but she was already sound asleep.

I started to watch the video but knew I was going to fall asleep any minute—as long as the capsules wore off and I could stop my mind going back to the same question over and over again.

There was an unholy alliance between PIRA and corrupt elements of the DEA, of that there was no doubt—and it very much looked as though Kev's boss was at the center of it. Kev had found out about the corruption, but not who was involved. He wanted to talk to somebody about it. Was it his boss whom he'd unwittingly phoned for an opinion the day I arrived in Washington? Very unlikely, because Kev would have had to include him on his list of suspects. Much more probable was that he'd spoken to someone unconnected with the DEA, someone who'd know what he was talking about and whose opinion he valued. Could it have been Luther? He knew Kev; would Kev have trusted him? Who knows? Whoever he had called, he was dead within an hour of putting down the phone.

The cabin lights came on a couple of hours before landing, and we were served breakfast. I tried to wake Kelly, but she groaned and buried herself under her blanket. I didn't bother with the food. From feeling almost elated at having gotten past security, I awoke profoundly depressed. My mood was as black as the coffee in front of me. I'd been crazy to let myself feel relieved. We weren't out of the woods by a long shot; if they knew we were on the aircraft, of course they wouldn't do anything about it until we landed. It was at the point that I walked off and stepped onto the ramp that they'd lift me. Even if that didn't happen, there was Immigration. The officials trying to keep out undesirables are much tougher and a lot more on the ball than those in charge of waving you off. They vet your documents much more closely, scrutinize your body language, read your eyes. Kelly and I were on a stolen passport. We'd gotten through at Dulles, but that didn't mean we could pull it off again.

I took four capsules and finished my coffee. I remembered

that I was an American citizen now. When the attendant came past I asked her for an immigration card. Kelly was still asleep.

Filling in the card, I decided that the Glazars had just moved and now lived next door to Mr. and Mrs. Brown. Hunting Bear Path was the only address I could talk about convincingly.

If I was lifted at Immigration, it wouldn't be the first time. I'd come into Gatwick airport once from a job. I gave my passport to the Immigration officer, and while he was inspecting it a boy came up on either side, gripped my arms and took the passport from the official. "Mr. Stamford? Special Branch. Come with us." I wasn't going to argue; my cover was good, I was in the UK now, everything was going to be fine.

They strip-searched me in an interview room, firing questions left, right, and center. I went through the whole routine of my cover story: where I'd been, what I'd been doing, why I'd been doing it. They telephoned my cover, and James supported my story. Everything was going swimmingly.

Then I got put in the airport detention cells, and three policemen came in. They wasted no time; two held my arms, one threw punches; they then took turns. They beat the shit out of me. No word of explanation.

Next I got taken for an interview and was accused of being a pedophile and procuring kids in Thailand—which was strange, considering I'd been on a deniable op in Russia. There was nothing I could say; it was just down to denying, and waiting for the system to get me out.

After about four hours of interviews I was sitting in my cell. In came people from the intelligence service, to debrief me on my performance. It had been a fucking exercise. They'd been testing all the operators as we came back into the UK; the only trouble was, they'd picked the wrong charge to pull us up on. The police don't wait for niceties like courtrooms when it comes to dealing with child molesters, so everyone who was lifted got taken to one side and given the good news. One bloke got such a severe kicking he ended up in the hospital.

* * *

Kelly looked as if she'd been sleeping in a hedge. She yawned and made an attempt to stretch. As she opened her eyes and looked around, completely bewildered, I grinned and offered her the carton of orange juice. "How are you today, Louise?"

She still seemed lost for a second or two, then got back with the program. "I'm all right." She paused, grinned, and added, "Daddy." She closed her eyes and turned over, trying to sort herself out with the pillow and blanket. I didn't have the heart to tell her we were landing soon.

At least I got to drink her orange juice as a Welcome to London video came on the screens: loads of pomp, circumstance, and pageantry, the Household Cavalry astride their horses, Guardsmen marching up and down, the Queen riding down the Mall in her carriage. To me, London had never looked so good.

Then the aircraft landed and we became actors again.

We taxied and stopped at our ramp. Everybody jumped out of their seat as if they were going to miss out on something. I leaned over to Kelly. "Wait here. We're in no rush." I wanted to get into the middle of the crowd.

We eventually got all the bits and pieces back into Kelly's daysack, organized the teddies, and joined the line. I was trying to look ahead but I couldn't see much.

We got to the galley area, turned left, and shuffled toward the door. On the ramp were three men—normal British Airports Authority reception staff in fluorescent jackets, who were manning the airbridge, helping a woman into a wheelchair. Things were looking good; freedom felt so close.

We walked up the ramp and joined the spur that led to the main terminal. Kelly didn't have a care in the world, which was good. I didn't want her to understand what was happening.

There was heavy foot traffic in both directions, people running with hand luggage, drifting in and out of shops, milling around at gates. I had the daysack and the laptop over my shoulder and held Kelly's hand. We reached the walkway.

Heathrow airport is the most monitored, most camera'd, most visually and physically secure airport in the world.

Untold pairs of eyes would already be on us; this was no time for looking furtive or guilty. The moving walkway stopped by Gates 43–47, then a new one started about ten yards later. As we trundled along I waited until there was a gap on each side of us and bent down to Kelly. "You mustn't forget I am your daddy today—OK, Louise Glazar?"

"As if!" she said with a big smile.

I just hoped we were both smiling in thirty minutes' time.

We came to the end of the walkway and took a down escalator, following signs for Passport Control and Baggage Reclaim. From halfway down the escalator I could see the Immigration hall straight ahead. This was where we'd stand or fall.

There were about four or five people waiting to go through the desks. I started joking with Kelly, trying to give myself something to do instead of just looking nervous. I'd entered countries illegally hundreds of times, but never so unprepared or under such pressure.

"All set, Louise?"

"I'm ready, Daddy."

I passed her the daysack so I could get the passport and immigration card out of my pocket. We ambled up to Passport Control and joined the end of a line. I kept reminding myself about an American friend who'd traveled from Boston to Canada, and then from Canada back to the UK. He'd picked up his friend's passport while they were sharing a hotel room; he couldn't get back to exchange it so he had to fake it. No one had even batted an eyelid.

We waited in line. Still with the laptop on my right shoulder, I was holding Kelly's hand with my left. I kept looking down at her and smiling, but not excessively so; that was suspicious behavior, and I knew that people would be watching on monitors and from behind two-way mirrors. The business type in front of us went through with a wave and a smile to the official. It was our turn. We approached the desk.

I handed my passport and visa waiver to the woman. She ran her eyes down the details on the card. She looked down at Kelly from her high desk. "Hello, welcome to England."

Kelly came back with a very American, "Hi!"

I guessed the woman was in her late thirties. Her hair was permed, but the perm had gone slightly wrong.

"Did you have a nice flight?" she asked.

Kelly had Jenny or Ricky in one hand, hanging by its ear, and the other one's head was sticking out from the top flap of the daysack on her back. She said, "Yes, it was fine, thank you."

The woman kept the conversation going. "And what's your name?" she asked, still checking the form.

Could I trust her to get it right, or should I butt in?

Kelly smiled and said, "Kelly!"

What a farce. We'd come so far, we'd come through so much, only to be caught by a line straight out of a B movie.

Right away I smiled down at Kelly. "No, it's not!" I didn't want to look at the woman; I could feel the smile drain from her face, could feel her eyes burning into the side of my head.

There was a pause that felt like an hour as I tried to think of what to do or say next. I pictured the woman's finger hovering over a concealed button.

Kelly got there before me. "I know, I'm joking." She giggled, holding out a teddy. "This is Kelly! My name is Louise. What's yours?"

"My name's Margaret." The smile was back. If only she'd known how close she'd been to a kill.

She opened the passport. Her eyes flicked up and down as she studied first the picture, then my face. She put the passport down below the level of the desk, and I saw the telltale glow of ultraviolet light. Then she looked back into my eyes and said, "When was this picture taken?"

"About four years ago, I guess." I gave a weak smile and said in a low voice that Kelly wasn't meant to overhear, "I've been having chemotherapy. The hair's just starting to grow back." I rubbed my head. My skin felt damp and cold. Hopefully I still looked like shit. The capsules certainly made me feel it. "I'm bringing Louise over to see my parents because it's been quite a traumatic time. My wife's staying with our other child because he's ill at the moment. When it rains, it pours!"

"Oh," she said, and it sounded genuinely sympathetic. But she didn't hand back the passport.

There was a big lull, as if she were waiting for me to fill the silence with a confession. Or maybe she was just trying to think of something helpful and human to say. Finally she said, "Have a good stay," and put the documents back on the desktop.

There was that urge just to grab them and run.

"Thank you very much," I said, picking them up and putting them back into my pocket, then carefully doing up the button, because that was what a normal dad would do. Only then did I turn to Kelly. "C'mon, Louise, let's go!"

I started to walk, but Kelly stood her ground. *Oh fuck, now what?*

" 'Bye, Margaret." She beamed. "Have a nice day!"

That was it. We were nearly there. I knew there wasn't going to be a problem with the luggage, because I wasn't going to collect it.

I checked the carousels. There was a flight from Brussels that was also unloading, so I headed for the blue channel. Even if they were watching and stopped us because Kelly had a Virgin Atlantic bag, I would play the stupid person routine.

But there weren't any Customs officers on duty in the blue channel. We were free.

37

The large sliding doors opened up into the arrivals hall. We walked through into a throng of chauffeurs holding up cards and people waiting for their loved ones. Nobody gave us a second look.

I went straight to the currency exchange. I found I'd done well last night with Ron, Melvin, and the Glazars, ending up with more than three hundred pounds in cash. Like a dickhead, I forgot to ask for a smaller bill for the subway ticket machine, so we had to stand in line for ages to get to the kiosk. It didn't seem to matter; even the hour-long ride to Bank station was enjoyable. I was a free man. I was among ordinary people, none of whom knew who we were or was going to pull a gun on us.

The central London district known as the City is a strange mixture of architecture. As we left the subway station, we passed grand buildings made up of columns and puritanically straight lines—the old Establishment. Turn a corner and we were confronted by monstrosities that were built in the sixties and early seventies by architects who must have taken a "Let's go fuck up the City" pill. One of these buildings was the one I was heading for, the NatWest bank on Lombard Street, a road so narrow that just one car could squeeze down it.

We went through the revolving steel and glass doors into the banking hall, where rows of cashiers sat behind protective screens. But I wasn't there for money.

The reception desk was staffed by a man and a woman, both in their early twenties, both wearing NatWest suits; they even had little corporate logos sewn into the material of their breast pockets, probably so staff wouldn't wear them after hours. As Kelly would have said, "As if!"

I saw both of them give Kelly and me an instant appraisal and could feel them turning up their noses. I gave them a cheery, "Hi, how are you?" and asked to speak with Guy Bexley.

The woman said, "Can I have your name, please?" as she picked up the phone.

"Nick Stevenson."

The girl called an extension. The man went back to being efficient on the other side of the reception desk.

I bent down and whispered to Kelly, "I'll explain later."

"He'll be along in a minute. Would you like to sit down?"

We waited on a couch that was very long, very deep, very plastic. I could sense Kelly's cogs turning.

Sure enough. "Nick, am I Louise Stevenson now, or Louise Glazar?"

I screwed up my face and scratched my head. "Umm . . . Kelly!"

Guy Bexley came down. Guy was my "relationship manager," whatever that was. All I knew was that he was the man I asked for when I wanted to get my security blanket out. He was in his late twenties, and you could see by his hairstyle and goatee that he felt uncomfortable in the issued suit and would be far happier wearing PVC pants, holding a bottle of water, and partying all night bare-chested.

We shook hands. "Hello, Mr. Stevenson, haven't seen you for a long time."

I shrugged my shoulders. "Work. This is Kelly."

He bent down and said, "Hello there, Kelly," in his best "I've been trained how to introduce myself to kids" manner.

"I just need my locked box for five minutes, mate."

I followed him toward the row of partitioned offices on the other side of the hall. I'd been in them many times before. They were all identical; each contained just a round table, four chairs, and a telephone. It was where people went to count money or beg for a loan. He started to leave.

"Could I also have a statement on my savings account, please?"

Guy nodded and left. Kelly said, "What are we doing here?"

I should have known by now that she hated to be left out of things. Just like her dad. "Wait and see." I winked.

A few minutes later Guy reappeared, put the box on the table, and gave me a folded printout of my account. I felt nervous as I opened up the paper. My eyes went straight for the bottom right-hand corner.

It read four hundred twenty-six thousand, five hundred seventy dollars, converted at a rate of 1.58 dollars to the pound.

Big Al had done it. I had to control myself, as I remembered Bexley was still standing there. "I'll just be about five minutes," I said.

"Tell reception when you're ready. They'll put it back in the vault for you." He left with a shake of my hand and a "'Bye, Kelly!" and closed the door behind him.

The box was eighteen inches by twelve, a metal file container I'd bought for ten pounds in Woolworth's, with a very cheap lock on the top that opened under pressure. It meant that I didn't have to turn up with a key every time—I couldn't always guarantee I was going to have that with me. The only problem was that if I had to make a run out of the country, it could only be during banking hours.

I flipped the lock and pulled out a couple of old soccer fanzines I'd put on top in case it accidentally opened. I threw them over to Kelly. "See if you can make any sense of those." She picked one up and started to flip through the pages.

The first thing I took out was the mobile phone and recharger. I switched it on. The battery was still working, but I put it in the recharger anyway and plugged it into the wall.

Next I pulled out a clear plastic freezer bag that contained bundles of US dollar bills and pounds sterling, five South African Krugerrands, and ten half-sovereigns that I'd stolen after the Persian Gulf War. All troops who were behind enemy lines in Iraq were issued twenty of the things as bribes for the locals in case we got in heavy shit. In my patrol we'd managed to keep ten of them each; we said we'd lost the rest in a contact. To begin with I'd kept them only as souvenirs, but they'd soon increased in value. I left them in the bag; I was interested only in the sterling.

I dug out a French leather *porte-monnaie* with a strap, in which I had a complete set of ID: passport, credit cards, driver's license, all the stuff I needed to become Nicholas Duncan Stevenson. It had taken years to get cover in such depth, all originating from a social security number I'd bought in a pub in Brixton for fifty pounds.

I then got out an electronic notebook. It was great; it meant that I could fax, send memos, word process, and maintain a database anywhere in the world. The problem was I didn't have a clue how to use it. I used only the phone number and address section facility because it could be accessed only with a password.

I had a quick look over at Kelly. She was thumbing through the magazines, not understanding a word. I pushed my hand to the bottom of the box and extracted the 9mm semiautomatic Browning I'd liberated from Africa in the late eighties. Loading the mags with rounds from a small Tupperware box, I made ready and checked chamber. Kelly looked up but didn't give it a second glance.

I powered up the notebook, tapped in 2422, and found the number I wanted. I picked up the telephone on the table. Kelly looked up again. "Who are you calling?"

"Euan."

"Who is he?"

I could see the confusion on her face.

"He's my best friend." I carried on pressing the phone number.

"But . . ."

I put my finger to my lips. "Shhh."

He wasn't in. I left a message on the answering machine in veiled speech. I then put the laptop into the box, together with everything that I wasn't taking with me—including the printout.

Kelly was bored with the fanzines now, so I put them back in the box. I knew there was a question on its way.

"Nick?"

I just carried on packing. "Yes?"

"I thought David was your best friend."

"Ah yes. Well, Euan is my best friend. It's just that sometimes I have to call him David because—" I started to think of
a lie, but why? "I told you to make sure you wouldn't know
his real name if we got caught. That way you couldn't tell
anyone. It's something that is done all the time. It's called
OPSEC—operational security." I finished packing and
closed the box. She thought about it.

"Oh, OK. His name's Euan then."

"When you see him he might even show you the floor I told
you about."

I poked my head around the corner and waved at the receptionist. She came in, picked up the box, and left.

I turned to Kelly. "Right, then, time for a shopping frenzy.
Let me see; we'd better buy some nice new clothes for us
both, and then we'll go and stay in a hotel and wait for Euan
to call. Sound good to you?"

Her face brightened. "OK!"

Once this was all over I would have to set up a different
named account and move the money, and I'd stop being
Stevenson. A pain in the ass to organize, but I could live with
that for $426,072.

The cab ride to Trafalgar Square became a tour given by me
to Kelly. I was more into it than she was, and I could tell by
the taxi driver's expression in his rearview mirror that I was
getting most of the details wrong.

We were going down the Strand when I spotted clothes
stores on both sides of the road. We paid off the taxi and
shopped for jeans, T-shirts, and a washing kit. Once that was
done, we took another cab to Brown's Hotel.

I said to Kelly, "You'll like this place. It's got two entrances, so you can enter from Dover Street and come out the
other side, on Albermarle Street. Very important for spies
like us."

I switched on the phone, got hold of information, and
called the hotel to make a reservation. Less than half an hour
later we were in our room, but only after discovering that the
Dover Street exit was no longer open. Finger on the pulse.

The room was a world removed from the ones we had been used to. It was plush, comfortable, and, best of all, had a minibar with Toblerones. I could have killed for a beer, but not yet; there was work to do.

Jet lag was starting to kick in. Kelly looked exhausted. She flopped onto the bed and I helped undress her, then threw her between the sheets. "You can take a bath tomorrow," I said. She was a starfish in about two minutes flat.

I checked that the phone had a good signal and that the charger was working. Euan knew my voice, so the "It's John the plumber, when do you want me to come and fix that tap? Give me a ring on . . ." would have done the trick.

I decided to have a quick nap for ten minutes, maybe shower, have something to eat, then go to bed. After all, it was only 5 P.M.

At a quarter to six in the morning, the phone rang. I pressed Receive. I heard "Hello?" in that very low, very controlled voice I knew so well.

"I need a hand, mate," I said. I didn't want to give him time to talk. "I need you to help me. Can you get to London?"

"When do you want me?"

"Now."

"I'm in Wales. It'll take a bit of time."

"I'll wait out on this number."

"No problem. I'll get a train; it'll be quicker."

"Thanks, mate. Give me a call about an hour before you get into Paddington."

"Yep, OK."

The phone went dead.

I had never felt so relieved. It was like putting the phone down after a doctor's just told you the cancer test was negative.

The train journey alone would take more than three hours, so there wasn't much to do apart from enjoy the lull in the battle. Kelly awoke as I caught up with some international news in the copy of the *Times* that had been slipped under the door—no walk to the street corner with a couple of quarters at Brown's Hotel. I phoned room service and tried out the hotel TV channels. No *Power Rangers*. Great.

Lazily, we both eventually got up, showered, changed, and were looking good. We took a leisurely stroll through Piccadilly Circus and Leicester Square. I delivered another tour lecture that Kelly didn't listen to. I kept on looking at my watch, waiting for Euan to call. While Kelly was being overrun by pigeons having a feeding frenzy in Trafalgar Square, the phone rang. It was 9:50 A.M. I put my finger in my other ear to block out the traffic and the screams of delight from Kelly and the other kids as birds tried to peck their eyes out.

"I'm an hour from Paddington."

"That's great. I'll meet you at Platform Three, Charing Cross station, OK, mate?"

"See you there."

The Charing Cross hotel was part of the station complex, just two minutes' walk from Trafalgar Square. I'd picked it because I knew that from the foyer you could see the taxis pull into the station and drop off their fares.

We waited and watched. The place was full of package-tour Americans and Italians. The Americans were at the tour-guide desk, reserving every show in town, and the Italians just moved from the elevator to the exit door in one loud, arm-waving mob, shouting at each other and all trying to get through the glass doors at the same time.

It was about half an hour later when I saw a cab with a familiar figure in the back. I pointed him out to Kelly.

"Aren't we going to go and meet him?"

"No, we're going to stay here and look, because we're going to surprise him. Just like we did with Frankie in Daytona, remember?"

"Oh, yes. We have to stand off."

I watched him get out. It was so wonderful to see him that I wanted to jump up and run outside. He was dressed in jeans and wearing the kind of shoes you see advertised in a Sunday supplement. Hush Puppies were positively cutting-edge fashion compared to these. He was also wearing a black nylon bomber jacket, so he'd be easy enough to pick out in the station. I said to Kelly, "We'll give him a couple of minutes, then we'll go and surprise him, shall we?"

"Yeah!" She sounded quite excited. She had two lumps of bird shit on the back of her coat. I was waiting for them to dry before picking them off.

I waited for five minutes, watching his back for him. Then we walked toward the station and through a couple of arches to the ticket offices. We looked for Platform 3 and there he was, leaning against the wall, reading a paper. The same feeling: I wanted to run over there and hug him. We walked slowly.

He looked up and saw me. We both smiled and said, "Hi, how's it going!" He looked at me, then at Kelly, but he didn't say anything; he knew that I'd tell him at some stage. We went off to the side of the station to steps that led down toward the river. As we walked he looked at my head and tried to hide a grin. "Good haircut!"

Outside Embankment station we got into a taxi. Drills are drills—they're there for a reason, and that is to protect you: the moment you start falling down on drills, you start fucking up. We took the driver on a roundabout route, covering our tracks, taking twenty minutes to Brown's instead of the straight-line ten. As soon as we got back to the room I turned the TV on for Kelly and phoned room service. Everyone was hungry.

Euan was already chatting away with Kelly. She looked pleased to have somebody else to talk to, even if it was only another grown-up and a man. That was good—they were getting a relationship going; she was feeling comfortable with him.

The food came; there was a hamburger and fries for Kelly, and two club sandwiches for us. I said to Kelly, "We'll let you eat in peace. We're going into the bathroom because you're watching TV, and I want to talk to Euan about some stuff. Is that all right?"

She nodded, mouth already full.

Euan smiled. "See you in a minute, Kelly. Save us some fries."

We went into the bathroom with our coffees and sandwiches, the noise of the TV dying the moment I closed the door.

I started to tell him the story. Euan listened intently. He was visibly upset about Kev and Marsha. I'd got as far as the lift by Luther and Co. when he cut in. By now he was sitting on the edge of the bath.

"Bastards! Who were they? Do you think it was the same group that zapped Kev?"

"Must be." I sat next to him. "Kev knew the three who killed him. Kelly confirmed that Luther worked with Kev. Then there's the question of that phone call to 'get the ball rolling.' "

"You reckon it was Luther?"

I nodded. "Who the fuck knows where he fits into the picture, but my guess is he's DEA, and also corrupt. It looks like some of the DEA are bent and working for drug money." I told him about the McGear killing and what I had found on the backup disk once de Sabatino had loaded the GIFs.

Euan understood so far. "So it all has to do with PIRA running drugs into Europe? To keep the route open it needs bribes, blackmail, and threats. But what about McGear—did he say anything?"

"Not a word. He knew he was going to die anyway."

"This guy de Sabatino? Does he have any copies of the intelligence?"

I laughed. "You know I'm not going to tell you that. OPSEC, mate, OPSEC!"

"Fair one." He shrugged. "Just being nosy."

I explained what I had found in Kev's house. Euan didn't speak. He just sat there, letting it all soak in. I felt exhausted, as if by somehow passing on the baton to Euan everything that had happened in the last ten days could now catch up with me and take its toll.

I looked at him. He seemed pretty drained himself.

"I can see only one thing wrong with what you're saying."

"What's that, mate?"

"Wouldn't the Colombians have anticipated that a bomb

would heighten security in Gibraltar, making it harder to get the drugs in?"

"It was a warning. They were sending it out to anyone who might not want to keep business going. I tell you, mate, this is far too big for me to be messing around with. I just want to get it to Simmonds and wash my hands of it."

"I'll help any way I can." He opened a pack of Benson & Hedges; he'd obviously taken up smoking again. I stood up, out of the way.

"I don't want to get you directly involved. Kev, Pat, me, we've all been fucked over—but I'm going to need you to back me if things go wrong."

"You just have to name it."

I could smell the sulfur from his match. He smiled as I started to wave the smoke from my face. He knew I hated that. Even under extreme pressure some things never changed.

I said, "Tomorrow afternoon, you should receive copies of the files by FedEx. If anything happens to me or Simmonds, it's basically down to you." By now we were in a cloud of smoke. The alarm was going to go off any minute.

"No problems with that, mate," he said in his very slow, very calm, very calculating way. If you told Euan he'd won the lottery he'd say, "That's nice," then go back to stacking his coins or folding his socks.

"How many copies of the disk are there besides the ones you're sending me?"

"I'm not going to tell you, mate. Need-to-know!"

He smiled. He knew I was protecting him.

"One more thing," I said. "I don't want to take Kelly with me to the Simmonds meet. He wasn't too pleased with me the last time we spoke. If this turns into a gang fuck, I don't want her caught in the crossfire. You're the only person I can trust her with. It's going to be for only one night, maybe two. Can you do that for me?"

I expected an immediate answer and I got one. "No problem." He smiled. He knew I'd let him talk freely with Kelly so they'd get to know each other.

"Will you take her back to Brecon?"

"Yeah. Have you told her I live in Wales?"

"I've told her you live in a sheep pen."

He threw the butt into the toilet because he knew I hated that smell, too.

I put both my hands on his shoulders. "This has been a fucking shit week, mate."

"Don't worry about it. Let's just go back in the room and finish the coffee. Then you just go and sort your shit out with Simmonds and get it over and done with."

"How was the burger?"

"Fine. I saved Euan some fries."

I sat on the bed next to her. "Listen, Kelly, me and Euan have been talking, and because I've got to do some stuff in London, we reckon it's a good idea if you go to the country-side with him and stay at his house. It's only for one night; I'll be back tomorrow. What do you think? Hey, you can even see the floor we laid—remember I talked about it?"

She suspected she wasn't being offered any option, and her face said so.

I said, "I won't be long, and Euan's house has sheep all around it."

She looked down at her fingers and mumbled, "I want to stay with you."

I said with mock surprise, "What, don't you want to go? You'll see all the sheep!"

She was embarrassed. She was too polite to say no in front of Euan.

I said, "It won't be for long." Then, like a bastard, I closed the trap. "You like Euan, don't you?"

She nodded, never losing eye contact with me in case she made it with Euan.

"It's just going to be for one night. I'll be calling you anyway; I'll be able to talk to you."

She looked very unhappy about it. After all, I'd promised not to leave her again. I caught sight of my mobile and had an idea. "How about I give you my mobile phone. I'll show you how to use it." I started playing with the buttons. "Here you are, you have a go. If I show you how to use it, you can put that under your pillow tonight, all right?"

I looked up at Euan, trying to bring him in. "Because she'll have her own bedroom, won't she?"

"That's right. She'll have her own bedroom, the one that overlooks the sheep pen."

I said, "And I believe there's a TV in her bedroom, isn't there?"

"Yes, there's a TV in there." He nodded and agreed, wondering where he was going to get one from.

There was an acceptance; she wasn't wild about it, but that was good enough. I switched on the phone, tapped in my PIN number, and handed it over. "Just plug the charger into the wall when you get there and it'll work, OK?"

"OK."

"Then put it underneath your pillow so when it rings you'll be sure to hear it. All right?"

"Whatever." By now she understood that she definitely had no choice.

Euan said, "I'll tell you what. We'd better get your teddies organized if we're going to the country. What are their names? Have they ever been on a train before?"

She warmed to him. We went downstairs and got into a taxi to Paddington station.

38

We bought Kelly ice cream, candy, soda, anything to keep her mind off what was happening. She was still deciding what comic to buy as Euan looked at his watch and said, "Wheels turning soon, mate."

I went with them along the platform and gave her a big hug at the door of the train car. "I'll call you tonight, Kelly. I promise."

As she climbed up, Jenny and Ricky were looking at me from the Virgin Atlantic daysack on her back. "OK."

The guard was walking the length of the train, closing the doors. Euan lowered the window so Kelly could wave.

"Nick?" She leaned toward me through the open window and beckoned as if she wanted to whisper something.

"What?" I put my face near hers.

"This." She threw her arms around my neck, squeezed, and planted a big kiss on my cheek. I was so taken aback I just stood there.

The train started moving.

"I'll see you tomorrow," Euan called. "Don't worry about us. We'll be OK."

As the train slowly disappeared from the platform, I felt the same wrench as I had at the moment I'd seen Pat's body being loaded into the ambulance. But this time I couldn't figure out why. After all, it was for the best and she was in safe hands. Forcing myself to see it as one more problem out of the way, I headed for the pay phones.

I got a very businesslike reply from Vauxhall: "Extension please?"

"Two-six-one-two."

There was a pause, then a voice I recognized at once. "Hello, two-six-one-two?"

"It's Stone. I've got what you needed."

"Nick! Where are you?"

I put my finger in my ear as a departure was announced.

"I'm in England." Not that he needed me to say that when he could hear that the Exeter train was leaving in five minutes.

"Excellent."

"I'm pretty desperate to see you."

"Likewise. But I'm tied up here until the early hours." He paused to think. "Perhaps we can go for a walk and a talk. Let's say three-thirty tomorrow morning?"

"Where?"

"I'll walk toward the station. I presume you'll find me."

"I'll do that."

I put the phone down with a feeling that at long last the dice were rolling for me. Kelly was safe, Simmonds sounded amenable. With luck I was only hours from sorting out this mess.

Back at the hotel I rented a car so I could pick up Kelly from Brecon after the meeting, and had something to eat. In my head I ran through exactly what I was going to say to Simmonds, and the way I was going to say it. Without a doubt, I had in my possession precisely the sort of evidence Simmonds had asked for. It was a shame I didn't have the video-tape to back up some of it, but, even so, the stuff I had was probably more than he could have hoped for. The worst-case scenario now was that I'd get the slate wiped clean and be let loose. At least I had a few quid to start a new life with.

I thought about Kelly. What would become of her? Where would she go? Would she have been affected by everything she'd seen and all that had happened to her and her family? I tried to cut away from that, telling myself that it would all get sorted out—somehow. Simmonds could help there. Perhaps he could orchestrate the reunion with her grandparents, or at least point me in the direction of the right kind of expert help.

I tried to get some sleep but failed. At 2 A.M. I retrieved the rental car and headed for Vauxhall Bridge.

I went a long way around, going all the way down the King's Road to World's End, then turning for the river and heading east again, mainly because I wanted to organize my thoughts one last time, but also because to me, the drive along the deserted Embankment and past all the historic, floodlit bridges offered one of the most beautiful sights in the world. This particular night the lights seemed to shine a bit brighter, and the bridges seemed more sharply in focus; I found myself wishing Kelly was there to see it with me.

I got to Vauxhall Bridge early. I drove east along the road that follows the river toward the next bridge, Lambeth. Nothing looked suspicious at the RV point on the drive-by. The gas station on the opposite side of the road, about halfway toward Lambeth bridge, had about four cars by the pumps, groups of kids buying fuel and Mars bars, and some early-morning office cleaning vans filling up before their shift.

Farther along the river, and on the other side, I could see the Houses of Parliament. I smiled to myself. If only the MPs really knew what the intelligence services got up to.

I did a full circle and headed back on the same road toward Vauxhall for one more drive-by. I still had time to kill, so I stopped at the station and bought a drink and a sandwich.

The RV point still looked fine. My plan was to pick up Simmonds, make distance and angles as we walked to my car, and go for a drive. That way I controlled the environment. I could protect myself as well as him.

I parked about four hundred yards west of the RV. While eating my sandwich I checked my route back to the car. I got out and walked down the road, arriving at five minutes to three. There was still nothing to do but wait, so I window-shopped at the motorcycle shop, resolving that I really would buy one as a gift to myself. No, more than a gift—a reward.

At twenty after three I moved into the shadows of the railway arches opposite the exit point I knew Simmonds would use. There were one or two people wandering about, clubbers on their way home, or to another club. Their drunken laughs shattered the still morning air, then there was silence again.

I could tell it was him right off, leaning slightly forward as he bounced along on the balls of his feet. I watched him branch right from the exit and stand at the pedestrian crossing, intending to head for the metal footbridge over the five-way road intersection to the railway station. I waited. There was no rush; I'd let him come to me.

As he crossed the road I came out of the shadows at the bottom of the footbridge steps.

He smiled. "Nick, how are you?" He kept walking, nodding left toward Lambeth bridge. "Shall we walk?" It wasn't a question.

I nodded the opposite way, toward my car. "I've arranged a pickup."

Simmonds stopped and looked at me with the expression of a disappointed schoolteacher. "No, I think we'll walk."

I was sponsoring the RV; he should have known that I'd organize for our safety. He stared at me a few more moments and then, as if he knew I was going to follow, continued on walking. I fell into step beside him.

Simmonds looked the same as ever, his tie about half an inch loose, the shirt and suit looking as if his wardrobe were a carrier bag.

"So, Nick, what have you got?" He smiled but didn't look at me, and as I told him the story he didn't interrupt, just kept his eyes on the ground, nodding. I felt like a son unloading his problems onto his dad, and it felt good.

We'd been walking for about fifteen minutes when I'd come to the end of my presentation. It was his turn to talk. I somehow expected him to stop, or at least find a bench where we could sit, but he kept on walking.

He turned his head toward me and smiled again. "Nick, I had no idea you'd be so thorough. Who else have you spoken to about this?"

"No one else, only de Sabatino and Euan."

"And has Euan or this de Sabatino also got copies of the disks?"

I lied. "No, no one apart from me." Even when you come to someone for help, you never play your full hand. You never know when you might need an edge.

He remained incredibly calm. "What we have to ensure is that no one else finds out—not for the moment, anyway. This is more than low-level corruption. The links with PIRA, Gibraltar, and, it seems, the DEA mean this is very grave indeed. You seem to have a pretty good grasp of this so far, so let me ask you something." He paused as if he were a judge about to hand down his decision. "Do you think it goes further?"

"Who the fuck knows," I said. "But you can't be too careful. It's why I wanted to talk to you on your own."

"And where is the Brown child now?"

"In a hotel, fast asleep. I'll be needing some help to pass her on to her grandparents."

"Of course, Nick. All in good time."

We walked on a while in silence. We got to a bar on the corner of a car tunnel under the railway line. Simmonds turned to the right, taking us under the arches. Then he spoke again, and it was as if there was no question of me not complying with his demand. "Before I can do anything to help you, what I need from you, of course, is the evidence." He was still not looking at me, making sure he avoided the puddles of water stained with engine oil.

"I haven't brought the disks with me, if that's what you mean."

"Nick, I shall do my best to see that you both have protection. But I do need the proof—and all copies of it. Can you get them for me now?"

"Not possible. Not for a few hours."

"Nick, I cannot do anything without them. I need all copies. Even ones you'd normally leave in that security blanket of yours."

I shrugged. "You must understand that it's for my own protection."

We turned right again and were now heading back toward the train station, paralleling the railway. For a couple of minutes we moved along narrow, warehoused streets in silence. Simmonds was deep in thought. He wasn't happy about the disks. A freight train rumbled above us on its way to waking up the residents of southwest London. Why the fuck was it so important for him to know how many copies there were and get his hands on all of them?

"Believe me," I shouted above the noise, "I've got that side all under control. I've been fucked over enough. You know as well as I do that I've got to protect everyone, including you."

"Yes, of course, but I need to control all the information. Not even you should have it. There is too much risk involved."

This was getting stupid. "I understand that. But what if you get zapped? There would be nothing to back up what I'm saying. It's not only the DEA corruption, don't you see? Gibraltar was a setup. It includes us."

Simmonds slowly nodded at a puddle in the gutter.

"A few things puzzle me," I said. "Why were we briefed that the bomb would be initiated by remote control? How come the intelligence was so good about the ASU, but so wrong about there being no bomb?"

Still he gave no reply.

Things weren't adding up here.

Oh fuck.

I felt as if I'd been hit on the back of the head by a fire extinguisher again. Why hadn't I thought of it? The freight train's rumbling was now in the distance. The early-morning silence had returned. "But you know all this, don't you?"

No reply. He didn't even break his stride.

Who had briefed us that the Gibraltar bomb was going to be initiated by remote control? Simmonds, who was there at Alpha to oversee it. Why the fuck hadn't I thought of it before?

I stopped. Simmonds kept walking. "This isn't just an American-PIRA thing, is it? It's much bigger. You are part of it, aren't you?"

The rear arches were more light industrial than retail—auto repair shops, sheetmetal works, and storage units, most with company vans that had been parked outside for the night.

He turned to face me and took the six steps back to where I stood. For the first time, we had eye-to-eye. "Nick, I think you need to be aware of something. You will give me all the information—and I mean all of it. We cannot take the risk of other copies being in circulation."

The look on his face was of a chess grand master about to make the decisive move. The shock in mine must have been plain to see.

"We didn't necessarily go along with the Americans' determination to kill you, but you should be in no doubt that we will do so now if we have to."

"We?"

"It's much bigger than you think, Nick. You're intelligent. You must realize the commercial and political implications of a ceasefire. Exposing what is on the disks would mess up much more than just what you know. It's unfortunate about Kevin and his family, I grant you. When he told me what he'd discovered, I did try to talk my American colleagues into a subtler course of action."

So that was why I'd been ordered back to the UK so abruptly. Once Simmonds had talked with Kev, he wanted me out of the US—and quick. He didn't want me speaking to Kev—or interrupting his murder.

I thought of Kelly. At least she was safe.

It was almost as if he were reading my mind. "If you decide not to give me all the information, we will kill the child. And then we will kill you—after extracting what we need. Don't be naive, Nick. You and I, we're the same. This isn't about emotion; this is business, Nick, business. You really have no choice."

I tried to fight it. He had to be bluffing.

"Euan sends his regards, by the way, and says that he managed to get a television set for her bedroom. Believe me, Nick, Euan will kill her. He rather likes the financial benefits."

I shook my head slowly from side to side.

"Think back. Who initiated the contact?"

He was right, it was Euan. Simmonds was there to direct it, Euan was there to pull the trigger. But I still fought against the idea.

He opened his jacket and pulled a mobile phone from his

inside pocket. "Let Euan explain; he was expecting a call later anyway."

He turned on the power and waited to put in his PIN number. He smiled as he looked down at the phone's display. "This is how the Americans found you, you know. People think that detection can take place only when the phone is in use. Not so. As long as they're switched on, these things are miniature tracking devices, even if no calls are made or received. It's actually a form of electronic tagging. We find it terribly useful."

He tapped in his PIN number, the tones blaring out of his hand. "However, once you'd given them the slip at Lorton, our only option was to let you make entry back into the UK. I needed to know what you'd found out. I have to say, I'm so glad your cancer treatment was successful."

Fuck! He hadn't even mentioned my lack of hair. That was because he already knew. But Euan. He'd been aware enough to mention it. I felt sick knowing he was using his skills against me.

Simmonds smiled. He knew he had me by the balls.

"Nick, I'll say this again. I really do need all the disks. You know the child would suffer greatly; it's not something that we would enjoy, but there are important matters at stake."

I wanted so much for him to get through to Euan. I wanted to speak to him, wanted him to confirm that it was a bluff. But in my heart of hearts I knew that it wasn't.

Simmonds had nearly finished tapping in the number.

I had no choice. I couldn't risk Kelly. He wasn't going to make this call.

With my right arm in a hooked position, I swung around hard and connected with his nose. There was a dull crunch of fracturing bone as he went down with a muffled moan. While he writhed on the ground I kicked his case under one of the vans and, in the same motion, picked up the phone in my left hand, got behind him, and positioned it at the front of his throat. Grabbing the other side with my right hand, I jammed it firmly under his Adam's apple.

I looked to the right and left. We were too exposed where we were; what I had in mind would take several minutes to complete. I shuffled backward, dragging him in between two of the trucks. I got down onto my knees, all the time pulling back on the phone. He was kicking out, his arms flailing, trying to rip my face apart.

His whimpers and chokes filled the air. I responded by leaning forward, using the weight of my upper body to bend his head down so that his chin was more or less on his chest. At the same time I pulled even harder. Just another two minutes and I'd be done.

After thirty seconds he started to struggle furiously, with all the frenzied strength that a man draws on when he knows he is dying. But no matter what he did now, he wouldn't be getting up.

His hands still scratched at my face. I bobbed and weaved to avoid them but maintained the pressure on his throat. Already the scabs from the fight with McGear had been pulled off, but I couldn't feel much blood. Then Simmonds managed to get his fingernails into the cut just below my eye. I stifled a scream as his three nails started into the already damaged soft skin. I made the injury worse by pulling my face away; as I did, Simmonds's nails took my skin with them.

I didn't bother now to see if anyone was watching. I was beyond caring. I was fighting for breath myself with the effort, as sweat stung the injuries on my face.

Gradually at first, his movements subsided to no more than a spasmodic twitching in his legs. His hands stopped grasping. Seconds later he was unconscious. It crossed my mind just to get up and walk away, to leave him to suffer the effects of hypoxia and be brain-damaged for life. I decided against that. I wanted this fucker dead.

I gave it another thirty seconds. His chest stopped moving. I put my fingers on the carotid pulse and felt nothing.

I dragged him to the wall and sat him up against the doors of a unit. Then I got to my feet and started dusting myself off. Keeping to the shadows, I tucked my shirt in and wiped away the sweat and blood with my sleeve. I checked the phone. It had been turned off in the fight. I wiped my prints off it, then just left everything where it was and casually walked away. If anybody had seen me, so what? It didn't really matter. I had more important things to worry about.

I drove west, holding my coat cuff against my eye to stop the bleeding.

The whole situation was still spinning around inside my head, slowly beginning to make sense.

I now knew how Luther and his lot had found me—they must have beaten the number out of Pat and traced the signal while I had it switched on waiting for his call.

If I'd let on to Euan or Simmonds that there was just one more set of backups in my laptop and had handed it over, I'd have been dead. They were covering their asses by retrieving the information.

Had Simmonds arranged to phone Euan some time after our meeting? Euan was more than three hours away, and Simmonds's body would be discovered soon. If Euan found out, he wouldn't take any chances. He would change location, maybe even kill Kelly right away. Either way, I'd have lost her. This time there was no question of just leaving her. I could call her on the mobile and tell her to run, but what would that achieve? She was in the middle of nowhere; even if she ran for half an hour, it would make no difference. Euan's cottage was in the middle of acres of mountains, grass, rocks, and sheep shit. He would find her.

I could call the police, but would they believe me? I could waste hours trying to convince them, by which time it would be too late. Or they might take it on themselves to raid Euan's house, and the result would be the same.

For a fleeting second I thought about Big Al. I hoped he'd be well out of it by now. He didn't have getaway accounts for nothing. If he'd transferred four hundred grand into mine, for sure he'd have taken eight hundred for himself. Old Watermelon would be OK. I cut him from my mind.

The highway services just before Heathrow were just coming up. I had a thought.

I pulled off and drove into the parking lot. Now all I had to do was get to a phone and make a call.

39

The service station was busy. I'd had to park a hundred yards from the main entrance. I got out of the car just as the heavens opened. By the time I reached the bank of four telephones outside Burger King, I was soaked. The first two I tried accepted only cards. I had about three pounds in change in my pocket—not enough. I ran into the shop, wiping my face to get some of the blood off. I bought a newspaper with a fiver, walked out, the woman looking worried at the state of my face. I then went back in and got a packet of M&Ms with a tenner. The woman looked even more scared. She was just happy for me to take my change and get out.

As I dialed the number I felt a knot in my stomach, as if I were a teenager phoning to arrange his very first date. Would she have charged it and left it switched on? Why wouldn't she? She had never let me down before.

It started to ring.

For a moment I felt like a child in a candy store with his dad, hardly able to contain my excitement. Then I had new things to worry about. What if Euan had the phone now? Did I hang up or did I try to bluff it and maybe find out where she was?

It was too late to think. The ringing stopped; there was a pause, then I heard a quiet, hesitant, "Hello, who is it?"

"Hi, Kelly, it's me, Nick," I said, trying for all the world to sound like Mr. Casual. "Are you on your own?"

"Yes, you woke me up. Are you coming back now?" She sounded tired and confused. I was trying hard to think of an answer; thankfully she went on. "Euan said that I might be staying with him longer, because you have to go away. It isn't true, is it, Nick? You said you wouldn't leave me."

It was a bad connection. I had to put a finger in my other ear to hear her above the noise of the rain on the glass of the phone booth. A truck driver in the next one along was shouting loudly and angrily, arguing with his boss that he couldn't go any farther because of his odometer, and he wasn't going to lose his license just to get a few boxes of bloody anoraks up to Carlisle. On top of that was the steady boom of traffic on the highway, and the noises of people coming in and out of the station. I had to block all that out and concentrate on the phone call, because there was no way I could ask Kelly to speak up.

I said, "Yes, of course, you're right, I will never leave you. Euan is lying to you. I have found out some bad things about him, Kelly. Are you still in the house?"

"Yes, I'm in bed."

"Is Euan in his bed?"

"Yes. Do you want to speak with him?"

"No, no. Let me think for a minute."

My mind was racing now, trying to think of the best way to say what I wanted.

"Of course I'm coming to get you. In fact, I'll be there very soon. Now listen. I need you to do something very difficult and very dangerous. You only have to do this one last thing for me and everything will be over." The moment I said it I felt like a lowlife.

"I don't have to run away again, do I?"

"No, no, no—it's not like that this time. But it's the most special job a spy ever does." I didn't want to give her time to think, so I just went on. "But I want to check something first, OK? You're in bed, aren't you? Get under the covers and talk to me only in a whisper, OK?"

I could hear the rustling, then she said, "What are we going to do, Nick?"

"First, I want you to press a number and look at the front of the telephone. Can you see it light up? Tell me if there's a picture of a battery. How many blocks are there where the battery sign is? Can you see it?"

I heard some scuffling.

"I can see that."

"How many blocks are there in the picture?"

"Three. There's three blocks. One of them is flashing."

"That's good."

It wasn't really. I was sweating: two blocks meant she hadn't recharged it and the battery was down to less than half-power, and I was going to need a lot of air time to talk her through the whole process.

"What's that noise?" she said.

The truck driver was now really pissed off and hollering into the phone, the cigarette in his hand making the phone booth look like a steam room.

"Nothing to worry about. Kelly, I'm going to tell you what to do, but you need to keep listening to me on the telephone. Can you do that?"

"Why is Euan bad, Nick? What . . ."

"Listen, Kelly, Euan wants to hurt me. If he finds you doing this thing for me, he will hurt you, too. Do you understand that?"

I could hear lots of rustling; she was obviously still under the bedcovers. Then there was a very quiet "Yes."

She wasn't sounding like a happy bunny. I was sure there was a better way I could be going about all this, I just didn't have time to think what it might be.

"If Euan wakes up," I said, "or if the telephone stops working, I want you to leave the house very, very quietly. I want you to go down the track to the road and hide behind the trees, just by the big gate that Euan drove through to get to his cottage. Know where I mean?"

"Yeah."

"You must hide there until you hear a car come and stop, but don't get out from your hiding place unless it toots its horn two times. Then come out. Do you understand that? I'll be in the car. It's a blue Astra, OK?"

There was a pause. "What's an As—Astra, Nick?"

Shit, she was seven years old and American. What was I expecting?

"OK. I'll stop in a blue car and come and get you."

I got her to repeat it, and for good measure I said, "So if Euan wakes up and sees you, I want you to run to the trees as fast as you can and hide. Because if Euan catches you doing what I want you to do, we will never see each other again. Don't let me down, OK? And remember, don't you come out from behind those trees, even if Euan calls for you, OK?"

"OK. You will come and get me, won't you?"

There was a bit of doubt in her mind.

"Of course I will. Now, first of all, what I want you to do is get out of bed, then put the phone on the bed and get dressed, very quietly. Put on a nice thick coat. And you know those sneakers we bought? Make sure you take those as well, but don't put them on yet."

I heard her put the phone down and start rummaging around the room.

For God's sake, hurry up!

I forced myself to calm down.

It was almost two minutes before I heard: "I'm ready, Nick."

"Now listen to me very carefully. Euan is not a friend; he has tried to kill me. Do you understand, Kelly? He has tried to kill me."

There was a pause.

"Why? I—I don't understand, Nick. I thought he was your best friend."

"I know, I know, but things change. Do you want to help me?"

"Yes."

"Good. Then you must do exactly what I tell you. I want you to put your sneakers in your coat pockets. OK, now it's time to go downstairs. I want you to keep the telephone with you. All right?"

"Yeah."

Time was running short, and so was my money.

"Just remember, you must be very, very quiet, because otherwise you will wake Euan. If that happens, you run out of the house toward the hidey-hole—promise?"

"Cross my heart."

"OK, I want you to creep very, very gently down the stairs.

Don't talk to me again until you're in the kitchen; and remember, from now on, what we must do is whisper all the time. OK?"

"OK."

I heard the door open. As she came out of the room I imagined her passing the bathroom on her left. Ahead of her, up a half-landing and about twelve feet away, would be the door to Euan's room. Was it open or closed? Too late to ask her. A few steps now and she'd be at the top of the main stairs and next to the old grandfather clock. On cue, I heard its slow, ponderous tick-tock; it was like something out of a Hitchcock movie.

The sound receded very slowly: good girl, she must be going down the stairs very carefully. Only once did I hear the creak of a board and I wondered again about Euan's door. Did he usually sleep with it open? I couldn't remember.

At the bottom of the stairs she'd be turning back to the right, heading toward the kitchen.

I tried to imagine where she was but lost her in the silence. At last I heard the barely perceptible sound of a protesting hinge; that was the kitchen door. I felt a stab of guilt for using the girl like this, but she knew the score—well, sort of. Fuck it, the decision was made; I just had to do it. If it worked, fine; if it didn't, she was dead. But if I didn't try it, she was dead anyway, so let's get on with it.

"I'm in the kitchen, but I can't see very much. Am I allowed to turn the light on?"

It was the loudest whisper I'd ever heard.

"No, no, no, Kelly, you've got to speak very slowly and very quietly—like this," I demonstrated. "And don't put the light on; that would wake Euan up. Just go more slowly, and listen to me all the time. If you don't understand anything, just ask, and remember, if anything goes wrong or you hear a noise, stop and we will both listen. OK?"

"OK."

The problem with her being quieter on the phone was that it was harder to hear her. The truck driver had now finished, slamming the phone down and storming into the

Burger King. A woman took his place and was yammering
to a girlfriend.

The kitchen was two areas knocked into one, the old back
room of the house and what had used to be an alley between
the cottage and the old sheep-pen wall. The alley had been
closed in by a sunroom, with all the kitchen units arranged
galley-style in one long range beneath it. There were plants
on pedestals and a large circular wooden table in the middle
of the area; I hoped Kelly wouldn't knock anything over
onto the squash-court floor. Thinking of the night we'd
spent "rescuing" the wood made me shudder at all those
years of friendship, trust, and even love. I felt let down,
used, fucked over.

There couldn't be much battery time left.

"Everything OK?" I said. I tried hard not to convey any
sense of panic, but I knew we would be in trouble soon. If the
phone went dead, would she remember what I'd told her
to do?

"I can't see a thing, Nick."

I thought for a few seconds, trying to remember more of
the layout. "OK, Kelly, go very slowly to where the sink is.
Go and stand by the hob."

"What's that?"

"It's the bit you cook on with saucepans. You see it?"

"Yeah."

"OK, there's a switch on the right-hand side. Can you see
that?"

"I'll look."

A second or two later she said, "I can see now."

She must have switched on the small fluorescent light that
illuminated the stove top; she sounded relieved.

"Good girl. Now I want you to go back and very gently
close the kitchen door. Will you do that for me?"

"OK. You are coming for me, Nick?"

I wasn't feeling confident about this at all. Should I stop it
now and just get her to open the door for me and wait? No,
fuck it. He might be getting a phone call any minute about
Simmonds's death.

"Of course I am, but I can't come unless you do what I say,

OK? Keep the telephone to your ear and very gently close that door."

I heard the telltale click.

"What I want you to do now is go and have a look under the sink and put all the bottles and things on the table. Will you do that for me?"

"OK."

There was silence, then a soft clatter as she moved bottles and cans around.

"Everything's out now."

"Well done! Now, very quietly, read out the labels to me. Can you do that?"

"I can't."

"Why not?"

"There's too many things and it's too dark. I can't do it."

She was sounding under pressure now; there was that wobble in her voice.

Fuck, this is taking too long.

"It's OK, Kelly, just walk over to the light switch by the door and turn the light on. Don't rush. Will you do that?"

"OK." It sounded as if her nose was stuffed up. I knew the sound so well by now. The next stage, if I wasn't very careful, would be tears—and failure.

I heard her shuffling toward the light switch.

"I can see now, Nick."

"OK, go back and read to me what the labels say, OK?"

"OK." She moved back to the table. I could hear her pick up the cleaning products.

"Ajax."

"OK, Kelly, what's the next one?"

Fucking hell, this was outrageous. I held the phone hard against my ear, almost holding my breath as I silently willed her to succeed. I was really pumped; I could feel my heart going. I was writhing like a madman in a straitjacket, twisting and turning in the kiosk, miming Kelly's actions to myself. I looked across at the other booth; the woman who was talking to her friend had wiped the condensation from the glass to get a better view of me and now seemed to be relaying a running commentary. I must have looked like a mass murderer, with cuts and scratches on my face, and my hair and clothes soaking wet.

The loud noise of metal clattering onto wood made me jump.

"Kelly? Kelly? . . ."

Silence, then the phone was picked up.

"Sorry, Nick. I knocked a spoon off. I didn't see it. I'm scared. I don't want to do this. Please come and get me."

It wasn't long before the crying was going to start.

"Kelly, don't worry, it's OK, it's OK."

No, not now, for Christ's sake! I heard sniffing on the phone.

"It's OK, Kelly, it's OK. I can't get you unless you help me. You must be brave. Euan is trying to kill me; only you can help me. Can you do that for me?"

"Please hurry, Nick. I want to be with you."

"It's all right, it's all right."

It wasn't all right, Nick, because Nick's fucking money was disappearing. I was down to my last few coins. They weren't going to last. I put another coin in and it rattled out into the coin return; I had to scramble for another one.

Kelly started to go through more of the labels. Most of the words she couldn't read. I asked her to spell them. As she got three letters out I worked out the rest. "No, that one's no good. Read the next."

My mind was now racing, trying to remember ingredients and formulas. At last she read out something I could use.

"Kelly, you must listen very carefully. That's a green can, isn't it? Put it where you can find it again. Then I want you to creep out to the room next door, where the washing machine is. You know the one?"

"Yes."

Euan had a place for everything, and everything had its place. I even knew that his forks would be lined up beside each other in the drawer.

"Just by the door is a cabinet, and in it there's a blue bottle. The label says antifreeze."

"What?"

"Antifreeze. A-N-T-I . . . I want you to bring it to the table, OK?"

The phone clunked onto the stove. I started to sweat even more.

After what seemed like an eternity she came back on. "I've got it."

"Put it on the table and then open it."

I heard the phone go down again and lots of heavy breathing and sniffing as she struggled with the bottle top.

"I don't know how to do it."

"Just twist it. You know how to open a bottle."

"I can't. It won't move. I am trying, Nick, but my hands are shaking."

I then heard a soft, long moan. I was sure it was going to turn into crying.

Shit, I don't need this. It isn't going to work.

"Kelly? Kelly? Are you OK? Talk to me, come on, talk to me."

I was getting nothing.

Come on, Kelly, come on.

Nothing. All I could hear was her holding back tears and sniffing.

"Nick . . . I want you to get me. Please, Nick, please." She was sobbing now.

"Just take your time, Kelly, just take your time. It's OK, everything's OK. I'm here, don't worry. OK, let's just stand and listen. If you can hear anything, you tell me on the phone, OK, and I'll try to listen at the same time."

I listened. I wanted to make sure Euan wasn't awake. I also wanted a break: there needs to be a cut in the action at a time like this, otherwise the errors snowball and people start tripping over themselves; so let's take our time, but at the same time be as fast as possible. I knew exactly what I needed to do, but the frustration lay in trying to interpret it to this child, under pressure, and to get her to work quietly—and all the time I was running out of money and the mobile was running out of battery life.

The woman left her booth and gave me a grin of appeasement in case I was going to lunge at her with a meat cleaver.

"Are you OK now, Kelly?"

"Yes, do you want me to unscrew the bottle still?"

I couldn't understand why she couldn't do it. I started giving her more instructions. Then I remembered: the bottle had a childproof top. As I started to tell her how to undo it, there was a soft bleep.

Battery. Shit!

"Yes, remember to push the top down before you turn. We just have to be a bit quicker or the phone is going to stop before we finish."

"Now what?"

"Is it on the table with the top undone?"

Nothing.

"Kelly? Kelly? Are you there?"

Was the battery dead?

Then I heard, "What do I do now?"

"Thank goodness, I thought the battery had gone. Is there anything you can open that green can with? I know, use the spoon, Kelly. Very, very carefully now, pick it up, put the phone on the table, and then open the can. OK?"

I listened, running through all the different options there were left if this scheme fucked up. I came to the conclusion there were none.

"Now here comes the hard part. Do you think you can do this? You've got to be pretty special to do this bit."

"Yes, I'm OK now. I didn't mean to cry, it's just that I am—"

"I know, I know, Kelly. I am, too, but we will do this together. What I need you to do now is put the phone in your pocket with your sneakers. Then take one of those big bottles from the table and walk to the front door of the house and open it just a little bit. Not wide open, just a little bit. Then put the bottle behind the door, to stop it swinging shut. Now remember, it's a big heavy door, so I want you to do it really slowly, really, really gently so it doesn't make a noise. Can you do that for me?"

"Yeah, I can do that. Then what?"

"I'll tell you in a minute. Now don't forget, if the phone stops working and you can't hear me anymore, I want you to run to the trees and hide."

Chances were Euan would find her, but what else was there to do?

"OK."

This was going to be the tough part. Even if he was sound asleep, Euan's subconscious was likely to detect the change in air pressure and ambient noise when the front door was opened and make something of it in a dream, giving him a sort of sixth sense that something was wrong.

If so, at least she'd have a head start—as long as she remembered what I'd told her.

"I'm back in the kitchen—what do I do now?"

"Listen to me. This bit's very important. What number can you count up to?"

"I can count to ten thousand."

She was sounding a little happier now, sensing the end was in sight.

"I only want you to count up to three hundred. Can you do that?"

"Yeah."

"You've got to do it in your head."

"OK."

"First, I want you to go to the hob again. You know how to turn the gas on?"

"Of course! Sometimes I help Mommy with the cooking."

I had never felt so sad.

I made myself concentrate again. There was no room for distractions. She might be dead soon anyway. I felt enough of a shit for getting her to do my dirty work; while I was at it, I might as well make sure she did the job properly.

"That's good, so you know how to turn on the gas in the oven, and all the rings on the hob?"

"I told you, I can help cook."

A coachload of teenage kids returning from a school trip was streaming into the Burger King. A gang of six or seven of them hung back and headed for the phones, laughing and shouting in newly broken voices, all trying to cram into the one vacant booth. The noise was horrendous; I couldn't hear a thing Kelly was saying. I had to do something. "Kelly, just wait a minute."

I put my hand over the mouthpiece, leaned out of the booth, and shouted, "You—shut the fuck up! I've got my aunty here, her husband's just died and I'm trying to talk to her, OK? Give us some time!"

The kids went quiet, their cheeks red. They slunk off to join their friends, sniggering with mock bravado to disguise their embarrassment.

I got back on the phone.

"Kelly, this is very important. The phone might stop soon because the battery is running out. I want you to turn on all the gas jets on the stove. Take the phone with you so I can hear the gas. Go there now while I talk to you."

I heard the hiss of the bottled propane that Euan used.

"It's very stinky, Nick."

"That's good. Now, just walk out of the kitchen and close the door. But be very quiet in the foyer. Remember, we don't want to wake Euan. Don't talk to me anymore, just listen. Ready?"

"OK."

I heard the door close.

"Nick?"

I tried to keep calm. "Yes, Kelly?"

"Can I get Jenny and Ricky to take with me, please?"

I tried hard to keep myself in check. "No, Kelly, there is no time! Just listen to me. There isn't time for you to talk. I want you to count up to three hundred in your head. Then I want you to take a really, really deep breath and walk back into the kitchen. Don't run. You must walk. Go into the kitchen and pour all the antifreeze in the blue bottle into the green can. Then I want you to walk out of the kitchen—don't run!—I don't want you to wake Euan."

If she tripped up and hurt herself, she could get engulfed by what was about to happen.

"Walk out very slowly, close the door behind you, then go out of the house and close the front door, really, really gently. Do not go back for Jenny or Ricky."

"But I want them—please, Nick?"

I ignored her. "Then I want you to run as fast as you can up to the trees and hide. When you're running you will hear a big bang and there will be a fire. Don't stop and don't look back. And don't come out until I get there, no matter what happens. I promise I will be there soon."

It was at times like this that I was pleased I'd done all the laborious, rote learning of mixtures and formulas for making incendiaries. At the time, many years ago, it had been mind-bogglingly boring, but it had to be done because you can't take a notebook on the job with you. I learned, by heart, how to make bombs from everyday ingredients and how to make improvised electrical devices. As clearly as even atheists remember the Lord's Prayer from the time it was drummed into them at school, I remembered the formulas and step-by-step instructions for making everything from a simple incendiary like the one I was using to try to kill Euan—Mixture Number 5—to a bomb that I could initiate by using a pager from the other side of the world.

The phone started bleeping urgently, and then it just went dead. I visualized the glycerine in the antifreeze working on the mixture. In forty or fifty seconds it would ignite. If it was damp, maybe a little longer.

Kelly had less than a minute to get out of the house; the instant the gas was ignited there was going to be a massive explosion and then a fire. Hopefully, it would take Euan down, but would it take her with it?

Please, please, please don't go after those fucking teddy bears!

I ran back to the car and started driving west. First light was just trying to fight its way through the clouds.

40

It was the worst journey of my life.

I saw a sign saying it was seventy miles to Wales. I raced along at warp speed for what I guessed was thirty miles, then another sign told me that Wales was sixty miles away. I felt as if I were running on a treadmill to nowhere and the treadmill was waist-deep in water.

My body had calmed down from all the excitement and was telling me I was hurt. My neck was in agony. The flow of blood had stopped, but the eye Simmonds had gouged was starting to swell up and affect my vision.

Euan, the fucker. The friend I had trusted for years. It was almost too painful to think about. I felt numb. I felt bereaved. In time, maybe that numbness would turn to anger or grief or some other thing, but not yet. In my mind's eye all I could see was the look on Kelly's face as the train left the station—and the smile on Euan's.

Where did I go from here? No fucker was going to move against me because they'd know that I still had the files. If the plan worked, Euan's package would sit in the post office now that there was no one to deliver it to. The killing of Simmonds would be covered up, no matter what. If some zealous policeman started getting too close to the truth, he'd be removed.

It all made sense to me, now, that every time peace talks began, PIRA, or someone claiming to be PIRA, had dropped a soldier or a policeman or bombed the mainland UK. And why? Because it was good business to keep the Troubles alive.

There were plenty on our side who profited from conflicts

such as Northern Ireland and didn't want them to end. The Royal Ulster Constabulary is probably the highest-paid police force in Europe, if not the world. If you're its chief constable, it's your duty to say that you want an end to the war, but the reality is that you've got a massive police force under your command and limitless amounts of resources and power.

The British army doesn't want it to stop, either. The province is a fantastic testing ground for equipment and training ground for troops—and, as with the RUC, it means the army gets a bigger slice of the cake. Every year the army has to justify its budget, and it's up against the navy, which is asking for more funds for Trident submarines, and the air force, which is banging on about needing to buy the Eurofighter 2000. With Northern Ireland on the agenda, the army can talk about a "now" commitment, an operational imperative—and nobody's going to argue against the need for funds to fight terrorism.

British industry stood to lose substantially from a cease-fire, too. Major defense manufacturers design equipment specifically for internal security and make fortunes out of the operational conditions. Equipment that was battle-proven in Northern Ireland was eagerly sought after by foreign buyers. No wonder the conflict had made Britain one of the top three arms exporters in the world, with beneficial effects on the UK balance of payments.

I knew now why McCann, Farrell, and Savage had had to die. Enniskillen. The backlash against PIRA. People signing books of condolence. Irish Americans stopping their donations. Dialogue and reconciliation must have looked a real prospect. Simmonds and his mates couldn't have that. They had to create martyrs to keep the pot boiling.

Me? I was probably just a very small glitch in a well-oiled machine. Come to that, Northern Ireland was probably only one item among many in their company accounts. For all I knew, these guys also provoked killings and riots in Hebron, stirred up Croats against Serbs, and even got Kennedy killed because he wanted to stop the Vietnam War. As Simmonds had said, it was business. There was nothing I could do to stop them. But I wasn't worried about that. What was the point? The only thing I had achieved—perhaps—was revenge for Kev's and Pat's deaths. That would have to be enough.

I got off the freeway and onto the secondary highway to Abergavenny. The rain had stopped, but it was a stretch of road notorious for repair works. Euan's house was about ten miles on the other side of the town, on the road toward Brecon.

I weaved in and out of traffic, the other drivers hooting and waving their fists. Then, in the distance, I saw the red of brake lights. The morning rush hour had started. I slowed with the volume of traffic heading into the town and eventually came to a complete standstill. The jam was caused by resurfacing work; it looked as though there was a mile-long backup.

I drove onto the shoulder. As I sped past them on the inside, stationary motorists honked angrily. The noise alerted the workers laying the asphalt up ahead. They ran and shouted, trying to wave me down, gesticulating at the roadwork sign. I didn't even acknowledge them. I only hoped I didn't get caught by the police. I dropped a gear, picked up speed, and shifted back up.

I got to Abergavenny and stayed on the ring road. The traffic slowed at a long set of stoplights, so I had to bump up onto the curb and edge my way to the front of the line.

Once I was on the other side of the town I was in the sticks and the road narrowed to a single lane in each direction. I put my foot down and bombed along at seventy to eighty, using the whole road as if it were my own. Seeing a left-hand bend, I moved over to the far right-hand side. I could hear the hedgerow screech against the side of the car. From this position I could see more of the dead ground around the bend. Not bothering with brakes, I banged down through the gears to second just before turning. Once on the bend I put my foot down and made use of rubber on asphalt. Out of the bend, I shifted into fourth and stayed there.

After a mile, a slow-moving truck was taking up most of the road. Its large trailer of sheep on two levels had a sticker asking me if I thought the driving was OK—if not, to call the

head office. I had plenty of time to read it, laboring behind the
fucker at twenty miles an hour.

The road twisted and turned; the trucker could see me in
his mirrors, but there was no way he was going to pull over
for me to pass. The speedo dropped to fifteen m.p.h. and I
looked at my watch. It was 9:05; I'd been on the road for just
under three hours.

I kept pulling out, looking and tucking back in again. Even
the sheep were staring at me now. The truck driver was enjoying himself; we had eye-to-eye in his side mirror, and I
could see he was laughing. I knew this road, and I knew that
unless he let me pass I was doomed to several miles of
driving at his pace. By now the road had a two-foot mud bank
on each side, then trees and hedges. It was wet and slippery,
with small streams running along each side. I'd have to take a
chance, just hope that nothing was coming. On this road, all
corners were blind.

Preparing for the next bend, the truck driver shifted slowly
down through the gears, and I accelerated past him on the
wrong side of the road. If there was anything coming around
the bend, we'd both be killed. He flashed his lights and
honked, probably doing his best to distract me and force me
off the road. For the first time today, I was in luck. The road
was clear; I'd soon left the truck far behind.

Fifteen minutes later I was at the turnoff for Euan's valley. I
hung a left, and within a hundred yards the road petered out
into a single lane. If I came up behind a tractor or farm machinery, there would be few passing places, but luck stayed
with me and there was nothing ahead. Another twenty minutes and I got to the valley.

As I approached the brow of the hill I could already see the
spiral of smoke.

41

The walls were still intact but most of the roof had collapsed, and there were smoke and scorch marks around the window frames. Two fire engines were there, and the firemen were still damping down. They looked wet, tired, and stressed. On the other side of the house was an ambulance.

A handful of people had gathered, locals in their slickers and boots, who'd driven from the other side of the valley to rubberneck.

I drove on and stopped by the gate. A couple of firemen turned around, but they didn't say anything; they were too busy doing their work.

I got out of the car and ran across the road to the small copse about fifty yards away, hollering and shouting like a madman.

"Kelly! Kelly!"

Nothing.

"It's me—it's Nick! You can come out now!"

But she wasn't there. Deep down, I'd probably known all along that she wouldn't be. She'd been dead from the moment she'd picked up the phone.

I turned away and walked slowly up the track toward the throng of spectators. They gave me the once-over, obviously not liking the look of my damaged face, then turned back, more interested in the remains of the house.

"Was there anyone in there?" I asked nobody in particular.

A woman spoke. "His lights were on last night. The ambulance crew has been inside already. Oh, it's such a shame. He was such a nice young man."

I walked beyond the group and a fireman came toward me,

lifting a gloved hand. "Excuse me, sir, if you could stay well back. We haven't made the area safe yet."

"Radio Wales," I said. "Can you tell me what happened?"

I looked over his shoulder. Other firefighters were dragging out charred remains of Euan's house and placing them on a pile that was being damped down. I could now smell the burning.

I looked back at the fireman. He said, "It looks as if there was a fire and then the gas bottles blew up. If you could move back, sir."

"Was anyone killed or injured?"

As I asked, something one of them threw on the pile caught my eye. It was Jenny or Ricky, one or the other—I never could tell which was which. Not that it mattered now. Whichever one it was, it was now burned black with only half an arm left.

"It will take some time before we'll know for sure. But no one could have survived that blast."

He was right. In any other circumstances, it would have been an explosion to be proud of.

Kelly was dead. Maybe it wouldn't be too bad. It would be a bitch, but I'd get over it. What could I have offered her?

Kelly would have been in bad shape when she realized what had happened to her; she would probably need psychiatric treatment. Besides, she'd been starting to like the way we'd been living. Her death would tidy things up. I wouldn't have to protect or worry about her anymore.

I started back toward the car, deep in my thoughts. What was done was done; I couldn't change it, couldn't turn the clock back. I'd find out more from the news.

Behind me, in the distance, I heard the squawk of a bird, maybe a crow. It almost sounded like my name.

I stopped and turned.

And there she was, running toward me from beyond the trees.

I started to run toward her but checked myself. I wanted to make it look casual, even if my insides were shaking off the Richter scale.

She flew into my arms, burying her face in my neck. I

pulled her back and held her at arm's length. "Why weren't you at the trees?" I was half-angry, half-relieved, like a parent who thinks he's lost a child in a crowd and then finds her again and doesn't know whether to give her a good old chewing out or just a hug and a kiss. I didn't know what to do, but it felt good.

"Why weren't you by the trees where I said?"

She looked at me in disbelief. "As if! Because you always make sure you stand off and watch. You taught me that!"

I got hold of her hand, grinned, and said, "Yeah, that's fair."

Still smiling, we walked toward the car. She was soaked, her hair matted to her head.

We reached the car and got in without exchanging another word.

I looked at her in the rearview mirror. We had eye-to-eye. She smiled, and I snapped, "Put your seat belt on!"

I turned the ignition and we drove off.

A preview excerpt from
CRISIS FOUR
by Andy McNab

Coming in hardcover from
Ballantine Books in July 2000.

MONDAY 16 OCTOBER 1995

The Syrians don't fuck around if they think you're invading their air space. Within minutes of crossing the border, your aircraft will be greeted by a three-ship intercept, flying so close you can wave at the pilots. They won't wave back; they've come to get a visual ID on you, and if they don't like what they see they'll hose you down with their air-to-air missiles.

The same rule doesn't apply, of course, when friendly commercial aircraft blip onto their radar screens, and that was why our team of four had opted for this particular method of infiltration. If Damascus had had the slightest clue about what was about to happen aboard our British Airways flight from Delhi to London, their fighters would have been scrambled the moment the Boeing 747 left Saudi Arabian territory.

I was twisting and turning, trying to get comfortable, feeling jealous of all the people sitting upstairs behind the driver, probably on their fifth gin and tonic since take off, watching their second movie and tucking into their third helping of *boeuf en croute*.

Reg 1 was in front of me. Six feet two, and built like a brick shithouse, he was probably having an even worse time in the cramped conditions. His curly black hair, going a bit grey at the sides, was all over the place. Like me, before I left in '93, he had been selected to do work for the intelligence and security services, including the sort of job for the US that Congress would never sanction. I had done similar jobs myself while in the Regiment, but this was the first I'd been on since becoming a K. Given who we were going in against, none of us was giving odds on whether we'd get to do another.

I found myself facing Sarah again. She was rubbing her eyes with her fists, like a sleepy child. I tried to doze off; thirty minutes later I was still kidding myself I was asleep when I got a kick on the back of my legs. It was Sarah.

I sat up in my sleeping bag and peered into the semi-darkness. Three loadies (load masters) were moving around with orienteering torches attached to their heads, glowing a dim red so as not to destroy our night vision. Each of them had an umbilical cord trailing from his face mask, and their hands moved instinctively to make sure it didn't get snagged or detached from the aircraft's oxygen supply.

I unzipped the bag and, even through my all-weather sniper suit, immediately felt the freezing cold in the unpressurized 747 cargo hold. None of the passengers or cabin crew would have known there were people down here, tucked away in the belly of the aircraft. Nor would our names have appeared anywhere on a manifest.

I folded the bag in half, leaving inside the two "aircrew bags" I'd filled during the flight—plastic bags with a one-way valve which you insert yourself into and piss away to your heart's content. I wondered how Sarah had been getting on. It was bad enough for me because my cock was still extremely sore, but it must be hard being female aircrew on a long flight with a device designed only for males—or the female commander of a deniable op. I put a Post-It on my mental bulletin board, reminding myself to ask her how she got round the problem. That was if we survived, of course, and were still on speaking terms.

I could never remember which was starboard or port; all I knew was that, as you looked at the aircraft from the front, we were in the small hold at the rear and the door was on the left-hand side. I clutched my oxygen tube as a loadie crossed over it, and adjusted my mask as his leg caught it, pulling it slightly from my face. The inside was wet, clammy and cold now the seal had been broken.

I picked up my Car 15, a version of the M16 Armalite

5.56mm with a telescopic butt and a shorter barrel, cocked it and applied the safety. The Car had a length of green para-cord tied to it like a sling; I strapped it over my left shoulder so the barrel faced down and it ran along the rear of my body. The rig (parachute) would go over that.

I pushed my hand under the sniper suit to get hold of the Beretta 9mm that was on a leg holster against my right thigh. I cocked that, too, and pulled back the topslide a few millime-ters to check chamber. Turning the weapon so it caught one of the loadies' red glows, I saw the glint of a correctly fed round, ready to go.

This was my first "false flag" job posing as a member of Israeli special forces, and as I adjusted my leg straps I wished I'd had a little more time to recover from the circumcision. It hadn't healed as quickly as we'd been told. I looked around me as we got our kit on, hoping the others were in as much pain.

We were about to carry out a "lift" to find out what the West's new bogeyman, Osama Bin Laden, a Saudi multi-millionaire turned terrorist, was getting up to in Syria. Satel-lite photography had shown earthmoving and other heavy equipment from Bin Laden's construction company near the source of the river Jordan. Downstream lay Israel, and if its main source of water was about to be dammed, diverted or otherwise tampered with, the West needed to know. They feared a repeat of the 1967 war, and with Bin Laden around it was never going to be a good day out. He hadn't been dubbed America's "public enemy number one" by Clinton, for nothing.

Our task was to lift Osama's right-hand man—known to us only as the "Source" for op sec (operational security) reasons—from on site. His private jet had been spotted at a nearby airfield. The US needed to know what was happening in Syria, and, more to the point, maybe learn how to lay their hands on Osama. As the briefing guy had said, "Bin Laden represents a completely new phenomenon: non-state-supported terrorism backed by an extremely rich and reli-giously motivated leader with an intense hatred of the West, mainly America, as well as Israel and the secular Arab world. He must be stopped."

Once ready and checked by the loadies, it was just a question of holding on to the airframe and waiting. There was nothing to do for the next few minutes but daydream or get scared. Each of us was in his or her own little world now. Before any operation some people are frightened, some are excited. Now and again I could see reflections from the red torches in people's eyes; they were staring at their boots or at some other fixed point, maybe thinking about their wives, or girlfriends, or kids, or what they were going to do after this, or maybe even wondering what the fuck they were doing here in the first place.

Me, I didn't know what to think really. I'd never been able to get sparked up about the thought of dying and not seeing anyone else again. Not even my wife, when I was married. I always felt I was a gambler with nothing to lose. Most people who gamble do so with the things that are important to them; I gambled knowing that if I lost I wouldn't break the bank.

I watched the glowing redheads pack our kit away into the large aluminum Lacon boxes. Once we'd been thrown out and the door had closed again, they'd stow all other evidence that we had been there in the boxes and just sit it out until they were taken care of in London.

Two of the loadies started a sweep with their torch lights to make sure there was nothing loose which could be sucked out as soon as the door opened. Nothing must compromise this job.

We got the order to turn on our own oxygen, disconnect from the aircraft supply and stand by. Sarah was standing in front of Reg 1, who was to tandem jump with her. She had never failed to amaze me. She was an IG (Intelligence Group), the very top of the intelligence-service food chain, people who usually spend their lives in embassies, posing as diplomats. Their lives should be one long round of receptions and recruiting sources through the cocktail circuit, not running around, weapon strong. Then again, Sarah had always made a point of finishing the jobs herself.

She was masked and goggled up, looking for all the world

as if she'd done this a thousand times. She hadn't; her first jump ever had been three weeks before, but she took her job so seriously that she'd probably read ten books on freefall and knew more facts and figures than all of us lot put together.

She turned and looked for me. We got eye-to-eye and I gave her an everything-is-OK nod. After all, that was part of this job, to look after her.

The loadie motioned us towards the door. Our bergens, each containing forty pounds of equipment, were hanging from our rigs and down the back of our legs. We waddled forward like a gaggle of geese, putting weight on each foot in turn. Thankfully the bergens hadn't needed to be fully laden. If everything went to plan, we'd only be on the ground for a few hours.

There was a pause of about five seconds as the loadie by the door spoke into his mike to the British Airways navigator, then he nodded to himself and swung into action. The door was about half the size of an average up-and-over garage door. Pulling out all the levers, he swung them anticlockwise, then pulled the handles towards him. Even though I had a helmet on, I heard the massive rush of air, and then a gale was thrashing at my sniper suit. Where the door had been there was now just a black hole. The tags on the aircraft's luggage containers fluttered frantically. The freezing cold wind whipped at the parts of my face that weren't covered by my mask. I pulled my jockey's goggles over my eyes, fighting against the blast, gripping hard on to the airframe.

Seven miles below us lay Syria—enemy territory. We did our final checks. I wanted to get this jump out of the way, get the job done and be in Cyprus for tea and toast tomorrow morning.

We rammed up close to each other at the exit, the roar of the wind and the jet engines so loud I could hardly think. At last came a handheld red light from the loadie. We all joined in with a loud scream: *"Red on, red on!"* I didn't know why, no-one could hear anything; it was just something we always did.

The loadie's light changed to green and he shouted, *"Green on!"*

He moved back as we all shouted to ourselves, *"Ready!"*

We rocked forward, trying to scream above the roar: *"Set!"*

Then we rocked back. *"Go!"*

Out and out we spilled, four people on three rigs, tumbling towards Syria. Being the last man, I was pushed by the loadie to make sure there wasn't too much of a gap between us in the sky.

You can now freefall from an aircraft flying at high altitude and miles from the target area and land with pinpoint accuracy. The HAHO (high altitude, high opening) technique calls for extreme weather clothing and oxygen equipment to survive temperatures as low as minus 40°C, especially when a fifty-mile cross-country descent can take nearly two hours. It has now largely replaced the old HALO (high altitude, low opening) approach, for the simple reason that, instead of hurtling towards the ground at warp speed, with no real idea of where you're going to land or where the rest of the team are once you're on the ground, you can glide gently onto the target sitting in a comfortable rig. Unless, of course, a man in a white coat has recently clipped a bit off the end of your cock.

I felt the jet stream pick me up and take me with it. As the aircraft thunders over you at 500 miles an hour you think you're going to collide with the tailplane, but in fact you're falling and never hit it.

Once I was out of the jet stream it was time to sort myself out. I could tell by the wind force, and the fact that I could see the aircraft lights flashing three or four hundred feet above me, that I was upside down. I spread my arms and legs and arched my back, banging myself over into a stable position.

I looked around—moving your head during freefall is about the only thing that doesn't have an effect on your stability—trying to see where everyone else was. I could just about see a figure over on my right-hand side; I didn't know who it was, and it didn't matter. As I looked up I saw the taillights of the 747 disappearing way above us, and downstairs, on the floor, there was nothing, I couldn't see a single light.

All I could hear was the rush of air; it was like sticking your head out of a car travelling at 120 mph. What I had to do now was keep stable and wait for the AOD (automatic opening device) to do its bit. The drill is just to assume that it's going to work, but to get in the pull position just in case. I thought, Fuck that. I knew my pull height—30,000 feet, an 8,000-foot drop. I moved my left hand up, just above my head, and my right hand down to the pull handle. There has to be symmetry with everything. If you're in freefall and just put one hand out, that will hit the air and you're going to tumble.

For the next thirty minutes we minced along the sky, controlling the rig, checking height and the sat nav. I started to see lights now. Small towns and villages with street lights following the roads out of the built-up areas for about half a mile, then darkness, only car lights giving away the road.

I looked at my alti. I was about 16,200 feet. I thought, I'll just go for a few more minutes and I'll take my oxygen mask off. The fucking thing was a pain in the ass. If I started feeling the effects of hypoxia, dizziness, I'd bring the mask back to my face and take a couple of deep breaths. By now I was just under 16 grand; my mouth was full of saliva and it felt all clammy. I got hold of the clip with my right hand and pulled the press stud off, and the thing just fell down and dangled by the left-hand side of my face.

I could feel the cold around my mouth where all the moisture from the mask had been. I was freezing, but it was nice; I could stretch my mouth and chew my jaw around a bit.

After about ten minutes I checked my alti again: 6,500 feet, time to start working. I put on my NVG (night viewing goggles), which had been hanging round my neck on paracord, and started looking for the flash on an IR Firefly (infrared detecting system). It was the same flashing light that you would expect to see on the top of a tall tower to warn aircraft, but these are just little hand-held things that throw out a brilliant quick flash of light, through an IR filter. No-one would see it apart from us—or anyone else with NVG, of course. I kept looking in the darkness. It would be easy to pick out. Bang—there it was to my half right.

We were coming in on finals. I was concentrating on keeping myself positioned right on top and to the rear of

Reg 1's canopy, which was larger than mine as he had the extra weight to jump with. I heard him below me sounding like an infant-school teacher. "Right, any minute now, keep your legs bent and under your hips. Are your legs bent?"

She must have acknowledged. I pulled the NVGs off my face and let them hang.

"OK, put your hands up by me." I imagined her with her hands up, holding Reg 1's wrists on the brake lines to keep them out of the way so she didn't damage herself if they took a bad landing.

I couldn't see any ground yet—it was far too dark—but I heard: "Standby, standby. Flaring soon . . . flaring . . . flaring . . ."

Then the sound of his bergen thumping into the ground, and his command to Sarah: "Now!"

His canopy started to collapse below me as I flew past. My bergen was dangling by the straps from my feet; I kicked it off and it fell beneath me on a three-meter line. As soon as I heard it land, I flared too. Hitting the deck, I ran along for three or four steps, turned quickly and pulled my lines to collapse the canopy.

A body appeared behind me. Regs 3 to 6 had been on the ground for five days preparing the job and were manning the DZ (drop zone). Fuck knows how they'd inserted in-country, and I didn't care.

"You all right, mate?" I recognized his voice. Glen, the only one whose name I knew, was the ground commander. He looked as if you'd hear steely Clint Eastwood when he opened his mouth, but in fact what you got was softly spoken David Essex.

"Yeah. Fine, mate, fine."

"Then let's get all this shit off."